The Ne

Daniel Faust, Book Eight

by Craig Schaefer

Publisher's Note: This is a work of fiction. Names, characters, places, and incidents are a product of the author's imagination. Locales and public names are sometimes used for atmospheric purposes. Any resemblance to actual people, living or dead, or to businesses, companies, events, institutions, or locales is completely coincidental.

Cover Design by James T. Egan of Bookfly Design LLC.
Author Photo ©2014 by Karen Forsythe Photography
Craig Schaefer / The Neon Boneyard
ISBN 978-1-944806-11-8

Contents

The Story So Far

Daniel Faust was an occult gangster, a professional thief, and a merchant of vengeance for hire. Then he landed behind bars. A prison break did more than leave his old identity legally dead; it gave him the drive he needed to pull his life out of a tailspin and claw his way back to the top. Now he has a new job to add to his resume: underboss of the New Commission, the criminal syndicate taking control of Las Vegas one block at a time.

Daniel's nemesis, known as the man with the Cheshire smile—or simply the Enemy—is on the move. He's the villain of the first story ever told, a piece of fiction made real, and he's out to fulfill the purpose his author wrote for him: to burn the entire multiverse down, one parallel Earth at a time. He's turned countless worlds into horror-infested cinders, and now he's preparing for a repeat performance.

Daniel has ruined his plans twice, and in the process uncovered a key to the Enemy's secrets: a wand owned by 1940s stage magician Howard Canton. The wand has the power to create and banish illusions, and one slight flaw. It only works when you're trying to do something heroic. Considering Daniel is a con artist and a killer, he and his new tool haven't been getting along. Now he's trying to find a loophole and learn more about Canton, namely, why the Enemy is obsessed with the dead magician's legacy.

His other rivals haven't been sleeping, and one just sprang a trap long in the making. The shape-shifting cannibal Naavarasi made a play to snare Daniel's soul along with enslaving his lover Caitlin, the right hand of a demon prince. Daniel and Caitlin fought side by side, found a way out, and left Naavarasi humiliated. Meanwhile, a mysterious syndicate of criminal sorcerers called the Network has been carving out a foothold in Las Vegas.

What Daniel doesn't know is that his three greatest adversaries—the Enemy, the Network, and Naavarasi—have joined forces. All three are using each other for their own ends, weaving a web of lies, but they share a common goal: to destroy Daniel Faust and all that he holds dear.

Prologue

The man with the Cheshire smile made a deal with the devil.

Ironic, considering how many humans would be quick to give him that title on sight alone: a flickering, photonegative blur of a man. White scratches crackled across his shadowy hands as he pored over a leather-bound book in the darkness of his penthouse office. Given his legacy and his calling, it was a title he'd normally wear with amusement.

Normally.

Tonight he was too distracted to take pleasure in his work, and the pages before him offered up no answers.

THE ENEMY studies the play, read the faded type on the page, *seeking insight into his suspicious ally. He doesn't notice MR. SMITH, ESQUIRE, sitting behind him. Then he speaks.*

SMITH: So, most of your power is still trapped inside that thing?

"So, most of your power—" said the agreeable voice at his back.

"*Yes*," he snapped. His shadowy feet stayed rooted facing the desk, while the upper half of his body swiveled around to face his uninvited guest. "We've unlocked a handful of acts, enough to restore a generous portion of my magic, but we appear to have reached an impasse. It was bad enough that Faust couldn't just die in prison like he was supposed to. No, he had the gall to attack me in my own home and ruin *another* sundering. The man is a curse."

Mr. Smith sat in a chair in the corner of the room, his forgettable, bland suit a gray smear in the shadows. He crossed one leg over the other.

"No use crying over spilled milk and all that," Smith said, "but perhaps this could have been averted with slightly better crisis-planning techniques?"

"*Excuse* me?"

The lawyer shrugged. "Your time was running out, you knew you were cornered, and you put most of your power into that reliquary before your enemies could steal it from you. That I understand. But why make it so difficult to open? You could have just, I don't know, password-protected it. 'Open sesame' or something."

The man's permanent, pearly smile twisted into a grimace, set deep in his eyeless face.

"I had no idea how long I'd be imprisoned in that miserable void. I couldn't take the chance that someone would steal the book before I managed to escape, and open it for themselves. No, the keys had to be unique, titanic, complex; difficult was the *point*. And I broke my magic into pieces so that even if someone did manage to unlock an act, all they'd steal was a small portion of my power and I could eventually reclaim the rest. Still...it wasn't supposed to be quite this infuriating."

"Faust," Smith said.

"Ruiner. Do you know how long it took me to lay hands on a Cutting Knife? There are only nine of the damned things and they're scattered across the entire multiverse. And he waltzed into my inner sanctum and stole it from me."

"To be fair," Smith said with a glance to the office doors, "you do have another one handy."

The shadow crackled, head blurring as it shook.

"No. Fleiss is my right hand. She's served me faithfully for a dozen lifetimes. This particular ritual would leave the knife...broken. Damaged beyond repair. She's too useful to squander like that."

"Even if it means never getting the rest of your magic back? Fleiss might be loyal, but she hasn't been hitting too many home runs for you lately, has she? Is she carrying your bags, or are you carrying hers?"

The man with the Cheshire smile turned away. His thoughtful silence was his only answer.

"As it happens," Smith said, "it may not be an issue. We've got one, you know."

"One what?"

"A Cutting Knife." The genial man spread his baby-soft hands. "The Network. We've got one. We could probably work out an arrangement. Of course, since we wouldn't be getting it back—not in working condition—we couldn't do it for free."

"Name your price."

"Oh, I couldn't possibly arrange a contract on the spur of the moment," Smith said. "I have to run it up the flagpole, talk to the gentlemen in the home office—"

The shadow dashed across the room in the blink of an eye, trailing streamers of jet-black smoke. He loomed over the lawyer. White scratches flickered across his body like flashes of lightning.

"Name. Your. Price."

Smith didn't answer right away. A tiny sliver of tongue ran across his lips, and he appraised the man like an auctioneer sizing up a piece of exotic art.

"Rumor has it," he said, "you found a little something-something down in Mexico. A real, honest-to-goodness interdimensional gateway. A gate leading straight to the heart of the Garden of Eden."

"I found three," the shadow replied. "I had two of them destroyed. The third is mine."

"The Network would very much appreciate access to that gateway. I'd like you to consider granting it to us as a token of goodwill, to celebrate our newly founded partnership."

"Access? To do what? Have you *seen* that place? Do you have any idea what kind of a nightmare you'd be walking into?"

Smith rose to his feet. He ran smooth fingertips down the sharp folds of his jacket.

"One man's trash is another man's treasure, sir. But I can understand your hesitancy; you want to see results, am I right? So let's deal with the problem at hand, first and foremost. Give me a chance to impress you with what the Network can accomplish."

"Faust."

"Correct." Smith inclined his head, offering a reserved smile. "We have a team on the ground in Las Vegas, and if my watch is correct...well, they've already made their first move."

* * *

Is she carrying your bags, or are you carrying hers?

The memory of the lawyer's voice, drifting muffled through the office doors, cut Ms. Fleiss like a scalpel across her heart. She knew she shouldn't have been eavesdropping, but she was only looking out for her lord's best interests. Smith and his people were a dangerous wild card, interlopers with their own agenda.

And now Smith was trying to turn her lord against her. Fleiss had burned entire worlds in service to this holy crusade. She'd burn him, too.

At least she wasn't the only injured party. Sitting across from her, sunk deep in the limousine's leather bucket seats, Naavarasi looked like someone had used her as a punching bag. The sullen, raven-haired woman cradled an arm blotched with bone-deep bruises, and her oversized dark glasses couldn't conceal the beating her face had taken.

"I don't like you," Fleiss said, "and I don't trust you."

Naavarasi shifted in her seat. She winced. "The feeling is mutual, but we've established this."

"What I do trust is your motivation. Your kingdom was stolen and your family, your entire *species*, was put to the torch while you were forced to watch. You want to see this universe burn. And you know that serving my lord's cause is the way to victory."

"Your point?"

Fleiss slid forward on her seat. The limousine rumbled over a pothole and the cabin jolted. Outside, the cold night streets drifted by behind panes of smoked glass.

"This 'Network' and their man Smith, we don't know what their ambitions are. They're sowing discord, brewing trouble. And that gives you and me a reason to work together."

"Smith," Naavarasi mused. Her voice was drowsy, like she'd popped a handful of painkillers before crawling into the car. "What do we know about him?"

"He doesn't have fingerprints. According to my lord, he doesn't have a *history*. No timeline, like he was born twenty minutes ago. I offered him a glass of water, so our scientists could study the DNA he left behind."

"What is he?"

"Human," Fleiss said. "A perfectly average human. *Too* average. There are no flaws, no odd markers, no genetic defects of any kind. He's the kind of average that doesn't exist in nature. The point is, we have to deal with Daniel Faust before the Network does, in case they're planning a betrayal."

Naavarasi held up one jade-nailed hand and grimaced.

"Let me stop you there. Word has it that Faust has been anointed a knight of hell. Specifically, by one of *my* court's rivals. I can't make a direct move against him now. It would violate the Cold Peace; that's an act of war. I wouldn't survive my prince's retribution."

"I would hardly expect you to make a *direct* move against anyone," Fleiss replied. "But you intimated to my lord that you have a servant in play. A skilled assassin who can act as a deniable proxy."

"I might," Naavarasi said.

"What if you were to...lend this servant to the Network, to support their efforts in Las Vegas? He could keep an eye on things for us. And when the time comes to take Daniel Faust off the table, he could ensure things are done properly. No tricks from our new 'allies.'"

"And you and I share the credit?"

Fleiss hovered on the edge of her seat. Her hands clenched

her knees as the limousine swayed. Her eyes were fervent pits of smoldering coal.

"That so-called lawyer is pouring poison in my lord's ears," she said. "I need a victory, do you understand? I need him to remember how valuable I am to his cause. I need him to need me. I need him to *love* me."

Naavarasi tugged down her sunglasses. Her bruised, bleary eyes stared at the woman as the limousine slid up to the curb.

"I'll make a few calls," she said. "This is your stop."

1.

I swore I'd never see the inside of a jail again. When I made that vow, just after escaping from Eisenberg Correctional, I didn't take visitation into account. Or the possibility that some teenager hopped up on a new designer drug would ask for me by name. My real name, the one I'd left dead and buried in Eisenberg's burning ruins.

So tonight I was breaking my promise to myself, standing silent while Detective Gary Kemper—a cop with demon blood, an ax to grind, and blackmail hanging over my head—talked Jennifer and me past the night-duty sergeant at the City of Las Vegas Detention Center. The place could have passed for a bank on the outside, with pristine white stucco walls and a bright robin's-egg-blue rooftop. You had to look closer to notice the ten-foot fence ringing the back of the compound, topped with spools of shiny barbed wire, and the slim gray cameras poking out from every nook and cranny.

The paranoid who lived in the back of my brain wondered if this wasn't some elaborate ruse to take Jennifer and me off the street. That once we passed through the heavy beige security door—past two layers of metal detectors, so we had to leave our steel outside—we'd find a swarm of guns in our faces and empty cells waiting for us. I had to give it a moment's contemplation; that paranoid voice had saved my life more than once.

I wasn't too worried, though. As he'd made clear time and time again, Kemper could end my life with a single phone call to the

FBI. I was more useful to him on the streets, for now, dealing with problems Metro wasn't equipped to handle. As for Jennifer, well, she'd clawed her way to the top of the underworld's food chain and brought Vegas's feuding gangs, the Chicago mob, and city hall to heel.

Kemper wasn't stupid. He could lock Jennifer in a cell, but he knew it would take an army to keep her there. An army bigger than hers.

"Lawyers," he told the sergeant with a less-than-friendly nod in our general direction. "Here to see a juvie who got picked up in that bust on Eagle Glen tonight. Helms, William H."

The sarge rattled a few keys, pulling up the prisoner files, and glanced our way. "Lawyers, plural? Gotta be a trust-fund kid."

"Good for him. He's gonna need all the help he can get."

No argument there. A whole bunch of trust-fund kids had been partying in that house on Eagle Glen Road, and somebody had added a twist to the usual mix of alcohol and Adderall: a new designer drug sweeping the nation at the speed of crack cocaine. On the street, they called it ink. The kids at Eagle Glen had gotten their hands on a bad batch.

Twelve of them were dead. Three were in a rubber room, under observation after their psychotic break and the ensuing murderous rampage. One—Helms, William H.—was possessed.

"Gotta sign in," the sergeant grunted, shoving a tattered logbook in front of us. I signed it as "Cary Grant." Jennifer buried a smirk behind her hand and scribbled "Grace Kelly." The sarge didn't even glance at the page. He took the book back, pocketed his twenty-cent ballpoint pen, and went back to surfing the web.

Kemper passed me an unlabeled manila folder as we walked. "Mayor wanted you to see these."

I opened up the folder, took a look at the crime-scene photos, and wished I hadn't. I pictured them as an art-gallery exhibition: *Fragments of an Atrocity*. Here was a sheet of glass, unread coffee-table books tilted at the perfect angle, drenched in so much blood it looked like a glaze of raspberry jam. Here was a designer lamp, spattered red, a handful of severed fingertips scattered around the base with an interior decorator's touch. Feng shui with body parts. A shadowy, naked body stood in an open closet, arms stretched above his head, wrists bent and dangling from rust-red ropes. No, not ropes. I squinted at the photo.

"Are those...his tendons?"

Kemper kept his eyes forward, stone-faced. "One of the survivors says he did it to himself. Opened himself up with a kitchen knife and started pulling. He couldn't get 'em tied to the closet bar on his own, once his arms were useless, so he asked for help and two of the ones who went psycho stopped in the middle of their murder spree to help him out."

A barred gate painted mint-green rattled shut behind us. A klaxon rang out, like the drone of a truck horn, and another gate opened just ahead. We passed through the tiger trap and into the slumbering cellblock.

"You were right to call us," Jennifer told him.

"*I* didn't call you. Mayor Seabrook did. I'm just the messenger." Kemper jabbed a finger at the folder in my hands. "Get the message?"

"Loud and clear," I said.

After a short and bloody war with the Chicago Outfit, the New Commission—Jennifer's bid to unify the Vegas underworld—was the last power standing. Seabrook was willing to work with us, to a certain deniable extent. She could turn a blind eye to our rackets, authorizing the occasional token bust but leaving our real operations alone, so long as we kept the peace.

Twelve dead teenagers, scions of some of Vegas's wealthiest and most powerful families, was the exact opposite of keeping the peace. Seabrook wanted the city's ink pipeline sealed up tight, as of yesterday, and the dealers...well, she couldn't come right out and say what she wanted us to do, but then again, she didn't need to. We were all grown-ups here.

"I had 'em stick the kid in an interview room once he started dropping your name to anybody who would listen," Kemper told us. He shot me a withering look. "Not to protect your little back-from-the-dead routine, either. It's obvious he's got something rattling around inside his brain that shouldn't be there, and I didn't want him spouting off anything he shouldn't in front of civilians."

The occult underground protects its secrets, a hard job in an age where everyone carries a video camera in their pocket. Sometimes I wondered if we were living at the end of the line, counting down the final days of the greatest scam in history. It was only a matter of time before something big went down, something undeniable under the light of day, and showed the whole world what kind of nightmare they were living in.

Don't get me wrong. We don't keep magic a secret as a public service. We keep it a secret because it makes us money.

A jangling hoop of keys dangled on Kemper's belt. He stopped at a reinforced and double-locked door, fumbling with the borrowed keys, trying them one at a time. I glanced left, to an observation mirror set into the wall. A kid, maybe seventeen, sat with his wrists shackled to a ring in a stainless-steel table. Dried blood spattered his high cheekbones and his preppy clothes, none of it his. As I watched, he turned his head and locked eyes with me through the glass.

Kemper glanced over his shoulder at me, still fighting with the keys. "You got your kit? You're gonna exorcise him, right?"

"Little problem there. Demons I can exorcise."

He frowned. "Point being?"

"He told you he was the 'King of Worms,' right?"

"Yeah."

The kid spread his lips in a sneering smile, still holding my gaze through the one-way mirror. Then his left front tooth began to buckle under the pressure of his tongue. It pushed outward and slowly tore from his gums like a lifting drawbridge.

His tooth fell out. It bounced across the interview table, trailing droplets of blood in its wake. The tip of the kid's tongue, glistening red, poked out through the gap and wriggled at me like the head of a newborn maggot.

"Far as I can tell," I said, "that's not a demon."

Kemper opened the door, saw the blood and the tooth. His face went sweaty-pale. I spotted an unplugged security camera in the corner of the room, dangling dead.

"Aw shit, Faust, don't let him do that—"

Jennifer patted his shoulder and skirted around him. "Stand clear, sugar. We got this."

"A bold claim," the teenager said in a voice older, more sonorous, than his spindly chest should have been capable of. Blood from the freshly yanked tooth drooled down his chin and spattered the stainless-steel table. He swung his reptilian gaze my way. "*Lazarus.*"

"Heard you were looking for me," I said, trying to sound more nonchalant than I felt.

"He who believes in me will live, even though he dies. And you believed in me, in the bowels of that mortal prison."

Eisenberg. Trapped behind bars with a target on my back and hired killers closing in, I'd done the only thing I could: reached out, for the second time in my life, to the King of Worms.

The king defied occult taxonomy. He wasn't a demon, wasn't a corrupted human soul or some ancient, undead sorcerer. He was something *else*, with names and epithets half-whispered down through centuries of occult grimoires. And as he had told me, when his desiccated, eternally rotting servants buried a lethal one-shot curse inside my brain, his gifts were free for the asking.

His "gifts" had nearly killed me, twice, and what they'd done to my targets was a fate worse than death. I was young, angry, and reckless the first time I called upon the king. The second time, I was desperate. There wouldn't be a third.

"And lo," he said, "you died within those prison walls. And rose again, resurrected and free. Thanks to me."

"I thought there weren't any strings attached to that deal," I said.

"There weren't. But how did you repay me? You lured my poor emissary into the desert and murdered him."

My hand throbbed with the memory. I was flat on my back in the dirt, inches from my fallen shotgun as Damien Ecko ground his heel against my broken fingers. Storm clouds roiled in the night sky and blotted out the stars as he raised one clawed hand. He spat out an incantation, a ritual call to the shadows, and then...nothing.

"You abandoned him," I said. "Ecko prayed to you, and you abandoned him."

"The necromancer had grown complacent with the passing of centuries. Lazy. Against anyone else, I might have aided him, but you...you I've been keeping a curious eye upon. I wanted to see who would win. If he had slain you with his own magic, I would have considered him worthy of my continued investment. Instead, you've forced me to seek a new servant."

"Let me guess," I said. "This is the part where you tell me that you've chosen me to become your next emissary."

He let out a wheezing, raspy laugh. "You think too highly of yourself. Lazarus *received* a miracle. He didn't perform them. Arguably, his greatest contribution was testimony. Telling people of the glory he'd beheld."

I leaned in. My splayed fingertips brushed the cold steel of the interview table. I stared down at the kid's torn-out tooth and swallowed a surge of anger.

"I'll be happy to tell everybody in town about you," I said, "as soon as I figure out what the hell you really are. But to be honest, right now I just want to know what it's going to take to get you out of that kid's body without doing any more damage."

He shook his head with a half-hearted snort. "The child is lost and damned. Not to your hell, but to mine. It was fated to be so, the moment the tainted sacrament melted upon his tongue."

2.

The sacrament. Ink. The kids at the party had gotten a bad batch, all right, but even that didn't explain the spontaneous possession. Thanks to Jennifer's chemists, we'd sussed out the ingredients. Mostly a mild opiate, a dash of LSD for spice, and trace amounts of a magically active alchemical reagent. Why it was in there at all, we didn't know. I was starting to get an idea, though.

Ink had boomed onto the drug scene overnight, but all the usual suspects were coming up empty-handed. The Five Families, the Bratva, the Cali Cartel—none of them were involved in the trade or the pipeline, and everybody wanted to know who was slinging the stuff. I'd found the answer. It was an urban legend come to life, an outfit called the Network whose operatives had a knack for melting into thin air. Their foot soldiers had their minds and their tongues bound with curses, and they were recruiting world-class sorcerers for upper management.

The Network had tendrils everywhere, and I had a feeling we'd only seen the tip of the iceberg. We didn't have a clue who was pulling the outfit's strings, not until now.

"It's you." I glanced sidelong at Jennifer. "The man at the top."

Her eyes narrowed. "We were looking for *human* gangsters, or maybe some demons who went rogue from the courts of hell. No wonder nobody can find the Network's head honchos. They're runnin' the show from...well. Dunno. Not *here*, anyway."

"The Network," the creature in the teenager's body said, "is a clockwork toy. My brother kings and I wound it up many, many years ago and let it spin. We watch it, for amusement. Guide it where it needs guidance, answer the occasional prayer. And every now and then they come up with something to surprise and delight. Like this wondrous chemical that makes it so easy for us to slip into your world. Not the *intended* effect, but I won't let it go to waste. I'd almost forgotten the tiny pleasures of mortal flesh."

He pressed the tip of his index finger against the edge of the steel table.

Then he shoved down. The fingernail ripped up by the roots, tearing flesh, and oozed crimson along the exposed nail bed. Kemper shouted. He ran in and grabbed the kid's shackled wrists, trying to stop the king from hurting him again. Then a sound like a thunderclap exploded in the interview room and Kemper went flying. He hit the cinder-block wall and crumpled to the floor in a daze.

Steel flashed in the corner of my eye. I wasn't sure how Jennifer had slipped her razor blade through the metal detectors, but the edge slashed across her forearm. Her blood and her power burst forth, each fueling the other, and a ribbon of spilled scarlet twisted in the air above her open palm like a cobra ready to strike. I hooked my fingers, hissing the opening words of an exorcism chant in bastard Latin. Pressure swelled in my sinuses, the feeling of three magical fronts converging to brew a violent storm.

"*Leave. The kid. Alone*," I said through gritted teeth.

The king gave us an almost-pitying smile. "He is beyond mortal sensation now. And I cannot be contained."

He twirled his wrists. The shackles fell free, unlocked, clattering to the blood-spattered table. The kid's body rose, chair scraping back. Then his sneakers lifted from the concrete floor. His arms and legs dangled slack and his shoulders slumped as he levitated, hovering a foot off the ground.

I leaned down and gave Kemper a hand. He winced, rubbing one bruised shoulder, as I hauled him to his feet. The kid's head lolled to the left and right while his unholy passenger surveyed the three of us in amused silence.

"You didn't do this for shits and giggles," I told him. "You want something. Spill it."

"You weren't entirely wrong before. Damien Ecko failed me. With his death, I require a new emissary. Every king needs a prince. Or a court jester."

"Not interested," I said.

"You aren't first in line for the crown. There is a man, a prominent mover within the Network, who craves my personal attention. A magus of rot, deeply devoted, with great potential. I'm thinking of anointing him as my chosen servant."

"Might have better luck with a temp agency," Jennifer said. "Maybe hire two or three this time, so you've got a spare handy. Your 'chosen servants' don't last too long when they get in our way."

"That is the case." The possessed teenager's head bobbed, his sneakers swaying above the floor. "And so, I think I'd like to play a game. With you, Daniel Faust."

I didn't like the sound of that. "What if I don't want to play?"

"You possess every freedom, except for that one. The game has already begun. If this ambitious necromancer manages to slay you, I'll grant him the honor of becoming my servant. If you defeat him, the honor will be yours instead. In three nights' time, one of you will be dead, and one of you will be anointed. Either way, I benefit."

"Call off your dog. Already told you, I'm not interested."

"I won't try to tempt you with occult majesty," the king said. "You already know I could grant you the power of a charnel god. If that isn't enough to make your mouth water, what about the greatest power of all? *Knowledge*. You could share in the resources of the Network. A thousand eyes and ears. You could confound your enemies, and lay their plans to ruin."

"I already do pretty well in that department," I told him.

"Ah, but what about...*the* Enemy?"

That got my attention. The kid's lips curled back in a sneer of triumph.

"Now you're listening," he said. "The mantle of the Thief has been forced upon your head. And as the story always repeats itself—always—it *will* kill you if you don't find a means of returning the role to its rightful owner. You don't know how. But I do. And I could tell you."

"We'll figure it out," I said.

"Time is not on your side. And what about your wondrous new discovery, Howard Canton's wand? Why is the Enemy so afraid of Howard Canton, a man who lived and died while he was trapped in a prison-world, a man he never met? I could tell you. That wand isn't his only legacy. I could *show* you. And lead you to a treasure beyond imagining."

"And all I have to do is serve you and get cozy with the Network." I put one hand on my hip. "We still don't know what your endgame is, but as far as I can tell, you're just as bad as the Enemy."

"Hardly. Do you know what the Enemy desires?"

I did. I'd come face-to-face with the bastard at long last, in a blood-soaked vault beneath a Texas ranch. He wasn't shy about his intentions.

"He wants to burn it all," I said. "Everything. Every world, every life, every spark of hope. He wants to be the last man standing."

"Our ambitions are unkind," the king said, "but far less nihilistic. We—my brother kings and I—have use for this world, and for humanity. We have use for you."

"Don't hold your breath."

He inhaled. The teenager's chest swelled. And kept swelling, as his lungs expanded to the point of bursting. His ribs made a faint crackling sound as they began to fracture.

"Ahh," the king sighed, letting the air out in a long, sultry hiss.

"You're done here," I said. "I don't know exactly what you and your 'brother kings' are, but I'm pretty damn sure that Jennifer and I have *something* in our collective arsenal that can hurt you.

Get out of that kid's body, or we go nuclear on your ass. You've got five seconds."

"The child is dead. His soul is mine."

"Four seconds."

"Find my would-be protégé," he said. "Slay him, before he slays you. His plans are already in motion. The game has begun."

"Two seconds."

"No worries," the king rasped.

The teenager's arms shot up. He grabbed the sides of his head and his fingers curled tight in his unruly hair.

"I'll see myself out."

The kid's neck cracked like a gunshot as his hands wrenched his head to one side. His feet hit the floor, then the rest of him, collapsing glass-eyed and stone dead.

Kemper raced to the kid's side. He dropped to one knee and leaned over him, feeling for a pulse, hammering his motionless chest in a haze of denial and hope. I was past both of those things, standing stock-still with a breath trapped in my throat.

"Sugar," Jennifer said.

"I know. These Network assholes. Priority one."

"With a bullet," she said.

"With as many bullets as it takes." I turned to face her. "We need a meeting. Full Commission."

Kemper waved a flustered hand at us. His eyes were yellow-tinged, his half-blood nature rising to the surface with his stress. Glistening with the tears he was fighting to hold back.

Gary Kemper cared too much. He was a good cop.

"Don't say this shit in front of me," he snapped. "Just...not another fuckin' word. I don't wanna hear anything I'll have to lie about later. And before you do whatever you're gonna do, you need to see Mayor Seabrook. I was supposed to take you to her once...once you *fixed* this."

"Yeah," I said. "Okay, Gary."

"Just go. Damn it, I need to take care of this, make this shit disappear. Just *go*."

So we left. Jennifer and I held our silence until we were out in the parking lot. She clicked her key fob and an alarm system squawked. Headlights flicked to life and painted the stucco walls in gauzy white. After her Prius had gone out in a blaze of dubious glory, she'd upgraded; her new ride was a sleek Tesla Model S in metallic blue, with a jet-black leather interior and ash wood trim. Business was good.

"Plan of attack?" Jennifer asked me.

"We track that bad batch of ink to the source. *Somebody* sold it to those kids. And there's a good chance the rest of his supply is just as tainted. We need to get that shit off the streets before more people end up dead."

"Or worse."

I opened the passenger-side door. "Or worse."

"What about all that other stuff he said, this 'game' he wants to play?" She slid behind the wheel and I got in alongside her. The seat molded itself around my shoulders. "If he's sending another killer like Damien Ecko your way, you need to get ready to scrap."

"I can't worry about that right now. Can't let myself get distracted. Finding whatever's left of that bad ink has to be our top priority. And if we play our cards right, we'll take the dealer alive."

"He'll probably be like the last one we caught. With the, uh—" She gestured at her belly and winced. So did I. The last dealer had been bound by a geas—a magically enforced taboo to seal his lips—and we'd gotten a nasty surprise when I tried to set him free.

"We'll be ready for it this time. These people aren't untouchable, Jennifer. Every clue we dig up, every scrap of intel we gather, puts us one step closer to taking them down. There's a gap in their armor. *Every* organization has a gap in its armor. We've just got to find it."

She pushed a button on the dash. The panel lit up, glowing in the dark, the engine running silent.

"Agreed. So. Seabrook's office?"

"Seabrook's office." I sagged against the seat. "Let's get this over with."

3.

A lone security guard waited for us at the doors to city hall. He locked up behind us and pointed the way down a half-lit corridor without a word. A janitor buffed the gleaming marble with a floor polisher, his eyes down and his ears buried under orange plastic headphones. He bobbed his head to a song I couldn't make out, just the thrumming traces of a steady bass beat, as we skirted around him. At the end of the hall, white light shone against the pebbled glass of the mayor's office door.

The glass rattled under my knuckles. "It's open," called out a tired voice from the other side.

Mayor Seabrook was at the tail end of a very long day or the beginning of a new one. This far past midnight, it was hard to tell the difference. Either way, she'd been hitting the hard stuff; her fresh-roasted coffee was strong enough to perk me up with the smell alone, no cream or sugar to get in the way of her caffeine fix. Steam curled from an electric kettle on the credenza behind her desk, one foil bag of whole beans crumpled and empty, a second one freshly torn open and ready to serve.

She didn't offer us any. I didn't expect her to. She waved us toward the pair of low lemon-colored chairs opposite her desk, then turned her back on us while she poured herself a fresh cup.

"Children," she said.

"We don't like it any more than you do," I told her.

"And yet, you've done nothing."

"There was an ink lab in Albuquerque. *Was*. Past tense."

The mayor turned around and stared daggers at me over the rim of her mug. She took a long, slow sip and pointed to the darkness outside her office window.

"Is this Albuquerque?"

"What my associate means is," Jennifer said, "we're takin' steps to address the situation."

Seabrook took her seat. Shoulders hunched forward, nose wrinkled like a bulldog's.

"Let me give you a history lesson," she said. "In the eighties, my office, the FBI, and various civic and corporate interests came together, and we broke the Mafia's back. It took an enormous expenditure of time and resources, but it was done. And if it was done once, it can be done again."

"Let's keep this friendly," Jennifer said.

"Give me a reason to. I don't mind playing ball with you people, so long as you toe the line. It's a simple arrangement: you don't hurt the tourist trade, no public displays of violence, and you toss us the occasional bust so Commissioner Harding can keep his numbers up. I only had one other request. One simple, tiny request: that you keep this 'ink' shit out of my city. Now I have to give a press conference to explain why a dozen teenagers just died from a tainted batch of drugs on my administration's watch."

Thirteen, but apparently Gary hadn't called her yet. I didn't correct her. I looked her square in the eye and laid my cards down.

"You've heard of the Network," I said.

"I've heard of the bogeyman too," she said, drinking her coffee. "Doesn't make him real."

"This particular bogeyman is. The organization exists, it's nationwide—if not global—and it's behind the ink pipeline."

She chewed on that for a minute, face scrunched up like she didn't enjoy the taste. She washed it down with a swig of black coffee.

"Then bring me proof," she said. "I'm getting ready to leave for Boulder City in a couple of days. The United Conference of

Mayors is holding a special session to address the ink epidemic. We'll shine a spotlight on them, drag them out of hiding—"

I held up a hand. "No. Bad idea. When people poke around the Network's business, they end up dead, and they don't draw lines like we do. Cops, district attorneys, *mayors*—they'll bury anyone who looks at them sideways. You shouldn't even go to this thing. Stay home, and don't make waves."

That got her hackles up. "I haven't held my office this long by *not* making waves. My constituents expect action. And once people wake up to the morning headlines, you'd better believe they'll be demanding results."

"Which is why you need us," I said. "I've seen some of the Network's playbook. Trust me when I say that the cops and the feds combined can't handle this fight."

"But you can." Her tone made it clear just how much confidence she had in me. A little less than the coffee left in her mug. She pushed her chair back and got up to pour another cup.

Jennifer had her phone out, flipping through her photo gallery like she'd checked out of the discussion entirely. Odd, but I left her to it.

"We have resources the law doesn't," I said, "and needless to say, we don't have the same limitations—"

Seabrook cut me off with an irritated flick of her fingers. "Words. I'm hearing words. Meanwhile I've got twelve dead kids on my hands, a designer-drug epidemic, and a contaminated batch out on the streets about to kill *more* users. Harding warned me that I shouldn't get into bed with gangsters. I'm not sure you people even qualify for the title."

"Few months back," Jennifer drawled, still staring at her phone, "had a dealer on my payroll who decided to cut his supply with baby powder. Stretch it out, make more money with less product, and pocket the surplus behind my back, you know? Only he didn't know how to do it right. Killed three of his best customers. And instead of coming clean about it, telling me what he did so we could fix the situation, the wet-brained son of a biscuit panicked and sold the *rest* of the batch to get rid of it. Maybe six people died before we figured out what was what."

She found the photo she was looking for. Then she stood up, leaned over the mayor's desk, and turned her phone to give her a good look. Seabrook's lips slowly parted. The color ran from her face.

"That's what I did to him," Jennifer said.

"Why..." the mayor said, her voice a strained whisper. "Why did you take a *picture* of that?"

Jennifer put her phone away and gave her a smile.

"Simple. Now, when someone new joins my crew, I explain Jennifer's easy rules for success. And then I show 'em that picture, so they understand what happens when those rules get broken."

She leaned farther over the desk, closer. The smile never left her face, but her eyes went colder than a Siberian sunset as her voice dropped low.

"That *gangster* enough for you? Or do I need to show you the rest of my photo collection?"

I watched Seabrook's throat bulge as she swallowed, hard.

"We'll find the dealer those kids bought from," I said. "And if any of the bad batch is still around, it'll disappear without a trace. Just like the dealer."

* * *

On the other side of the mayor's office door, I shot Jennifer a dubious look.

"Seriously, you probably shouldn't carry that picture around on your phone."

"Can't prove it's real. Special effects, a Halloween decoration..." She hip-bumped me as we walked. "Ain't like they're ever gonna find his body."

"True, true. So, were you *trying* to scare the hell out of her? Because mission accomplished and well done."

"I was tired of her sass," she said. "One of Jennifer's rules for success: Jennifer gives the sass. She does not receive the sass. Seabrook just needed a little reminder of who's wearing the pants in this particular domestic arrangement. And you weren't wrong about keeping her away from that conference. I'd rather we had a scared mayor than a dead one."

"Scared only goes so far. We need some results, to show we're holding up our end of the bargain. I wasn't even going to ask her about the liquor license for the American."

The American was my pet project. A nightclub on the fringes of the Vegas Strip, built from the ground up to be a safe harbor for the city's underworld. Whether you carried a gun or a wand, no matter what color your blood ran, we'd be waiting with open arms and your favorite poison on tap. Not to mention a high-stakes backroom game or two, with no pesky IRS forms for the winners to fill out, and a secure vault to facilitate the exchange of contraband. I'd convinced every member of the New Commission's board of directors to kick in some seed money, guaranteeing that each of the city's biggest crews had a stake in the place and a vested interest in keeping it safe.

All we needed now, once construction wrapped up, was a liquor license. I'd breezed through a forest of red tape with ease, crafting a shell company with reams of fake paper (not to mention the American's fictional owner, one Mr. Rick Blaine), but the Board of Liquor and Gaming was a tough nut to crack. One phone call from Mayor Seabrook would grease the wheels, but she needed a little encouragement to play along.

I figured she'd cooperate if we made a show of good faith and drove the Network out of Vegas. Fine by me. We were going to do that anyway.

"Y'know, if we *have* to wait, it's not the biggest problem in the world," Jennifer told me. "Yeah, everybody on the Commission wants to see a return on their investment, but now that we're getting a grip on Nicky's old rackets, we're starting to see some real cash rolling in. The American's a small splash in a big pool."

Our footsteps echoed off the polished sweep of white marble, echoing down a long and lonely hallway lined with doors of pebbled glass. We traveled in that strange space just before dawn, when the bars and strip clubs had kicked out their last stragglers, the neon went cold, and the city took one slow, deep breath before the party started all over again. At this hour, only sharks kept swimming.

"It's not the money," I said. What was it, then? I fumbled for an answer, figuring it out as the words came to me. "I turn forty in a few months."

She put a hand on my shoulder. "Oh, I know. Believe me, I've been plannin' your party. We're going to have black balloons, black candles on the cake..."

"I've been thinking about it, is all."

"Getting older, or just getting old?"

"Both," I said. "But it's more like...I've ghosted my way through life. I pay cash, I carry fake paper, I don't leave footprints. And that's always been fine, that always worked for me."

"We *are* career criminals," Jennifer said. "It kinda goes with the lifestyle."

"And if I died tomorrow, outside of a few people's memories, there'd be nothing to show I ever existed at all." I dug deeper and found the words I was looking for. "I want to build something."

"Like a legacy," she said.

"I guess, yeah. I want to put my mark on this city. I want to build something so I can stand back and point to it and say, see that? That's *mine*. I made that."

"Sugar," Jennifer said, "you're havin' a midlife crisis. You know that, right?"

"Maybe."

We pushed out through the double doors and onto the granite steps. It was a desert night in early November; the bone-dry chill wasn't taking any prisoners. The bitter wind ruffled my hair and slipped an icy finger along the back of my neck, leaving goose bumps in its wake. A cold and loveless glow touched the mountains in the distance with the shimmer of false dawn.

"I'll shake a few trees, see if I can figure out an alternative option if Seabrook doesn't come through." She stifled a yawn behind her fist. "I'm bushed, gonna hit the sack for a few hours. You oughta do the same. Feels like one of those 'calm before the storm' situations."

I promised myself four hours of shut-eye, but I break promises all the time. I was up and moving in two, blasting my drowsiness away under the spray of an ice-cold shower and knotting a fresh tie around my neck as I headed for the door. I had work to do, and the warning of the King of Worms—that his would-be prince was on the move and gunning for my head—lingered at the back of my thoughts.

So did his offer.

I was used to being on the defensive, but never like this. The Enemy was coming after me, and if that wasn't bad enough, I'd been sucked into the same cosmic nightmare that spawned him. As far as the universe was concerned, I was the Thief, one of the characters in his endlessly repeating story. And the Thief's story always ended with a knife in his back. If I didn't get this curse off my head, and soon, the Enemy wouldn't have to knock me off; the fabric of reality itself would do it for him.

On the other side, we had the Network, a criminal occult cartel with ambitions we couldn't begin to decipher and a reach longer than the edges of the world. And Naavarasi, who had her own plans in motion. It felt like everyone wanted to use me, kill me, or both.

Taking the king's offer would solve all my problems. Attractive, but his pitch smelled as sour as month-old milk. If there was one thing a life of running con games had taught me, it was that when someone offered you the perfect solution, it was usually the perfect lie.

I didn't need help from the King of Worms. All I needed was a little breathing room. Just enough space to start throwing punches.

4.

I was still renting my wheels. The last I'd heard, my Barracuda had been "requisitioned" by Special Agent Harmony Black, an act I considered tantamount to grave robbery. And then dancing on my grave after robbing it.

The point is, I loved that car.

I had feelers out, trying to track it down so I could steal it back. At the moment, though, my ride was a dirty-silver Hyundai Elantra. Good mileage, good cargo space, and forgettable enough to vanish like a ghost in the city's arteries. I drove off the edge of the Vegas Strip and straight down, down into the neighborhoods the tourists never saw.

St. Jude's was open for breakfast. The place had been a dance hall in its heyday; now the wooden floors were scuffed and scarred, dust clung to the cathedral-style arches, and a skeleton crew of volunteers played host to the city's lost souls. Most mornings I could find Pixie working the soup kitchen's serving line. When I first met her, I assumed she was doing penance for some unbearable sin, trying to make amends.

Turned out she just liked to help people and make the world a little better. I guess that should have been my first assumption. Says something about me that it wasn't. But if I were a good person, I'd have been rolling up my sleeves and helping out, not waving cash under her nose to lure her away from her work.

"Ten minutes," she told me, passing her ladle to another volunteer and stepping out from behind the serving line. She led me over to an open spot at the end of a row of folding tables, lugging her laptop under one arm.

The recap took me five. I left out the part about the King of Worms. Just the bare and bloody facts, more or less how they'd be splashed across the morning's papers.

"I need to know where they got that bad batch," I said. "And who sold it to them, before any more of that shit hits the streets."

She flipped up the lid of her laptop, all business, and slipped on a chunky pair of Buddy Holly glasses.

"Keep your money," she told me. "This one's a freebie."

"I figure our first step is to figure out who was at that house. Not everybody took the ink, and the kids who weren't affected—or killed by the ones who did—scattered before the cops showed up. If I can track one of them down, they can at least tell me who brought the drugs to the party. I'm thinking...teenagers, they're all on social media, right? Should I look on Facebook?"

She arched an eyebrow at me. "Facebook? Seriously? They're in high school. What are you going to check next, MySpace? Ooh, maybe try LiveJournal too."

"Is...is that a thing I should be doing?"

I was treated to the most extravagant of eyerolls.

"Instagram," she said. "Everyone's on Instagram now."

"I'm not."

Her fingers danced across the keyboard. "Everyone who isn't old. Got a name, somebody you know was there?"

"Helms, H-e-l-m-s, William, middle initial H. He was one of the victims."

It took some searching. And longer than ten minutes, more like forty, but she wasn't watching the clock anymore. Pixie was a hunter in her element, plowing through waves of data like a torpedo. Finally, she struck gold: one of William's classmates had been on the scene. She'd left early—lucky for her—and apparently she hadn't heard about the massacre yet because her Instagram feed was chock-full of pictures from the party. *Best night of the year*, she called it.

Lots of smiles, lots of goofing around, lots of illegally bought beer sloshing in red Solo cups, but no names and nothing that even hinted at who brought the drugs. Lots of happy teenagers who were currently lying on cold slabs down at the city morgue. My stomach went tight. All they wanted was to blow off some steam, have a little fun. They hadn't done anything to deserve this.

"Tell me something," Pixie said as we studied the photographs in silence.

"The answer is yes," I told her.

She was looking for reassurance, asking if I was going to get my hands on the person who did this. I was. Then she would have asked me, if I'd let her, if I was going to kill him. I was. We'd known each other long enough that all she needed was the shorthand. She nodded and clicked through to the next picture.

"Hold it," I said. "There. That one."

She squinted at the shot. It was just like the others, a couple of kids clowning around and almost spilling their beer on a floral-upholstered couch while the party swirled around them.

"What do you see?" she asked me.

"An eyewitness." pointed to the corner of the shot, where a girl was dancing like a dervish, whirling too fast for the camera to catch her face. Just her short-cut mop of cobalt-blue hair.

* * *

There are places where a man pushing forty shouldn't be seen hanging out alone. Toy stores, for instance. Playgrounds. Or in my case, cruising slow along the curb outside Palo Verde High School. Students walked in tight clumps along the sidewalk, heads low, voices hushed. Word about last night was spreading. I waited around, catching a few looks from parents dropping off their kids, until I spotted my target. My passenger-side window hissed down.

"Melanie," I called out. "Get in."

She was walking with a trio of friends. They all looked like they'd survived an earthquake, but Melanie wore the only face that blended a little guilt with the loss. Her buddies looked from her to me and back again.

"Is this...like, your uncle?" one asked her.

"Yes," I said. "Melanie, Uncle Daniel needs you to get in the goddamn car."

She jerked a shaky thumb over her shoulder. "I...I have to get to school."

"You can talk to me now, or you can talk to your mother later. Your choice."

I waited, as patiently as I could manage, while she stuttered out an excuse I couldn't hear and sent her friends on ahead of her.

High school was hard. Facing it as a cambion—half human, half demon—was even harder. A while back, Melanie, was running with a gang of would-be rebels suffering from delusions of competency. That I could hide from her mom. When I caught her getting drunk at Winter on a fake ID, chasing clues to her dad's murder in the bottom of a cocktail glass, I decided I could keep my lips sealed once I was sure she'd gotten her head on straight.

This was different.

This time I wasn't sure what I was going to do. I figured I'd hear the kid out, then decide. She got in and sat there with her head bowed and her hands in her lap. The faintest outline of blue veins pulsed across her face like the pattern of a butterfly's wings; cambion blood exerts itself under stress. Normally they can keep it under control, keep their true nature hidden from the world, but Melanie was still learning. And I could only imagine how much stress she was feeling right about then.

"You're putting me in a lousy position, you know that?"

She flicked her gaze at me. "How do you mean?"

"I just got off your mom's shit list. I mean, *just* got off it. Now I find out you were at a party where twelve kids overdosed and killed each other. If I don't tell Emma—"

"Please." Her hand shot out and grabbed my wrist, squeezing hard. "You *can't*."

"Calm. Down. Take deep breaths. Your face is showing."

She checked herself in the rearview mirror and ducked low in the seat, doing breathing exercises until the web of blue veins faded away. Four seconds in, four seconds out.

"I'm not looking to bust you," I told her, "but you're one of the only living witnesses and I need to know what happened out there. What were you even doing at that party? I mean, drugs? That's not the kind of crowd you run with."

She found something interesting on her knees to stare at. "You don't know what kind of crowd I run with."

"I know you've got a four-point-oh grade average and you're the star of the school paper *and* the track team. Trust me, Emma makes sure we know about these things."

"Oh God." She slumped lower in her seat.

"You think I'm kidding? The biggest crime bosses in Las Vegas are regularly appraised of your academic prowess. The Bishops and the Calles are very impressed." Deadpan, I waggled my hand from side to side. "The Inagawa-kai think you need to study harder and add some more extracurriculars, but you know the yakuza, those guys are hardcore."

Melanie mashed her face into her hand. "I was just…partying, okay? That's all."

"And drinking. Melanie, you know the rules. You can't be doing that around outsiders, not until you get older and you can keep your blood under control. You flash your real face to the wrong person and then it's not just your mother who has to fix things. That's when Caitlin gets involved. What about the ink, did you take any?"

"What? *No!*" She glared at me like I'd slapped her across the face. "I don't do that stuff, okay? But…that's why I was there. I was undercover."

"You're going to have to explain that one."

She took another deep breath. It gusted loose in an exhausted sigh.

"We've never had a big drug problem at my school—a little beer, a little pot, normal high school stuff, but not, like, *drugs.*

A couple months ago, though, ink started going around. I mean, everybody's doing it. But everybody's getting it third- or fourth-hand, buying it off somebody who knows somebody who knows somebody else. And I was thinking, if I could break a really big story for the school paper, I mean, real-world-journalism big, it'd look amazing on my college applications."

I connected the dots. "You've been trying to track down the source. The dealer at the top of the food chain."

"Exactly. If I could find the student bringing it in—or maybe it's even a faculty member—can you imagine? It would be huge. Maybe even the 'full-ride scholarship and job offers after I graduate' kind of huge."

"Okay," I told her. "First thing, your Nancy Drew adventure is officially over. Drop the story."

"Dan, you can't—"

"Oh, I can. We've been doing some digging too. Ink isn't just a designer drug. It's mixed with alchemical reagents. Nasty stuff."

Her brow scrunched up. "There's magic in it? Why? What does it do?"

"We don't know yet, and that's a big problem. What we do know is the cartel pushing this stuff isn't any ordinary gang. You do *not* want to land in their crosshairs. I'm sorry, I know this was a big deal to you, but you need to leave the sleuthing to me. What did you find out?"

"I don't know," she said, sullen, talking to her knees again. "Not much."

"Melanie."

Her shoulders sagged. "Okay, fine. This kid named Rob Ackerman is in my algebra class. It was his house, his party. I heard he was going to have ink, a lot of it, so I bugged him until he threw me a pity invite. I thought he might be the source."

"Was he?"

"No. And he...he didn't make it out." She folded her arms, hugging herself as her lips curled. "He was the first one to, you know, lose it when the crazy hit. But I snooped around before everything went bad and found out *his* supplier is a guy named Todd. Todd something, I don't even know his last name, but everybody knows him. Major burnout. He drives this van from the eighties, and I think he actually lives in it."

"Another student?" I asked.

"No. I mean, he was. He dropped out last year, but he still hangs around campus, mostly trying to pick up freshman girls. Gross. I think he works at the Burger Barn on Lake Mead Boulevard when he's not being Creeper McCreeperson."

"Did he take the ink too?"

"No," Melanie said. "He wasn't even there. Which was weird, because Rob invited him, and Todd *always* shows up at parties. Like, whether he's invited or not. He sold Rob the ink and said he'd drop by later, but he never showed up."

It wasn't weird, not if you saw the world like I did. The pieces clicked into place clear as the desert sky. Melanie was a good kid, too good, too much heart to see the obvious answer.

"We've been treating this like somebody slipped up, contaminated the ink by accident. Wrong assumption."

She tilted her head at me. "What do you mean?"

"Todd wasn't there because he knew what was going to happen," I said. "The batch was tainted on purpose. This wasn't a mistake. It was mass murder."

5.

Melanie sat ash-faced in the passenger seat, looking like a shell-shocked soldier pulled from the trenches.

"What they did, when they took that stuff," she said in a small voice. "What they did to each other...I barely got out. If I hadn't been able to barricade the bathroom door when everyone went crazy then slip out the window...*why?* Why would anyone *do* that?"

Damn good question. The Network was an oiled precision machine, built for stealth. It operated in the deepest waters, and we had no idea how long it had been around. Lurking in silence, an urban legend. If the law or the media managed to swing a spotlight in their direction, they smashed it without hesitation.

Thirteen dead kids, killed in some of the worst ways imaginable thanks to a bad batch of ink, was a disaster in the making. In one night's work they'd guaranteed more cops, more feds, more public funding to fight them tooth and nail. It was equal parts pointless and stupid, and the Network wasn't stupid.

I tried to put myself in their shoes, work out a reason why I'd pull that move, and I came up empty. If I wanted somebody dead, I put a gun to their head and pulled the trigger; I didn't toss a hand grenade into a crowded room and hope I hit the one person I was aiming for. Then again, maybe that was the point: to obfuscate the intended target.

Like the child of somebody they wanted to send a message to.

"Any of your classmates, the kids at the party," I said, "do any of their parents work in law enforcement? Or work for the city, maybe?"

Melanie walked back through her memories. Aching, and I ached right with her. I knew from experience that she was picturing her friends two ways right now: before, and after.

"Jenna...her dad's a lawyer, I think. There's this one guy—I don't really know him, he's in my social studies class—his dad's a lobbyist, I'm pretty sure. I don't know."

"I'll figure it out," I told her. "You should get to class. They'll probably dismiss early, anyway. Considering."

She put her hand on the door and froze.

"Something I've been wanting to ask you," she said.

"Shoot."

Melanie turned in her seat and looked my way. Her eyes glistened. The threat of tears brought out the red, bloodshot from loss and lack of sleep.

"Teach me."

"Teach you?"

"Magic," she said.

"That's...that's not a good idea."

She perked up, intense, like she was asking permission to go to a rock concert and had a list of preplanned arguments.

"My mom would be okay with it! I asked her! I mean, not about you, specifically—she wants to set me up in a mentoring program with this guy she works with, ew, no thanks—but in general she's okay—"

I cut her off with a distracted wave. "That's not the issue. I had an apprentice, once."

A little of her energy faded, and I saw the look in her eyes; she had her junior reporter hat back on.

"What happened?"

Then it was my turn to look back and see the before and after.

Before: thick as thieves, my arm around Desi Srivastava's shoulders, snapping a selfie with a disposable camera in front of the dancing fountains at the Medici. I still had the photograph. I took it out sometimes, when I was drunk and felt like torturing myself.

After: sand swirled across the floor of a deserted office lobby, rising up in a whirlwind, taking on form. A drooling crocodile snout, shimmering armored hide. A custom-built trap for me and my crew, at the end of a heist we were never supposed to survive.

"*I can do this, Dan!*" Desi's voice echoed off the inside of my skull. "*I can do this!*"

Her head hit the floor, bouncing across the blood-streaked tile, two seconds before the rest of her body did.

"It ended badly," I told Melanie.

"That doesn't mean this will! I'm a good student. You know I'm a good student."

"I know you are. I'm not a good teacher."

"I don't believe that. And I don't want to learn from my mom's friends. She's already pushing me to intern at Southern Tropics over the summer, and I..." She shook her head, her bottom lip trapped between her teeth. "I don't want to work for those people, okay? I don't want that."

Southern Tropics Import-Export, aka the shell company that covered the Court of Jade Tears' operations on earth. Emma was the queen of the boardroom, handling Prince Sitri's cash, and she expected Melanie to follow in her footsteps.

"Don't know if you heard," I said, "but apparently *I* work for 'those people' now."

"That's not the same thing. You know why Prince Sitri knighted you."

"Do I?" I arched an eyebrow. "Clue me in."

"Because he thought it would be funny, and he wanted to screw with you. Duh. Come on, even I know that. You can mostly still do whatever you want. I mean, you're Daniel Faust. Nobody really expects you to toe the line. *Any* line. For me, it's...it's different. I'm supposed to be all on board." She shook invisible pom-poms. "Yay, hell. I'm supposed to be all excited about spending the rest of my life working for my mom's shitty company, surrounded by jerks, which will put me on an *amazing* fast track to spending all of eternity being surrounded by even bigger jerks. I know, I'm a cambion, that's supposed to be my thing—"

"Your thing is whatever you *want* your thing to be," I said. "Your blood doesn't get a say in the matter."

"See? See, that's what I'm talking about. You don't try to put me in a box like that. When I'm talking to you I never feel like I'm...I don't know. Wrong inside."

I decided to shift gears. Melanie was a pressure cooker about to burst, and there was more going on than a sudden desire to expand her studies.

"You know," I said, "knowing magic doesn't make anything easier. Life is tough, especially at your age. There aren't any cheat codes."

"I don't care about easier. It would make me *safer*. Hello? I could have gotten killed last night. And it's not the first time. Remember the Redemption Choir? Or when Damien Ecko set a zombie loose in my house?"

"You got through it okay."

"I was lucky. I can't count on luck."

"You can't count on magic," I told her. "Why do you think I carry a gun?"

She pushed her head back against the seat and balled her hands into fists. Out of words, out of oxygen.

"Hey," I said. "What's going on with you? Talk to me."

She forced a breath, but her muscles stayed taut, like she had steel cables under her skin.

"You know where I want to go to college? Emerson. Their journalism school is the best, okay? God tier."

"Okay."

"And Emerson," she said, "is in Boston. About two thousand miles outside Prince Sitri's borders. And my mother is a dignitary in his court. Which means I *can't* go to Emerson, because I'd probably be kidnapped or killed the second I got off the plane. I can't go *anywhere*."

"You've got options—"

"No," she said. "I...I don't. I don't. My entire world is Jade Tears territory, because *I can't leave*. Because I'm a cambion, because I'm Emma Loomis's daughter—I was born with a target on my back and I can never, ever take it off. And all my friends? They're leaving. They're going to Chicago, and New York, and Boston, and Florida. They're going to all these places I can never go, *will* never go, and I'm never going to—"

The dam broke and the tears flowed at the end of a ragged, strangled word. I pulled her close and she let me, and she shook for a while. I held her shoulders and felt my shirt grow damp.

"Once we graduate, I'm never going to see any of my friends again," she whispered into my chest. "And my mom is like, it's fine, you'll make new friends at Southern Tropics, and I *hate* those people. I need...I need to be able to make my own choices. I need something that's *mine*."

I understood. Just like I knew I couldn't give her what she needed. I let her finish, holding her until there was nothing but a few wet sniffles left. I wiped her eyes with my sleeve. A stray, salty drop splashed across my fingers.

"I'm here for you," I told her. "I will always be here for you. Know that. But...I can't teach you, Melanie. It's not you. It's me. I can't do that again."

The hope in her eyes sputtered out and died. Her smudged tears felt like fresh blood on my hand.

"Fine," she said. "Thanks for nothing."

"Melanie—"

She shoved open the door and turned her face away.

"I'm late for class."

She was gone before I could think of a way to make her stay. I understood better than she thought. I wasn't far from her age when Bentley and Corman took me under their wing. They did more than teach me: they gave me confidence, an anchor in the world, a source of strength.

Something that was mine.

I could have said yes, could have passed the torch along, but I'd tried that once before. When I looked into Melanie's eyes, all I could see was Desi. I cared too much about Melanie to ever let her get that close to me.

6.

The sunset bled tangerine in long streaks across the desert sky. The Vegas Strip came to life and fired up the neon, unleashing its clarion call to the gamblers, the pleasure-hunters, the hungry of all appetites. I looked at the ghost of my reflection in a floor-length window. Suited up, Italian loafers, paisley silk handkerchief with a razor-sharp crease.

We'd rented a conference room at the Flamenco. Pixie came early, swept for bugs, and jetted before the meeting started. I did my part at the same time, hunting for witch-eyes and scrying spells. The room was clean. The attendees weren't, and most of them were wearing a small stolen fortune on their backs or their wrists. We'd turned the place into a den of thieves, the head honchos of the city's biggest crews coming together for our regular sit-down.

"You look upset. I get nervous when you look upset."

Chou Yong, the recently promoted Red Pole of the 14K Triad, stood on my right. He'd earned his stripes in the field after his boss got eaten by a shape-shifting assassin, so I could understand where he was coming from. His double chin bobbed as he looked me up and down.

"Had to disappoint somebody today," I told him.

"I do that every day." Yong rolled his eyes to the darkening sky outside the window. "My mother. And she makes sure to remind me."

"Think we're about ready to get rollin'," Jennifer called out.

She took her seat at the head of the long, oval conference table, mahogany inlaid with black leather and an alligator-hide sheen.

I sat at her left hand and took a long, slow look around the room as everyone got settled. In the wake of Nicky Agnelli's downfall, the self-proclaimed King of Las Vegas escaping just ahead of a federal dragnet, Jennifer had taken the feuding factions of the city and forged them into a more or less united front. We had the top men in the Cinco Calles and the Fine Upstanding Crew sitting side by side, after five years of scrapping. The 14K and the Inagawa-kai were being civil to each other. Even the Blood Eagles had come to the table, taking time out from their busy schedule of roaring down the desert highways and stomping anyone who looked at them sideways. Our feud with the Chicago Outfit had cost us, but we came out on top and tighter than before.

"We're starting to look like a serious threat," I murmured.

Jennifer cracked a bottle of Perrier and gave me the side-eye. "Sure thing, sugar. Thanks to...*the guy*."

I struggled not to bury my face in my palm. On the far side of the table, Emma Loomis was getting settled in; we'd exchanged a brief hello when she arrived and not much else, while I tried to decide how much to tell her about Melanie's little adventure last night. I was still deciding. Emma looked like a wealthy, coiffed suburban soccer mom, but the demon that lived under her stolen skin didn't take prisoners.

Jennifer waited until everyone simmered down, pushed her chair back, and took command of the room.

"Let's tackle the elephant, first things first," she said. "Did my damned best to stop it, but Nevada made pot legal and that's just how it is. Good news is, saw this comin' way back when, and made nice with a couple of our congress critters. My people were first, second, and twentieth in line for dispensary licenses."

Eddie Stone, war chief of the Bishops, smoothed the lapels of his peacock-blue suit. His upper lip curled back and flashed a golden tooth.

"How many we talking?" he asked.

"Enough to recoup *some* of what we're losing in street deals. Low risk, pure profit. For the ones we don't control, I reckon we shift gears and move into...helpin' these good folks take proper care of their income."

"You're talking about protection."

"Sure," Jennifer said. "It's a cash business, and most banks won't do business with dispensaries. They'll be needing our help to keep that money tidy and safe. And if they don't want our help, well...lots of bad things can happen."

Chou Yong raised one stubby finger. "Can we talk about the reclamation?"

That was what we were calling the slow, grindstone march toward taking back all of Nicky Agnelli's former rackets. His overnight downfall had created a power vacuum in the city and a gigantic mess. Lots of smaller crews and independent operators going rogue, carving out their own little fiefdoms. There were a lot of people who had faithfully paid out to Nicky for years but didn't quite grasp the change in management. Yet. We were working hard to convince them.

Jennifer looked his way. "Whatcha got, sugar?"

"My people have been focusing our efforts on the Transport Workers Union. Taking control of McCarran Airport—quietly and seamlessly—is key to any number of future endeavors."

Winslow leaned back in his chair and waved his long-necked bottle of Bud at Yong. The grizzled biker was the top dog of the Blood Eagles, not to mention the personal firearms concierge to almost everyone in the room.

"Lotta cargo coming in and out of McCarran. Be nice to have somebody on the inside who can finger the best stuff, get us schedules and plate numbers."

"My thoughts exactly," Yong replied. "The union has a board election scheduled next month, and two seats are up for the taking. If we can place a pair of faithful hands—"

"Pick your dogs," Winslow rumbled. "Anybody who doesn't

look like they're gonna vote right, my boys'll be happy to point out the error of their ways."

"Where are we on Donaghy Waste Management?" Jennifer asked.

Eddie shook his head and stared at the table. "We're nowhere. Can't even get these people to take a meeting, let alone get any leverage and dig our hooks in. Their corporate structure's all kinds of screwed up. Managers that don't exist, paper trails that all lead offshore...pretty sure these dudes are more crooked than we are."

"Don't fret," Jennifer said. "As I recall, Nicky never managed to dip his beak in neither. We'll crack 'em sooner or later. Somebody give me an update on—"

Three sharp knocks sounded at the door. One of Jennifer's hired hands poked his head in; he'd traded his street gear for an off-the-rack suit that bulged in all the wrong places. She waved him close. He whispered in her ear, and one of her eyebrows lifted.

"Speak of the devil," she said. "Looks like we've got a special guest. Send him on in."

The last time I saw Nicky Agnelli, he was being raced into Sunrise Hospital by a team of paramedics. We'd both gotten bushwhacked by the Chicago Outfit, hauled off to be tortured, killed, and dumped out with tomorrow's trash. I managed to cut myself loose, the hard way. Habit made me glance down. One sleeve of my dress shirt rode up just far enough to flash the ugly webwork of scars on my wrist. A permanent reminder marking where the soldering iron had scorched through the duct tape and charred my skin.

Just a bad memory now. Before that week was over, Winslow's boys managed to track down the Outfit's torture specialist. They served him up to me on a platter and I made sure to pay him back with accrued interest, for me and Nicky both, before I buried him.

For a man who had nearly been beaten into a coma—not to mention fleeing Vegas with the feds hot on his heels—Nicky was looking good. That's the nice thing about being half demon, I'm told: the blood keeps you young and healthy. He had his hair greased back, his Porsche Design glasses in place, and a new suit tailored to fit. His escorts didn't hurt, either. Juliette and Justine, the twin blondes poured into little black cocktail dresses.

I wasn't fooled. Skintight dresses or not, they were both armed and deadly. Not that they needed weapons to turn a meeting into a massacre at the drop of a hat. The rest of the room was feeling the same vibe. Shoulders tensed up, eyes narrowed, and a few hands dipped dangerously under the conference table.

"So, uh...hi," Nicky said.

He cringed under the weight of a roomful of silent stares.

"All right." He nodded. "This is awkward as shit, not going to deny it. Seeing as you all used to, you know, work for me. And now you don't. Hey, we had some good times though, right?"

Eddie Stone folded his arms tight and snorted. "Bitch, please."

That looked like the general sentiment. Jennifer hovered her palms a few inches over the table and pushed down the rising tide of dissent.

"Hear him out," she said. "We can give him that much."

Juliette flung out her hand and pointed. "Listen to her. Listen to the voice of reason. Even if she sounds like a total hick with that accent. Which she does."

"And she smells like patchouli," her twin added. "Patchouli, sadness, and failure."

"And she dresses like she shops at thrift stores. Not good ones. Cheap ones for poor people."

Jennifer closed her eyes and took a slow, deep breath.

"I will shoot you both," she said.

"*Ladies*," Nicky said. He regrouped and tried again. "Look, I ain't trying to come back. That ship's sailed and we all know it. I'm starting fresh. Setting my sights up north."

"How far north?" Winslow asked. "Canada?"

"Reno," he replied.

Not that far north, then. Four hundred and forty-odd miles northwest, a hop and a skip from the California border. Within grabbing distance of Carson City, too. I flicked my gaze across the table and took the temperature of the room. Cold skies, light turbulence.

"The city's primed to pump gold," Nicky said, "and right now it's just some old-school Vegas Mob refugees from the eighties and a handful of feuding crews running the place. One good push could drive 'em all out, easy."

Jennifer tilted her head, sizing him up. "And you're tellin' us as a courtesy, or...?"

He dug deep, looking like a kid who couldn't leave the table until he ate his broccoli.

"I need your help. The damn feds took everything; they cleaned me out. I had contingencies on contingencies, but they foxed me good. To make this happen, I need liquid cash and I need shooters." Nicky glanced my way. "Some occult firepower wouldn't hurt, either."

Nobody said a word. Nicky wrung his hands and shifted his weight from foot to foot.

"I'm not asking for old times' sake, okay? This is pay for play. You help me out, then once I get a foothold you can...you have no idea how much it fuckin' pains me to say this, but you can dip your beak in Reno. You'll be repaid with interest. More importantly, let's talk long-term strategy. We'll be partners, with a mutual defense pact. After the spanking we just gave Chicago—"

"'We'?" Jennifer asked.

Nicky pouted at her. "I was here. I did my part. Anyway, you're making waves now. You've got people talking, and bigger sets than the Outfit—I'm talking about the Detroit Combination, I'm talking about the Five Families—are sizing you up. Maybe you don't *need* a friend close to Vegas—a friend who can move fast to cover your back, and keep an extra ear out for trouble—but can you really say you wouldn't *want* one?"

"Give us a minute," Jennifer told him.

7.

Organized crime is a trust-based operation. Every deal you make, every choice, boils down to predicting your business partners' moves. Guess right and you make some money. Guess wrong and you get a gun in your face or cuffs on your wrists. We had one advantage, once the conference-room door swung shut and we were left to make a decision: we all knew Nicky Agnelli. Which meant we knew how he operated, what his pressure points were, and how likely he was to keep his word.

"If the weasel's gonna be out there," Eddie said, "I'd rather have him where I can keep an eye on him. Besides, hate to say it, but he has a point. After Chicago, it's only a matter of time before somebody else steps up to test us. Be nice to have a little backup."

Yong steepled his fingers on the table and frowned. "He was invested in being the 'King of Las Vegas.' His ego is more precious to him than his bank balance. How long, once he gets his footing back, before he comes to reclaim his old kingdom? Reno is a poor man's throne by comparison."

"Don't forget," Jennifer said, "that was before the feds made their move and pushed him into the shadows. Nicky is a fugitive now; his old lifestyle, that wannabe-celebrity-out-on-the-town deal, is over and done. He *can't* have it back. He knows that. Nicky's hungry, but he's not stupid."

A hush fell, the room settling into an uneasy impasse. Winslow took a pull on his bottle of beer and looked my way.

"I ain't gonna kick one stray bullet into the pot before I see a plan that makes sense," he said. "And he's gonna need more than bullets. You in or out?"

He was right. Nicky was going to need my kind of help to get a foothold in Reno. There were only two magicians on the Commission, me and Jennifer. Jennifer was our chair; she couldn't be running off to fight a border war. Which meant the entire decision—work with Nicky, or tell him to go pound sand—had just been dumped in my lap. If I backed out, that was that. No deal.

If Nicky had approached me alone, one on one, I knew what my answer would have been: no and *hell* no. Too much risk for the reward. But this decision would affect the entire Commission, our future, everything we were trying to build in Vegas.

Building a strong coalition, with a mutual-defense pact that swept the Mojave from north to south, was the smart-money play. Bad and risky for me, but good for the team. I had decided, along the line, that I wanted to be part of something bigger than myself. Turned out stepping up was the easy part. Following through was where the real work came in.

"*If* Nicky's plan checks out," I said, "I'll lend a hand. We could use a strong partner. And like Eddie said, at least this way we know where Nicky is and what he's up to. My vote is a yes."

Winslow snorted at me over his bottle. "*The guy* has spoken."

* * *

We gave Nicky the good news and he gave us a promise to deliver a full plan of attack. That's where we left it for the night. Jennifer banged the gavel, hotel staff wheeled a drink cart in, and we broke up into little pockets of conversation. I was mostly there for the booze. I was nursing a gin and tonic by the window, looking out over the neon wilderness, when Nicky sidled up alongside me.

"That couldn't have been easy," I said.

He clinked his glass against mine and tossed back a swig of deep-brown liquor.

"Easier than playing the punching bag for those Chicago

pricks," he said. "Never got the chance to thank you for getting me out of there."

"You bounced back, looks like."

"Physically." He glanced over his shoulder, spotting the twins across the room. "Didn't have much of a choice but to rest up for a while."

"What'd they do, tie you to the bed, stick a funnel in your mouth, and pour chicken soup in until you felt better?"

He squinted at me. "How'd you know?"

"Lucky guess."

Neither of us had anything to say after that. We were going to be working together in Reno, for a few days anyway. Just like old times. But bringing up old times meant bringing up the reasons we'd burned the bridge between us.

Then again, maybe that made him the best person to talk to.

"You remember Melanie?" I asked him. "Emma Loomis's daughter."

He nodded, thinking back. "Yeah. Met her once or twice. Good kid."

"She wants me to teach her."

"Teach—" He paused, uncertain. Then the light went on. "Oh. Wow. How'd she take it when you turned her down?"

"How do you know I turned her down?"

He curled his lips into a humorless hook of a smile.

"C'mon, Dan. How long have we known each other?"

"Long time."

"Long time." He sipped his drink and looked to the city lights, glimmering in the dark like a carnival. "I've seen you low, I've seen you down and out...but I've only seen you broken once. Just the once."

"It's not just about the past. You know as well as I do that magic and the life go hand in hand. Melanie's too smart, too good to get caught up in this gangster shit. She can do better for herself than we did."

"Doesn't have to go hand in hand." He gave me an impish look. "I hear the FBI's hiring."

"Don't even joke about that."

"It's not mandatory is all I'm saying. And c'mon. Don't kid a kidder. It's got nothing to do with wanting to keep Melanie pure and clean and away from a life of crime. It's about Dizzy."

I thought I caught the shadow of her ghost in the window glass. Desi's easy stride, always with a little swagger. A smile that lit up the darkest of dive bars, two seconds before the crack of a pool cue. I drank my gin and tonic.

"She died on my watch."

"She died because she didn't listen to her teacher," Nicky said.

My grip tightened on the glass. "Careful."

"Am I lying? Why's Melanie want to learn the trade, anyway?"

"She feels like she's got a target on her back."

"Does she?" Nicky asked.

Between being born a cambion—the absolute bottom rung of hell's legions, free game for the monsters higher up the ladder—and the daughter of a ranking court official...yeah, she did. That was the one thing I couldn't argue.

"She could use a little extra help," I said. "The kid's got to deal with the consequences of other people's bad choices. Not her fault, but she still has to deal with it. That's life."

"And you could give her the tools she needs to survive. Just sayin'."

"I gave Dizzy the tools, too," I said.

"You can't control what other people do, Dan." Nicky chuckled into his glass. "Believe me, if I knew how to do that, I wouldn't be standing here like a bum with my hat in my hand. All you can do is help, or not help."

"You think I should teach her."

"Didn't say that. Do what you want. I just think you need to remember something. You know that thing you just said, about how Melanie's got to deal with other people's bad choices?"

"Yeah?"

"Dizzy made a bad choice, too. What happened to her wasn't your fault. Wasn't my fault, either. She just made a bad choice, a long time ago. Don't make Melanie pay for it."

I had to think about that. I nodded to his glass.

"Look at you, being insightful for a change. Must be the liquor talking."

"A little lubrication greases the mental wheels," he said. "So. Me and you in Reno. We're getting the band back together, man."

"With a few changes this time around. Number one, I'll be there to work *with* you, not take orders—"

He held up his free hand in surrender. "Understood."

"Number two, I'm not promising anything until I see the battle plan. If everything checks out, I'll do what I can to help."

"Also understood." He looked to the window again. His gaze went distant, wistful behind his titanium glasses. "Won't be the same. God. *Reno*. Was a time I wouldn't have wiped my feet in that town. I hope you're taking notes."

"I'm not enjoying this, if that's what you mean."

"What I mean is learn from my mistakes. You know that poem by, who was it, Shelley? 'Ozymandias.'"

"Look who's all cultured tonight," I said.

"I'm serious. It's about this fallen, broken statue in the middle of a wasteland, and on the pedestal it reads, 'My name is Ozymandias, king of kings. Look on my works, ye mighty, and despair.'"

"Never heard of him."

"That's the point," Nicky said. "This Ozymandias guy, he was hot shit in his day, right? King of *kings*. Then the desert blew in, and the sandstorms raged, and...*pfft*. Nothing left but a pedestal with some broken legs and a name that the world forgot."

He rapped his glass against the window. Dark liquor sloshed like dirty water, leaving an oily sheen in its wake. He swept his hand along the shining neon, slow, taking it all in.

"There was a time, all of this was mine. Every door in town was open to me. Every restaurant had a prime table with my name on it, seven nights a week. Everybody had an envelope stuffed with green, and everybody smiled when they handed it over. I was the king of kings."

He tore his gaze from the window and looked my way.

"Then one day I woke up and everything was gone. *Everything*. Then I realized the truth. This city is a boneyard, Dan. And the vultures are always circling. There's always someone, someone younger, hungrier, ready to swoop in and eat you for dinner. Vegas is yours now, you and your pals. And that's fair. That's fair and square. But you'd better keep one eye over your shoulder and never ever sleep, because the second you do, what happened to me is gonna happen to you."

"Cheerful thought," I said.

"What do you want, I should blow sunshine up your ass? I respect you too much to lie."

I caught sight of Emma across the room, saying her goodbyes and easing her way to the door.

"Speaking of," I told him, "need to show some respect of my own. Call me, okay?"

"I got your number."

I crossed the conference room on an intercept course, bracing myself for a discussion I didn't want to have.

8.

I caught up with Emma. Two minutes later, she was tugging me out the door by my sleeve. We caught the elevator and shared the ride down with a couple of tourists who smelled like suntan lotion and cheap cologne.

"I wasn't—" I started to say.

She waved her hand, sharp, like she was thinking of chopping it across my throat. I stopped talking.

We made our way down to the hotel lounge. Speakers, hidden high behind dangling plastic ferns in brass buckets, played a stream of canned piano music. Not much to see at this hour: a couple of weary travelers bellied up to the bar, one with a carry-on at his feet, and on the far end a plump businessman was trying to make time with a woman five brackets out of his league. Emma guided me over to a high-top table in the corner and pointed to a stool.

"Sit. I'm calling Caitlin."

"I really wasn't—"

She made a *zzt* sound, drew her finger across her lips like a zipper, and got her phone out.

Caitlin showed up to save the day. I hoped. She cut across the lobby like a shark, dressed for business; her spill of curly scarlet hair fell across one shoulder of her jacket, charcoal black over an ivory silk blouse. A floppy black ribbon dangled at her throat, tying her ensemble up with a bow. She leaned in for a perfunctory kiss—cheek, not lips, which told me I was really in trouble this time.

"Tell her." Emma yanked back a stool and sat down. "Tell her what you told me."

"You promised not to overreact."

Emma tensed her cheeks until her face bent in a ghoulish facsimile of a smile.

"Daniel, are your intestines where they should be?"

I patted my belly, just to be sure. "I think so?"

"Then clearly, I'm not overreacting. You'll know when I do."

Caitlin sat in contemplative silence, a judge on her barstool bench, as I walked her through it: the house party gone wrong and my encounter with the King of Worms, spotting Melanie in the party photos, and hearing her confession at school.

"My daughter," Emma added, "was nearly killed last night, and he *just now* decided to tell me about it."

"Maybe because I knew how you'd react."

The second I said it, I wished I could claw those words from the air and shove them back into my mouth. Now I had two women giving me the death eye, from both sides of the table. Emma took a slow, deep breath.

"Caitlin," she said, "give me five minutes alone with him. Just five minutes."

"*I* dispense the discipline around here." Caitlin looked my way. "You should have called Emma right away."

Know what the worst thing about a two-on-one argument is? When you're wrong and you know it. I laid my hands on the table and bowed my head in defeat.

"I know," I said. "I screwed up, okay? I'm sorry."

"Keeping this from me?" Emma snapped. "Talking to Melanie without me, at her school, no less? What were you thinking?"

"Honestly? I was thinking I needed answers. C'mon, Emma. She's your kid."

"Exactly."

"Exactly," I echoed. "And if you confronted her with that

photograph—which, I remind you, just showed a blur with hair like hers, not exactly a smoking gun—she would have denied everything. You know this."

Her gaze flicked to one side. "I would have gotten it out of her eventually."

"Or *I* would have," Caitlin said.

"Sure, but not as fast as I did, and not without a headache. Look, you're both authority figures. I'm cool Uncle Dan." I paused. "I think I'm cool. Point is, I'm not her mom, or the enforcer for a prince of hell for that matter. It's easy for her to talk to me. And in the process, I did you a favor."

Emma gave me a suspicious look. "How do you figure that?"

"If you had confronted her, what do you think the status quo at your house would look like right now?"

"Based on our last few spats," she said, "after loudly informing me that she hates me, Melanie would stomp off to her room, slam the door, and refuse to speak to me until...next Tuesday, most likely."

"Yeah, well, now you don't have to have that conversation. Tell her that I ratted her out. She'll be so mad at me, she won't even think of being mad at you. Meanwhile, you can sit her down, tell her how much you care about her and how worried you are—"

"Or I can ground her for a month," Emma said.

"Also an option," I said. "Or do both. But I just spared you the entire shouting match. I'm the bad guy for betraying her trust, and you get to be the good guy. You're welcome."

The winter front behind Emma's eyes defrosted a little. She stuck out her bottom lip and drummed her manicured nails on the table.

"You...*may* have a point," she said.

"Every once in a while, I've been known to stumble onto one."

"I'm still miffed. Daniel, you're a knight of our court now. There are rules. A hierarchy."

I was still waiting for somebody to send me a copy of the rulebook. Prince Sitri had knighted me on a whim—that, and to force the rakshasi queen Naavarasi into a bind, torn between losing face or accepting my challenge to duel. Caitlin and I beat the trap she had set for us and got away clean...but a knighthood was forever. Literally. So far I'd sussed out the basics. Namely, that my gun hand was chained to my hip now. As a knight of hell, moving against another court's minions was an act of war, which meant I had to cancel my plan to punch Naavarasi's ticket for good.

Canceled for the moment, anyway. She wrote her own death sentence when she went after Caitlin. Sooner or later, I'd find a way to carry it out.

"I'm a lousy team player," I said. "To be fair, Sitri knew this when he knighted me."

"Five minutes," Emma said to Caitlin. "Me and him alone."

Caitlin found something interesting to stare at on the ceiling. "If it will make you happy and let us all move on, I'll punish him myself. Five lashes."

"Twenty."

"Wait," I said, "what?"

"Ten," Caitlin said.

"Ten," Emma fired back, "and I get to do it."

"Wait," I said again, feeling distinctly left out of the negotiation. "Lashes with what?"

"With my whip, obviously. What else would I use?" Caitlin turned to Emma. "You are *not* doing it yourself. Twelve lashes."

"Fifteen and I get to watch."

"I don't—" I stumbled over my own words. "I don't think this is a thing you can actually bargain over."

They ignored me. Caitlin shook her head. "Twelve. Final offer."

"I suppose," Emma said, "I can accept that as a fair recompense for the insult."

"Good. Matter resolved, then. Now shake hands."

I blinked, taking Emma's outstretched hand and feeling like I'd just been sideswiped by a truck.

"What...what just happened here?" I asked.

"A learning experience," Caitlin told me. "Actions have consequences, and infernal society is highly centered around caste and reciprocity. As your senior in the court, Emma is entitled to petition me for redress when she feels slighted. I offered to punish you for it and she accepted my terms, which means she has no reason or excuse to carry a grudge against you going forward. Thus societal balance is restored."

"Yeah, but that—that's an example, right? I mean, this was a hypothetical exercise. You're not actually going to *do* it."

She looked at me like I'd sprouted a second head. "Daniel, darling, have you ever known me to make an empty threat? You know better. But we can discuss that later; for the moment we should focus on this...what was his name? Todd?"

The ink dealer. I nodded, suddenly eager for a change of subject.

"The Network's gone silent since our last run-in," I said. "This guy's the best and only lead we've got. And he can tell us why they put a batch of toxic product on the street."

"You think it was deliberate," Emma said.

"I'd bet money on it. The dealer's a burnout who shows up at high school parties uninvited—except for this particular party, where he made sure his ink would be passed out like candy. He stayed clear because he knew what was going to happen. The Network *wanted* those kids dead."

Emma's lips tightened. "Including my daughter. Still, it doesn't make sense. They're sabotaging their own business."

"It almost feels like an act of terrorism," Caitlin mused, "but what's terrorism without an ideology behind it?"

"We've got a name and we know where he works," I said. "Let's scoop him up and ask him ourselves. And I don't mean 'ask nicely.'"

"If he's able to speak," Caitlin said.

A shiver of revulsion ran down my spine. The last time we got our hands on a bottom-rung Network dealer, we discovered their anti-squealing policy. They used a kind of curse called a geas, basically a taboo enforced by magic. Their people would literally kill themselves, or chew their own tongues off, before giving up the goods.

They didn't use the garden-variety version of that spell, either. A Network geas came in the form of a six-inch cockroach, wriggling deep inside their agents' bodies. If you were lucky, pulling it out would only leave you with the mother of all sore throats. If you weren't, it'd chew a tunnel through your guts on its way to freedom. And maybe leave eggs behind.

"I'd say he's got a fifty-fifty shot at surviving the extraction," I told them. "I'm good with those odds if you are."

Nobody objected. Nothing we could do until the morning, so we called it. Caitlin walked me out, slipping her arm around mine as we crossed the casino lobby. The swath of flamingo-pink and lime carpet was our personal runway, flanked by walls of flashing, trilling slot machines.

"But just to be sure," I said, with a glance over my shoulder to make sure Emma was out of earshot, "you're not going to really do it."

"What?" She furrowed her brow. "Oh, your whipping? Of course I am. The law is all that keeps us from savagery, Daniel. I'd never lie about something like that. Breaking the rules carries a cost."

"C'mon. Every rule has a loophole."

"No, no, quite iron-clad, I'm afraid." She paused, flashing the tiniest hint of a smile. "Of course, I didn't say *when* I was going to carry out your punishment, did I? I suppose I'm obligated to do it sometime between right now and...oh, the heat death of the universe. Sometime in between there."

I leaned into her and savored the flood of relief.

"I knew you wouldn't do it."

She put on an almost-believable face of grave concern. "Well of course I will. Eventually. Probably in the middle of the night, with no warning. Maybe tomorrow. Maybe years from now. When you least expect it...expect it."

"You're clearly taking 'how to screw with people's heads' lessons from your father."

"Goodness," she said, "it's *almost* like fear and pain are two of my most essential management tools."

I gave an amiable shrug. "Well, you've got to go with what you're good at, that's what I always say. Any news on the Naavarasi front?"

We passed through a revolving door and out into the night. A clean, dry chill hung in the air. Tourists queued up in a serpentine line at the taxi stand, one yellow van after another trundling off to join the molasses-sludge traffic on the Strip.

"She retreated to lick her wounds," Caitlin said, "quite literally, I expect."

"You did stomp the hell out of her."

A pleased glimmer shone in her eyes. "That I did. Not nearly as much as I wanted to, but...rules. Now, remember: technically, your knighthood means she can't come after you—"

"But *technically*, she couldn't go after you either. She just had to bait a trap that left her hands clean."

"Precisely," Caitlin said, "and she'll likely try to do it again."

"At least we know her real stripes now. She tricked us by playing dumb; that won't work twice. Meanwhile, I'm digging up all the info I can. Jennifer's pulling the audio from when Naavarasi killed Kirmira at her stash house."

"Chicago's shape-shifter?" Caitlin glanced sidelong at me as we followed the curling ribbon of sidewalk. "She insisted he wasn't one of her kind."

"So she said. According to Naavarasi, she's the last rakshasi on earth. But Kirmira said something to her, just before she snapped his neck. And I saw the look on his face. The guy *knew* her, Cait. I'll admit, it's a hunch, but..."

"But your hunches are generally worth following up on."

"Maybe she already played her last hand. Maybe her scheme was all about snaring you." We rounded a pillar ringed with a band of pink and ducked into the clammy gloom of the parking garage. "I don't buy it, though. Naavarasi's got bigger plans than that. And I want to know what she's chasing *before* she takes her next shot."

"Follow your instincts. Just be careful. You're playing for higher stakes now. You know, I have a hunch of my own."

"Yeah?" I asked. "What's that?"

Her fingertips played like silken petals along the back of my neck, leaving an electric tingle in their wake.

"I have a hunch you're coming home with me tonight."

As it turned out, we were both right.

9.

The next morning I called the Burger Barn on Lake Mead Boulevard, posing as a human-resources flunky doing an employment verification. Had to make sure I was casting my bait into the right pond.

"His name is Todd...sorry," I said, "the application got smeared in the photocopier. I always tell them to make sure the ink is dry. Looks like a C or a K maybe—"

"Could it be an L?" asked the tired voice on the other end of the line.

"Yes! You're right, it's definitely an L."

"Todd Long. Yep, he works for us."

She didn't sound too enthused about that fact. She was quick to offer up all the information she could legally provide, with thinly veiled pleasure that some other company was poised to take a slacker off her hands. I relayed the info to Pixie and told her to cross-check it with the Palo Verde High School rolls for the last couple of years. Dig up enough bits and pieces of a person's life, sooner or later you have enough to draw a complete picture.

That said, I planned on getting most of what I needed straight from the horse's mouth. Today was Todd's last day at the Burger Barn.

It was a gritty, dry morning. I pulled in at the edge of the parking lot, under the bulbous plastic shell of a burger-shaped sign, and jumped down onto dusty asphalt. The air left a dirty taste in my mouth, like truck exhaust mingled with charred meat and old grease. It was a little after ten, too late for breakfast and too early for lunch, and the plate-glass windows looked in on a barren fast-food joint.

That meant most of the cars belonged to the doomed souls behind the counter. And one, down on the lot's far end by a stretch of chain-link fence, was a van that matched Melanie's description. It was a vintage GMC, beige with a ketchup-red swoop. Cheap white curtains hung in a dusty side window. The owner, amazingly enough, had no stickers decorating the rust-spotted bumper. This minor concession to taste was offset by his Playboy-bunny-silhouette mud flaps.

"Keep it classy," I muttered as I strolled on by. My gaze went up, prowling along the dead concrete lampposts and the eaves of the restaurant, hunting for security cameras. Not one glass eye pointed my way. I reached into my breast pocket and tugged out a pair of blue latex disposable gloves, slipping them on. Once I stepped around the side of the van, I was all but invisible. Invisible long enough to get my picks out, teach the cheap lock to roll over and play dead, and let myself inside.

I breathed deep and smelled a hellish chemical mélange of pine air freshener, Drakkar Noir, and Axe body spray. Underneath that, the musk of stale sweat and furtive sex. I crouched as I stepped into his little love nest. Sheets lay rumpled and storm-tossed on a narrow slab of mattress; the other side of the van sported a long, low counter and some shallow cupboards. He had a hot plate, a half-full box of Honey Smacks next to an empty bowl caked with dried milk, a few scattered muscle-car magazines...and that was most of his worldly belongings. Todd was not living his best life.

A footlocker near the bed caught my eye. I crouched down, ears perked for anyone approaching the van, and flipped open the hasps. Inside, some mismatched, unwashed socks and wrinkled underwear shared space with more magazines. Porn, mostly, tawdry and tattered. I'd worn the gloves to conceal my fingerprints; now I wished I'd brought a second pair just to add another layer between my hands and Todd's fantasies.

I found what I was looking for at the bottom of the locker. A fat sock concealed a fistful of tiny plastic packets, each about the size of a condom wrapper, stuffed with spiky black grains. Ink. I held up one of the packets and took a closer look. The granules glistened like bubbles of oil with hair-fine bristles, ready to be slipped under a user's tongue or melted down with a lighter and a spoon.

Ink was America's new favorite party drug, a guaranteed good time for all. Except when somebody skunked the product and turned a houseful of teenagers into homicidal maniacs. I wondered if this was more of the bad batch or Todd's personal stash.

I walked to my rented car and came back with a duffel bag. Just the essentials inside: handcuffs, duct tape, a foursome of beeswax candles with brass stands, and two tubs of Tupperware. One held a few fistfuls of coarse white sea salt. The other, fresh blood from a butcher's shop, syrupy and thick. Removing a geas was essentially a kind of exorcism, and a good exorcism had two key objectives: to make the host's body an unpleasant place to live, and to give the creature under his skin a more attractive option.

I crouched down in the back of the van and waited, like a trapdoor spider.

* * *

It was around five o'clock when Todd got off his final shift at the Burger Barn. The autumn sky had gone dirt-brown dark with streaks of grimy clouds, cars casting cold shadows across the parking-lot asphalt. He was a tall guy, gangly, with arms and legs that seemed a little too long for his body. He clambered into the front seat of the van and tossed his yellow-and-red paper hat onto the passenger seat.

Todd was sliding the keys into the ignition when I put the muzzle of my nine-millimeter against the back of his skull. He turned to stone. The only part of him that moved were his eyes, flicking to the rearview mirror.

"You scream, you die," I told him. "You try to run, you die. If you do exactly what I tell you, when I tell you, you have a very good chance of living through this."

I was lying about that last part. He was desperate enough to believe me, though, and that was all that mattered. I tossed the handcuffs into his lap.

"Put 'em on," I told him. "Nice and tight."

He almost dropped them, but with time and some gentle coaching, he managed to lock the steel bracelets around his wrists. I stepped back. I nodded my head where I wanted him to go, keeping the gun fixed and level.

"In back. Not one word."

He had to brush past me, closer than I ever wanted to get to a desperate hostage. If he was going to try to jump me, wrestle for the gun, that was when it would happen. I kept my finger firm on the trigger and braced for it.

Todd didn't even try to make a move. He was cowed enough to plod right past me, into the back of the van.

"Lie down on the bed," I told him.

That got a reaction. He turned to face me, his wrists flexing against the cuffs.

"H-hey," he said, "you don't want to do this. I've got AIDS. Swear to God, I've got full-blown AIDS. And syphilis. And the mumps."

I stared at him. "I'm not going to lay a hand on you. Relax. Lie down."

He stood his ground until I thumbed back the hammer on the gun. The universal symbol for "this is your last chance." He lay on the bed and stared at the roof of the van, his sweaty face turning pale.

"I need to ask you some questions," I told him, setting up my duffel bag on the narrow ledge next to his hot plate, "but the thing inside you isn't going to let you answer. So getting that out, that's the first order of business."

He stared at me like he thought I was crazy, and his eyes only bulged harder when I took out the Tupperware.

"Thing?" he stammered. "Inside me? What...what thing?"

"You might not remember it going in, but your employers—and I do *not* mean the Burger Barn—implanted a fail-safe to keep your lips shut. The bad news is, the next fifteen minutes aren't going to be much fun for you. The good news is, I have done this once before, and the guy is...well, he *was* still breathing when I got finished with him."

"What employers? Man, I flip burgers for a living, that's all! I mean, yeah, I do some dealing on the side, but that's just to pay for my own habit. I'm nobody, swear to God!"

I barely heard him, too busy sinking into my preparations for the ritual. Years of occult practice had left me with layers of mental shortcuts, mnemonics, patterns of breathing and thought that eased me into a waking meditation like I was sliding into a warm tub of water. I focused on symbols, following jagged curves and flashes of color, forcibly rerouting the neurons in my brain. Electric impulses woke old, sleeping nodes, buried knots of gray matter whose purpose was lost in the primordial.

My senses stretched out, glimmering in my third eye like violet sea anemones, their stalks brushing and tasting everything around them. I drank in the remnants of a life that failed to launch, fragmented memories of empty beer cans and Todd's father's belt curled around a hairy-knuckled fist. Hopes broken, dreams he stopped bothering to reach for. The van's tires were mired in an oily residue of *this is good enough*.

What I didn't sense from Todd was the one thing I was looking for.

He didn't have a geas.

My psychic tendrils pushed their needle-thin feelers under his skin, peeled back the layers of his mind like skinning an onion, and found...nothing. I squinted my physical eyes at him. Then I took my roll of duct tape, sliced off a strip with a box cutter, and slapped it over his mouth.

"Either this just got a lot easier than I thought it was going to be," I said, "or a lot more complicated. And given the way my week is going so far, smart money is on 'complicated.' Sit tight. You and me, we're going for a little ride."

* * *

I took his keys and took the wheel, making phone calls on the road to set everything up. Our destination was on the west side of town: the Rosewood Funeral Home. Doc Savoy, everybody's favorite off-the-record patch-up man, ran his operation out of the back room. He had, anyway, until the Chicago Outfit decided they didn't respect the rules of neutrality and pitched a firebomb through his window.

The Doc and his nurse got out fine; we were in the process of finding them a new place to hang their scalpels. For now, the van's headlights swept across yellow strands of police tape and shattered glass, wooden walls charred black. The fire had destroyed the front of the house, but the rooms in back survived just fine. Specifically, the one room I needed.

Half an hour later, Todd wasn't a happy man. I didn't blame him. I'd laid him out in a pine box, not even a pillow to rest his head. Cocoons of duct tape looped his ankles and his wrists and bound his arms to his sides, so he couldn't do much more than wriggle like a pinned bug. I left him there while I went downstairs to find the circuit breaker.

The power came on with a rattling thrum, and stark white light gleamed across a speckled tile floor. I loomed over the box, reached in, and tore the tape off Todd's mouth.

"So," I said, "about those questions I need answered."

"I'm telling you, I don't *know* anything—"

I held up a finger for silence.

"First, let's establish your situation. You're in a coffin. That coffin, though you can't see it from where you're at, is on a conveyor belt. Now pay attention, Todd, this part is important."

I held his gaze, stepping back toward his feet, and reached up to rap my fist against a shell of black iron.

"That conveyor belt," I said as a grate clanked open, "feeds into this crematory furnace."

I flicked a few switches. The gas jets hissed to life.

"So that's your situation," I told him. "Let's chat."

10.

"Man, I swear, I don't know anything—"

I pulled a lever. The conveyor belt rattled and the pine box lurched toward the open grate. Todd screamed like he was on the world's deadliest roller coaster. I stopped the belt.

"The ink, Todd. Where do you get it?"

Beads of greasy sweat ran down the side of his face. He had his eyes squeezed shut, tighter than his mummy wrap of duct tape, and he mouthed a prayer with no breath behind it.

"You're about...I'm going to say eight feet from the furnace door," I said. "Oh, hey, speaking of, it's not a coincidence that you're going in feet-first. See, first thing that'll happen is, the rubber on your shoes is going to melt. It'll be like...hot tar, searing the soles of your feet."

I knew what he was wrestling with. I'd seen it before: he was asking himself if his bosses would do worse things to him, if he talked, than I would. My job was to convince him that they couldn't. He had to believe this was his worst-case scenario, here and now, and giving me what I wanted was his only way out.

"The skin is next," I told him. "You ever see a chicken rotisserie with the oven set too high, Todd? The flesh chars, then it just...*sloughs* off the bone."

"Santiago!" he yelped.

"Pardon?"

"S-Santiago. That's the name of the guy I get my shit from. That's the name he gave me, anyway."

"And he's tight with the Network?" I asked.

He shook his head. "I don't know what that is. I swear, please, I don't know!"

I believed him. There comes a point when a man is too afraid to lie, and Todd was about ten feet over that line. It was looking more and more like I'd netted a guppy; he'd been played, too dumb to realize what he'd done. I wanted the people who were playing him.

Hell, I was starting to think Todd might live to go back to the Burger Barn. I wasn't done wringing him out yet, though.

"Tell me about Santiago."

"Not much to tell, man. He's...he's a short guy, built like a football player, bushy black mustache. He's—he's Spanish. I know because I asked if he was from Mexico once and he got really pissed at me. I thought it was the same thing."

"Spaniards are from Spain," I told him. "Mexicans are from Mexico."

"That's what he said. I thought Spain was *in* Mexico."

I cocked my head at him. "Let's move on. How do you get in touch with him?"

"I don't. He gets in touch with me. Once a month, he texts me and tells me where to meet up. Always a different place. He brings my supply, I bring his cut of the money from last month's sales. He gets ninety percent. I keep the rest, and he kicks me a little junk on the side, you know, for personal use."

Ninety percent. No wonder the kid was living in a van and flipping burgers. There was something else there, though. Not a lie, but the whiff of something he was holding back, like he had an ace card squeezed to his chest under the duct tape.

"There's something you want to tell me, Todd."

I phrased it as a statement, not a question, and gave a knowing look to the crematory oven.

"You...you aren't going to believe me."

"Try me. You might be surprised."

He breathed as deep as the bands of tape would let him and stared at his feet like he could imagine the first kiss of the flames.

"This dude, Santiago...he's not human. It sounds crazy, I know, but he's not human."

"I'm still listening," I said. "How do you know?"

"When he brought me on board, you know, he was laying down the law. How much money I had to kick back to him every month, and how he'd be checking up on me, making sure I didn't screw him." One of Todd's hands jerked, pointing up to his face. "His eyes, man. The dude's eyes...*changed*. The color drained out and they went all yellow and pus-white, like a couple of rotten eggs."

Cambion eyes. Todd's supplier, his pipeline into the Network, had demon blood. That was interesting; the feuding courts of hell were united in agreement that the Network wasn't their creation. The members we'd faced off against until now, as far as I knew, were *human* magicians.

By the looks of it, they'd expanded their recruitment. Caitlin would want to hear about this. More importantly, if this "Santiago" was a local, she might even know where to find him.

"I believe you," I said. "You're doing good, Todd. Real good."

"So you'll—you'll let me go?"

I pulled the lever and sent the pine box rattling toward the mouth of the furnace. He shrieked at the top of his lungs. I yanked the lever back, my eardrums stinging, and the belt jolted to a stop.

"Maybe."

A dark stain spread across the crotch of his acid-washed jeans. He'd survive. I'd already decided to cut the poor dope loose, but I needed to squeeze any last lies out of him.

"Let's talk about the house party on Eagle Glen Road. You sold a bad batch, Todd."

His face was slug-belly white, glistening and pale. He stared at something a million miles away.

"That...that wasn't my fault. It wasn't my fault—"

"The stuff you sold to the guy throwing the party—was that all of it? Is there more tainted ink floating around out there? I need to know, Todd. I need to gather it all up before somebody else gets hurt. This is really important, okay?"

I put my hand on the control lever.

"No," he wheezed. "No, it was...I met with Santiago that morning, he gave me the ink, I sold the whole batch to Rob, and that was it. There's no more, I swear!"

He was on the home stretch. And if he had kept his mouth shut, he might have made it.

"I sold it to Rob," he said, "just like Santiago told me to."

I narrowed my eyes at him. I had been starting to wonder if my theory about the ink being tainted on purpose was off base. Maybe not.

"He told you exactly who to sell it to? Does he do that a lot?"

"N-never, but this was, you know, circumstances, and I mean, I..." He thumped the back of his skull against the coffin. "I didn't *want* to hurt those kids! But Jesus, he was gonna pay me ten grand. Cash. You know how much money that is to a guy like me? I could get a new van, pay off my bills—"

I stood over him and searched his eyes.

"You knew. You knew the ink was bad."

"He told me, get it to Rob before his house party, stay cool, don't blow it. And don't go. I was—I was planning on going. So I asked him why. And he told me. He told me his boss needed to take somebody out, and this was how they wanted it done. I said I wasn't gonna do that, that's not me, and that's when he offered me the money. All I had to do was sell Rob the stuff and walk away. It wasn't like I had to kill anybody with my own hands. I just had to sell it and walk away."

He knew. He'd lobbed a bomb made of madness into a house filled with kids. And he did it for ten thousand measly bucks. I didn't lose my temper. I was too angry for that. All I felt was cold, like a sheath of ice crackling its way down my spine, frost flooding my veins. I was cold enough to do anything.

"Who was the target?" I asked, my voice soft now. "Was it Rob?"

"N-no," he stammered. "It was this chick, Mel...Melanie something. Loomis! Melanie Loomis. Santiago said she was going to be at the party, and his boss wanted her dead. Dead in a way that would look like an accident."

I set my hand on the edge of the pine box and took a slow, deep breath. Four seconds in, four seconds out.

"Sit tight," I told him. "I need to make a phone call."

* * *

I came back half an hour later, and I wasn't alone.

"I want you to meet some people," I told him.

Todd's eyes flicked from me to Caitlin to Emma and back again. He was too scared to open his mouth. That suited me fine. I needed him to hear every word I was about to say.

"First of all, this 'chick' you were paid to kill with tainted drugs? I know her. In fact, I'm really, really protective of her. I suppose you could almost say I'm her"—I glanced sidelong at Emma—"godfather? Is that fair?"

"Against my better judgment," she replied. Her eyes were locked onto Todd like a pair of diamond-tipped drills.

"Now, this lady on my right, her name is Caitlin. Here's a fun fact, Todd. He might not have gone into specifics, but your buddy Santiago has demon blood."

"Demon blood," Todd echoed, breathing the words.

"Yep. But just a little. Just enough for a tiny kick. A little spice. But Caitlin, here? She's the real thing."

Caitlin's eyes blossomed with swirling motes of copper. They gusted across her pupils like a storm of burning embers, blotting everything out until nothing remained but two seething orbs of molten metal. She parted her lips, showing double rows of jagged shark's teeth.

"Part of Caitlin's job is watching out for people under her prince's protection. People like Melanie. She takes her job very seriously."

Todd squirmed in his duct-tape cocoon, thrashing against the walls of the pine coffin like a fish drowning in air. "I didn't know. I swear, I didn't *know*—"

"Now, on my left," I said, "here's someone you really need to meet. This is Emma Loomis. Melanie's mother. She also works for the courts of hell. Emma, you had the best idea just now, out in the hallway. Want to tell him about it?"

She curled her lips into a razor-thin smile.

"Absolutely. I was just saying that we're in a mortuary filled with autopsy tools. Scalpels, saws, caustic chemicals, *so* much to play with…and I was thinking that unless you tell us everything we want to know, and I do mean everything, we'd take turns tearing you apart, one little piece at a time. And I get to go first."

Emma leaned in close and dropped her voice to a whisper.

"You tried to murder my daughter. I've already decided what I'm going to cut off first and what tool I'm going to use. Would you like to guess, or should I make it a surprise?"

He talked after that. He talked plenty.

What we mostly got out of him—between frantic, babbling apologies—was that he didn't know why Melanie had been targeted. All Santiago told Todd was that she'd been green-lit, they wanted it to look like a tragic accident, and the Network had no problem murdering an entire houseful of teenagers to get at a single target.

Santiago had set him up with a dedicated burner phone, for business only. He kept it stashed under the passenger seat of his van. He gave up the phone, the unlock code, and the password he always started texts with so Santiago would know it was really him. They used a custom-built app to talk, set to erase each message after it had been read, so I couldn't get at their past chats to verify that. Still, at this point I had no doubt that every word on Todd's lips was the purest truth. He was a drowning man, clutching at imaginary life preservers.

We also found out Todd was as incompetent a hit man as he was a drug dealer. He hadn't gotten the money up-front. Santiago gave him the tainted batch of ink and told him he'd be paid once the job was done. I could use that.

The three of us peppered him with questions until we'd wrung him dry. There wasn't anything left inside of him after that, nothing but fear and the faintest, most distant glimmer of hope.

I saved the hope for last.

"That's it, then," I told him and turned to walk away. Caitlin curled her arm around mine and followed suit.

"Wait!" he called out. "What...what now? Are you going to let me go?"

I glanced back at him, then looked to Emma.

"Not really my place to say. I mean, under the circumstances, I think that's Melanie's mom's decision. What do you say, Emma? Should we let him go?"

She lingered beside a tray of autopsy tools. Her outstretched fingers glided across the implements while she thought it over. Her hand stopped. She scooped up a long pair of stainless-steel jaws, designed to crack open a corpse's rib cage, and held them up to the light.

"I don't think so," she said.

Todd started to scream. Caitlin and I walked out. As the door swung shut, my last glimpse was of Emma leaning over the pine box, slowly reaching inside.

11.

I needed some air. I sat in the front seat of Todd's van, sideways, legs dangling out the open door as I huddled over his burner phone. I'd have one shot at approaching Santiago and setting up a meet. If I got it wrong, he'd dive underground, too deep to follow.

"It's like submarine warfare," I muttered.

Caitlin leaned against the side of the van. She stretched, languid, one hand raised like she was beckoning to the cold and starless sky.

"How's that?"

"We're prowling around each other, aiming for a direct shot. When we de-roached one of their dealers, and I had my run-in with that lawyer from Weishaupt and Associates, Smith...that was the opening salvo. We know the Network exists. They know that we know. The outstanding question now is, how much do they know about us?"

"You're straddling two worlds these days, pet. Do you mean how much do they know about our court, or how much do they know about your criminal friends?"

"Both," I said. "Look, I think we can agree that Melanie wasn't targeted because of that article she was trying to write. There's no chance the Network murdered over a dozen people—with their own product, no less—to knock off a teenager who wants to be an investigative journalist. The most Melanie could have possibly uncovered was...well, *Todd.* And that's as far as the cops would have gotten, too."

Caitlin nodded, taking that in as she got on my wavelength. "Not remotely worth the risk or the cost. Which suggests the real target was Emma."

"Exactly. Kill a family member to send a message. But here's the kicker: Emma works for your court—"

"Our court," Caitlin corrected.

"—*and* she has a seat on the New Commission. So who were these people trying to attack? The infernal underworld? The criminal underworld? Both? And what's the message supposed to be, anyway? Remember what Santiago said to Todd: they wanted it to look like an accident. This whole scheme, it seems solid from a distance, but the second you start poking at it the entire thing falls apart. There's something we're missing here. Something we're not supposed to see."

And under it all, the taunts of the King of Worms kept drifting back to me. I eyed the phone again and clicked the custom app Todd used to communicate with his boss. I tapped in his password—*geronimo*—and a message.

Job's done, just like you told me to do it, I wrote. *I want my money.*

Three minutes later, a response pinged in. One word. *Patience.*

Fuck your patience, I wrote back. *I need that money. I kicked over a hornet's nest, cops everywhere. I want to get out of town for a while.*

Cops looking at you? came the reply.

I had to be careful here and put just enough pressure on Santiago to push him into a face-to-face meeting. If I pushed too hard, he might cut his losses and run.

No, I typed. *I'm careful. Careful enough that I want to split town before they do start looking. And it's in your best interest to help me do it. If I go down, you go down.*

Are you threatening me, Todd?

I felt that tinge of *wrongness* again. Yes—as Todd I was absolutely threatening him. And I shouldn't have been able to. The Network was careful, obsessive, neurotic about protecting itself. Not long ago we'd pulled a bottom-tier dealer from Albuquerque off the street, a guy who knew less than nothing; he'd been implanted with a geas-roach just to be safe. Todd had been commissioned to commit mass murder for hire, and they'd left him free as a bird. It didn't make sense.

No, I replied, choosing every word carefully. *I'm just saying, I gotta get paid. Tonight. Help me out, I'll disappear, and neither of us has anything to worry about.*

If I were in Santiago's shoes, I'd be thinking of ways to make Todd disappear for good right about now. Minutes drifted by in the dark, just listening to the occasional car rumbling by, and I started to worry I'd overplayed my hand. Then the app let out a happy ping.

Container Park, 11 tonight. Be at the benches closest to the soundstage. Don't be late.

"He took the bait." I showed Caitlin the screen. The message history slowly erased itself, line by line. "He's either coming to give Todd his money, or he's coming to kill him. I figure it's even odds."

"Todd won't be able to make it," Emma told us. She came out the side door alone. Her hands had the pink sheen of blood after a vigorous bout of scrubbing, the stains faded but not quite clean.

"Have a good time?" Caitlin asked.

"I did, as a matter of fact. You could have stayed and joined in, you know."

"You needed to vent some frustration. Next time we'll share." She glanced my way. "So, shall we arrange a welcoming party for our new Network friend? Santiago should have all the answers we want, and then some."

Sure. It was the natural next move. The obvious next move.

And then I saw it.

"They weren't after Melanie," I said. "Whether she lived or died, it didn't matter. It was the *attempt* that mattered. They weren't sending Emma a message. They weren't sending a message at all."

Emma put her ruddy hands on her hips, frowning. "Could have fooled me."

"Fooling us. *That* was the point. Look, do we all agree that none of this makes any damn sense? For starters, regardless of who they wanted dead, why would the Network use a tainted batch of their own designer drug to kill people? We know they have assassins, they have magic—spiking a batch of ink at a house party isn't just pointlessly risky, it's going to undercut their business. So I asked myself—what *does* using poisoned ink accomplish?"

"Considering they're the only people who know how to make the drug," Caitlin mused, "it tells us that they're the ones responsible. Breaking their usual patterns of stealth and sticking their necks out for no good reason. Which...tells us that being seen was entirely the point."

I pointed at her. "Bingo. Now, Todd said that Melanie was the target. Problem number one, and this is a biggie: Melanie doesn't do drugs. Let's not kid ourselves, it's not like she never gets in trouble, she's a typical teenager—"

"Lucifer save us all," Emma muttered, rolling her eyes to the night sky.

"—but 'trouble,' for Melanie, means staying out after curfew or sneaking a beer when she can get away with it. Anyone who knows anything about her knows she wouldn't take ink. So not only is it a stupid way of killing anybody, spiking the batch was a *spectacularly* stupid way of trying to kill *her*."

Caitlin moved closer to me. Hovering, eyes narrowed, catlike. She was prowling along in the wake of my thoughts and overtaking me fast.

"And the Network isn't stupid," she said. "Thus we can surmise that their goal was to put Melanie in a dangerous situation—as you said, it didn't matter if she actually died or not, only that she was threatened—and put their stamp on it so we'd know exactly who to pursue."

Emma glanced back at the side door. "Not just them. Todd."

"Todd," I said. "He knew that Melanie was the target. But why would Santiago even need to tell him that? Why tell him that the drugs were poisoned at all? Not a huge loss if he went to the party and died there with everybody else."

"So he would tell us," Caitlin said.

"Exactly. Which is also why he didn't have a roach inside of him, when as far as we know, all of the Network's flunkies get one. Because the extraction process has a fifty-fifty chance of killing the patient, and they *needed* him to talk to us." I held up the burner phone. "We followed the trail of clues, asked all the right questions, and ended up right where they wanted us."

"It's a trap," Emma said. "But...why me? I'm a ranking member of the Court of Jade Tears and I have a seat on the New Commission—which group are they targeting?"

"Most likely both," Caitlin told her. "You're an intelligence asset. If you fell into enemy hands, anything they could wring out of you would be valuable."

I had to smile. "There's one more layer to this thing. We know the Network isn't stupid. Can we assume they know that we aren't, either? We followed the clues, then we realized the whole thing was a house of cards and took it apart with one good poke. They're counting on that."

"This is feeling like a game of speed chess," Caitlin said. "I approve. So, they never really expected to fool us. We were supposed to realize that this is a trap. And they're expecting us to act accordingly, in the mistaken belief that we're a step ahead of them."

"Let's say we figured out everything except that last part. We know it's a setup, we know we were supposed to figure it out, but we *don't* know that's actually the key to whatever surprise they're planning to spring on us. How would we react? What would our next move be?"

Emma paced the driveway, slow, hands clasped behind her back.

"The one thing we need most right now," she said, "is information. The Network thrives in the shadows, and we can't fight them until we drag them into the light. So we'd still show up at the 'meeting,' one way or another, hoping to capture at least one of their people for interrogation."

"And since they went after your daughter?" I asked.

"I'd be the one to show up," Emma said. "If I offered myself up as a target—assuming that they'll want to capture me, not kill me—it would be the easiest way to spot their people. Surround me with covert operatives, and when the Network moves in to grab me, our people move in to grab *them*."

"A counter-ambush," Caitlin said. "But now we have a problem: if we were supposed to work out their scheme, and they're expecting us to respond in the most likely manner...what's the point? If they want to abduct Emma, they've just made their job that much harder."

"That's because she's not the target," I said. "I am."

Emma stopped pacing. They both looked my way.

"Emma's going to need backup, watching from a safe distance. You asked whether they're targeting your court—"

"Our court," Caitlin said.

"—or the Commission. Doesn't matter, because there's only one other person with a foot in both worlds. Me. No matter which side I'm repping, if Emma decided to play the bait, I'd be there to watch over her. See, the King of Worms overplayed his hand. He wanted to pitch me on his 'game,' this death match with his wannabe disciple. But he slipped when he said the guy's a big deal in the Network, and that he'd already started making his move."

"That's what this is all about," Caitlin said. "This entire scheme, from start to finish, was intended to draw you out and distract you. While we're watching Emma, expecting that she's the target, they'll be coming for you instead."

"Exactly. So we get a line of sight and backup on both of us. We can surround Emma with obvious muscle, so it looks like we took the bait, while everybody else keeps their eyes on me. When they pounce, we pounce."

"One problem," Emma said. "This man who's trying to impress the king...he's been ordered to murder you, yes?"

"Well, I'm hoping he'll want to snatch me and kill me someplace less public." I jammed my hands in my pockets and stared up at the onyx sky. "Hoping. If I'm wrong, this could get messy. We may have to improvise."

12.

I wanted to keep improvisation to a minimum. I'm good at thinking on my feet, but knowing somebody out there wanted me dead put a chill on my adventurous spirit.

I wasn't sure why it should matter. *Lots* of people wanted me dead. All the same, it wasn't every night that I willingly walked into a trap orchestrated by a necromancer who planned to kill me for a job promotion.

"I want coverage at all high points," I said to Jennifer. "My worst nightmare is this guy turning out to be a sniper. If he jumps me, I can roll with that. A shot from a few hundred yards away, not so much."

Her voice crackled over the phone. Tired, and I could hear a strain as she scribbled frantic notes.

"Done and done. I'll see if I can round up some of those Triad boys who helped us out at the Cobalt Lounge. Nobody spots a sniper like another sniper. They won't be able to carry long arms, though, not without starting a stampede. Best you're gonna get is a heads-up."

"Long as my head stays intact, I'll take what I can get."

"I'm not sure *what* we can get, not until I make a dozen last-minute phone calls. You know we're cuttin' this down to the wire, right?"

I glanced to the dashboard clock. I was back in Todd's van, latex gloves gripping the dusty wheel as I muscled through nighttime traffic. I kept to the side streets, staying away from the congestion on the Strip as I hunted for a good place to dump the ride, but taking the long way around wasn't helping my time-crunch problem. The clock read 10:14, which gave us just over forty-five minutes to round up as many guns as we could, set up a counter-ambush, and plan for every contingency.

Like Caitlin said, it felt like a game of speed chess.

I almost called the whole thing off. The opposition couldn't make their next move if we didn't show up to play. But this was our best shot yet at digging up some serious intel on the Network and their so-called "kings," and I couldn't let it go to waste. If I blew this, there was no telling when we'd get another chance.

The King of Worms expected me to kill his protégé before he killed me. Forget that. I planned on taking him alive. Then, once we got him locked down someplace nice and far off the grid, we could have a chat.

My next call bounced through two other extensions before I finally landed on Mayor Seabrook's desk phone. She was burning the midnight oil again, just like I hoped she would be.

"I'm listening," she said. Not exactly a warm hello. We weren't there yet.

"Need you to use your leverage with Commissioner Harding," I told her. "We've got a thing. Kind of thing where it would be good to keep Metro clear of the area until we're finished."

"When and where?"

"Container Park," I said. "Forty-five minutes. We'll need...maybe half an hour of clear sailing and closed eyes. Call it an hour to be safe."

"Park's open to the public until midnight," she said, cagey now.

I read between her lines. The place would be crowded with civilians, and I'd just asked her to pull the cops away.

"No rough stuff," I said. "Nothing in public, nothing that breaks our agreement. We need to have a word with some people about the ink epidemic in our fair city. If the fine members of law enforcement saw us politely escorting them from the park, they might get the wrong idea. We wouldn't want to make a scene."

The line went dead quiet. I could hear her gears turning.

"I'll make the call. One thing."

"Yeah?" I said.

"If anything happens that makes the papers tomorrow, in any way, shape, or form, I'll be making a second call to the commissioner."

"Don't worry," I told her. "The papers never print good news."

* * *

Container Park was an open-air mall on the end of Fremont Street. The architecture coined its name; the three-level walls ringing the rectangular park, lined with shops and cafes, were all built from recycled shipping containers. A riot of colors adorned the ridged steel, ivory and hornet yellow and Halloween orange, giving the place a funky, art-hipster vibe. Like a wasteland settlement from a Mad Max movie, but more boutiques and Frappuccinos than leather and spikes.

A geodesic dome out front lit up like a giant glowing beach ball, next to a towering metal sculpture of a praying mantis. As I walked past, blending in with the evening crowds, twin gouts of flame erupted from the mantis's antennae.

A soundstage stood at the far end of the park, where throngs of people packed an artificial lawn. Raw, grinding guitar chords drifted through the chilly night air. It took a second, picking up the lead singer's warbly, underwater voice, before I realized it was an Aerosmith cover band. Not a good one, though the audience was too raucous and too drunk to care. I found a spot to stand out of the way of foot traffic, ducking under a steel awning. Caitlin sidled up a moment later, her gaze tracking faces in the crowd.

"Well, now I know everything's going to be all right."

"How's that?" she asked me.

"Because I have too much self-respect to die to an Aerosmith tune. I just won't do it. How's Emma?"

"Eager," Caitlin said. "I called up everyone I could reach; she's surrounded by some of our finest, who are all under orders to be very obvious while pretending to be discreet. They'll stick out like a sore thumb."

Good. If I was somehow wrong, if I'd overthought this entire plan or given the Network too much credit for being clever, that should stave off any would-be kidnappers.

Her kidnappers, anyway. If I was right about all this, I still didn't know if my mysterious adversary was going to try to grab me off the street or just kill me right here in the park. I scouted the tiers, looking up at the container-built shops, trying to spot Jennifer's people. They were doing a good job of blending in. Or they were late. I wouldn't know until I needed them. I flexed my wrist. Howard Canton's wand—my wand now—dropped from its concealed sheath and into my outstretched hand. I palmed it and passed it to Caitlin.

"Hang on to it," I told her. "We know the Enemy is hot to get his hands on this thing; the Network might want it, too. Can't risk losing it if they grab me."

"I don't like you going unarmed."

"I'm armed just fine." I patted my breast pocket, feeling the hard edges of a fresh packet of playing cards. A .22 automatic rode on my hip for backup, just the right size for close-up work. "I can replace my cards and my gun. I can't replace the wand. Besides, it only works when I'm protecting someone from danger. Someone who isn't me."

"It's a stubborn wand," she said.

"Stupid jerk wand." I cast a baleful look at the stick as she slipped it into her purse. "Yeah, you heard me, jerk wand."

A little forced levity made me feel better. For a few seconds, anyway. My watch said 10:58, time to go to work.

"We'd better split up," I said to Caitlin. "If they know me, they know you. They won't make a move if you're close enough to save me."

She took my hand and gave it a squeeze.

"I'm always close enough," she told me.

Then she let go and cast me out like a worm on a hook.

Walking alone, I angled my way toward the benches near the soundstage where the meet between Todd and Santiago was supposed to take place. I kept to the shadows, but not too deep. Away from the crowds, but not too far. I had to walk the fine line between making myself look like an easy target and making sure my own people didn't lose sight of me.

I counted my breaths and listened to the cover band butcher another vintage track. I wanted a drink. I worked hard at keeping my moves slow and easy. Couldn't give away the game. I watched over Emma from a distance, trailing her shadow while she prowled near the benches, pretending I was her guardian angel.

Something was wrong.

My watch said it was thirty-six minutes past the hour, and nobody had made a move yet. I could only figure that we'd been made, that I'd given something away with my body language, and the Network had decided to fight another day. I didn't want to go home empty-handed, and I tried to figure out where we'd gone wrong. Where had—

A hard electronic squawk jarred my thoughts. The music from the soundstage sputtered and died, leaving the fist-pumping audience milling in sudden confusion. Then a voice boomed from the loudspeakers perched throughout the park.

"By order of the Metropolitan Police Department, Container Park is closed for the evening. Please make your way directly to the exit at this time in a calm and orderly manner. Thank you."

Deflated tourists joined a mob shuffling to the front archway, clutching their beer cups like trophies of war. I jogged up, getting closer, and saw a wall of colored lights lining Fremont Street. And a wall of beige uniforms at the park's exit. A sergeant with a walkie-talkie was coordinating, pointing, and I watched a couple of cops snatch people from the front of the crowd when they tried to leave.

I walked backward, repelled like a flipped-over magnet, and speed-dialed Jennifer's number while I hunted for a wastebasket.

"Sugar? I got five guys all shouting in my ear at once. What's—"

"Harding," I said. "He fucked us. He was supposed to keep his guys clear. Apparently he decided to go for a big bust instead. I bet he's feeling the pressure after that house party; getting a few ink dealers off the street would make for good press."

"He doesn't even know who he's looking for."

I saw the cops grab a lanky guy from the pack and put him up against a cruiser's hood, patting him down.

"I think they're just grabbing anybody who doesn't fit the tourist profile and hoping to catch them carrying. *Idiot.* He just blew this entire operation on a fishing expedition. Forget it. Jen, get your guys out of here, tell 'em to keep their heads down and we'll bail out anybody who gets nabbed. You and me, let's meet up at the Tiger's Garden later. We need to have a long hard think about our *relationship* with Commissioner Harding."

I could worry about that later. Right now, I needed to get out of here without ending up in handcuffs. Daniel Faust was legally dead, but my fingerprints were still in the national ViCAP database. One background check and I'd be back on the law's radar for good.

I glanced over my shoulder. There were more uniforms taking up the rear now—they must have circled the edge of the park—and herding everybody toward the exit in a slow, firm march. I wasn't worried about Caitlin and Emma. Caitlin could go over the side of the park if she had to—I'd seen her take a three-story drop and land with the kind of grace a cat would envy—and Emma could talk or buy her way out of most trouble. As for me, my concealed .22 had just transformed from a backup plan to a deadly liability. I had to lose it, fast.

I joined the crowd's listless march, another lemming in the pack, and angled my stride toward a trash can up ahead. A deputy was standing five feet away, hands clasped at parade rest as he scanned every passing face. My fingers slipped under my jacket and brushed against steel. I'd have to pull the gun to toss it.

I watched the slow sway of his head, holding my breath, and timed my approach like a plane trying to land on a ten-foot runway. Five steps from the can, four, three, his gaze swung left as I turned my hip and plucked the pistol loose and—

—it disappeared, plastic lid swinging in its wake, as he locked eyes with me. I gave him a friendly nod in passing.

"Evening, officer."

He didn't respond. I didn't care. There was nothing on me now but a deck of cards. Even if the cops on watch singled me out for a search, I was free and clear.

I took a deep breath and congratulated myself on a move well done. That's when they pulled me out of the crowd, five feet past the exit archway.

A pair of uniforms grabbed me by the elbows and marched me over to a squad car. I gave them a genial laugh, playing up the "slightly drunk and confused" act. "Hey, fellas, I know the band sucked, but that's no reason to break up the party. What gives?"

Neither of them said a word. One bent me over their squad car while the other gave me a brisk pat-down. He plucked the cardboard pack from my breast pocket, shook it a few times like he was expecting to hear something besides cards inside, then tossed it onto the hood.

"Careful," I said, "that pack is loaded."

They weren't in a chatty mood. The cop finished searching me, running his hands along both legs from my inseam down to my ankles. I waited, patient, figuring they'd cut me loose with an apology.

Handcuffs clinched tight around my wrists. I barely got a word out before they shoved me into the back of their car.

13.

My stint at Eisenberg Correctional flooded back in a heartbeat and stole the breath from my lungs. I was standing on a yellow line, shoulder to shoulder with hardened felons, stripping down on command and tossing our clothes into a cardboard box. My prison uniform was tight in some places, baggy in others, scratchy as the barber ran his shears across my scalp. I watched my curls fall to the floor, mingled with all the other fresh convicts', while they turned me into a man with a number for a name.

I was lying in the dark in my prison cell, listening to the snoring, the whispers, the faint sound of someone in tears, shivering under my paper-thin blanket. Still aching from the beating I'd taken earlier that day, and realizing that this was the shape of every single night for the rest of my life. Realizing that I was going to die in this cell and never breathe free air again.

I closed my eyes.

I felt my cuffed hands behind my back, brushed my fingertips together, then patted the cruiser's seat. I wasn't in Eisenberg. I was here. Now. And I wasn't going back inside.

"What am I being arrested for?" I asked.

The two cops in the front seat didn't say a word. Keeping up the silent act.

"I want to know why I'm being detained."

Nothing. The sedan rolled through a green light. If they took me to the lockup and ran my fingerprints, I was finished. So I calmly, rationally decided that wasn't going to happen.

"I don't know what your game is," I said, "but I'm guessing you were given an arrest quota tonight, am I right? So you figured you'd find some tourist and run him in on a drunk and disorderly."

Silence. The driver's face was a shadow in the rearview mirror, a dark-eyed sliver that flicked a glance at me then back to the road.

"I'm not a tourist," I told them. "And ten minutes after you book me, you're going to have everybody from the mayor's office on down burning your phone up. The best thing you can do right now is pull over and let me out."

Another glance in the rearview. No words.

"I'm trying to help you guys out, okay? Listen, you don't want to—"

"Shut up, Faust."

I stared at the driver's reflection. A chill crept its way up from the base of my spine, where my cuffed wrists rested against my belt.

"You've got the wrong guy," I said. "My name's Emerson. Check my wallet, look at my driver's license. You'll see."

"We know who you are." His voice carried the trace of a Spanish accent. A passing streetlight strobed against the windshield, casting a glow across his face in the rearview. I caught the curve of a sneer and his black bristle-brush mustache.

I slumped back in my seat.

"Santiago," I said.

He didn't answer. He didn't have to. I sensed an invisible hand moving pieces around a chessboard.

Check.

Either the Network had dirty cops on their payroll or access to fake badges and a stolen cruiser. I'd predicted every layer of their trap except one. The one where they staged a police raid, swooped in, and grabbed me in the confusion.

I laughed. I couldn't help it.

Santiago's partner, with eczema on his cheeks and a beetle brow, glanced back over his shoulder at me. "Something funny?"

"No, just...kind of relieved."

"You shouldn't be."

"No, I really am," I said. "See, I don't hurt cops if I don't have to. It's not a moral thing, it's just good business; I try not to mess with the biggest gang in town. So here I am, trying to figure out how I'm going to deal with you two, you know, with the least necessary mess. But I'm guessing you're not taking me to lockup, are you?"

The cruiser swerved at the next intersection. We jetted down a side road, leaving downtown behind.

"You're not cops. You're a couple of Network thugs. Which means I don't have to decide if I'm going to kill you. I am. The only question is how and when."

Santiago's partner snorted at me and turned back around.

"We got a file on you half an inch thick," he said. "We know you can't do shit without your cards. Now pipe down, we're almost there."

I tried not to be offended. True, most of my magic was long-form and required a handy prop or two, but I wasn't without a few emergency resources. For instance, their file apparently didn't warn them about how one of the men who taught me magic was also a former stage magician with a sideline in escapology.

I remembered the day Bentley taught me Houdini's mailbag escape, demonstrating it himself before walking me through it. He sprang from the canvas sack with his cuffs, three padlocks, and a serpentine coil of chains all lying at his feet.

"*The first key to success,*" he had said, brandishing a tiny twist of steel, "*is exactly that. Standard-issue handcuffs open with a universal, generic key; the design hasn't changed in decades. I'll show you a few ways to shim cuffs open with common objects you might find lying around, but you'll never need to if you keep a key handy at all times.*"

Bentley had turned and pulled at his faded leather belt. There, square at the center of his back and hidden against his slacks, a handcuff key sat nestled in a blob of beige putty.

"Never leave home without one. You never know when you'll need a handcuff key...and if you ever need one and don't have one, well, that's when you're really in trouble."

The technique was harder than it looked. Getting at a fingernail-sized key, prying it from its hiding spot without dropping it, then opening a pair of cuffs all with your hands behind your back demanded serious practice.

But I had a great teacher. And I practiced.

I almost went for the key; then I stopped myself. They'd snatched my cards, they both had guns on their hips, and I didn't care for the odds. Besides, even if I took them by surprise and won, I'd probably have to kill them to do it. Which meant no prisoners, no new intel, and this entire night would be a wash.

On the other hand, they were probably driving me straight into the Network's den. At least the Vegas branch. If I was willing to risk it, and if I timed my moves just right, I wouldn't be empty-handed when I made my escape. I might even find out who the King of Worms' little friend was and take him off the board before he got another shot at me.

I made my choice in the space of a single red light. I had to risk it. My key stayed hidden where it was, for now, while I played the helpless prisoner.

Santiago showed off his tradecraft. He pulled all the usual tricks to shake a pursuer: doubling back, sudden bursts of speed, weaving through parking lots to jump onto adjacent roads, the works. I didn't know if any of my people had managed to track the cruiser, but if they had, they'd turned invisible. Not a single pair of headlights on our tail, just a dark and lonely road.

I couldn't count on the cavalry showing up. Getting out of here was all on me now.

"Call and make sure we're good," Santiago told his partner.

"We're good."

"*Call*," he said, "and make *sure*."

His buddy tugged out a phone. I perked my ears, but all I could make out on the other end was a faint, unintelligible squawking.

"It's us. We've got the package. Night shift on the scene yet? Can we bring him inside?"

More squawking. He hung up the phone and looked at Santiago.

"No civvies for a mile around. We're good. I said we were good."

"The man likes things done in a very specific manner," Santiago told him. "Very. Specific. You start half-assing this job, it's not me you're going to have a problem with."

"Sounds like your boss is a micro-manager," I said. "That's never fun. Look, it might be pointless, but I'm professionally obligated to make this pitch: leave the Network, come work for me. Whatever they're paying you, I'll beat it by five percent."

Santiago's partner arched a bushy eyebrow. "Aren't you supposed to say you'll double it, or triple it?"

"No, because that's what desperate people say when they're staring down the barrel of a gun, and they're always lying when they say it. I'm making you a serious business proposal. Five percent. If you want to make a counteroffer, I'm open to negotiation."

"I got a proposal," Santiago said. "*Shut up.*"

"Have it your way." I leaned back and got as comfortable as I could with the cuffs digging into the small of my back. "But trust me. Real soon now, I'm going to remind you we had this discussion. And you're going to wish you took the offer."

Of course, I was lying too. Santiago was Todd's handler and he'd orchestrated the house-party massacre. One way or another, he had a pine box and a crematory oven in his near future.

We drove past a rail yard, silent freight trains like jointed steel bones in the dark. Then a stretch of fence, prison-yard tall and topped with coils of concertina wire. A gate up ahead rumbled open. The sign beside it, pea-soup green with faded yellow letters, read Donaghy Waste Management.

The company Nicky never managed to get his hooks into, back when he was running this town. Now I knew why. How long had the Network been operating this place as a front? How long had they been in Vegas? Fighting these people was like punching at smoke. I could swing until my arms got tired and never hit a damn thing.

The gate rattled shut behind the squad car, sealing us inside.

A garbage truck backed up to a dimly lit loading dock. Electronic beeps split the cold night air. Men in blueprint-colored overalls were milling around, lugging barrels and boxes, directing more trucks along the asphalt lot. Donaghy's night crew had bloodless, slack faces and sunken eyes. They lurched and lumbered, like their brains couldn't quite deliver the orders to their arms and legs, something lost in synaptic translation.

I'd seen moves like that before, from dead men walking. Damien Ecko, the last emissary of the King of Worms, raised corpses to serve him. I wondered if his would-be successor had the same bag of tricks. I was studying the workers on the loading dock, trying to get a read on them, when I saw two of them pause for a short conversation.

Not zombies, then. Ecko's creations were relentless, not to mention capable of punching a hole through a man's rib cage, but they were basically machines made of meat. Still, something was off about the night crew. I tried relaxing enough to stretch out my psychic senses, then yanked them back like I'd touched a red-hot stove.

This place was radioactive. Maybe literally. A giant, festering boil of toxic power seeping into the ground, the sky, poisoning my city. The squad car pulled around the back of the building, and Santiago killed the engine.

Whatever was in there, I was about to meet it.

14.

At night, the recycling plant slumbered. Faded bars of light, sheathed under plastic grills, cast a dim glow along vast galleries of stained concrete. Machines for sorting and shredding sat motionless; the rusted metal bulks let out faint rumbling sounds, small things scurrying inside the fat and twisting pipes. An ammonia smell clung to the air, strong enough to burn the back of my nose, like the night crew had poured out bucket after bucket of bleach and left it to dry.

Santiago and his partner flanked me as they marched me through the complex, each one taking hold of an arm. The slack-faced watchmen didn't even look our way. They shambled along with their uneven, twitchy strides, heads swaying like their necks were on steel springs.

This place was a maze of faceless corridors. Emergency lighting cast long, angular shadows across bare stone and unmarked doors. Pipes ran along the walls, bulky and marred with tarnish, corrosion spreading like black mold at every welded seam. The farther we walked, the more patches I saw on the pipes, slabs of misshapen metal welded over blotches of rust.

There was something sick inside this place, an illness running behind its walls, through its pipes, and keeping it contained was a losing battle.

I was feeling sick, too, as the ammonia smell surrendered to the odor it was trying to conceal. It was the stench of roadkill on a sweltering summer day. Like someone had filled a bucket with rotten meat, poured in a gallon of sour milk, and mashed it together into an unholy meal. Bile rose in my throat and I swallowed it down, focusing on my breath.

I wasn't the only one having a hard time. My escorts were looking green, lips tight, a few flecks of sweat glistening on Santiago's mustache.

"Almost there," he breathed. I wasn't sure if he was telling us or reassuring himself.

Our final stop waited beyond an unmarked door clad in hammered metal sheeting. It was a vaulted chamber of bare concrete, long, dotted with a trio of pits. The holes were maybe ten feet across, smooth cylinders carved into the stone. A dirty yellow ring of paint surrounded each pit, and stenciled letters read Minimum Safe Clearance.

Beyond that, the room was spartan. By the door stood a card table, a couple of folding chairs, and a desk lamp that shed a puddle of hard white light. Santiago grabbed one of the chairs. It scraped, shrill, as he dragged it across the chamber. He plopped it down on the edge of the middle hole, right on the yellow clearance line.

They sat me down with my back to the pit.

"Go tell him," Santiago said to his partner. The other man left, fast, not bothering to hide how badly he wanted to get out of this room. That made two of us. I started planning my exit strategy.

Santiago tossed my deck of cards, my wallet, and my phone onto the table. Out of reach, but once I got the cuffs off, a good two-second sprint would close the gap. A quick spark of magic to wake the cards up, and I'd have a weapon. That said, two seconds was less time than it would take for Santiago to draw his sidearm and shoot me dead.

I couldn't be reckless. But with the air caked in that rancid, breath-stealing stench, and faint rustling sounds drifting up from the pit behind me, it took everything I had to keep my nerves in check. I focused on Santiago, trying to give my brain something to do besides worry.

"One question," I said. "You a real cop, or is that uniform bogus?"

He started poking through my wallet. "Real as the cruiser I drove you in."

"I've seen fake squad cars before."

"So have I." He plucked the cash from my wallet, a couple hundred in loose bills, and curled them around his index finger. "Hey, thanks for the donation."

"You ever hear the phrase 'adding insult to injury'?"

He shoved the cash into his pocket and flipped the wallet back onto the table.

"You're about get a lot more than injured, pal." He glanced my way. "Not by me. I'm just the babysitter."

"Do you even know who you really work for?"

"Sure," he said. "The winning team."

"You used your boy Todd to murder over a dozen innocent kids. That what you call 'winning'?"

Santiago rolled his eyes. "That's what I call 'overcomplicated,' but I don't give the orders around here. If it was up to me, you'd already be dead in a dumpster with two shots in your noggin. I like to keep things simple. But my boss has very specific plans to end your ass in a very specific way—don't ask me why, it's above my pay grade—and that meant luring you out and taking you alive and undamaged. Speaking of living, can I assume Todd's not coming back to work?"

"He died slow," I said. "Not as slow as you're going to, though."

"Look at me, I'm shaking."

The metal door whistled open and Santiago jerked his spine straight like a soldier snapping to attention. His partner hadn't come back. The new arrival, alone, rustled over the doorway on mismatched legs, one an inch or so shorter than the other. His entire shape was mismatched. Torso too squat, arms too long, a bulbous head oscillating on a spindly neck. He stepped into the light.

He was maybe sixty or so, wearing tufts of salt-and-pepper hair like a crown around his bald and wrinkled scalp. His amber eyes were moons set into his face, his chin a bony spear. He wore a three-piece suit, too big for his frame, and the sleeves dangled halfway down his narrow hands like he was a kid trying to wear his father's jacket.

Santiago grabbed the other folding chair and rushed it over, setting it down about six feet from mine. Facing me. The man folded himself onto the seat. He curled his knees against his chest and perched there like a bird.

"Hello," he chirped.

I wasn't sure what to make of him. Or any of this. "Uh…hi," I said.

"You can go now."

He was staring at me, but seeing as nobody moved to get my handcuffs off, I figured he meant Santiago. So did Santiago. The cop gave a nervous little nod of his head as he scampered for the door.

Just the two of us now.

"I'm being terribly rude," he said. "My name is Elmer Donaghy. It's a pleasure to meet you, Mr. Faust."

"Call me Dan. So…this is your place."

"The business I've been entrusted with, yes." His twitchy fingertips snatched at the air. "Of course, it's a front, but that doesn't mean we don't deliver quality performance! I'm very insistent on things being run properly. Your city's refuse is in good hands here. You could say that I…*refuse* to cut corners."

He giggled at his own joke. Great. The psycho had a sense of humor.

"You've been a lovely competitor," he added. "Tell me, I'm curious. This little contest of wits…in your mind, did you frame it as a chess metaphor or a more physical battle, like a boxing match?"

"Chess," I said. No reason to lie.

He smacked his palms together, a merry little golf clap, then hugged his knees tight.

"I thought you might. We're a good match. And I'm not much inclined toward the martial arts, I'm afraid." He held out his arms to his sides. His oversize coat draped over him like a bedsheet on a scarecrow. "I realize I don't look like much. You must be disappointed. You have to understand that where I come from, nine out of ten children die before their third birthday. I was the runt of my litter, but I survived. 'Healthy' is a very relative word."

"Where's that? Somewhere in the third world?"

"Not *your* third world," he said with a smile. "You are aware there are more worlds, in the literal sense, than this, yes?"

I was aware, all right. Twenty years ago, a black-budget science team inside Ausar Biomedical carried out a string of interdimensional incursions. They didn't like what they found. From what one of the survivors told me, they'd opened windows onto plenty of other Earths, parallel to ours, and most of the locals were anything but friendly.

They'd also found a place that looked a hell of a lot like the Garden of Eden. Abandoned, choked with cancerous and cannibalistic horrors, and toxic to human life. That survivor I interviewed realized the experiments were going too far; he tried to stop his former partners and managed to unleash something even worse in the process. He opened a crack in the prison world where the Enemy had been banished, and set the bastard loose.

"So how does a guy from a parallel Earth end up on this one?" I asked.

"Talent." Elmer giggled again. "As a young man I was banished from my village. I had a natural affinity for the occult arts, and I was foolish, too eager. Well, that, and my early experiments mostly centered around stealing the other children's health to sustain my own. I was present at one too many crib deaths, and rosy-cheeked when our village was suffering crop rot and drought."

"You're lucky they just banished you."

"Oh, far from it. Burning me at the stake would have been a more merciful punishment. I was cast into the wastes of a poisoned, *afflicted* world, without food or water. Soon I came upon the bones of a city, infested with the insatiable vermin we called 'gravers'—the wilding dead. But they had what I needed to live, and my spirit was not so broken as my body. I found that by coating myself in the rotten viscera of corpses and working a few charms, I could pass among them unscathed. With more practice, more experience, I could tame their animal minds and make them obey me."

"Did you teach 'em to roll over and shake hands?" I asked. "I suppose 'play dead' wasn't an option."

"I taught them, and they taught me. I was all alone in a kingdom of death. More of a playground, really. I immersed myself in decay as a survival tactic at first, but soon I understood the true beauty of rot. Decomposition is part of the cycle of nature, every bit as essential as growth. And one comes from the other. Did you know, with proper cultivation and care, certain flowers can actually grow upon corpses? It's wondrous to behold."

"I'm starting to see why they put you in charge of a garbage plant."

He grinned, wide, showing off yellowed and broken teeth.

"I wore a ceremonial robe made of human skin, my face smeared with a dead man's entrails, as I led the charge upon my former home. I punished the villagers for casting me out, then added their reanimated bodies to my ranks. We preyed on merchant caravans after that, mostly. A winning tactic until I ransacked a pilgrim train. They were escorting a safe filled with strange artifacts, including a knife made of a metal I'd never seen before. No wonder, as it turned out. It wasn't *from* my world. And then, on the dark of the moon, its owners came to reclaim their stolen property."

"The Network," I said. I had reason to believe the organization's reach stretched across parallel worlds. Now I had the proof.

Which didn't mean a thing if I died here tonight. Behind my back, my fingers slowly eased toward my belt, and the hidden handcuff key.

"Indeed," Elmer said. "They could have killed me out of hand, but my work impressed them. I never stopped experimenting, you see. Occult transmutations to reshape life—and death—into new and more useful forms. The Network saw value in my designs. You're already familiar with one of them, I believe."

"Am I?"

In response, he nodded at the air just above my left shoulder. I held my breath, tasting the chamber's stench, as I squirmed in the chair and looked behind me.

The pit at my back, with the legs of my chair perched on the edge of its yellow-painted rim, offered a sheer drop into a pool of rotting garbage. Trash bags had burst at the bottom, moldy food and waste spilling from their glossy black skin, mingling with heaps of wet cardboard boxes and smears of rancid grease.

A sheet of cardboard moved. Lifting, just a little, as a mottled brown cockroach the size of my fist squirmed out from underneath. Its mandibles twitched at the air, as if it could sense me watching it.

It let out a rattling, wet hiss and squirmed back under cover. More hisses rose up, joining the roach chorus, as the entire pit of garbage began to quiver and move.

15.

"I crafted my pets from raw clay," Elmer told me, "but the Network—they saw their true potential. For an organization whose survival depends on secrecy, what could be more useful than a parasite that can compel one's silence?"

I turned from the pit, fighting to ignore the hissing, squirming sounds echoing up from the shadows. I had to get out of here, but right now I needed to keep Elmer talking while I figured out an escape plan.

"Which is why all the Network's flunkies have them," I said. "They can't rat you out when they've got a magic roach nestled in their guts."

"We started with the lowest levels of our outer cells, yes. A proof-of-concept run, to make sure there were no long-term side effects. And I'm pleased to say it's been a smashing success. We're ready to move to phase two."

I shook my head. "Meaning?"

"Oh, Dan." He looked disappointed. "Use your imagination. My pets don't just compel silence, they compel *obedience*. Anyone, with a parasite and a little hypnotic conditioning, can be turned into a Network asset. If done properly, they don't even know they've been turned."

"Anyone." The skin of my chest prickled as the implication dawned on me. "Or *everyone*."

"Now you get it. Alas, it's not to be so. Not in the short-term. My pets don't reproduce as quickly as the roaches of your world.

Their incubation period is nearly a year long, and all attempts to modify them for faster breeding have failed utterly. We simply can't mass-produce the little beauties, let alone keep up with demand. Yet, anyhow. Phase two is about targeting more valuable hosts. Setting our sights a bit higher than the rabble we have pushing our narcotics."

Behind my back, my fingers felt along the rim of my belt. I'd done this move more times than I could count under Bentley's guidance. Theoretically, it was simple: dip my fingertips behind my belt, pry the tiny key loose from the blob of putty holding it in place, twist it around, and unlock my cuffs.

With an audience watching me like a hawk, that theory fell apart. Any hint that I was doing something suspicious—my shoulders shifting, my forearms wriggling—would give me away. I had to be slow, glacier slow, my every move perfectly natural.

"Is that why you're making nice with the King of Worms? Hoping he gives you the secret to better roach breeding?"

Elmer cupped his palm over his mouth and chortled. "No, no. I seek his blessing not for my glory, but for his. If he sees fit to reward me, of course I won't deny his will. And it's fair to say that becoming his emissary will boost my standing in the Network considerably. Why, I'd be a regular rock star. Imagine that."

I held his gaze and kept him talking. Not just for the information: if he was looking in my eyes, he wasn't watching the slight twitch of my arms as I hooked two fingers around my belt. One fingertip grazed the hard edge of the handcuff key.

"What *are* the kings?" I asked. Elmer gazed across the three pits in rapt contemplation, like a mystic composing a prayer.

"They're us, Dan. They're the original us. The *perfect* us. To commune with the kings is to find perfection within our mortal flesh. If you'd made more of an effort, well, our positions might be reversed right now. The King of Worms offered his gifts to you! Do you know how rare that is? You should have prayed to him when you had the chance."

"I'm not religious," I said. "Also, unlike you, I don't dance like a puppet when somebody puts a little fight music on. Don't be a chump, Elmer. This 'game' of his isn't about picking the best man for the job, because I was never going to *take* the job. He just wants me gone, and he's using you and the Network to do it. Once you kill me, don't be surprised if he stops taking your phone calls."

For the first time since he arrived, his cheerful smile wilted. The big moons of his eyes narrowed.

"I would say that you'll see the error of your ways, but, well, you won't. I think I'll re-animate your body after I sacrifice you, in the hopes that some tiny part of your brain retains just enough consciousness to feel regret."

Almost there. I had my fingers in position behind my back, ready to dip and pry the key loose. Once I had it, I'd be halfway home.

I still wasn't sure what I was going to do once I got my wrists free, or what Elmer was capable of, but I figured I'd start throwing punches and improvise from there.

"Diminished brain capacity?" I said. "Strong sense of regret? You just described how I wake up most mornings."

He wagged a finger at me and cracked a fresh smile. "This. I'm going to miss this. We had such a short time together. I really think we could have been friends. I don't have many. People around here, well, they find out you're from a parallel Earth and they start treating you like some kind of alien."

"Maybe you shouldn't tell 'em about how you used to wear a human-skin suit. That turns people off."

"Maybe so, maybe so."

"Tell me one thing," I said. "If all you have to do is off me, and the king—allegedly—is going to swoop down and put his holy halo on you, why the wait? If I was you, I would have killed me five times over by now."

"Alas, my hands in certain matters are tied. I oversee this particular branch of the Network's operations, but I answer to a higher—" He paused as three knocks sounded at the metal-sheeted door. "Ah, there we go. Enter, please!"

The door swung wide, and one of the last people I expected to see strode into the chamber. Ms. Fleiss, draped in her purple leather trench coat, eyes shrouded behind onyx shades.

"You're kidding me," I said, glancing between them. "The Enemy and the Network, teaming up."

"You're late," Elmer told her.

"Stuck in traffic."

"Where?" He squinted at her. "Three planets away?"

"If you must know, yes." Fleiss turned my way. My reflection doubled, trapped in the frames of her long, oval glasses. "We meet again. For the last time, thankfully. Howard Canton's wand—where is it?"

"The one place not even your boss will go looking for it," I said. "I hid it...in New Jersey."

Her gaze snapped to Elmer. "He hasn't been implanted with a parasite yet?"

"I was waiting for you," he sighed. "As I was instructed to, so don't get snippy with me. He'll answer all the questions you have for him—and truthfully—once one of my pets is snug inside his belly."

Fleiss's heels rang out on the concrete as she stepped closer. She loomed over me, wearing a withering scowl.

"What did you do with the Cutting Knife you stole from us?"

"You mean, what did I do with your sister?" I asked.

Even the impenetrable glasses couldn't keep the flicker-flood of emotions from Fleiss's face. Her lips twitched and her cheeks went tight, and she showed me every card she was holding: worry, pain, disgust, fear.

"I have no sister," she said. "I am unique."

I was sitting, handcuffed, between an immortal monster and a pit of giant roaches. Not the best place to push my luck, but she'd just shown me a crack in her armor. All I could do was drive a shiv right into it.

"Your sister," I said. "Circe. You remember her."

"I have. No. Sisters."

"Why did you say that?" I asked her.

"Because it's true."

"No. Your choice of words. I said sister. You said sisters. Plural. Like, say...eight of them? You remember, don't you? You know who you are. Who you were, before the Enemy sank his teeth into you."

Fleiss's hands curled into fists. "Shut up. Stop talking."

"To answer your question, I took Circe home, to the Low Liminal. To the Lady in Red. Your mother. Would you like to go home, too? I know the way. Say the word and I'll take you there right now. You can be home in an hour—"

Her coattails flared as she wheeled around. She flung out her hand and pointed at me as she turned her fury onto Elmer. "I want him implanted, muzzled, and ready for transport. I want it done *now!*"

Elmer's chair clattered back as he jumped to his feet. "Hold on. What? No. No, he's not being 'transported' anywhere. He's not leaving this facility. Not alive, at any rate. You're welcome to his remains once he's been sacrificed. I'll even reanimate them for you, so you don't have to carry the body. But he's not leaving."

"Oh, shit," I said, "looks like this weird little alliance is hitting a few rocks. Could it possibly be because...ooh, right. See, Elmer, you need to sacrifice me to the King of Worms to get your prize. But the Enemy, he needs me to die in a prison cell, per the terms of his little magical reliquary, or *he* doesn't get *his* prize. You can't both get what you want."

"We already thought of that." Elmer pouted at me. "I've had a cell, a perfect replica of your cell at Eisenberg Correctional, constructed here on-site. I kill you myself, inside the cell, and all conditions are satisfied."

Fleiss gaped at him. "No. Under no circumstances. I was *not* consulted about that. A replica cell, on land that's never been used as an actual prison? We have no guarantee that the ritual will succeed. We'll only get one shot at this. It has to be one hundred percent perfect."

"Well, Mr. Smith told me to build it. If your office and his aren't communicating, that's hardly my problem."

"I'm making it your problem." Fleiss punctuated her words with a finger jab to the breast of his oversized jacket. "Faust is coming with me. No arguments."

I felt the heat in the room rising between the two of them, and my life depended on fanning the flames.

"I wouldn't trust her, Elmer. All she cares about is making the Enemy happy. If he tells her to screw you over, you're gonna be screwed over royally. And if she kills me herself, well, you can kiss your new job goodbye."

"I did," he said, his voice on the edge of a whine, "exactly what Mr. Smith instructed me to do. I was promised I could kill him here, as long as it was done inside the replica cell, and after you were done questioning him."

"*I* didn't make that promise," she told him.

"Oh, hey," I said, "that reminds me. Fleiss? Why are you teaming up with the Network? I mean, they're building some kind of empire across...how many worlds, Elmer?"

He didn't take his eyes off her as he snapped his response. "*Many*."

"Okay. And the Enemy wants to burn the entire multiverse to ashes. Now, call me crazy, but it sounds like you folks have some serious irreconcilable differences there. The only way I see this working out is if both of you went in with the intention of pulling a double cross at some point. Hey, is that today, do you think? Fleiss, do you think the Network might be deliberately trying to screw this up, to make sure your boss never ever gets all of his power back? I've got no proof, but I mean, that's what I'd do if I was them."

Neither one answered me, but I could see from their faces that I was landing some direct hits.

"I'm calling Mr. Smith," Elmer said. Fleiss followed him to the door. He stopped short with his hand on the knob. "What are you doing?"

"Not letting you out of my sight. We will call Smith *and* my lord, at the same time, and the four of us will get this sorted out *together*. Just to make certain that there are no further 'misunderstandings.'"

"What about him?" Elmer asked, nodding my way.

Fleiss spun on her heel and stalked toward me.

"There is one thing we do agree upon," she told him.

Fleiss lifted one leg and pressed her spiked heel to my chest. Then she gave me a shove. I felt myself teeter back, then fall, wind roaring in my ears as I plummeted into the breeding pit.

"Let the roaches have him," she said. "They'll take good care of him until we return."

16.

The folding chair broke under my back when I hit the bottom of the pit. The cheap metal hinges buckled against my spine and sent a jolt of pain up my tailbone. I sank into a morass of rotting trash like it was a filth-encrusted sponge, embracing my struggling body, threatening to suck me down like quicksand. The stench stole my breath, leaving me gagging; my eyes watered like I'd rubbed them with chopped onions. Up above, out of sight, the chamber door slammed shut.

I wasn't alone. Soggy, decomposing cardboard shifted. Torn garbage bags rustled. Two feet away, I saw antennae wriggling in the corner of my blurry vision.

I squirmed, sitting up, and reached for my belt. I didn't have to be subtle now, but I had to be fast. And perfect. If I dropped the key into this slop, if I lost my grip for one second, I might never get it back.

I felt an itch along my left arm. I looked back and saw a six-inch roach wriggling up my shirtsleeve, climbing toward my face. I shook, violent, like a dog with a knotted rag, and knocked it loose. It landed on its shell, kicking its segmented legs in the air.

Another scurried over my sock and disappeared into my slacks, crawling up my leg. I forced myself to focus. Nothing mattered but getting my hands free. My fingers pulled my belt back and found the handcuff key. One slow, careful tug and it pried loose from the putty.

Roach legs rustled in my right ear. Antennae flicked at my

cheek as the roach's head pushed its way into my eardrum. I thrashed my head until the bug fell free. Another was on my shirt now, clambering up my chest.

Had to focus. I turned the key in my fingertips—gentle, gentle—shoving away a chitinous shell as a roach tried to skitter onto my hands.

I jabbed for the keyhole. Missed it, metal scraping against smooth metal. Legs crawled across the back of my neck. More on my shoulder. I shook hard, sinking deeper into the rotting muck, knocking it loose. The one on my neck was tenacious, digging in as it climbed my chin. It scambled up onto my face, my mouth, trying to squirm its way between my pursed lips. Another had made its way into my hair, hissing as it crawled toward my other ear.

Third try. The key slid in, turned, clicked, and my wrists were free. I leaped up, sinking knee-deep in the trash, and flailed at my face. I slapped the roaches from my cheeks, my hair, knocking another two from my sleeves. They kept coming, the trash roiling around me as the entire infested pit came to life. The roaches boiled up, mandibles clacking as they squirmed in from all directions, converging on me.

I set my sights on the lip of the pit, ran, and jumped.

My left hand missed, falling short, but I caught the concrete rim with the fingertips of my right. My shoes scrabbled on the sheer wall, struggling to get a hold, any kind of traction. One good heave and my left hand curled over the lip. My back screamed, muscles burning as I gave it everything I had, pulling one arm over the rim. From there I had enough leverage to keep fighting, keep pulling, hauling myself over the pit's edge one agonizing inch at a time.

I rolled and slapped at my arms and legs, sending stray roaches scattering. One came right back at me, relentless. I jumped to my feet and brought my heel down like a sledgehammer, bursting it like a balloon filled with yellow pus. Another still had a grip on my shirt. I grabbed it, ripped it from the grime-caked linen, and hurled it across the room.

The roaches were climbing the pit walls now, a rising, glistening brown tide. I sprinted to the table and snatched up my cards, my phone, and my wallet. The deck pulsed against my fingertips, sensing danger and eager to fight, but I was pretty sure I didn't have enough cards in the pack.

The desk light. I grabbed it, hoping the creatures had this much in common with the roaches of our world as I angled back the plastic hood and aimed the light at the pit's edge. The roaches cascaded down in hissing curtains, tumbling from their grip on the smooth concrete, and scurried into hiding to escape the glare. I used the light to cover my escape, sweeping it across the floor as I backed toward the metal-sheeted door, and drove back a few desperate stragglers.

The door clanged shut. Out in the hallway, I pressed my back to the sheet metal and took deep, gasping breaths of air.

I ran fingers through my hair and slapped at my clothes, muscles jerking with revulsion as I made sure I didn't have any stragglers clinging to my body. Clean. As clean as I could get, anyway, with my suit soaked in filth. My phone had two bars and maybe twenty minutes of charge time. I wouldn't even need half.

"Daniel." Caitlin's voice was breathless; she'd picked up on the first ring. "Where are you? Jennifer's men saw the police take you, but Harding is insisting you were never brought into custody."

"I wasn't, not by Metro. The Network grabbed me."

"Are you safe?"

I looked left and right. The boxy concrete corridor stretched in both directions, lit by a single thin bar of light under a white plastic shroud. As soon as Elmer and Fleiss finished their phone call, they'd be back. And then they'd come hunting for me.

"I'm nowhere near safe. I'm over at Donaghy Waste Management; the whole place is a Network front. They've got a necromancer on site, and Fleiss is here too."

"Fleiss?" Caitlin said. "Wait, you said this is a Network—you know what, never mind, we'll discuss it later. I'm on my way."

"Call Jennifer, have her round up everybody she can. We need a wrecking crew out here. Oh, and make sure everybody knows—the night shift is clued-in and loyal to the Network. As far as I know there aren't any civilians here, so come in hard."

"As I said, pet...I'm on my way."

The cavalry was coming. I only had one job now: survive until they got here. I picked a direction at random and ran, jogging up the corridor and into the shadows. I had seen Fleiss in her battle form once before; it had taken two rifles firing on full auto, plus my cards, just to drive her off. I didn't know what it would take to actually kill her. Or if she could even be killed.

Then again, maybe I wouldn't have to. I remembered the look on her face when I reminded her of Circe. And her slip, how she'd denied her sisters—plural—before I'd said the word. Whoever she was before the Enemy corrupted her...part of her was still in there. Close to the surface but trapped under the ice and drowning, trying to get out.

Landmarks started to look familiar. The great steel vats rusting away in the dark, conveyor belts, engines for sorting and shredding the city's cast-off waste. The echo of heavy, jerky footsteps up ahead jolted me to a stop. I didn't think the night crew were Ecko-style walking dead, but *something* was off about these guys. I changed course, darting down a side passage.

A pair of swinging doors opened onto a break room. Rumpled magazines littered the long Formica tables, and a soda machine hummed away in the dark. A dry-erase calendar on the wall charted employee birthdays and what day the communal fridge would be cleaned out. Aggressively mundane, an artifact of the day shift. On the far side of the break room, a stub of a hallway ended in a door marked Emergency Exit Only. A sticker on the push bar warned that opening it would trigger an alarm.

Did I chance it? No telling what was on the other side, beyond a shot at freedom. I ran through the layout of the lot in my head.

The perimeter fence had been topped with spools of concertina wire. Once I was outside, I'd have to fight my way to the main gate, or jack a truck and crash the fence.

Speakers crackled to life. Elmer's voice drifted from a recessed grille in the ceiling, a slow and singsong chant.

"Dan. *Daaan.* Daniel. You see, this is exactly why I didn't want to leave you alone for a second, much less allow Ms. Fleiss to take you outside this facility. I have far too much respect for you as an adversary to give you an opportunity like that. She's looking for you, by the way. I hadn't seen her other form before. I'm impressed, I have to say. She's very fast for a...well, a plus-sized woman."

Elmer's nasal giggle echoed through the empty hallways. I put my ear to the emergency door, trying to get any kind of a fix on the other side. If Fleiss was in battle mode, I needed to be anywhere but here.

"You'll be happy to know we agreed on a solution," Elmer said. "Once she catches you, Ms. Fleiss is going to amputate your arms and legs, then sew your lips shut. You won't be playing any tricks after that. And you'll be nicely compact for travel."

I shoved the emergency door's bar and pushed on through. Crisp, cold night air embraced me under the halogen glow of a loading dock. A couple of Elmer's men were working on a garbage truck—the hood up but the engine humming, ready to roll. I formed my plan in a heartbeat: kill them, steal the truck, blast through the perimeter fence at full speed. The second I was clear I'd call Caitlin and meet up with the convoy, then do a one-eighty with some serious backup on my side. A spark of magic spurred my deck of cards to life. They leaped from my pocket in a fluttering stream, landing in my left palm and crackling with static electricity.

One of the slack-faced men turned my way. He threw his shoulders back, his torso wobbling like his spine had turned to jelly, and opened his mouth wide. His jaw cracked, disgorging a fat, filth-brown roach where his tongue should have been. Then he let out a shriek louder than a jet engine and so shrill it felt like a pair of icepicks had stabbed into my eardrums. The garbage truck's windows burst, imploding in a glittering spray of glass.

His partner spun and dropped to all fours, bouncing on his hands and feet as his maw yawned open. His tongue-roach quivered its mandibles at me as he joined in the skull-pounding screech. They charged as one, loping across the asphalt, fast as lions on the savanna.

I hauled the emergency door shut. The latch clicked a heartbeat before a body slammed against it from the other side. The reinforced wood rattled and shook under a hurricane of frenzied punches. I wasn't sure how long the door would hold up. I only knew I wasn't getting out that way. I turned and ran, deeper into the complex, closer to the immortal monster that was hunting for me.

17.

Staying mobile was my best hope. A janitor's broom closet beckoned to me, offering the temptation of a hiding place, but that was a sucker bet: sooner or later, either Fleiss or Elmer or his "night crew" would find me and drag me out of hiding, and then I'd be finished. Once Caitlin and my reinforcements rolled in I might have a fighting chance at living through this. Until then, nothing mattered but running down the clock.

A lonely doorway opened onto a stairwell. It rose up like a fat chimney along the back of the building, the concrete steps lined with black rubber runners. I bounded up two at a time, grabbing the iron rail with one hand and my phone with the other, thumbing the speed-dial.

"I'm with Jennifer," Caitlin said. "We're five minutes out. She rounded up a number of her Calles friends, and most of Winslow's associates just rendezvoused with us on the road. They're a bit inebriated, and eager for a fight."

"They're going to get one. Warn everybody: this necromancer goes in for some extreme body modification. His crew is faster and stronger than they look."

"Noted. Where are you?"

"On the move."

I rounded the next landing. A long, narrow window reinforced with chicken wire looked out over the company lot. Shapes bounded across the puddles of stark yellow light on all fours, more animal than man, the night crew hunting for prey.

"Gonna try the roof," I told her. "I'm hoping they won't think to look for me up there."

I hung up without telling her the second part of my plan. If they did find me, I wasn't going to let Fleiss take me alive. A three-story drop onto the asphalt was a better way to go than anything she had planned for me.

I burst out onto a flat rooftop covered in fine white gravel, stumbling to a stop, and put my hands on my knees as I doubled over and took deep breaths. My heart pounded a staccato rhythm against my ribs. Blood roared in my ears louder than the steady hum of the boxy air-conditioning units that studded the roof.

I could see the lights of the Strip from here. So bright, offering a world of normality and safety so close I could almost reach out and touch it. I could be sitting in a casino bar right now, nursing a Jack and Coke, or out strolling with the tourist crowds and enjoying the night air.

But I was here, trapped on a roof, neck-deep in a world of monsters, torture, and death.

"The fuck am I doing with my life?" I breathed.

It wasn't a rhetorical question. I had kicked off the lethargy, the self-doubt, the ennui that kept me couch-surfing and doing nothing for months on end. That was a victory. But what was I doing with it? Assuming I survived to see daylight, was this really how I wanted to spend the rest of my life? Living by the gun, down in the nightmare underbelly of the world?

Was I capable of doing anything else?

A swarm of headlights flared on the access road, coming in hot. Philosophy class was over. I crouched down low and got as close to the rooftop's edge as I dared.

A dirt-encrusted semi truck crashed the gate at sixty miles an hour, sending twisted metal flying in a shower of sparks. A pair of minivans in Calles brown and yellow—gunships, with the side doors yawning open so shooters could lean out and make the drive-by—were right on its tail, followed by a dozen Harleys. Their engines revved in a full-throated diesel shout.

The night crew answered with an air-splitting chorus of screeches. They raced from the shadows, swarming like ants, and my reinforcements answered with crackling gunfire. The darkness lit up with muzzle flashes like a fireworks show on the Fourth of July.

The motorcycles never stopped moving, roaring as they wheeled around and charged up and down the asphalt. One of Elmer's creations pounced from the darkness. He landed on a rider's back and dragged him down. The bike spun, out of control and crashing into a loading dock wall, while the feral creature pinned the rider down and ripped out his throat with its teeth. It raised its head to howl in a bloody-mouthed victory—and another biker streaked by, giving it both barrels of a sawed-off shotgun. The creature flipped onto its back, kicking like a dying bug, its headless neck ending in a stump of broken spine.

I caught a glimmer of white leather under the lamplight. It was Caitlin, her battle coat flaring out behind her as she darted into the building. Jennifer was out front with her crew; a razor blade glinted between her teeth. Her chromed .357 bucked in her hand, taking down one of Elmer's men in mid-leap, and she slashed her blade across her opposite arm. Blood boiled from her wound, a glittering wet cloud, then hardened into a cluster of deadly crystalline brambles. With a single guttural word, the ruby barbs fired in a buckshot blast.

I whirled around as a door slammed open at my back. Fleiss had found me.

Clawed hands latched on to the sides of the doorway, heaving as she squeezed her rubbery, elephantine bulk through one glistening inch at a time. Her head was an Easter Island idol with oval slabs of black onyx for eyes, swaying on a leathery serpentine neck, and her legs bent on backward joints.

I slid one foot back, the white pebbles rustling under my shoe as I moved closer to the rooftop's edge.

"I'll jump," I warned her.

Her squat feet thumped on the stony rooftop as she emerged from the door. Her head tilted, opaque eyes drinking me in.

"If you die," she hissed, "good chance the mantle of the Thief will return to Marcel Deschamps. We *have* Marcel. Same outcome."

My mind raced. I knew my cards would barely slow her down, and I didn't stand a chance in a fistfight. Violence wasn't going to win this one; I had to keep her talking, keep her off-balance.

"A good chance. You want to bet eternity on that? We both know part of the Enemy's power is locked up in the Thief's death. If I die here, tonight, without fulfilling the requirements and the Thief reincarnates on some other Earth...how long is it going to take you to find him again? A thousand years? A hundred thousand? A million? How about 'never'? How will your boss take the news, do you think?"

Fleiss wavered. Her frog mouth quivered. "I won't allow you to die here. Not like this. My lord's will must be obeyed."

She moved toward me, looming, and I stopped her with a single word.

"Why?"

The wrinkled skin around her onyx-lens eyes went tight.

"Why?" she echoed.

"Yeah. Why? You've been carrying a torch for that asshole for centuries. Why do it? What's he ever done to earn that kind of loyalty?"

She looked like the question had never occurred to her before. She spoke slow, piecing her words together with justifications and twine.

"He is...everything. He is my lord. Therefore I must serve him. I was...I was created to serve him."

"No," I said. "You weren't. He didn't create you. I think you know that, deep down inside. I *know* that you know that."

"You're lying," she grunted. "All you do is lie."

She took another ponderous step closer. Two more and she'd be close enough to grab me in those leathery, steel-cord arms and tear me to pieces. I held my ground, sensing the sheer drop at my back.

"I do lie a lot, true, but not about this." The words of the Lady in Red drifted back to me. I recited them to Fleiss. "Once upon a time, nine beasts emerged from the Shadow In-Between. Nine of the Lady's daughters, war-witches all, pledged to slay them. But they were tricked and led into an ambush."

"Stop. Stop talking."

"They were bound, trapped in the form of tools, their powers to be commanded by any man who wielded them." I gazed up at her. "But the Enemy didn't just wield you, did he? He knew he was about to be tossed into a prison dimension; his only hope was to store his magic in a reliquary, before his rivals could drain it from him, and give it to a servant he could trust. A servant who literally couldn't think of rebellion. A servant who thought she was in love with him and believed he loved her back."

"He *does* love me," she hissed.

"Has he ever told you that?"

She halted in mid-stride, one stumpy foot hovering an inch above the pebbled rooftop.

"No," I said. "He's never said he loves you. And you know, deep down, you know it's because he doesn't. He never will. He's not even capable of it. He twisted your memory, your mind, your body. He stole from you. He stole everything from you. But you can take it all back. You have a mother. You have a family that loves you, that *really* loves you. Let me take you to them. Let me help you."

Fleiss stood frozen. Her face twisted in an agony of indecision, buried doubts and fears racing to the surface as she warred with herself.

Then her foot slammed down, turning the white pebbles to broken powder. She lunged for me, stampeding in, and lashed out one elongated arm. Her claws latched tight around my throat. My breath cut off and she heaved me off my feet while I kicked frantically at the open air.

"No more lies." Her other hand clamped nails tight around my jaw. "I'm taking your tongue for a trophy."

"I wish you wouldn't," said the voice at her back, tinged with an amused Scottish burr.

Fleiss swung me around like a rag doll as she turned. Caitlin stood fifteen feet away, draped in her white leather coat, one hand casual on her hip.

"I'm fond of his tongue," Caitlin said. "He's very skilled with it."

Fleiss tossed me aside. I hit the roof, landed hard on my shoulder and rolled into a crumpled heap. Coughing, I gulped air back into my aching throat.

"She means my witty repartee," I croaked as I shoved myself to my feet.

"Oh. That too." Caitlin wriggled one scarlet eyebrow. Then she tossed back her coat like a gunslinger, baring the coil of a bullwhip on her belt. "As for you...kneel and face judgment. Cooperate, and I'll make it quick."

Fleiss flexed her claws, ten knives of black iron. "I won't be judged by the likes of you, demon. I answer to a higher authority."

Caitlin curled her lips into a pleased little smile.

"Right here, right now," she said, "I *am* the highest authority. But if you won't die with dignity, I suppose we can do this the entertaining way."

Fleiss bellowed as she charged. Her bulk thundered across the rooftop, kicking up a cloud of flying pebbles and white dust. Caitlin broke into a sprint, ran at her, and leaped to one side as Fleiss's claws made a wild swipe. Her boot caught the edge of an air-conditioning unit, and she used it for a launchpad, sending herself sailing at Fleiss heel-first. She drove a bone-crunching kick into the creature's face and Fleiss staggered backward. One of the lenses over her distended eyes sprouted a spiderweb of cracks.

Caitlin didn't have time to savor her victory. Fleiss was faster than she looked. She rallied, knocked Caitlin's next kick aside, and shoulder-charged her. Caitlin landed hard on her back and rolled to escape the pile-driver slam of Fleiss's foot.

I hurled my cards, one after another, a crackling swarm of magic-charged hornets. The pasteboard missiles sank into the blubber of Fleiss's back and dangled like a porcupine's quills. She wheeled around, slapping at them, and it gave Caitlin just enough time to jump back to her feet.

Her whip snaked free of her belt. She brought it down on the rooftop with a thunder-snap *crack*, and flames erupted from the brass grip. They raced down the leather like a gasoline trail, setting the whip alight. She swung it above her head, a blur that left a burning smear in my vision, then lashed it around Fleiss's neck.

Fleiss clawed at the snare as it burned blue-hot into her skin and the air filled with the stench of sizzling, rotten meat. Caitlin ran past her, springing from air conditioner to air conditioner, winding the whip tight as she sprinted around the bellowing creature. Then she leaped, yanking hard on the line and driving both heels into Fleiss's backbone.

Fleiss crashed down. She fought free of the whip, driving Caitlin back with frenzied slashes of her claws, and staggered back toward the far edge of the roof. The skin of her serpentine neck was charred black and weeping pus.

"Next time," she snapped, "I choose the battleground."

She dragged her claws through the open air in a vicious downward swipe and opened a rent in the universe. A black and starless void howled beyond the tear. The edges of reality flapped and rippled like canvas sails in the wind. I heard the faint sound of wind chimes, and the scent of roses kissed the night air.

"Stop her!" I shouted, racing in as I hurled another brace of cards. "Don't let her—"

Too late. Fleiss dove into the void. It whipped shut behind her as the world repaired itself. She left nothing behind, nothing but the fading floral aroma, dissolving away on a stiff, cold breeze.

18.

Caitlin and I stood on the rooftop alone. Both of us panting for breath, battered but still standing. The flames of her whip died out, a few last sparks fluttering free and going cold, and she coiled the supple leather around her forearm before hooking it back onto her belt. She looked my way, paused, and wrinkled her nose.

"You're, ah—"

"Covered in rotten garbage." I glanced down at my soiled clothes. "Yeah. This was a really nice outfit, too."

"It might be salvageable."

I shook my head. "I like my dry cleaner too much to do that to him."

Down below, the last few gunshots died out. The air filled with raucous voices and the rev of wide-bodied choppers. We might not have gotten our hands on Fleiss, but we'd still won the night. I only hoped my words had planted a few seeds under her skin. Maybe they would bear fruit later on. All the same, I knew better than to count on it. Life had taught me that when you show somebody proof that they've been conned, nine times out of ten they just dig their heels in harder.

"I would hug you, but—"

"Right," I said. "I'm gross. I wouldn't hug me either. Rain check?"

"Absolutely."

"Don't suppose you came across a creepy little guy on your way up here? Sixty-something, balding, wears an expensive suit that doesn't fit him?"

"Didn't have the pleasure," she said. "The creator of the welcoming party downstairs, I take it?"

I nodded, moving fast for the stairwell door, and she fell in at my side.

"Elmer Donaghy," I said. "Also, would-be emissary of the King of Worms. Once I catch him, he's going to be my *special* friend."

* * *

Elmer was either playing the best game of hide-and-seek ever or he'd seen which way the wind was blowing. He couldn't be found, but we were tearing the place apart just to be safe.

"Grab those computers," Jennifer shouted, sending soldiers in brown bandannas scattering in every direction. "Collect notebooks, tablets, anything that might have anything on it. This is the first Network front we've cracked, so we're snatchin' anything that ain't nailed down."

"How are we doing on time?" I asked her.

"Not great. These boys didn't call the cops when the shooting started—for obvious reasons—but a good citizen called in a noise complaint. We got fifteen minutes, tops."

"Hey," one of Winslow's bikers called out. He kicked a corpse, its blue overalls peppered with bullet holes, and pointed. "What should we do with these ugly fuckers?"

I took a closer look. The man's mouth hung open, a dead roach lolling out between his blood-flecked teeth. I crouched low and studied the seam where it had been grafted onto the stump of his tongue. Elmer was nothing if not inventive.

"Burn it," I said. "Can't have civilians seeing this shit. Burn them all. On that note, anybody bring some extra Molotovs?"

Winslow swaggered over, shirtless under his leather vest, toting a canvas messenger bag over one shoulder. The bag rattled as he walked.

"How many you need?" he asked.

"Three ought to do it. Follow me."

The first breeding pit went up in a satisfying *whump* of flame. The roaches screamed. Their bleats filled the smoky air like a herd of dying sheep. I flicked a lighter and held the flame to a second rag-stuffed bottle.

"Hey, Jen," Winslow said. "Next time you wanna rally me and the boys for a midnight run?"

"Yeah, sugar?"

"Don't."

I threw the second bottle in. Burning moonshine smashed across rotting garbage and set the next pit alight.

"Good news is," I said, "according to Dr. Frankenstein himself, they're having trouble making more of these particular monsters. With their breeding pits gone and their stock reduced to charcoal, we won't have to worry about any bug infestations for a while."

In theory, anyway. I knew better than to hope that we'd killed off the last of the roaches. Just like I knew that if Elmer ran when the shooting started, he didn't run far. The King of Worms had dangled the perfect prize in front of the necromancer's greedy, moon-shaped eyes, and to get it, all he had to do was put me in the ground.

Glass shattered, burning alcohol spattered against concrete, and the final pit went up in flames. Fire licked the open air, hot enough to make me sweat through my filth-encrusted clothes, and the acrid black smoke drove us from the room. We shut the sheet-metal door, leaving the chamber to cook.

The rest of this mission was a smash-and-grab. Anybody not running out to the vans with armloads of stolen records and hard drives, anything that might hold a stray clue, was on arson detail. By the time the first police lights swam into view in the distance, red and blue strobes cutting the darkness, Donaghy Waste Management was burning. Flames blew out windows and spat plumes of smoke into the cloudless sky.

I didn't ask Caitlin if she could give me a ride. I knew she would, but I also knew how she felt about keeping her car seats pristine. Instead, I crammed into one of the loot-stuffed Calles vans with

Jennifer. Shooters piled in, high-fiving each other, celebrating their victory. A few of them gave me weird looks and wrinkled noses.

"You are a little ripe, hon," Jennifer told me.

I sighed. That was an understatement. At least I was alive, intact, and I didn't have any alien parasites making themselves at home in my intestinal tract. I counted that as a solid win.

"Yeah, just drop me off at Della's, and I'll remove my odor from your presence. First order of business is taking these clothes and burning them."

"And after that?"

"After that..."

Good question. I'd survived the night and escaped Elmer Donaghy's trap, but he was still out there. So was Fleiss, and now that the Network had joined forces with the Enemy—against the odds, given that one of them wanted to rule the multiverse and one wanted to burn it all down—the danger had effectively multiplied.

"After that, I'm taking a shower," I told her. "We'll see how things go from there."

* * *

I trudged into my apartment, a remodeled one-bedroom over Della's Pool Hall on the east side of town, and stripped down on the doormat. My clothes went into an extra-strength garbage bag. So did the doormat, just to be safe. Then, just like I said I would, I hit the shower like an athlete at the end of a long, hard game. The hot water and steam coursed over my aching muscles, pounding the knots out, and I ran my fingers through my slicked-back hair.

For a second I thought I might find a stray roach there, a hidden stowaway. The thought made my skin crawl and I had to pat my entire body down again until the jitters went away, but I was clean. Cleaner by the heartbeat as the water and the soap foam did its work, scrubbing away everything but my sins.

The pulse of the water drove out the sounds outside. It blanketed the world in white static and gave me some time alone with my thoughts. I spent a couple of idle minutes indulging in the One Last Score fantasy. Everybody in the life knows that one. It's the dream where you pull a single heist, *the* heist, then hang it up forever. The one where you take a score big enough to float you all the way to the end of the line. It always has a happy ending, sipping frosty mixed drinks on a beach in Mexico or maybe Bora-Bora, dipping your toes in the warm surf.

Everybody has that fantasy. Most of us even have a target in mind, that big fish we could hook if all the planets lined up just right. The thing was, though, I'd known a lot of professional heisters in my day. Some were still working; some landed in a prison cell or ate a bullet. A couple retired and took on semi-legit jobs, hanging out at the edges of the underworld. Those guys, they understood: once you're in, you can't ever get all the way out. The life calls to you like a siren song.

Maybe that's why not a single one of them had ever made that fantasy real. The One Last Score doesn't exist, not really. And if it did, most of us would find some excuse not to reach for it. Because we don't *want* to quit.

I wondered if it was the rush that kept me going. Every day I rubbed shoulders with solid citizens. People who lived in the daylight Vegas, far from the underbelly I called home. They could go their entire lives without someone sticking a gun in their faces, or taking the kind of job that ended with spilled blood and closed caskets. For that matter, they'd never find themselves forced into a death match with a necromancer from another dimension because some alien "king" wanted to see what would happen.

No. It wasn't the rush. I was never much of an adrenaline junkie—I didn't even like roller coasters that much—and I'd survived this long as a career criminal by balancing every risk against the potential for reward. That wasn't it.

So why, then?

Answers eluded me as the shower steam wrapped warm arms around my weary flesh, tempting me with the pleasures of sleep. I wasn't going to figure anything out tonight. I toweled off, stumbled to my bed, and crawled under a storm-gray comforter, losing myself in an oasis of soft linen.

19.

I dreamed of suburbia.

I recognized it on instinct, even as my sleeping mind took the scene—manicured lawns and white picket fences scrolling past my car window—for reality. I'd had this dream before. It usually popped up when I wasn't feeling sure of my way. More and more, lately.

Neighbors were out and enjoying the warm desert sunshine. Cooking burgers on a grill, throwing footballs around. A couple of cherub-cheeked tots ran a lemonade stand on the corner. The air was clean and crisp, and on the other side of a plate-glass window, I watched a dad kick back on the couch with his kids to watch the big game.

I guess everyone dreams of the things you can never have.

My car stopped at the corner. I glanced to the kids at the lemonade stand.

They didn't have faces.

The skin had been carved away with surgical precision, leaving wet ovals and glistening cherry bone behind. They grinned at me with skeleton mouths.

The car was gone. The street was gone. This was new. I ran along a corridor of black marble, walls yawning and twisting ahead of me like a fun-house mirror.

I emerged into a parlor, jolting to a stop. The only sound was the metronome *tick-tick-tick* of a grandfather clock. Elmer

Donaghy perched on a regal chair, rubbing his spear of a chin as he studied a chessboard set out upon a French-styled dais.

"Check," he said.

I stared at myself in the chair opposite his. The stumps of my arms and legs, cauterized black by fire, twitched as my sewn-together lips struggled to form words.

"Time's up," Elmer said to my mutilated twin. He reached over and moved another piece. "You can't win if you don't play."

"He's right," said the voice behind me.

I turned and the parlor ripped away, dissolving to gossamer smoke. Now I stood at a forest crossroads, torches burning at the three points of the path.

"He's a figment of your imagination, as your brain struggles to parse the events of the day through the process of dreaming," the Lady in Red told me, "but he's still right."

She was a vision in scarlet, the train of her vintage dress sweeping out behind her as the pale woman strode toward me. A spill of raven curls flowed down her shoulders, and her pomegranate lips curled in a vaguely taunting smile. A silver antique key dangled from a chain at her throat.

"As for his unfortunate chess partner," she said, "Elmer's threat must have resonated with you."

I didn't look behind me. I didn't know if the tableau was still there, but I didn't want to see it again.

"I think the threat of getting turned into a living torso would resonate with anybody," I said, trying to play it cool.

"True, but for you…I think it speaks to a fear you've carried for a very long time."

She took hold of my shoulders. Then she spun me around and yanked me close, so I could feel her body against mine, her hot breath gusting against my ear.

"It was born in this room," she whispered.

A plastic lamp with a tattered lampshade cast a puddle of yellow light across peeling powder-blue wallpaper. I knew this place by heart. The cheap beds, the toy chest with the broken lid, the two boys shivering under thin blankets.

"Dan," my brother whispered, "I think Dad's gonna kill us."

I could hear him downstairs. Stomping, slamming the refrigerator. He'd gone on a beer run after work. Beer-run days were the worst. He'd come home with a case, half of it gone by dinnertime. He couldn't drink on his meds, so he just wouldn't take the meds. By midnight, the New World Order would be sending him commands through the television and the neighbors would be spying from electrical sockets.

"Teddy," twelve-year-old me said from the bed by the door, "you know I'll protect you, right? We're brothers. You can always count on me."

Downstairs, my father threw a lamp through the television screen. I knew he'd be here soon.

"I don't want to see this," I breathed. The Lady's hands, long-fingered and cold, held my shoulders tight.

"You made your brother a promise."

"I tried. I slept with a butcher knife under my goddamn pillow. I *tried*."

"How did that work out for you?" she asked.

Court day. My father's lawyer had dressed him up in an off-the-rack suit from Sears, gotten him a twenty-dollar haircut, and made sure he was on his medication. We were all wearing suits that day. I couldn't remember where mine had even come from. It was too heavy, too scratchy, and I tried not to fidget while Teddy, eight and a half years old, took the stand.

"So you saw your brother, Daniel, attack your father without provocation," the lawyer told him.

Teddy bobbed his head. "Without provo...provo...he did it."

"And your father never hit you, did he?"

Teddy's head swayed. He bit his bottom lip.

"Teddy," the lawyer said. He crouched down, all fatherly now. "Tell us who broke your arm."

My brother pointed at me. "Dan did it."

I stood on the edge of the court now, invisible. I felt more tired than anything.

"I never blamed him," I said. "Even then, I understood. I was going away, and he was going back to that house. Alone, with the man who probably killed our mother. The fuck was he supposed to do? He had to protect himself."

"You blamed yourself, though," the Lady said.

"Sure I did. If I'd stabbed my father two inches to the left, he would have died that night. First time I ever tried to kill a man, and I blew it."

I watched the courtroom turn to smoke. Outlines of people wavered, gelatinous, their voices fading to indistinct murmurs.

"Why are you doing this?" I asked her.

"Maybe I'm not real," she whispered in my ear. "Just another figment of your imagination. You are dreaming, aren't you?"

"No. I've dreamwalked with other people before. You're really here. Why are you doing this to me?"

"Nightmares are gifts. They can show you the problems in the waking world you've failed to correct, or don't even know that you're struggling with. Tell me the core of your fear."

"I don't understand the question."

We slipped sideways. Sideways into a room with white peeling paint and a barred window and a locked door. No furniture but a bare mattress on a wire frame, and there was me, fifteen years old, naked, facedown with my arms and legs in hospital restraints.

The orderly, a kid in his early twenties with long, greasy hair and a jackal's eyes, lit a cigarette.

"The fuck is it with you, Faust?" he asked in a lazy drawl. "We only have a few simple rules around here, and you can't go three days without starting a fight."

"I didn't *start* it," younger me snarled, yanking hard enough to make the bed frame rattle. "Syd and his asshole buddies were shaking down that new kid. It was three against one and he's half their size. It wasn't fair."

"Everybody says you threw the first punch. And now you gotta be segregated, and I gotta work more unpaid overtime and fill out an incident report. And every time reviews come around, we get graded on how many incident reports we had to fill out, you get me? So not only did you make me cancel a date tonight, you're directly fucking with my chances of getting a raise."

I tried to turn around, didn't want to see this, didn't want to go back, but the Lady's grip was made of iron.

"*Watch*," she hissed in my ear.

I watched the orderly shove a knotted rag in my mouth. Then I watched him put his cigarette out on the small of my back.

"Maybe this time you'll listen," he said as my teenage self screamed through the dirty rag and thrashed on the mattress. The flesh under the cigarette, when he finally pulled it away, was beet-red and blistering. It would leave a fresh scar to join the other three.

"Oh, and that new little shit, the one you were 'protecting'?" the orderly said. "He's two rooms down. And I'm going to go down there now and give him the same treatment, and then I'm going to tell him it's your fault."

"What are you feeling?" the Lady whispered.

I tried to shut my eyes but my body wouldn't do it. I was feeling the cigarette sear into my back like it was happening all over again, the plastic restraints cutting off the flow of blood in my hands and feet, the rage coursing through my veins like gasoline.

Mostly the rage.

"I want to kill him."

"Why don't you?" she asked.

The restraints pinned me to the soiled mattress. My younger self was still screaming through the knotted rag—not in pain, not now—as the orderly sauntered out of the room and the door slammed shut.

"I *can't*."

"What are you feeling?"

My rage splashed like fire against a wall of iron, pinning me in, trapping me. I couldn't move, couldn't change anything, couldn't save anyone.

"*Helpless*," I tried to scream.

The word came out in a brittle whisper, then turned to ash. The world turned to ash, cascading, spinning, a snow globe from a mausoleum.

I was on my knees, in darkness. Head bowed, shoulders slumped, all of my rage gone cold and turned to sludge inside of me.

The Lady in Red crouched down, and her fingertips gently lifted my chin.

"It's good to know the things we fear most," she told me, "and the wellspring that birthed them. The things that can be used against us."

"I don't understand," I said.

"You will, when the time is right. I'm not often cruel without reason. And there's one last thing to see. Come."

She took me by the hand. We walked through darkness, into darkness, something soft and loamy under our feet. Then, up ahead, a single gray spotlight captured our destination.

"You aren't the only one sleeping right now," the Lady said. "Though he denies her freedom, even in her dreams."

Under the spotlight, Fleiss hung suspended from a column of liquid iron. Her torso dangled from the molten black pillar, her arms behind her and her hands and feet trapped inside the goo. The iron burbled as it slowly flowed, like a living blob of soot-stained mucus. Her eyes were closed and her head lolled from side to side.

"Mother," she whimpered.

The Lady reached for her. As her pale hand brushed the edge of the light, the entire column rippled. The iron went rigid, yanking Fleiss's arms tighter, wrenching her shoulders. The trapped woman groaned in pain. As she lifted her head, I realized her eyes weren't only closed: dribbles of the liquid iron had welded them shut.

"I try to comfort her as best I can," the Lady said, "but the Enemy is a diligent warden."

"So...I was right." I stood at the edge of the light, careful not to cross it, as I looked between them. "The real her, before the Enemy twisted her around his finger—she's still in there, somewhere."

"And aware." The Lady folded her arms, storms behind her eyes as she stared at the pillar of iron. "I promise you that. Every vile thing he forces her to do, every waking second of being under his dominion—part of her is aware. And screaming, but no one can hear her voice. Those memories I just walked you through, the helplessness you felt? That's what my daughter feels, awake or dreaming, every moment of her life."

I knew what she was going to ask me next. She didn't even have to say it. I sealed the pact between us with six words.

"Tell me how to save her."

She favored me with the faintest smile.

"You've already started the work. She has to be forced to confront the contradictions that surround her. She'll dig her heels in, no doubt; he's grafted a mask to her face. Push her until it shatters. Here's something you can use: she's an accomplished witch."

"Well, I knew that much," I said. "How does that help?"

The Lady wore a faint twinkle in her eyes.

"Ask her who her teacher was. And remember what I teach all of my daughters: that freedom is a witch's creed."

Her fingertips brushed my cheek.

"I'll be watching you, Daniel."

20.

Morning in Las Vegas was a weird place to be, even if you hadn't spent the night in the hands of a goddess. The free-floating party on Fremont Street started early, although the real show didn't begin until the sun went down. I moved among packs of wandering tourists, most of them bleary-eyed and clutching plastic cups of cheap beer to stave off the hangovers they'd worked so hard to earn last night. Elderly gamblers roamed under open casino archways, queuing up for the penny slots. Off to my left, by a sound stage that wouldn't see any action for another twelve hours or so, a busker dressed as Gandalf the Grey was trying to get sightseers to pay for a photograph.

Fremont felt wrong by daylight. It had the self-destructive earnestness of a guy in his forties at a frat party, egging everyone on to keep drinking past dawn just to prove he could still hang. I wasn't here for the crowds, anyway, or the penny slots or the two-dollar margaritas for that matter. I let my mind go blank as I strolled, thoughts drifting on an aimless sea—

—and a copper bell chimed as I crossed a stained, worn-out carpet, suddenly surrounded by cool air and the aroma of Indian food. The Tiger's Garden had sensed me on its street, decided I was worthy, and pulled me in like a fish on a line. Past the three-seater bar, lit by dangling paper lanterns from a '70s garage sale, the tiny dining room only had three occupants. Jennifer was already here along with Bentley and Corman, and all three were starting the day off with a proper magician's breakfast: greasy food and alcohol.

Jennifer tore off a hunk of tandoori chicken, waving the bright scarlet meat at me in greeting. "Hey, sleepyhead. I was just tellin' the guys about your entomological adventure."

"Better you than me," Corman said, arching a bushy eyebrow as he sucked on a bottle of beer. "Good to see ya, kiddo."

Bentley got up before I could protest. His frail arms pulled me into a tight hug.

"Be *careful*," he fretted. "You should have called us."

"C'mon, I can't be bothering you guys every time I run into trouble—"

"You mean you don't want to *bug* them?" Jennifer asked.

I shot her a look and pulled out a chair.

"Besides, you were there in spirit," I said to Bentley. "The mailbag escape saved my life last night."

He lit up at that. "Handcuff key behind the belt?"

"Never leave home without it."

Bentley saluted me with his gin and tonic. "That's our boy."

Amar, the Garden's only employee and maybe owner, swooped by with a brass-rimmed tray. There were no menus at the Tiger's Garden; Amar always knew what you were going to order, and more often than not, it would be waiting for you when you arrived. We didn't know how he did it, and he wouldn't tell us. He set a champagne flute in front of me, garnished with a perfectly cut wedge of orange.

Corman snorted. "A mimosa?"

"Hey," I said, "it's a classic brunch cocktail. Pass the chicken."

Between bites, Jennifer brought us up to speed. "Commissioner Harding's ducking my phone calls, but Seabrook was apoplectic. Accordin' to her, she did just what we told her and passed down a no-touch order on Container Park. And, like you suspected, Harding saw the chance to bust a few ink dealers and get some good press."

"And Santiago and his buddy blended in, just waiting to grab me." I frowned. "Still don't know if they're real cops or just playing the part. Santiago wouldn't give me a straight answer."

"Does it make a difference?" Bentley asked.

"Insofar as how we're going to handle it." I sipped my mimosa. It went down like a boozy-sparkly waterfall. "Santiago got a dozen kids killed, for no reason but to draw me out. As far as I'm concerned, he's a dead man walking. If his badge is real, though, we have to be a little more delicate; you can't just green-light a cop. Also, if he's legit, there's a good chance's he's not the only real cop on the Network's payroll. We need to root them *all* out. And preferably replace them with our own people."

"I'm still not feeling this weirdo alliance," Jennifer said. "The Network and the Enemy joining forces? Far as we can tell, they're after totally different things."

I had been doing a lot of thinking about that since last night, and I kept circling around to the same answers.

"The Enemy's got something the Network wants. Something they want bad enough to offer him a short-term alliance, but I guarantee it's only a matter of time before somebody gets stabbed in the back. If we're lucky, we'll be able to spin it to our advantage. In the meantime, though, they're a lot more dangerous united than they were on their own. Our number-one priority right now is tracking down Elmer Donaghy. If we can squeeze him for information—"

Jennifer cut me off, holding up a slender iPad.

"Gotta stop you there, hon. My boys are still combing through the loot we jacked from Donaghy's place, with Pixie's help on the computer end, and so far it's a lot of nothing. These Network critters raise paranoia to a high art. Pixie tried telling me about the security they use—some kinda double-triple self-destruct fourteen-jillion-bit encryption—and it made my eyes glaze over."

"They're cautious," I said. "On the plus side, caution slows them down. I'd hate to think what kind of damage they could do if they dropped the cloak-and-dagger act and went all-out."

She tapped the tablet and spun it around, scooting aside a plate of half-gnawed chicken bones to make room.

"When he made his exit, Elmer didn't have time to be discreet. This purchase went through on his company AmEx, right about two minutes after the gunfire started."

I read the blurry scan, black type on stark white. Elmer had bought a first-class ticket on a Delta flight to Paris. His takeoff time was two in the morning. I looked up from the screen.

"We missed him."

She nodded and took the tablet back. "He fled in style, on the first flight out of the country that would have him. I did some checkin', and Donaghy Waste Management has municipal contracts in some far-flung places. Vegas, Cheyenne, Miami..."

I finished the thought. "And Paris."

"Paris, France, registered home of his corporate HQ. Sorry, sugar, he's gone. And while you could hop on a plane and chase him down, there are probably more important things needing your attention here on the homestead."

She was right. Besides, I saw the lure, glimmering bright in the water.

"Fool me once," I murmured.

"Meaning?" Corman asked.

"He's not gone for good. He can't be. We know the King of Worms is dangling a nice fat promotion over Donaghy's head, and he's got to kill me—with his own hands—to get it. The guy's a fanatic, and true believers never quit until they get what they're after. No." I pointed at the tablet. "He wasn't in a hurry. We were *supposed* to find this. And he took a flight straight to his corporate headquarters, which of course we can easily find a registered address for."

"He's hoping you chase after him," Corman said.

"Straight into the belly of the beast, on his turf, where he can lay another trap for me." I sipped my cocktail. "Nope. Denied. He'll come back for round two eventually, and in the meantime, I can get ready for him. Like Jen said, I've got better things to do.

And things I don't want to do but apparently don't have a choice about."

"Your, uh, party," Corman said. "That tonight?"

"Yep." I tapped the side of my champagne flute. "Another six or seven of these, I'll be almost ready."

"You sure you don't want us to come?" Jennifer asked.

"Nah. I mean, I do, but number one, I wouldn't do that to you, and number two, it's apparently a private function. Courts of hell and aristocracy only."

"Ooh, aristocracy." Jennifer put her finger under her nose, forming a mustache. "Yes, yes, do pass the caviar, my good man. And did you see what Lady Wembley Shuffleboard-Smythe is wearing? Simply *preposterous*."

I slouched in my chair. "Yeah. I'm thinking it's going to be a lot like that, plus everybody but me is a demon. Caitlin says I have to be on my best behavior."

"She's gonna settle for that? Has she *seen* your best behavior?"

"I know, right?" I shrugged, resigned to my fate.

"Almost forgot." Jennifer wriggled in her chair, tugging a slim tape recorder from her jeans pocket. "I pulled that surveillance-feed audio, from when Naavarasi ganked Chicago's shape-shifter for us."

"Get anything good?" I asked.

"Not sure, seeing as I don't understand a word of it."

She hit Play, and the micro-cassette's wheels spun. I leaned close to try to make out the grainy audio. We heard sounds of a scuffle and strained, raspy breath.

"To think," Naavarasi's voice said, "you actually believed this pathetic creature was one of my kin."

Kirmira said something soft, desperate, in a language that sounded like Hindi. Then came the sudden, sharp snap of bone as Naavarasi broke his neck with one hand. The recording stopped.

"Can I borrow this?" I asked her. "I've got some free time this afternoon before the party. Figure I'll run it over to one of the local colleges and track down a language instructor."

"May I assist?" Amar asked. I hadn't seen him come back, but there he was—at my shoulder, swapping my drained glass for a fresh mimosa.

"Sure, if you don't mind."

"Play it again?" He leaned in. His brow furrowed as he listened to the muffled words. "Once more?"

Jennifer rewound the tape and gave it a third play. This time Amar stood straight and nodded.

"The man said," Amar told us, "'Why, Mother? I did everything you told me to.'"

The table fell quiet.

"Was that helpful?" Amar asked.

"Yeah," I said, my appetite gone. "Thanks, Amar. Appreciate it."

Nobody said a word after that, as we weighed the implications. Amar vanished with his tray. Eventually Jennifer broke the silence.

"That heinous *bitch*."

"Sounds like Kirmira was a rakshasa after all," Corman said. "Which means her whole spiel about being 'the last of her kind' after Prince Malphas sieged her jungle was a load of crap all along. What do we actually know about Naavarasi?"

"We know she's a heinous bitch," Jennifer snapped, glaring down at the tape recorder. "Her own kid. She set up her own kid and killed him, just to make us think she was on our side."

"And so I'd owe her a favor," I said, "which she then used to bait her trap for Caitlin later down the line. Kirmira didn't just start working for the Chicago Outfit last month; he'd been serving the boss's kid for *years*. How long ago did she start setting this up?"

"Well, did her a fat lot of good in the end," Jennifer said.

I wished I could believe that. I wanted to think we'd blown Naavarasi's plans apart and left her bleeding, bleeding bad enough that it'd be a dog's age before she tried anything like that again, but I didn't buy it. Mainly because I suspected enslaving Caitlin wasn't her endgame. It was just another layer of her plan.

"Sit on the tape for now." I pushed my chair back. That second drink beckoned to me, but I needed a clear head. "I'm going to try to be productive tonight and learn as much as I can about the rules of my new 'honored position' in Sitri's court."

"Like where the loopholes are?" Corman asked.

"Just like you taught me. And in the meantime, I'm looking for Santiago. Something tells me Elmer Donaghy didn't spirit him and his partner away on a first-class jet to Paris, which means there's a good chance they're still in town. And if they're here, I want them."

21.

I had one solid source in Metro, though he had a strangely lopsided view of our relationship. Just because Gary Kemper had blackmail on me and could end my life with a single phone call to the FBI, he seemed to believe he was the one in charge. People get strange ideas sometimes.

We met in the parking lot of a Five Guys a few blocks from the Strip. No particular reason for the choice of rendezvous spot, except I was in the mood for a cheeseburger. I wasn't sure if the party tonight was going to have catering, or if the food would be anything I'd want to eat, so stocking up ahead of time felt like my best move. He pulled his unmarked car up facing opposite to my rented Elantra, so we could talk between our driver-side windows.

My first thought, as his window rolled down, was that seeing that kid break his own neck in holding had rattled Gary deep and hard. Usually he'd greet me with annoyance and a reminder that I wasn't calling the shots anymore. Today all he had was a terse "What've you got?" and a furtive glance at the passing cars.

"The ink from the house party was tainted on purpose," I told him. "It was a long-range hit, courtesy of the Network."

I didn't tell him that I was the one they were trying to lure out. Gary already thought he might be right to make that call to the FBI, and I didn't need to give him any more reasons to burn me.

"Who was the target?"

"Still working on that. I can tell you that the man in charge of the Vegas Network cell left the country last night."

"'Left the country'? That a euphemism?" he asked.

"No. He ran, but he'll be back. And we'll be waiting for him. In the meantime, you might have a couple of rats in your house. One of these rats is a part-time dealer; he's the guy who made sure the tainted drugs would be at that party. On the other hand, he might just have a bogus uniform and a squad car to go with it. If that's the case, I'll have to cast a wider net, but I figure Metro is the best place to start hunting. That's where you come in."

I expected an argument. Something about how he didn't know every uniform in Metro and I was asking too much, at the very least. Instead, he locked eyes with me.

"Tell me what you know. If the bastard's on the job, I'll find him."

"He goes by Santiago. Only name I know. He was at the Container Park shakedown last night."

Gary rubbed his chin. "Container Park's under the downtown division's command, pretty sure it's Sector A. That narrows it down. I'm good with the watch captain over there. I'll drop by this afternoon and do some digging."

"Watch yourself," I told him. "You've seen how the Network plugs leaks, especially when it comes to law enforcement. They don't take chances. You'd better not, either."

"I'm touched by your show of concern. Don't worry, this isn't my first rodeo."

"I know. All the same." I hesitated, but I couldn't send him off without making sure we were on the same page. "If you find him, you do realize this can't be handled through legal channels, correct?"

"Clarify for me." He wore an open challenge in his eyes.

"The people pulling his strings won't—*can't*—let him be questioned by the police. If you arrest him, he'll be dead in an hour. And you'll be dead right alongside him. They'll probably bury you in the same ditch."

He sank in his seat and watched the road, sullen now.

"I have a job, Faust. When the city gave me a badge, I promised to treat it right."

"You didn't promise to die for it. Nobody could ask that of you. Hey, Gary. Look at me. *Look at me*. You've got a responsibility here."

"That's what I'm telling you."

"You've got a responsibility to *stay alive*. That shiny badge of yours isn't worth shit if it's pinned to your corpse. If you find Santiago, I want you to call me. Let us handle it."

"You want me to hand him over to you," he said. "Which basically makes me an accomplice to murder."

"It makes you a person who did the right thing, got a guy who killed a dozen kids off the streets for good, struck a blow against the Network, *and* lived to fight another day. Now, I'm nobody to lecture on morality, but that sounds like pretty decent behavior. If I were you, I'd make that call and I wouldn't lose a minute of sleep over it."

He turned the key and fired up his engine.

"That's the thing," he said. "You aren't me."

His window hummed up and he rolled out onto the boulevard. I watched him go. Nothing I could do now, for him or about him, except hope he made the right choice.

* * *

After that, I had nothing to do until sunset. I'm lousy at doing nothing. I ended up back at my place, setting the groundwork for a science experiment. I had borrowed a couple of oversized mail sacks from Bentley, the stiff fabric bags that were a staple of any escape artist's kit. One went in my living room nook beside the television set. The other I positioned fifteen feet away in the open kitchen, right next to the granite-topped cooking island.

I studied Howard Canton's wand, turning it in my hand. It was mahogany, inlaid with caps of polished bone at each tip, a tool of a more elegant age. And a more macabre one: the bone, I had learned, was human. One cap of the wand, enchanted to weave illusions, came from the skull of an ancient Egyptian sorcerer.

The other, designed to tear them down and reveal the truth, was from Harry Houdini himself.

I toted the wand into the living room and fiddled with the remote, launching Netflix and fast-forwarding through a movie until I got to the part I'd been looking for. I was about to begin the experiment when a knock sounded at the door.

"Just so you know," Melanie told me, "I'm grounded for a month."

"You want to come in?" I asked her.

She puffed air up at her neon-blue bangs, making them flutter, and breezed past me. I shut the door.

"I can't help but notice it's two in the afternoon on a Thursday," I said.

Melanie leaned against the kitchen island. "Yeah?"

"Isn't there someplace you're supposed to be right now? Like...school?"

She spread her hands. "Seriously. A month. What the hell, Dan? I told you everything you wanted to know, and you still ratted me out."

"Hey, it's not all sunshine for me, either. I'm in trouble, too."

"What? Is Caitlin going to spank you?" She dropped her voice and murmured out one side of her mouth. "Not like she doesn't do that already."

"Hey now—"

"What?" She shrugged and gave me an innocent look. "I'm just saying, people talk. Whatever floats your boat, you do you. I don't judge."

"Did you come all the way over here just to take cheap shots at me, or are you hiding from the truant officer?"

"I came because I want to know what gives." She sighed. "Seriously. I thought we were cool. I thought we were friends."

"We are friends."

"Friends don't tell other friends' mothers that they were out at house parties without permission. Even ones where people got killed. *Especially* those."

What could I tell her? I'd already kicked her legs out from under her once this week, refusing to take her on as my apprentice. I didn't want to do it twice. Ultimately, this was one of those rare cases where the truth was the best policy.

"I'm your friend," I told her. "I'm your mom's friend, too. And I'm also allegedly a grown adult, which means I've got responsibilities. Yes, Emma can be a little..."

"Abrasive? Overbearing? Insufferable?"

"It seems that way right now, sure. But...can you see how I've got a different perspective? I hear how she talks about you when you're not in the room. And she gets frustrated with you about as much as you get frustrated with her—"

"Zero surprise there, since she never listens."

"—but it comes from a place of love," I said. "If she didn't care, she *wouldn't* care. She's trying her best to do right by you, Melanie. And I can't promise anything, but I really think five, ten years from now, you and her are going to relate to each other a lot better and be a lot closer. It just takes some growing to get there. Maybe...a little less trying to drive each other nuts. A *little* less. A teensy bit."

"Whatever." My tenuous grasp of teenagerese told me that was the best I'd get from her. She glanced down at the mailbag. "What's this?"

"Little experiment. I'm having a problem with my wand."

"They make medication for that now."

"Cute." I showed her the mahogany stick. "There's some serious magic locked in this thing; so far I've seen two of its moves, and I'm betting it's capable of more than that. Anyway, one of the wand's powers is a short-range translocation."

"Translocation?" Melanie's eyes widened. "Wait, like a transporter beam, like on *Star Trek*?"

"Sort of. I've only gotten it to work once. In theory, I jump into a confined space like a bag or a cabinet, trigger the effect, and the wand moves me elsewhere. See, Howard Canton, the guy who created the wand, he was a stage magician back in the forties. He designed a lot of his spellwork to replicate classic illusions."

"Holy shit," she said. "Show me. I've got to see this. Can I try it?"

"Well, therein lies the rub."

I walked into the living room and she trailed behind me.

"If you start rubbing your wand, I'm leaving."

I chose to ignore that. "Canton's wand has one very weird restriction. It doesn't just work when you want it to; it only wakes up when it senses its owner is trying to save someone in danger."

"Not seeing a problem," she said. "Don't people try to kill you, like, twice a day on average? You're in danger all the time."

"Ah, that's the thing. It won't lift a magical finger to save its *owner*. Damien Ecko murdered Canton sometime in the fifties, and Canton didn't even bother bringing the wand to their showdown. He knew it wouldn't help. He hid it away instead."

"What? That's nuts. Why create this super-powerful doohickey and wire it so it wouldn't even help the guy who *made* it? If I had my own transporter beam, I'd use that thing all the time."

"Would you use it to go back to class, where you're supposed to be right now?" I asked.

"You haven't kicked me out yet."

"I'm a bad role model. And I don't know why he did it, except to keep it out of the hands of somebody like me."

Melanie frowned at the wand. She tilted her head, contemplating. "Maybe it's like dog training."

"How do you mean?"

"You get the behavior you reward," she said. "Maybe this Canton guy wanted to encourage himself to go out and save people."

"Yeah, well, Canton's dead now, like most people who think they can use magic to be a hero. It doesn't work that way."

"Power corrupts?"

"Absolutely," I said. "And more importantly, every system has a flaw, and every set of rules has a loophole. A real bad guy is scarfing up all of Canton's relics, and he's hot to get his hands on this wand. If he thinks he can unlock its power, I *definitely* can. Just have to figure out how."

I reached for the remote control and offered it to her.

"So I'm going to try to hack this thing. Wanna help?"

22.

"I'm not sure exactly what the wand is responding to when it decides to work," I said to Melanie. "It might be something as simple as the sound of someone in distress, or something that looks like real violence."

She looked from the remote in her hands to the television. I'd cued it up halfway into a horror flick. On the screen, a hockey-masked killer was frozen in the rain, mid-rampage, holding a machete high over his head.

"I hate horror movies," she muttered.

"You just don't appreciate classic cinema."

"Seriously," Melanie said. "We are surrounded by literal, actual monsters. All day. Every day. Some of my mom's coworkers *eat people*. Why would you want to watch make-believe psychos on top of that?"

"At the end of the day, the make-believe psychos usually lose. I find it refreshing."

I walked over to the kitchen nook and stepped into the first mailbag, pulling it up over my shoes.

"Okay, when I say go, hit Play. I'm going to try to wake up the wand. If this works—*if*—I should pop out of the bag right next to you."

"Ready," she said.

I concentrated, closing my eyes, and felt the smooth mahogany wand under my fingertips. This was a game, at heart—a battle of wits between me and a dead magician. I was good at games.

I breathed fast, almost hyperventilating, trying to push my heartbeat. The brain is an impressionable organ, which is why horror movies and roller coasters work in the first place: even when you know you're perfectly safe, a little trickery can convince your body that you're in danger and trigger those sweet fight-or-flight chemicals to flow.

Running out of time, I told myself. *If I don't get over there in the next two seconds—*

"Now!" I said.

Melanie tapped the remote and a shrill scream burst from the television speakers. I dropped to a crouch and hauled the mail sack over my head, burying myself in canvas and darkness. A pulse of magic jolted along my spine, sizzling down my arm and into the wand, kick-starting it to life. Then I jumped to my feet, bursting from the bag—

—and found myself standing exactly where I'd started, in the kitchen. On the screen, the machete buried itself in a wayward camp counselor's skull while sharp violin chords screamed.

"You're too late," Melanie said. The remote dangled from her hand as she gave me a dubious look. "Freddy claimed another victim."

"That's Jason."

"I don't care." She turned off the TV and tossed the remote onto the couch. "So the wand is smart enough to know the difference between fake danger and real danger."

"We learned something. That's progress. Even if it doesn't go the way you want, an experiment is never a failure if you learn something from it."

Melanie strolled into the kitchen. "Where do you keep your silverware?"

"Drawer on the left, why?"

"Got an idea. I'll stand here. You get into the bag by the TV."

While I swapped places, she rummaged around in the drawer and came up with a salad fork.

"If you don't teleport over here in the next five seconds," she declared, "I'm going to poke myself with this fork."

I glanced up at her while I pulled the second sack over my feet. "I'm not sure I'm comfortable with that."

"I'm not going to, like, open an artery or anything. Geez." She put on a face of grim resolve. "But I'm going to poke myself really hard, and it's going to hurt a *lot*. So you'd better get over here and save me from this evil fork."

"Melanie—"

"Five. Four. C'mon, stop me. Please stop me? Three."

I dove into the sack. I dug deep, down in the stifling darkness, willing myself to *move*. I waved the wand with a flourish, hurled the fabric back...and hadn't budged an inch. On the other side of the apartment, Melanie jabbed the fork into her arm.

"Ow," she said.

"Okay. So, self-inflicted harm doesn't trigger it either."

"Maybe if it's lethal harm," she said, "but I'm not going to cut my wrists to find out."

She tossed the fork. It rattled into the sink as she dusted off her hands.

"Progress, though," I said.

I was already putting together what we'd learned, trying to come up with a plan of attack. Melanie watched me as I paced the carpet. Something must have shown on my face.

"You really get into this, don't you?"

I really did. It was nice to have a puzzle to sink my teeth into, a problem I could solve. Not doing it alone was nice for a change, too. Reminded me of the old days, when Desi and I would grab a pizza and a bottle of wine and stay up until two in the morning arguing the finer points of occult theory.

I stopped pacing.

"You should probably get back to class," I said.

"Heck, I'm *in* class. This is—" She paused. Her excitement shriveled like a deflated balloon. "What is it? Seriously. All of a sudden you look like somebody ran over your dog."

"I shouldn't have gotten you involved. I've got no idea what this wand's really capable of. It's dangerous."

"Well, if you'd *teach* me..."

I put my fingers to the bridge of my nose and pinched. I felt a headache coming on.

"We're not having this discussion right now," I said.

"Come on, weren't we just having fun? And learning things? We could be a great team!"

The shrill buzz of my phone saved me. I showed Melanie the screen.

"Caitlin's on the line, so unless you want *real* trouble, don't make a sound." I tapped the screen and put the phone to my ear. "Hey, beautiful."

"I hope you're polishing your dancing shoes, pet."

Right. The party. I would have been more excited about a trip to the dentist. Filling a cavity would probably hurt less, too. All the same, I tried to inject some excitement into my voice. I knew Caitlin had been putting a lot of work into setting this up, and even if I wasn't thrilled about my new knighthood, I wanted her to feel appreciated.

"I wouldn't miss it," I said. "We've still got a few hours left though, don't we?"

"I'd like to see you ahead of time. We need to go over some...finer points of etiquette you need to be aware of. This is your first court function and I don't want you to be surprised. Not by anything that isn't supposed to be a surprise, at any rate."

"You make that sound slightly ominous."

"Oh, it'll be fun. I've been looking forward to this."

"I'll swing by the club," I told her. "Let me get cleaned up and presentable. See you in an hour, maybe?"

"Wonderful. Oh, and one last thing? Put Melanie on the phone."

"Oh." I looked over at Melanie. Her eyes bulged and she fluttered her hands at me. "She's, uh...I mean she's not exactly..."

"Daniel," Caitlin said. "Are you really going to lie to me right now?"

I gave Melanie the phone. She held it like a venomous asp as it hovered beside her ear.

"Yes, ma'am," she said. "No, but I—yes, ma'am. No, but why can't—" Her shoulders slumped. "No, ma'am. Yes, ma'am. Right now."

She hung up and handed me the phone.

"Busted?" I said.

"Busted. How does she *know* these things?"

"Hey, just be thankful she's looking out for you. You could do a lot worse in the guardian angel department."

"Yeah." She sighed. "Whatever. I gotta go. And hey, Dan?"

"What's up?"

"Thanks," Melanie said. "For...I don't know. Being here."

"Always."

I saw her out, and then I turned a discerning eye to my closet. It wasn't every day I got an invitation to an infernal shindig, much less one where I was the guest of honor.

All in all, things were looking up. We'd taken out a Network front and stalled their plans, Elmer Donaghy was in Paris for the moment—I knew he'd be back once he figured out I wasn't going to chase him, but it bought us some breathing room—and the powder keg of Las Vegas was more or less under control for once. I didn't have a whole lot to worry about.

Of course, times like this were when I really started getting nervous. Call it a bad habit, but I always expected something to come out of nowhere and wreck my tranquility. And with a posse of hell's elite in town, all converging on the same nightclub for a party, I didn't trust the relative peace and quiet to last.

But I was apparently a knight of hell now, so whatever happened, it would probably be my fault, my job to fix it, or both. What an honor.

* * *

Autumn currents and air pollution worked magic at twilight,

painting the sky in streaks of lavender and casting long shadows beyond the russet mountains. It was beautiful, until you remembered the world wasn't supposed to look like that. Maybe the atmosphere was just trying to get into the game, adding its own razzle-dazzle to the city of illusions. A little warm-up act before darkness fell and the real show got underway.

I was equally armed to handle illusions and flesh-and-blood threats tonight. Canton's wand sat snug up my sleeve, nestled in the spring-loaded sheath Caitlin had bought for me. A fresh deck of cards rode in the breast pocket of my Brunello Cucinelli jacket. Style-wise, I'd opted for corporate chic: tailored black suit, crisp ivory shirt, and a tie and pocket square the color of hammered brass.

Winter, a club a couple of blocks off the Strip, was marked with a single blue neon arrow that pointed to an anonymous set of double doors. If you didn't know where it was or what it was, you weren't hip enough to get in. Even so, while the place didn't officially open until nine—or get roaring until eleven—partygoers were already lining up along the sapphire velvet ropes. I jumped the line, like usual, and one of the bouncers unhooked the rope for me.

"Mr. Faust," he said, "welcome. Ms. Brody is up in the DJ booth. She asked if you'd see her before going downstairs."

"Thanks. Lot of people on the party list?"

He showed me his clipboard. A passel of names had already been scratched off. Some I recognized, most I didn't. He dropped his voice and shot a furtive glance toward the line.

"You, ah, resolved your situation with the Order of Chainmen, right, sir?"

"Situation" was a good word for it. Thanks to Naavarasi, I'd earned a price on my head, with demonic bounty hunters from Vegas to Chicago competing to cash in. Caitlin and I dueled her to put an end to it. We'd barely survived, but at least we limped off the battlefield arm in arm, while the rakshasi queen had to be carried off on a stretcher. I'd call that a win.

"I am officially bounty free," I told the bouncer.

"Good, it's just, well, a few of the Order's members are on the guest list. Wanted to make sure we didn't need extra security downstairs."

"I've got everything under control," I said. "Haven't you heard? I'm a knight now."

"Right." He nodded, slow, and made a note on his clipboard. "So, we'll have extra security on standby."

A title and nobility, and I still got no respect. At least he held the door for me. I took one last deep breath and headed in.

23.

I was used to pulsating crowds and bone-jarring bass inside Winter's confines. Instead, I was greeted by the hum of a vacuum cleaner as staff scurried in all directions, getting the place ready for opening. I dodged a delivery guy rolling a steel keg on a lift and climbed the long, circular staircase that ringed the outer edge of the dance floor. Ice-blue runners and bars of light guided me to the top, while the LED screens along the wall hung dark and dead. At the top, a balcony curled like a painter's palette, up to the edge of a glass DJ booth that hung from steel cables over the floor below.

"Stop fidgeting, darling," said a familiar voice.

"I am *not* fidgeting," Caitlin replied.

Caitlin stood with her arms wide, a vision of designer elegance. Her dress was pure couture, a shimmering gown of silk tailored to her curves, midnight-black, with a quality that caught the light and turned it into a faint rainbow sheen. A ruffled drape drew the eye down to an asymmetrical hem, perfect for a tango under the stars. Fredrika Vinter knelt at her side, dressed to kill and squinting behind a pair of bifocals as she adjusted pins along the fabric.

"*Really*, darling. Just another minute or two and you'll be all set. I'm almost done, I promise." Freddie looked my way and broke into a grin. "*Dahling*. You caught me with my glasses on. That's mortifying. Go away. No. Come here. Come here and hug me once I'm finished making your lover a vision of absolute beauty."

I stepped around her, leaned in, and Caitlin's lips brushed against mine. "Too late, she already is."

"You know my policy: all women are beautiful, but a House of Vinter gown can improve even upon perfection." Freddie stood up, took a step back, and looked Caitlin up and down with a dubious eye. "Maybe the hem isn't *exactly* right—"

Caitlin laughed. "Dances, you've been fussing for an hour. Enough. It's wonderful, I promise."

"Well, if you say so." She slipped off her bifocals and yanked me into a bone-crushing hug. Her lips felt like chips of ice against my cheek. "And you. Look at you. You're moving up in the world, darling."

"That's what they tell me. I didn't expect to see you here tonight. I mean, you're not part of the courts."

Freddie trailed her fingertips across her emerald décolletage. "No, but I *am* nobility. I'm the Queen of Chicago."

"I'm pretty sure that's not a real thing."

"I wanted to wear something special tonight," Caitlin told me. "And seeing as Dances has been asking me to model at one of her shows..."

"Quid pro quo," Freddie said. "Caitlin gets me tonight, I get her in Chicago next month. This party is a test run for my new design. And I'm still not sure about that hemline. Maybe another tenth of an inch?"

"Perfectionist." Caitlin offered me her arm. Tailored suit or not, I felt like a dumpster fire standing next to her. That, and the luckiest man on Earth.

"Guilty." Freddie fell in on my other side as we walked to the stairs. "Also, my always-wise BFF thought you might want another friendly face in the room. And while *you* are now obliged to follow the rules of demonic high society—"

"You give no fucks," I said.

Freddie put her hand over her mouth and gasped. "Darling. Such coarse language. But no, I left all my fucks in Chicago for safekeeping. So point out anyone who dampens your sunshine, and I'll be happy to eat them for you."

"You will *not*," Caitlin said. "You're here as my guest. Please remember that."

"I'll eat them outside, of course. *Clearly* I wouldn't do it here."

"Okay," I said, "what do I need to know?"

Caitlin contemplated the question for a moment as we descended the winding staircase.

"Obviously, be on your best behavior. And then some. Decorum is everything. Now, throughout the evening people will be giving you gifts; that's the traditional method of honoring a new inductee to the infernal courts."

"I like presents," I said.

"Also, the gifts are all cursed."

I gave her the side-eye. She shrugged.

"That is also tradition," she said. "Everything is lethal and will most likely kill you. Sort of a...welcome to demonic politics. Poison in every gift, a dagger behind every smile. It's all meant in good fun, really."

"And at the end of the night, I have a big pile of cursed junk."

"Well, that's the second part of the tradition," she explained. "Now that you're one of us, you'll get invitations to other parties, where you'll be expected to pass on the gifts you received tonight. Some of these tokens have been circulating for centuries; they accumulate little stories, a legacy of sorts. Passing along a cursed gift that was given to you by someone in high esteem is a sign of great respect to its new recipient."

Now Freddie looked genuinely shocked. "You...*regift?* You *all* regift? Caitlin, darling...there's evil, and then there's just simply *unacceptable.*"

"So be on my best behavior, and don't touch anything," I said. "Got it. Fun city."

Caitlin gave me a long, almost wistful look.

"I really am proud of you, you know."

I knew. And even though I wasn't feeling it, I mirrored her smile and gave her arm a squeeze. I didn't know why Prince Sitri had knighted me—beyond his usual deranged sense of humor—but it was a big deal to Caitlin and her people. She wanted to celebrate. So we'd celebrate.

* * *

While Winter prepared to open its doors to the public, the party down below was in full swing. Past a code-locked door, down a sweeping staircase, the second level of the nightclub was by invitation only. It was a maze of honeycomb-shaped rooms, onyx lit with pipes of golden neon. Tonight the central chamber had a fresh addition: an open bar and long tables piled high with catering dishes.

"Don't eat anything from the table with the red cloth," Caitlin murmured in my ear. "It's...not for you. The food on the table with the black cloth is human food."

"What's on the red table?" I asked, not sure I wanted to know.

On my other side, Freddie sniffed the air and grinned.

"If my nose doesn't betray me," she said, "some of it is *human* food."

She split off to investigate. Caitlin and I descended into the social whirl, moving between knots of conversation as she introduced me around. At one point she needed to catch up with Emma, so she left me to my own devices. Never a good idea.

"Oh," she said in parting, "Emma doesn't know about Melanie's little field trip this afternoon. And she doesn't need to, agreed? Let's not add any extra friction, considering recent events."

I locked my lips and threw away the key. I was checking out the spread at the black-draped table—and trying to ignore the spicy, inviting smells drifting over from its red-draped twin—when a couple of familiar faces came by to say hello. Nadine, poured into a tiny black dress, with Royce serving as her arm candy. The aristocrats from Prince Malphas's court both carried ring boxes wrapped in golden foil and tied with bows.

"Welcome to the big leagues," Nadine told me. "How long do you think you'll last?"

I took the box from her outstretched hand and gave her a casual smile in return. "Time me. Let's find out."

Royce shook his head. "Poor choice, signing up with the Jade Tears. We could have made you a better offer."

"Hey, you were there when Sitri knighted me. Did it look like I had a choice in the matter?"

"No, fair enough." He leaned in, conspiratorial as he clapped me on the shoulder. "Just remember, old sport, defection is *always* an option."

"I'll keep that in mind."

"And if you sign up willingly," Nadine said, her attention on the milling crowd, "Royce and I can protect you from whatever horrible scheme of vengeance Naavarasi is undoubtedly cooking up at this very moment. Now where is...Nyx! Come *here*."

Nadine's daughter—thankfully in her Nordic-goddess human disguise, not the monster I knew was lurking under her porcelain skin—trudged across the room. She had a box in her hands, wrapped in black, and her fingers squeezed it hard enough to crush the edges.

"Be appropriate," Nadine told her.

Nyx thrust the box at me and stared at the floor.

"This one," she grumbled, "offers you congratulations on the auspicious victory of your knighthood."

She was sore, and it wasn't hard to see why. She'd been one of the hunters on my tail when Naavarasi slapped me with a bounty, and I slipped out from under her claws just before the contract was revoked. Then I'd bluffed her, in this very room, and embarrassed her in front of her rivals. I would have felt raw about it too. I figured it wouldn't cost me anything to play nice.

"Hey," I said as I took the box, slowly building a pile in my arms, "Thanks, Nyx. You didn't have to say that, and I really appreciate it."

"This one *did* have to say it," she snapped, then stomped away. Okay, we weren't going to be friends. At least I tried.

I was looking for a table to set my growing collection of cursed presents down, when another familiar face dropped by. Well, a familiar voice. I didn't recognize the guy—a surfer type in his twenties, fish-belly pale, with the Y-shaped stitch of an autopsy incision showing at the collar of his over-starched dress shirt—but I knew him the second he opened his mouth.

"Have to tell you, friend, this is not the future I saw in the ol' crystal ball."

"Hey. Fontaine, right?"

"In the borrowed flesh," he drawled. "Congrats on the big promotion. You're a smart cookie, though. You know your new prince just slapped a juicy target on your back."

"I hope you're not here to take a shot," I said.

He cracked a smile. "Not unless it's a legal contract and I'm getting paid to do it. Nah, I came by to make sure there weren't any hard feelings. I mean, I did almost bleed you out like a prize hog."

"Forget about it," I said. "You were just doing your job."

"And thankfully," Caitlin said, returning with Emma in tow, "now we're all one big, happy family. Hello, Fontaine."

"Ah! *Ma chère, enchanté.*" He kissed her hand, bowing low, then turned my way. He held out a business card: pale cream, with a single monogram F in black. "And now that you're an esteemed member of the courts, hang on to this. You can always call upon me for your bounty-hunting needs, be it a formal challenge through the Order or a bit of freelance work."

Emma folded her arms and glared at him. "Really? You came by to drum up business?"

"It's a hard life out there for a working man, darlin'. Always gotta be hustling. And who better to solicit than a person who knows the quality of your work firsthand?"

"True," I said. "You *did* capture me when nobody else could. So where's your little friend?"

Fontaine curled his lips, irritated. "My partner? She murdered somebody she wasn't supposed to. Had to put her in time-out."

Emma brushed past him with a small box cupped in her palm, like the evil queen with a poisoned apple. She offered it to me.

"Congratulations, Daniel. We've had our differences, but you've been a good friend to our court, and more importantly—to me, anyway—a good friend to Caitlin. I'm glad you're one of us now."

I wasn't on board with the "one of us" thing, but I thanked her as I took the present.

"Go on," she said, "unwrap it."

We parked by a spot of empty table so I could set down the rest of the gifts. I tore into Emma's, peeling the paper back, and lifted the gray velvety lid of a jewelry box. Inside, a platinum tie clip, studded with diamonds, glimmered on a bed of white satin.

Caitlin's jaw dropped and she pulled her friend into a hug. "Oh. *Emma.* You're the *sweetest.*"

I glanced between them, looking for an explanation.

"That clip was given to Emma by her mentor, when she was just finding her feet," Caitlin told me.

"And it was given to my mentor by..." Emma said with a grin.

"Me," Caitlin said. "And now it's home again, full circle. Deliberate full circle. Oh, Emma. Seriously. You're wonderful."

I felt the cultural divide shift beneath my feet like tectonic plates. Across worlds, across species. I understood enough to grasp that Emma had just honored me, big-time, but without the social cues I would have been lost. This was the world Sitri's knighthood had hauled me into, with customs and rules and expectations I was barely beginning to understand.

If those plates kept shifting underneath me, they could tear me in half. I needed to find my footing fast. I was looking for something to say, to show my thanks, when I saw another familiar face on the far side of the party.

My blood ran cold. Then burning hot.

"Pet?" Caitlin asked, catching the expression on my face. "What is it?"

"Naavarasi," I said.

24.

Naavarasi hadn't come as herself. That would have been enough of an insult, after what she'd just done—tried to do—to me and Caitlin. No, her guise was for my eyes only. She flitted through the party in Gothic black lace and leather, her auburn hair in tight ringlets, antique rings dripping from her fingers. The shape-shifter had worn that face once before to trick me—the face of my ex-girlfriend Roxy, a reminder of the relationship I'd managed to send crashing down in flames before I met Caitlin.

I cut through the crowd, steaming toward her, and she had the nerve to smile when she saw me. I stopped dead in front of her, with Caitlin, Emma, and Fontaine in tow.

"The last time you took on that form," Caitlin told her, "I backhanded you across the room. Are you eager for a second taste?"

Naavarasi sipped her cocktail and chuckled. "Try me. Here and now."

I took another step toward her, and Emma's hand clamped down on my wrist. She yanked me back.

"Uh-uh," Emma said. "You know the rules. No fighting between members of the courts."

"After what she pulled—"

"The things we can prove she did were all perfectly legal," Emma said. "What we can't prove, we can't prove, so they don't count. As far as the laws of the Cold Peace are concerned, she's in the clear. And so are you, as long as you keep your hands to yourself."

Fontaine rubbed his chin, glancing between us. "Afraid Emma's got the right of it. I'd like to be workin' *with* you next time we cross paths. You take one swing and you're right back on the Chainmen's target list."

Which was why she wore Roxy's face. Naavarasi was baiting me. Trying to push me into making a dumb mistake before I found my footing as a newly minted knight. Cheap trick, but I knew from firsthand experience that cheap tricks were usually the most effective ones in the book.

"And to think," she said, turning her attention to Caitlin, "that I promised to walk you through this very room on a leash. It's going to happen eventually. You could save yourself so much pain by just surrendering here and now."

Caitlin's stony silence was her only reply. I took a deep breath to steady myself, to find my cool.

"I know what you're doing and it's not going to work," I told her. "Now, this is officially my party, and I don't think your name was on the invite list. So turn around and walk away. The stairs are right behind you."

Naavarasi smirked. She looked to Caitlin. "He doesn't know anything, does he? Tell him."

"Terms of the Cold Peace," Caitlin said, her teeth clenched. "A feast or revel open to members of multiple courts is open to all members of *all* recognized courts, as a means of preventing collusion. Remember how we crashed Prince Malphas's poker tournament in Chicago and they weren't allowed to throw us out? Naavarasi is allowed to be here, under the same rule. So long as she minds herself."

"I wouldn't dream of disturbing the peace," she said.

I was thinking about the recording Jennifer had dug up. The proof that Kirmira was one of Naavarasi's children, and how she'd orchestrated his murder just to get her hooks into me. Mostly I wanted to throw it at her to see how she'd react. I was dying to wipe that smug look off her borrowed face.

Then I counted to five under my breath. The Kirmira tape was a hole card, and hole cards were meant to be played facedown, to keep your opponent guessing. For once we knew something Naavarasi didn't. I aimed to keep it that way until I figured out how to take advantage.

I didn't know how long Freddie had been hovering and listening. I only knew that she swooped in, like a superheroine on her third martini, and put her icy hand on my shoulder.

"Some of my favorite people, all in one place," she said. "But the picture isn't quite right. Is it the lighting? The decor? No...no, it's definitely the two-dollar skank."

Naavarasi's lids went heavy as she stared at Freddie. "*What* did you just call me?"

"I'm sorry, I just understand there's this little legal thing where my BFF Caitlin and her ever-wonderful boyfriend can't actually give you the vicious beatdown you so richly deserve." Freddie broke into a hungry grin. "But I'm not a demon. And I can kick your ass until my legs get tired."

"I would peel your skin," Naavarasi told her, "cook your entrails, and pick my teeth with the splinters of your bones."

The temperature dropped. Plummeting, until my breath formed curlicues of white mist in the air. In the corner of my eye, Freddie's skin turned ashen gray, touched by black splotches of frostbite.

"Want to find out for sure?" Freddie asked her.

Naavarasi wrinkled her nose, turned, and stormed across the room. She disappeared into the crowd.

The warmth flooded back in, and Freddie's hand—normal now, if unnaturally cold to the touch—patted my shoulder. "You're welcome."

"I appreciate the assist," I told her, "but look, be careful, okay? I've seen Naavarasi in action. She's *really* dangerous."

"As if I was actually going to fight her. Please, darling, it's called a bluff, look it up. Do you know how much this gown costs? I do, because it's from my signature collection. I'm hardly going to get in a brawl and risk popping a seam."

"Still, appreciated."

"Also," Freddie added, "I'm drunk."

"I assumed."

"I should have anticipated this," Caitlin muttered, staring in the direction of Naavarasi's retreat. "A sad little last-ditch attempt to goad us into a foolish error."

I wished I could be that sure. The problem was, showing up and trying to egg us into throwing a punch, breaking the Cold Peace in front of a crowd, was the definition of a "sad little last-ditch attempt." And now I knew that Naavarasi was all about the bigger picture. No way she would have come all the way from her lair in Denver just to be a jerk at a party.

No. She had another reason to be here tonight. We just couldn't see it yet.

"I think we need a bit of merriment," Caitlin said. She strode to the heart of the room and held her wineglass high. "Kind gentles, loyal and true, may I have your attention? Your attention, please."

The din of the party fell to a low murmur. The waves parted, as people pressed to the edges of the gallery and gave her space.

"We are united tonight for an auspicious occasion. The elevation of Daniel Faust, my consort, as a knight of the Court of Jade Tears."

She paused for a smattering of polite applause, pinging through the room like popcorn.

"When I claimed this man for my own," she said, "I was met with...some skepticism. For a prince's hound to choose a human for a companion was, some felt, undignified. Unacceptable, even."

She flashed a wicked smile, daring anyone to say a word. Over to the left, I watched Nadine open her mouth. Royce jerked on her wrist, hard, and she closed it.

"But Daniel has proved himself time and time again. Not just to me, but to Prince Sitri and to our august court. He has shown himself to be capable, strong, loyal, unafraid. Despite his mortal blood, he embodies the qualities we should all expect from a knight of hell. And now, at long last, he is granted his rightful due. Come, Daniel. Stand beside me."

The applause washed over me from both sides of the room, a curtain of sound, raucous now. I walked to stand at Caitlin's side and she took my hand in hers. A tear glistened in her eye as she mouthed, "*I love you.*"

I didn't want this. Didn't want to be associated with Prince Sitri's court or any of them, didn't want to be sucked into the endless machinations of hell...but in that moment, I understood how much it meant to Caitlin.

So I'd make it work.

She raised my hand high, like the winner of a boxing match. "I give you Daniel Faust, knight of the Court of Jade Tears! Mark his name, and laud his victories!"

More waves of applause crashed in, thundering through the gallery and slowly fading away. All but one pair of hands.

Long after it ended, a single person was still clapping. Slow. Rhythmic. Sarcastic. The crowd parted, and he swaggered on through.

Whoever he was, he dressed like a rock star. Painted-on black leather pants and a vest with no shirt, and a purple cashmere scarf rounded out his ensemble. He wore his bleach-blond hair in a puffed-out pompadour. His left arm was sheathed in blue tattoos, the ink laid in dizzying swirls and loops like some Viking warrior's battle-woad. Energy radiated off him—dirty, erratic, electric. He stood in the middle of the room like he owned it.

"So you're the great Daniel Faust," he said.

"I'm *a* Daniel Faust," I told him. "Not sure if I'm the great one. I'll have to take a poll."

"Heard a lot about you. Underboss of the Vegas mob, making moves in the courts of hell. You get around, don't you?"

I wasn't sure what to make of this guy, but I didn't think he was here to give me a present. Caitlin watched him with her lips pursed, pensive, but she didn't make a move. From the looks on the faces of our audience, I understood why.

Like I'd said, this was my party. As Caitlin had warned me when Sitri gave me the nod, a lot of demons weren't so hot on the idea of a human getting a knighthood. She'd said they'd be looking to test me.

And here was my test. Everybody at the party was watching to see how I'd take care of business. Whatever I did, however I played it, tomorrow it'd be all over the demonic grapevine. Caitlin wasn't stepping in because that'd be the worst move possible, her fighting my battles for me. A knight should be able to carry his own weight.

I kept my hands easy at my sides, my voice pleasant, like this was no big deal. "I've gone some places. Seen some things."

"So modest," he said. "But I hear you're a real big shot. Everybody calls you *the guy.*"

"Yeah, but I really wish they wouldn't. I've been trying to get people to stop."

He took a step closer. Close enough to land a punch, if he felt like swinging. I didn't let myself brace for it. The last thing I wanted to do right now was show any hint of being nervous. He pitched his voice softer, but still loud enough for the entire room to hear him.

"After all that talk, I was expecting more," he said. "But as far as I'm concerned, you're nothing but a little bitch."

That got the reaction he was looking for. From the crowd, at least, as a chorus of oohs simmered through the gallery. All eyes on me now.

Clearly, I was going to have to deal with this. My way.

25.

I waited for the crowd to fall silent. I kept my eyes on the rock star, my stance loose, my expression calculatedly bland. He wanted payment in fear or anger—either would make him the top dog in the room. I gave him my apathy instead.

It was like prison all over again. Your first day on the yard defined who you were for the rest of your time behind bars. Inside Eisenberg I was tested just like this, by a guy who had a foot of height and a hundred pounds of muscle on me. I remembered facing that moment of uncertainty and fear, deciding my fate, and jumping in with both fists flying.

Getting my ass kicked, but showing I wasn't afraid and I was willing to scrap, earned me as much respect as it did pain. I'd do it again tonight, if I had to. I still didn't like the idea. Bottom line, whatever I did here would spread through the courts; this was my chance to make a name for myself and show them how I handled my problems.

"What's your name, buddy?" I asked.

"I'm not your buddy."

"Okay," I said. "What's your name, pal?"

"My name," he said, voice rising as he played to the room, "is Grimm. Hunter MacGregor Grimm."

I stared at him. He stared back.

"I..." I shook my head. "No. Really. What is it?"

"Hunter. MacGregor. Grimm."

I squinted. "Okay, I mean...if that's really what you want to go with. You might want to workshop it, though."

"My great-great-grandfather was the sire of all vampires. My great-great-grandmother was the queen of the werewolves."

"No. Stop." I held up a hand. "First of all, there's no such thing as vampires. Or werewolves. Seriously, what is this?"

While I was talking, my third eye was digging deep. Listening to the pulse of his blood, feeling for the texture of his soul. Whatever his real name was, "Hunter Grimm" was a cambion. I sensed something else there, too, buried in the barbed-wire twists of his half-demon soul, some hot and toxic energy, wild magic crammed into a container too small to hold it.

"They call me the Mystical Marauder, the Hard-Luck Harrower, the Demon Magic Sentry."

"That's three titles," I said, "and I bet twenty bucks *nobody* calls you that."

"I ride across these forsaken lands with my blade at the ready, in search of fools and pretenders. And when I find them, their heads join the collection on my trophy wall."

"Your blade. It's a katana, isn't it?" I glanced sidelong at Caitlin. "You know it's a katana."

Caitlin studied him, eyes narrowed to serpentine slits. I figured she sensed the same thing I did. I was being flippant, playing to the crowd and trying to get a smile—and frustrate Grimm into tipping more of his hand—but this wasn't just some puffed-up clown looking for the wrong kind of attention. I wasn't going to make a move until I was sure what I was dealing with. And despite the quips, I was taking him very seriously.

"Which court do you claim?" she asked him.

He turned, grimaced, and spat on the floor. The whole room had been whispering. Now it was holding one collective breath.

"A better one than this. Bad enough that a prince's hound would spread her legs for a human. Elevating one to knighthood? That's nothing but a sick joke, just like you, just like your entire court."

"This would be a good time to stop talking," I told him.

"Why? You're *weak*. If you claim otherwise...duel me. I wield the black blade of Masamune and the talisman of Thor. No pretender can stand against me."

Caitlin leaned close and murmured in my ear.

"He challenged you, after insulting your hound and your prince, pet. The Cold Peace will not protect him. Do as you will."

And he wanted it, almost as bad as I wanted to give it to him. Grimm had his footing squared and light, his fingers curling at his sides, just waiting for me to throw the first punch. Which was exactly why I didn't.

This guy was a joke at best, a nutcase at worst, and everything about this situation screamed *setup*. For all his goofy claims and posturing, he wasn't entirely harmless; the pulsing core of wild magic in his gut told me that much. Beyond that, I had to think about the message my next move would send.

When I saw the trap, I almost admired it.

Grimm—or whoever paid him to put on this act, most likely—had maneuvered me into a no-win situation. His wannabe tough-guy act meant that if I did beat him down, legal or not, I'd come off looking like a thug who punched out a harmless loser. On the other hand, if I backed down, I'd look like I was afraid of him—and that was infinitely worse.

Caitlin was right. Somebody here resented my promotion. But instead of testing me themselves, they sent in a chump who looked like he was in no way, shape, or form capable of doing the job. So I was damned if I fought him, damned if I didn't. Every eye in the room was on me. I needed to find a third option and I needed it fast.

"I'm not going to fight you," I told him.

He grinned in triumph, like a bully who just took over the playground. "See? You see, everyone? The human is *weak*. He's weak, just like his entire court, like his prince—"

"I wasn't done talking," I told him. "Shut the fuck up and listen. See, a couple of weeks ago, I was walking down the street and passed this mean-looking little kid. He was nine, ten years old maybe. He looked up at me and said, 'Your hair looks stupid, mister.'"

That got a tiny chuckle or two, but most of the guests were silent now; they were busy trying to follow my angle and figure out where I was aiming to land.

"Now, first of all, that kid was wrong. My hair is *flawless*." I ran my fingers through it to highlight the point. "But you might be wondering...what did I do to him? Did I beat him up? Kill him? Of course not. It doesn't matter what he said to me—he could have insulted my girlfriend, my mother, my family name—because there's absolutely no honor in a grown man retaliating against a child, and there's no weight in a child's insults. He was beneath me."

I jerked my thumb at Grimm.

"Just like this clown is, and I'm not going to degrade the dignity of the honor I've been given by dueling him."

From the blindsided look on his face, I figured Grimm had prepared for every response except that one.

"You're...you're afraid," he said, fumbling for his tough-guy act. "You know you can't beat me."

"Please. I'm a knight of hell. You're a pissant nobody. I don't have to prove myself to you." I turned my attention to the rest of the room. "And who am I supposed to be defending? Caitlin? Caitlin, the Wingtaker? You all know where she earned that title, and if you don't, you'd better ask somebody. Prince Sitri? The master of an entire court? Get real. I don't care if Hunter MacPfeiffer Granola here curses all three of us out, all day long. His words don't mean anything, because *he* doesn't mean anything."

I took a long, slow look around the room. Checking expressions, searching for the tell of a player whose gamble just went south. Mostly I was looking for Naavarasi. Either she'd left or she'd found another face to wear.

"One of you, though," I said. "One of you I *do* want to duel. Because somebody here hired this joker."

Grimm's left eyelid twitched. "That's not true. I'm a lone wolf. A one-man occult army—"

"Shut up, sparky. Grown-ups are talking." I made a circle, giving everyone a dose of eye contact and seeing who looked away. "One of you wanted to test me, didn't have the steel to do it yourself, and put this loser up to the job. Now that? That *is* an insult worth going toe to toe over. So step up."

Honestly, I didn't care if it was true or not. Even if Grimm was acting alone, I'd just reframed the narrative. Now the guests were looking at each other, whispering, pointing subtle fingers.

"Nobody?" I asked. "Have it your way. If you change your mind, and you want to bring a real challenge, you know where to find me. Until then, how about we all get back to the party? I hear the spread at the red table is really great, so definitely try some of...whatever that is."

A couple of bouncers were closing in, bracing Grimm from the sides. He was already yesterday's news. I'd given the partygoers something a lot more interesting to gossip about—his mysterious master, who might or might not exist—and they broke ranks to mingle and chat about it.

"This isn't over," Grimm told me.

"Get him out of here," I said and turned my back on him.

Outside, I was a picture of callous cool. Inside, I was sweating. If I'd gotten him wrong—if he really was a deadly menace in a jester's cap—I had just set myself up for a literal stab in the back. But people were still watching, casting discreet glances, and my act had to be picture perfect.

He didn't say another word as they hustled him up the stairs and out the door.

* * *

After the final gift was added to the table, the open bar shut down, and the last few guests drifted off into the night, it was just me and Caitlin in the abandoned party room. Light from the neon piping shimmered off her dress, painting her in shades of black and gold. We split the last bottle of chardonnay between us, glasses half-empty as we unwrapped presents together.

"Some of these have been floating around for centuries." She opened the lid of a small teak casket and nodded her approval. "A few of the guests were definitely trying to get on your good side. I'll make a list for you."

"Obliged." I glanced to Emma's gift, the diamond tie clip. "Okay, so all of these are basically cursed to kill their owners, right?"

"That's the tradition, yes."

I pointed to the clip. "So if I put this one on, what would it do to me?"

She gave me an impish smile. "The Curse of Xyl'kotis, if I remember correctly. It would cause your bowels to violently evacuate."

"That sounds bad, but not deadly."

"To evacuate *everything* inside your body. Including said bowels."

I pushed the box a little farther away.

"I know you didn't want this," she told me.

"A tie clip that makes you poop yourself to death? Well, it's not my ideal fashion statement..."

She gently swatted my arm. "No. This. The knighthood. Being drawn into my court. You've been putting on a game face, but I know you're not happy."

"It's not...that I'm not happy," I said. "It's just a responsibility that got dropped on me out of nowhere, and..."

"And you're not one of us. Daniel, it's all right. I understand. You've been charged with defending a court you feel no allegiance to. That's a burden."

I reached for her. My fingertips trailed along the curve of her chin.

"Hey. It's important to you. So I'm all in."

"Do you know why, though? Do you understand why this is important to me?"

I had to shake my head. She took my hand in hers.

"When we first met, you welcomed me into your family. Your circle of friends, these people you trust more than anyone in the world...and you welcomed me in. No one had ever done that for me before."

"At Margaritaville, as I recall." I glanced over her shoulder, into the distance. "Strange things are often afoot at Margaritaville."

She laughed and squeezed my hand. "Be serious. It meant a lot to me. And now...now it feels like you're a part of *my* family, too. I know you don't feel the same way, but...if you'll try, maybe in time, you might?"

"I think I get it," I told her.

My phone buzzed against my hip. Bentley calling.

"Hey," I said, "it's late. Everything okay?"

He sounded cagey, like he was holding something back. "Oh, certainly, everything is...everything is fine, fine indeed."

"Okay. And you're calling because...?"

"Oh! Yes. When you're free, could you swing by the bookstore? It won't take long. I just need...something."

A bad feeling loomed over my shoulder. Maybe tonight's encounters with Naavarasi and Hunter Grimm had me on edge, but this smelled fishier than last week's catch.

"I'll be there in twenty," I told him.

26.

I killed my headlights a block before my final destination, coasting in slow and careful along a back-alley strip. I pulled in behind the Scrivener's Nook and killed the engine, leaving the sedan's door cracked when I got out; shutting it would make too much noise. Then I padded across the dirty asphalt, shoes rustling on loose gravel, to the back door of the shop.

I had my own set of keys. They jangled softly, one sliding into the reinforced lock, the tumbler *thunk*ing as it rolled over. Too loud. I put one hand on the door, silently counted to twenty, then pushed it open.

It yawned onto a darkened stockroom. I felt my playing cards pulse against my chest, ready for a fight, as I stepped inside. I shut the door behind me and bathed in pitch darkness. That improved my odds, if somebody was lurking in here, assuming they couldn't see in the dark. I knew the layout of the back room by heart. I sidestepped to my right, figuring I'd follow the perimeter all the way around to the shop door. Then I held a breath and braced myself.

The lights flooded on and nearly a half dozen people shouted, "Surprise!"

Bentley, Corman, and Mama Margaux were in the middle of the room, flanking a folding table with a cake frosted in white and scarlet. Jennifer came in from the opposite door, toting two magnums of champagne, while Pixie popped a party noisemaker between her lips and blew a celebratory raspberry.

I had a half smile, half grimace pasted to my face, frozen while a burst of adrenaline rioted through my body. "What...what is this? It's not my birthday yet."

"Given recent events," Bentley said, "we just thought it would be good to pause and celebrate everything we—especially you—have been through these last few months."

Corman leaned back and jammed his thumbs in his pockets. "Lotta shit and gunfire. Sometimes you just have to take a few minutes and eat a slice of cake."

"Also," Margaux added, "we wanted to remind you what side you're on."

Bentley slashed his hand across his throat. "We weren't going to *say* that—"

"What? Danny's not stupid. He knows what this is." She shot me a look. "*I* wanted to do an intervention. They said, bring cake and booze, he'll be too distracted to figure it out."

I had to laugh. I held up my hands in surrender.

"Guys. C'mon, it's me. Same old Dan. I'm not plotting in cahoots with Prince Sitri to take over the planet."

Margaux folded her arms. "Mm-hmm. *Yet.*"

"I'm pretty sure this entire knighthood thing is the setup for an epic practical joke. Once Sitri springs the gag—assuming I survive it—he'll probably yank the job right out from under me."

I played it off, but deep down I was as worried as they were. Not long after Caitlin and I hooked up, Prince Sitri had played another one of his games, forcing her to choose between me and her sworn duties. The entire mess, starting with his challenge for me to kill a supposedly innocent priest, was a giant setup. It was a labyrinthine scam that the prince had under his complete control from start to finish, and no matter what choices I made along the way, the outcome would have landed in his favor.

Sitri could give lessons in the art of the con. Only problem was, it was impossible to tell if I was his student or his mark. Knowing him, the answer was probably both.

Jennifer held up a knife. "Can we distract you with cake?"

"Absolutely not, and I'm offended that you would think so." I nodded at the bottles. "You can distract me with cake *and* some of that bubbly."

The cake was butter cream with chocolate filling. It was also labeled "*Happy Birthday, Maurice.*"

"Okay," I said between bites, "who stole this cake?"

"Who says we stole it?" Corman asked.

"I'm just saying, whoever Maurice is, his birthday is ruined."

"Then he should have kept a better eye on his stuff," Jennifer said.

I couldn't argue that. The cake was too good. We got to drinking, and we got to talking, and fell into pockets of comfortable conversation. On my second flute of champagne, I pulled Bentley aside. I needed some fatherly advice. I would have grabbed Corman, too, but he and Margaux were busy arguing about tarot symbolism on the other side of the stockroom.

"So, about Melanie—" I started to say.

"She asked, I presume?"

"You knew?"

The crow's-feet crinkled at the corners of his eyes. "I did more than teach her a few card tricks that night you asked Corman and me to watch her. We sniffed out her magical potential. And she has potential."

"Did you tell her that? Because she's pretty dead set on rolling her sleeves up and diving in."

"Is there any reason she shouldn't?"

"Oh, I don't know," I said. "Let's look at the last few months. I've been thrown in prison, broken out of prison, fought a mummy, fought a mob war, got drawn into an ancient cosmic conflict waged between endlessly reincarnating fictional characters, traveled to another dimension and almost died there, and that's just a small sample of the joys a life of magic has laid upon my doorstep."

"And all of that would have knocked upon your door anyway, ready or not. When we first found you, before you'd had a lick of training, you'd fallen in with that vile little cult. Their leader, what was his name?"

"The Shepherd," I said. The word felt dirty on my tongue.

"He sensed your spark and set out to plunder it. You didn't choose a life of magic, Daniel. Magic chose you. What you did was learn, and study, and grow strong, so you could face the challenges it threw in your path. Melanie has the same spark, and if anything, she's twice as headstrong as you were at that age."

"That's a terrifying thought."

"She's going to find a teacher," Bentley said. "If not you, she'll find another. If she's lucky, that teacher will be half as skilled as you are. If she's not...well, she might find a Shepherd of her own."

He was right. I hated to admit it, but he was right. That didn't stop me from arguing.

"What about Desi?" I asked. "I couldn't keep her safe."

Bentley rested his hand on my shoulder. "And that's the real issue, isn't it?"

"*Shouldn't* it be? I had an apprentice. Once. She's dead now. I think that should disqualify me from taking the job again."

"What happened wasn't your fault," he said. "And heavens above, even if it was...Daniel, do you know how many mistakes, blunders, and absolute disasters I've caused in my lifetime? If I let each one close and lock a door forever, well, I'd be all out of doors. There's something to be said for getting back on the horse and trying again. If not for you, for Melanie's sake."

My resolve was a wall with a hundred cracks, the mortar crumbling with every strike of reason. All the same, it held fast, molding itself to the contours of Desi's face.

"I'll think about it," I told him. That much I could promise.

He patted my arm and reached behind him, rummaging through one of the storage shelves.

"Good. Now then. I suspect you received a number of terrible gifts tonight."

"How did you know about that?"

"I asked Caitlin if gift giving was appropriate, given

your...recent elevation, and she told me about the custom. Sounds dreadful."

"It was pretty bad, yeah," I said. "I now own a tie bar that induces death pooping. I've also got a poppet that'll come alive in the night and eat my eyes if I ever leave its box open. And those are just the *good* presents."

"Allow me to offer a counterbalance." Bentley handed me a black velvet pouch. I opened it and peered inside. My fingertip poked at a cluster of tiny balls, the size of marbles, rolled from chalky white clay. I felt a grin coming on.

"Alchemist's clay? *Nice*."

"I finally found time to whip up a fresh batch," he said. "Thought you might appreciate having a few to keep on hand for emergencies."

I put my arm around him and pulled him into a hug. Bentley's creations had saved my life inside Eisenberg, covering an escape attempt with clouds of billowing green smoke. Purely defensive, as far as occult weapons went, but essential for those times when you absolutely, positively needed to live and fight another day.

On the far side of the stockroom, Pixie had set her laptop up on a packing crate. Jennifer, standing at her shoulder, waved me over. I was glad to see them hanging out together. Jen had carried a torch for Pixie for months, not too discreetly, until I found out Pixie wasn't into the whole amorous-affection thing in any capacity. It didn't make much sense to me; as far as I was concerned, sex was one of the four essential food groups along with alcohol, red meat, and whatever the fourth one was. Coffee, probably. But that's the thing about your friends: you don't always have to understand them, you just have to respect them and love them for who they are.

Jennifer agreed with that sentiment. She'd waved a white flag on the romantic pursuit and settled into a comfortable friendship, which seemed to suit them both just fine. I ambled over.

"Your girl's a genius," Jennifer told me.

"Well, I knew that."

I squinted at the screen. Pixie was sifting streams of data between three different windows, juggling them back and forth with her mouse, tossing them underhand and doing tricks like a bartender in a tropical tourist trap.

"Okay," Pixie said, the words rat-a-tatting as fast as she could think. I always knew she was onto something when she developed motormouth. "Remember how you put me onto Weishaupt and Associates, that phony lawyers' office?"

"Sure," I said. Weishaupt was a shell company with Network ties and fake employees straight from a stock-photo website. They'd been sponsoring the gladiatorial games at Eisenberg, among any number of other dirty deeds, but it was impossible to pin them down. I'd only met one of their alleged lawyers in person, a shyster calling himself Mr. Smith. He came and went like smoke, sticking around just long enough to murder a former drug mule and stage it as a suicide. I got the impression he did that kind of thing a lot.

"So far, I've gotten nada from their company servers. They're like, Death Star levels of impenetrable."

"The first Death Star, which blew up, or the second Death Star, which also blew up?"

Pixie glared at me over the rims of her Buddy Holly glasses.

I shrugged. "I'm just saying, as analogies go..."

She ignored me and typed with one hand, holding up a finger with her other. "*But*. I started digging into the computers you and Jen liberated from Donaghy Waste Management and probing their Internet traffic."

"Liberated? You mean 'stole,'" I said.

"No, I mean liberated. I used to go after corporate polluters and pharma companies that ripped off poor people. That was a crusade. By comparison the Network, as far as we can tell, is basically trying to take over the entire planet. That makes this a *war*. It's not immoral to steal from the enemy in wartime. That's called 'liberation.'"

I didn't argue. I was used to Pixie's mental gymnastics, the moral calculus that let her feel righteous while hanging out with people like us, and I didn't see a need to fight her on it. The mercenary hacker could wear any halo she wanted, as long as she was on our side.

"So what did you find?" I asked.

The columns of numbers froze on her screen. Two of them, framed in white highlights, matched. I knew enough about computers to recognize it as an IP address, the Internet designation that any given server called "home."

"If I'm right," Pixie said, "I found a way to spy on the Network."

27.

"According to the network logs," Pixie told us, "right about the time you were busy laying waste to the garbage plant—pun intended—a tiny burst transmission passed from Elmer Donaghy's personal computer to a server—this one—which I've already identified as belonging to Weishaupt and Associates. He ran before he had time to purge his records, and the computer kept a copy of the outbound message."

I leaned in over her left shoulder. Jennifer mirrored me on the right.

"What's it say?" I asked.

Pixie shook her head. She opened a fresh window, a rectangle filled with random letters and characters.

"That's the problem. It was just a single two-hundred-byte text file, which is nothing. Like, your grocery list is probably longer than two hundred bytes. And as you can see, it's...this. Garbage data. Or it's supposed to look like that, anyway."

She ran her cursor over a string of repeating numbers in the middle of the file, highlighting it.

"But this isn't. This numeric string isn't random garbage. It's just buried and obfuscated."

"Like some kind of code?" I said.

Pixie nodded. "That's my guess. You can fit a ton of information in an alphanumeric cypher."

"Like, 'oh no, we're gettin' our heinies kicked, send reinforcements,'" Jennifer said.

"So how does this help us?" I asked.

"On its own? It doesn't. But here's the thing: I think Weishaupt, if it isn't at the top of the Network, is at least a clearinghouse for signals traffic. Sort of the Network's central mail room."

"With you so far."

"If I can crack the code," Pixie said, "figure out what kind of encryption they're using, and how to reverse-engineer it, then I can focus on sniffing Weishaupt's server traffic for anything that matches the same criteria. As it stands, they're passing massive amounts of network traffic in and out all day long, most of it disguised. These little packets are the needles in the haystack. Learn to spot those needles..."

"And we can read their mail," I said.

"Bingo. Well, not their *actual* mail, but whatever's hidden in these messages. And the best part is, it'll be like the Enigma machine from World War Two: they won't even know we're reading their stuff. Heck, I could even spoof messages between Network computers. Maybe send fake emergency messages, or cancel real ones."

Progress. Real progress. We needed this.

"I'm sold," I said. "So what do you need from us to make this happen?"

Pixie waved a hand at the screen. "More samples. Hit a Network front, scare them into sending a distress call to Weishaupt, then grab their computers before they can erase anything. Ideally, hit every one of them you can find. The more data I have to work with, the more false positives I can weed out while I'm hunting down the pattern."

"Unfortunately," Jennifer said, "we only found the one. They don't exactly advertise."

I drummed my fingers on the back of Pixie's chair as I considered our options. The fight at Donaghy Waste Management had been a solid victory, for once, but that was where the trail dead-ended.

"Well, we know Elmer's going to come back for a rematch,"

I said. "He can't *not* come after me. Also, he told me about his 'phase two' project with the roaches, but without his old safe house—and without the breeding pits—he's going to have to start from scratch. If we can pick up his scent when he lands in Vegas and keep an eye on him from a safe distance, that'd be our way in."

Jennifer gave me a pat on the back. "Looks like you get to be the bait, sugar. It's your lucky week."

I had another slice of cake.

* * *

The next morning, reasonably refreshed and with only a mild hangover, I swung by city hall. I wanted to update Mayor Seabrook and see if her attitude on that liquor license was softening any now that we'd delivered some solid results. Also, I needed to know where she stood on this Metro thing. I knew Jennifer had read her the riot act over Commissioner Harding's impromptu raid at Container Park, but depending on what Gary's investigation turned up, this situation was primed to go nuclear.

Bottom line: if some cops were on the Network's payroll, then some cops were about to disappear. I needed to know she'd yank tight on Harding's leash to keep him from retaliating.

The undercarriage of my Elantra had a rattle in it, just persistent enough to be annoying. I parked at the edge of the lot and made a note to run it over to the rental place, maybe see about swapping it out for another set of wheels. *And also get my damn Barracuda back*, I thought. My car was out there, somewhere, and I tried not to imagine Harmony Black enjoying it. It was like picturing your ex with a new lover.

The mayor had some new security on the scene: men in severe suits with Secret Service style earpieces, thick white coils snaking down into their starched collars. They stopped me in the hall outside her office door and asked for my bona fides. I told them my name was Emerson and flashed a fake driver's license to prove it. Two minutes later, they waved me inside.

"You're tightening things up around here," I said.

I shut the pebbled-glass door behind me. Seabrook was at the credenza, pouring herself a cup of coffee. She paused a moment, pot in hand, then poured a second mug. She slid it across her desk. I took a seat when she did, raised the mug in salute, and had a taste. Her peace offering went down bitter and strong.

"I hired Tall Pines to coordinate security for the United Conference of Mayors, since it's outside Metro's jurisdiction and I don't know how much I trust the locals in Boulder City." She paused. "After recent events, not sure how much I trust anyone. This is a shakedown cruise, showing me how they do things. They're sweeping for bugs this morning. One's in the bathroom, finishing up."

Her sharp glance to the mahogany-paneled door drove the point home: mind my words until the hired help left.

"Do you trust the commissioner?" I asked her.

"With my life. I've known Earl for twenty years. But men have their pride. Once the news ran with that story about the house party massacre, it didn't take long for the headlines to turn into 'Vegas Police Impotent in Face of Drug Crisis.' He needed a win. For the force's morale, he said, but...well."

"Men have their pride."

She sipped her coffee. "Your colleague said I should thank you for some forward momentum in the matter under discussion."

"We won a battle," I said. "The war is ongoing, but the people responsible for recent problems are being dealt with."

"That's what I like to see."

I couldn't say more on that subject until our company left. I heard rustling behind the bathroom door.

"So, about that other matter," I said. "The liquor license?"

"I like what I'm seeing. I'd like to see more of it. You're on the road to convincing me, Mr. Emerson. I'm just not quite there yet."

I had to smile. I'd earned a cup of coffee, but that was where the ride ended for now.

"You're no pushover, Mrs. Mayor. I'll give you that much."

"I haven't held my seat for this long by being an easy touch," she told me. "But I'm fair. Hold up your end, I'll hold up mine."

"On a side note, extra security or not, I still don't think you should go to the mayors' conference."

Seabrook was already sorting a stack of paperwork on her desk, the meeting half-dismissed. She opened her top desk drawer and took out a steel-rimmed pair of glasses, polishing them with a cloth as she glanced up at me.

"That's nonnegotiable. We need to show a unified front in the face of this epidemic."

"The problem with a unified front is that it puts you all in the same place at the same time."

"Tall Pines Security is renowned for their skill at managing public venues," she said. "Also, sweeping for explosives is a specialty. I've already considered the risks, believe me, and so have they. Everything is under control."

The bathroom door swung open. A short, tow-headed man in a black suit poked his head out, toting an aluminum briefcase.

"Sorry to interrupt, ma'am, you're all clear—"

He froze. So did I. Seabrook's world may have been under control, but mine spun right out from under me in a dizzying lurch. I knew her hired help. It had been over twenty years since we'd spoken, but I knew him.

You don't forget your brother's face.

"Um, that—that is—" Teddy stammered, eyes fixed on me while his cheeks went pale.

Seabrook glanced between us. "Do you know each other?"

"No," I said, hoping he could get his act together and follow my lead. "Sometimes people think they recognize me, until they look closer. I've just got that kind of face."

"Sorry, I'll get out of your way." Teddy hustled to the door. "I'll be outside."

That was more for me than for her. I slid my hands down below Seabrook's line of sight and squeezed my legs to keep myself steady. I couldn't let myself get distracted, couldn't let myself *care* right now. We were alone. Time to tackle the elephant in the room.

"One other thing," I said. "About Metro."

"Your colleague suggested the possibility that the man who sold that tainted ink is...in a position of public trust."

"We're looking into it now," I said.

Seabrook pushed her chair back. She walked to the credenza, her back turned as she prepared a fresh pot of coffee. Her hands worked slowly, deliberate, every movement precise.

"Earl is loyal to his men, to a fault. And he doesn't believe in extra-judicial measures."

"I understand that," I replied. "But the people we're dealing with...they can't be fought by legal means. And if we do uncover a mole in uniform—or several of them—conventional methods of questioning aren't going to yield results."

She didn't answer at first. The office fell silent save for the muted clinking of her coffee pot, the burble of fresh water flooding a chamber of glass.

"Earl won't get on board with that," she finally replied. "Which is why, if you need to take aggressive action, you will cover your tracks in a manner that doesn't point back to you. Or to my office."

Green light.

I finished my mug and pushed my chair back. "Thank you, Mrs. Mayor. We'll be in touch."

She didn't say goodbye. I'd earned coffee, not pleasantries. And we weren't friends. I let myself out, nodded to the two bruisers at the door, and made my way back out through the corridors of power.

My brother was waiting for me on the steps outside, just like I knew he would be.

28.

Out in the desert sunshine, Teddy rushed toward me. Then back two steps, bouncing like an overexcited terrier. The look on his face was somewhere between wonder and panic.

"Dan—"

I stopped him, fast, and shot a glance over my shoulder.

"Emerson. My name is Paul Emerson. Understand?"

He understood. I walked down the steps and followed the sidewalk at the edge of the parking lot, getting out of the path of foot traffic. He trailed me.

"I don't know where to start," he said.

I took him in, now that I could think clearly enough to see. He was fit, his broad shoulders holding up more muscle than flab. He'd spent a few bucks on his suit, but not too many, and his shoes were department-store leather.

I didn't spend a lot of time looking at his face. That's where all the bad memories were hiding.

"I don't know either," I said. "I guess I'm sorry. For not keeping in touch."

"Me too."

Silence fell, as if that was all we had to say to each other. It felt more like I had this torrent of words shoved down in my belly, a giant balloon stuffed with them, jammed up and twisted and knotted, too many to get a single one of them out.

"I tried to reach out once," I managed to say. "You were in the military, I guess? Navy?"

"Yeah." He smiled, sheepish, and rubbed the back of his neck. "Did a couple of tours to pay for college. Overseas. I would have been hard to reach."

"Yeah." I looked for something to add to that. "Were you on a ship?"

"Big one. I signed up to learn electronics. Got a little of that, but mostly I got really good at painting and cleaning." He ducked his head, still looking at me like maybe I wasn't really there. "Got married when I came home. We spent a few years out in Fort Collins; the company just transferred me to Vegas last month. You, uh...you have a niece. She's six years old. You want to see a picture?"

I had a niece. I didn't expect to get gut-punched out of nowhere, but that did the trick.

"I'd like that," I told him.

He tugged a photo from his wallet. She was gap-toothed with blond pigtails, riding a tire swing and grinning like a loon.

"Cute kid," I said. Hell with that. She was perfect. She was family.

"I gotta ask," he said.

"Sure."

"I tried to reach out to you, too. Couple of times. You were beyond off the grid. It took me a while, but eventually I figured out you wanted it that way. Then I found this guy, Jud Pankow. He told me his granddaughter had been murdered and you...fixed it for him."

"People say a lot of things."

"Then I tried again, and—" Teddy paused. He looked behind him, then hustled a little farther along the sidewalk, waving me close. His voice dropped to a whisper. "Dan, you were in *prison.* And then they said you were dead, that you died in that riot. Do you know you have a tombstone, in a potter's field? I left *flowers* there."

"Hence the new name. And it's really, really important that you keep the old one out of your mouth, all right?"

"Sure. Right. Of course." He stared at my shoes. "I never knew you even tried looking for me. I didn't expect you to."

"What? Because of what went down? Teddy, c'mon. I never blamed you for that."

He met my gaze then. I could see him forcing himself to do it. His neck muscles strained like steel cables.

"I sold you out. I *lied*."

"You were a scared kid, and Dad's lawyer told you that you were going home with him at the end of the day, no matter what you said on the stand."

Teddy's cheeks tightened in disgust. "Didn't understand until years later that he was full of shit, just trying to scare me into backing Dad's story. I could have saved you if I'd told the truth. I could have saved us both."

"Exactly. You didn't know, you didn't understand, and you were eight years old. You were never in my bad books. If you need me to say I forgive you...Teddy, I forgive you. It happened. We survived."

I took a breath and sighed it out one side of my mouth. There are some things you don't want to know, but you have to ask.

"Dad?"

"Seven years ago," Teddy said.

"Cirrhosis?"

"Pneumonia. Can you believe it? The booze didn't get him, a bad flu did."

I took that in. My father was dead.

I'd known he had to be, realistically, statistically, given the way the man lived from drink to drink. Maybe that was why I never went looking. Or maybe I was afraid I'd find out he was still alive, and then I'd start feeling like I had to do something about it.

But my father was dead, and he'd been in the ground for seven years now. I wondered if violent schizophrenics went to hell, if whatever machinery governed the cosmos held them responsible for their crimes, or if the bad wiring in their brains gave them a get-out-of-damnation-free card. Maybe I'd ask Caitlin sometime. Maybe I'd be happier not knowing.

"We buried him up at Colewood," my brother said. "Five people came to the funeral, and nobody really wanted to be there."

My face went hot. "Colewood? Jesus, Teddy."

"The plot and the headstone were already paid for—"

"He doesn't deserve to be buried next to Mom. That's fucking obscene and you know it."

"It was *paid for*," he snapped, throwing my anger back at me. "I'm not exactly made of money, okay? And you weren't there. I had to handle everything on my own, and pretend to be the grieving son when I would have been fine tossing his evil ass in a burlap sack and dumping it in the trash. *You weren't there.*"

His shoulders sagged as his fury drained away.

"I'm sorry," he said. "You didn't deserve—"

"Yes. I did. You're not wrong."

"Geez." He kicked his toe against the curb. "Still brothers, huh? Peas in a pod."

"Still brothers."

"So, the stuff they said about you." He hedged, slow, working his way to the question. "I mean, when you were in prison, the things they said you did. So you're some kind of..."

"You can say it," I told him.

Our eyes met. "Gangster?"

"That's a word for it. Let me put it this way: remember back in the day, when we'd boost food from that 7-Eleven down the street? You'd distract the clerk while I loaded up the backpack?"

Teddy looked to the sky and let out a sound somewhere between an empty laugh and a sigh. He put his hands on his hips.

"Of course," he said. "That was the only way we got any food at all, some nights."

"Turns out I've got a talent for taking things that don't belong to me. And I believe a person should play to their natural strengths."

He laughed again, this time with some affection behind it. "Do I even want to know why you were in Mayor Seabrook's office?"

"Believe it or not, doing my civic duty. Sometimes it takes a bad guy to catch a bad guy."

"That I don't believe."

"Oh, it's true," I said. "Let's just say I have access to avenues of information that the cops don't."

"No. Not that part. I don't believe that you're a bad guy."

Sweet, innocent Teddy. I could have shown him where the literal bodies were buried. I could have led him to a river of blood, my arms washed elbows deep in it. After all that, he'd probably still say the same. It was nice to have someone who believed in your better nature, even when you knew they were wrong.

"So," I said. "Security, huh?"

"Playing to my natural strengths, I guess. Ex-military and all that. It pays the bills, and it beats being stuck in an office all day."

"I hear that."

The conversation faded as we both worked toward the same question. He asked it first.

"So what now?"

"Now? Well, I've got to get back to work. I assume you've got to get back to work. And we shouldn't be seen talking in public because officially you don't know me—"

"But after?" He studied me, head tilted, pensive. He looked like a kid trying to find the confidence to ask a girl to prom. "Still brothers?"

"I'd like that," I told him.

"Would you...want to come around sometime? Dinner or something? You've got a sister-in-law and a niece you haven't met yet."

I hadn't been expecting the invitation. I figured we'd end this with a polite exchange of phone numbers before slipping out of each other's lives again.

"Is that okay?" I asked him. "Teddy, you know what I do for a living."

"Well, don't *tell* them that. Just...make something up. You used to be good at that."

"I'm still pretty good at it."

He reached out and took hold of my arm.

"I want you in my life," he said. "We can't make up for lost time, but we can start fresh, maybe."

We exchanged numbers. We went our separate ways. I cracked the car door to let the heat out and stood there and marveled at life for a little while. As I got behind the wheel, reality sawed through the wonder like a serrated knife.

I had a list of enemies as long as my arm, and any one of them would love to get their hands on my long-lost brother. They'd snatch him for leverage or just hurt him to hurt me. My recent promotion and induction into the courts of hell, where a stab in the back was how most people said hello, added a fresh layer of trouble to the mix. The best, smartest thing I could do—for Teddy and for myself—was to keep my brother as far away from me as humanly possible. Cut him off, change my phone number, disappear.

But I wasn't going to.

I was only human, and a chance to reconnect with Teddy—after my father and the world had torn us apart—was a treasure I couldn't forsake. So I'd find a way to make this work.

The undercarriage of the Elantra rattled again as I pulled out onto the street. I set the dashboard GPS for the rental place, and then I called Pixie.

"You found another Network safe house?" she said. "Already?"

"No, just wondering if my car's popped up anywhere."

"Seriously? That's what you're calling me about?"

"I miss my car," I said.

"So go buy another one."

"It's a painstakingly rebuilt 1970 Hemi Cuda," I said. "It's not a Honda Civic. You can't just 'buy another one.'"

"I've got feelers out, okay? I'm doing my best."

"That's all I ask—" I paused as the phone beeped. "Hold on, I've got another call coming in."

I tapped the screen, and an unwelcome voice growled in my ear.

"You shouldn't have made fun of me," Grimm said.

"How did you get this number?"

"When a *man* is challenged to a fight, he stands up and answers."

"I did answer," I told him, "and my answer is 'you're ridiculous.' That answer still stands, by the way."

"I'm going to expose you for the craven weakling you really are."

I sighed. "Look, what did you call yourself? Huffington Goofyman?"

"*Hunter. MacGregor. Grimm.*"

"That's what I said. Bottom line is, I just don't have time to deal with you right now. I'm supposed to be getting ready for a fight with a guy who is A, actually dangerous, and B, actually has a reason to want to kill me. It's a lousy reason, but that's more than you've got."

"Too bad he'll never get the chance," Grimm replied. "Bang. You're dead."

I stepped on the gas and wove through the midmorning traffic. I took Grimm seriously enough to cast an eye toward the rooftops on either side of the street, watching for the telltale glint of a riflescope catching the sunlight. If he was good enough to get my number, he was good enough to track my movements. All the same, there were a dozen directions I could have left city hall from, and the possibilities exploded with every intersection I passed.

I shouldn't have been nervous. And yet.

"I'm driving forty miles an hour," I said, keeping my tone light even as my nerves trilled like warning bells. "You'd have to be one hell of a sniper to hit me through the windshield, assuming you even know what street I'm going to take and have time to set up a perch before I get there."

Grimm chuckled. It was a long, slow, raspy sound, and entirely too confident for my liking.

"People always make that mistake," he said.

"Which one?"

"Thinking the word 'bang' implies a bullet."

The undercarriage of the sedan rattled again. Louder this time.

29.

Horns screamed as I spun the wheel hard. The Elantra lurched, swerving between lanes. I slammed against the seatbelt as my front wheel hit the curb, the car jumping, screeching to a stop halfway onto the sidewalk. Grimm's laughter burst over the phone, giddy and mad, the sound like electric claws raking down my spine. I snapped the belt open, threw open the door, and jumped out with the engine still running.

The sidewalk behind me was clear. A few people were walking up from the other direction, curious now, and I flailed my hands as I broke into an all-out sprint. "*Stay back!*" I shouted. "*Don't come any—*"

The bomb under the sedan erupted and painted the world in jagged streaks of hot white. A fist of concussive force slammed into my back and threw me to the pavement while metal screamed louder than thunder. The sound was a physical force, penetrating flesh and bone, reverberating in my ears and blotting out the power to think. I lay there, stunned, my shirt torn and my left arm scraped bloody on the pavement.

A shower of sparks and ash drifted down in a lazy, silent rain, kissing the scorched earth.

I wasn't sure how long it took before I was able to move again. My hearing slowly swam back. The *thrum-thrum-thrum* of the endlessly echoing blast faded, replaced by car horns and distant sirens.

My phone buzzed in my hand. Private number. Had to be

Grimm, calling back. I didn't pick up. Let him wonder if I was dead or alive.

I damn well knew which category he'd fall under, once I got my hands on him.

* * *

First things first. Damage control.

I limped off down an alley, waving off a couple of good Samaritans and putting some distance between me and the pile of twisted, smoking debris that used to be my ride. I made two phone calls. The first call was to Jennifer; I needed a pickup, fast. I also needed someone to hop onto the police and paramedic radio bands. I was pretty sure I'd bailed in a clear spot, that no bystanders had gone up in the blast, but I wanted to know for sure. My second call was to Pixie. I gave her a five-second recap.

"So you need the Avis rental database scrubbed," she said. "Got it. Why would you rent a car under your own name, anyway? I mean, your own fake name."

"Building credit. I'm trying to give 'Paul Emerson' a credible paper trail in case anyone ever pokes into his life, which entails buying and renting a lot of stuff as him. Which works great, until someone starts blowing up the aforementioned stuff. I don't think the standard insurance covers 'acts of mad bomber.'"

"I'm on it. Pix out."

A ragtop sedan with battered, Bondo-patched doors rumbled along the street. A couple of Calles bangers were up front and I dove in the back, stretching out along the vinyl bench seat. Partly to keep my face out of sight, just in case the first cops on the scene were working faster than usual, but mostly because I really, really needed to lie down for a minute.

Once the adrenaline ebbed away, leaving a jittery, empty ache in my veins, I was able to do a self-assessment. Wriggling toes, bending joints, checking for damage. I knew a guy who had been shot in a botched smash-and-grab once and didn't know it until half an hour later; he tried to scratch a nagging itch and chipped a fingernail on the slug in his back.

I'd gotten off easy by comparison. The scrapes along my left forearm were ugly to look at and stung like I'd dunked my arm in scalding water, but I'd only sacrificed a little skin. My knee twinged when I bent it, but I could walk that off. The injury to my pride would take longer to heal.

I still thought I'd made the right move at Winter, refusing to duel with this chump. My mistake had been thinking he'd slink off with his tail between his legs and that'd be the end of it. Whatever his malfunction was, he was bound and determined to come at me, and he'd keep coming until I shut him down for good.

I told the Calles to run me over to East Harmon Avenue. Winter wasn't far away—and neither was the parking garage where I'd left my rental on the night of the party. I walked in on foot, past the automated ticket box and glossy yellow swing-arm, and into the gallery of silent cars.

Jennifer met me there, and Caitlin wasn't far behind. Cait pulled me close. Her eyes narrowed, suddenly venomous, staring at my shredded and rust-spotted sleeve.

"He dies," she said.

I crouched in an empty parking spot, the concrete spattered with dried oil stains. From there, I looked to the rafters and the bare, industrial girders that laced the boxy garage like steel bones.

"That's a given," I said. "So, this is where I parked the night of the party. I didn't notice the rattling sound under the car until the next morning, so I think this is where he planted the bomb. Do you see any security cameras?"

They joined me in the search and came up empty. I had parked in a blind spot.

"He came to the party late," I said. "Good chance he stopped here first. Must have been watching me for a while, so he knew what car to look for. If he had a few minutes, uninterrupted, it'd be easy enough to slap something crude to the undercarriage."

Caitlin tapped her chin with a fingertip, following the timeline. "So you think he rigged your vehicle, *then* came and challenged you to a duel? Why?"

"Fail-safe, maybe?" Jennifer said. "We don't know if the bomb was triggered remotely or if it was on a timer. Could be he set it on a long timer, figuring that if you beat him at the party, he'd get ya from beyond the grave. So what do you know about this weirdo, anyway?"

"Very little," Caitlin replied. "I put out some discreet feelers after the party, but no court seems willing to claim him. Not surprising. The one thing we know for certain is that he's a cambion, and my court is one of the few that doesn't consider half-bloods a step above literal vermin."

We walked back to the garage entrance together. I spotted the gray nozzle of a camera pointed square at the gate.

"I know that he's got some very unlucky timing," I said.

Jen glanced my way. "How do you figure?"

"Because with Elmer Donaghy in Paris and the Network's plans on hold, the dumb bastard just made himself my one and only dance partner. He's earned my undivided attention." I gestured to the camera. "And if he did plant the bomb during the party, there's a good chance somebody caught him coming and going. Let's find the manager and ask."

The on-site manager was a bloated slug in a beer-stained tank top and jeans, squeezed into a tiny office behind a lopsided and broken-legged desk. A small bank of monitors showed grainy, flickering views of the garage entrances and exits.

"We need to see last night's surveillance footage," I told him.

He looked at me like I'd come in off the street and asked for his daughter's hand in marriage. "Who's 'we'? You ain't with the company."

I was deciding whether I was going to play nice or start bouncing him off the walls to relieve my pent-up irritation, when Jennifer caught the look in my eyes. She gently nudged me aside and stepped up to the desk.

"Let me, sugar." She looked at the manager and took out her wallet—white leather, with western fringe—then peeled off a couple of hundreds. She slapped the cash down on the desk. Her side, just out of his reach.

"What's this?" he said.

"That's what we're payin' you for access to that security-cam footage. Two hundred dollars, nonnegotiable. Now, you can take the money and have yourself a good time tonight. Or"—she pulled back her utility jacket and showed him her pistol, snug in a calfskin holster—"I can introduce the butt of this roscoe to your skull a half dozen times, and you can spend that money on stitches down at the ER when you wake up. Either way, you're taking the money, and we're getting that footage. Do we have a deal?"

He didn't take long to think about it.

"Yeah, deal." He paused. "Uh, the—the first choice, the good one, not the other one."

"Good thinkin'," Jennifer said.

* * *

I wasn't sure if Grimm was legitimately crazy or not, and that bothered me. He'd shown up with a bevy of made-up titles and a ridiculous legend to go with it, along with his pointless vendetta. Did he actually believe any of it? Was it all a smoke screen? And why did he want me dead, anyway? There's no opponent more dangerous than one you can't predict, and as it stood, Grimm was the deadliest kind of wild card. I needed to find out who he really was, what made him tick, where his lines were.

I only knew one thing for certain: the man was sloppy. If that bomb had been on a timer, he had no way of knowing I'd be anywhere near the sedan when it went off. If he triggered it remotely, that was even worse; he'd talked, and gloated, and given me just enough time to get clear of the blast, when he could have vaporized me with the push of a button. He needed attention more than he needed victory, and that was a weakness I could exploit.

More evidence of his sloppiness was right there on a flickering screen. We'd narrowed the footage down easily, starting from when I'd parked the car up to when Grimm had made his appearance at the party, and the security camera had caught a perfect shot of his arrival. He rolled in five minutes after I did, riding alone behind the wheel of a dirty white panel van.

"Okay," I said, "so let's jump it ahead an hour or so and see if we can catch him on the way out, too."

He obliged us at one hour and fourteen minutes on the dot. I froze the frame on a still of his license plate number.

"Gotcha," I said. "Well, maybe. If he's any kind of professional, that car is stolen—"

"But from what you've been tellin' me," Jennifer said, "he ain't any kind of professional."

"My thoughts exactly. I'm going to shoot the plate number over to Pixie. She can run a search and pull the registration info for us. Who knows? We might even find out Hunter McChucklenuts's real name."

I tugged out my phone. I was about to copy the plate down when a text pinged in. Then a second, and a third.

"Good man," I murmured. "You might hate yourself in the morning for this, but you made the right call."

Jennifer tilted her head at me. "Whatcha got, sugar?"

I turned the phone so she and Caitlin could read the messages, straight from Gary Kemper.

Santiago is a cop

at the Starbucks on n rancho dr, keeping him distracted

come pick him up before I change my mind

30.

"I really appreciate this," Santiago was telling Gary. "I mean, I got potential, you know? I could really make an impact if I got my detective's shield. All I need is a mentor to help me get there. Somebody who can put in a good word for me."

They were nestled in a two-seater by the window, talking shop over paper mugs of coffee. Both in plainclothes. I figured it was either Santiago's day off, or Gary had convinced him to call in sick. Either way, he was off the clock and nobody was going to come looking for him until tomorrow at the earliest.

"And that's why I offered," Gary told him. He didn't make eye contact. He did with me and Jennifer, though, when he saw us coming. Then he stared at his cup. Santiago had his back to us.

"You...you okay, man?" Santiago shrugged. "You look down all of a sudden."

Gary curled his lips in a bitter smile.

"Just wondering how to do this right. I think this is the part where I'm supposed to kiss you on both cheeks."

I clamped my hand on Santiago's shoulder. He looked at me, then at Gary, and I saw the pieces click together in his eyes.

"Don't make a scene," I told him.

"You son of a bitch," Santiago breathed. "You're with them?"

Gary's hand tightened around his cup. The cardboard started to buckle. Now he looked Santiago in the eye, cold and steady.

"I'm not with them, no. I'm with the dozen kids who died because of the tainted drugs you put on the street. And whatever these two do to you, it's probably better than you deserve." Gary looked to me. "Get him out of my sight."

Jennifer nudged Santiago to his feet. "C'mon," she said in a low voice. "We want you alive, but we don't need you alive. And if you don't think I'll put a bullet in you right here and now, think twice."

She was bluffing, but he bought it. Santiago rose and walked with us, a lamb to the slaughter.

"Faust," Gary said.

I looked back at him.

"Never ask me to do this again," he told me.

"Might not feel like it right now," I said, "but you did the best thing you could do, under the circumstances. You're still one of the good guys, Gary."

He drank his coffee and looked out the window.

* * *

We took him to the fortress. That was the nickname for Jennifer's place out by the airport, a U-shaped tenement block she'd bought up on the cheap and converted into a modern-day castle of crumbling stone and sheet-draped windows. Rusted cars parked along a side street formed a makeshift barricade, and corners in every direction were manned by Calles foot soldiers in brown and yellow. Up on the rooftops, more shooters stood with binoculars and hunting rifles, keeping a silent watch over her tiny kingdom.

Caitlin had gone ahead of us to get the room ready. When we marched Santiago inside, he knew what it was for. You don't lay plastic sheeting across dusty floorboards, let alone tack it up over the peeling floral wallpaper, unless you're planning on making a serious mess.

We cuffed his hands behind him, sat him down in a chair in the middle of the plastic tarp, and that's when he started to cry.

My kit was all laid out on a sawhorse on the side of the room. Tupperware containers of sea salt and cow's blood, white candles, all the fixings to purge his body of the Network roach in his guts. I could see it with my third eye, a black blotch like a fist-sized tumor in his abdomen.

I took the salt and started to trace a circle around his chair in glittering crystal lines. I focused on the spell-work to come—I had a fifty-fifty shot of pulling this off—and tried to ignore his blubbering.

"Have some damn dignity," Jennifer snapped at him. "All we want to do is ask you some questions. You tell us what we wanna know, maybe give up some of your buddies, you got a real good chance of walking out of here."

Of course, she was lying. After what Santiago had done—dancing to Elmer Donaghy's tune, sending Todd into the streets with a baggie of tainted ink and causing a massacre just to get my attention—there was no chance he was ever leaving this room alive. We were going to wring him dry, and then we were going to kill him, and that was that. The only question was how much he was going to suffer between those two points.

He should have known that, but desperation makes people stupid. He got himself under control and bobbed his head at Jennifer like an eager puppy. A blob of snot glistened in his mustache.

"Anything you want to know," he stammered. "Anything! I can help you. I can be real helpful!"

I finished the circle, tapped off a few last grains of salt from the Tupperware, and went to get the candles.

"Not yet," I told him. "Keep your mouth shut until I get this done."

"You want to know about Elmer, right, and phase two? I can tell you all about it. The dude is sick, you don't even know the half of it."

Santiago wrenched to one side, his words cut off in a choking sob of pain. I saw the hazy image of the roach stir inside of him—and bite, a punishment for his disobedience.

"*Stop talking*," I said. I laid down the candles as fast as I could, forming the points of a star around the circle of salt. Caitlin was right behind me with a book of matches. Wicks sizzled to life one by one, filling the air with the faint, musty scent of smoke. Sweat beaded Santiago's face. He was too desperate to think straight, too afraid to understand what was happening to him or connect his treason to the sudden pain in his belly.

"You didn't stop shit," he stammered. "Those pits were just where he keeps the roaches, not where he makes 'em. Oh God, what—"

He lurched forward, his spine bucking, and vomited a gout of blood. It splashed across his slacks and spattered the plastic sheeting. I ran and grabbed the plastic bucket of cow's blood, an offering to draw the geas-roach out.

"Jennifer," I shouted, "put something in his mouth to shut him up. Gag him with your belt or something!"

Santiago wheezed his words out. He was trying to save his own life by giving us something we could use. He didn't realize he was committing suicide by doing it.

"Elmer's got another site where he runs experiments," he said. "That's where he keeps the breeder. The breeder is a—"

His last words ended in a howl of agony. He threw his head back, shoulders quaking, and thrashed hard enough to bring the chair crashing down onto the plastic tarp. His throat swelled, rippled—and then burst, muscle and skin tearing as the roach, half a foot long and its mud-brown shell smeared with streaks of scarlet, dug its way out of him. Santiago was still alive, still trying to scream, his breaths coming out in a wet burble as his eyes bulged wildly.

Jennifer's hand cannon roared, and a copper-jacketed bullet put him out of his misery. It tore into Santiago's throat, shredding the roach, splintering vertebrae and splashing the remnants of two lives across four feet of plastic tarp. I stood over the carnage and waited for my ears to stop ringing.

"Swear to God," I told her—still barely able to hear my own voice, like I was standing under five feet of water—"do *not* fire that thing indoors."

"What?" she shouted. I think she was shouting.

Eventually we were able to communicate again. Caitlin nudged Santiago's cheek with the toe of her shoe. The head lolled, only clinging to his body by a Swiss-cheese scrap of cartilage.

"That's new," she said lightly. "I've been half-convinced that certain people might talk me to death, given the chance, but I've never seen a man talk *himself* to death before."

"Next time, we gag 'em first," Jennifer said.

"Next time," I told her, "you warn me before you start shooting."

"Hey, you've seen how fast those critters move. I didn't want that sucker getting loose and escaping into the vents. Not in *my* house. I'd have to start sleepin' with a helmet on."

She had a point. My ears still stung, but she had a point.

"Well, we got...something before he croaked," I said. "Not much, but something. We know there's another Network hideout in town. Which is good news, in a way. If we can track it down and take it by surprise, we might get the data Pixie needs to work on her decoder thingy."

"As far as that last bit," Jennifer said, "you know what he was about to say, right?"

"'The breeder is a—'" I replied.

"Giant cockroach." She pushed out her bottom lip and stared at Santiago's dead body. "You know it. I know it. Caitlin knows it. It's gonna be a giant roach. Let's just prepare for that right now so we're not surprised when we see it."

Caitlin considered that and gave an agreeable nod. "The only question is...cow-sized? Truck-sized? House-sized? Now I'm curious."

"Well," I said, "on the bright side, it'll keep. Anything in Elmer's second hideout is *staying* in Elmer's second hideout until he comes back from Paris. I don't imagine the flunkies he has left are going to move forward on this 'phase two' thing without him."

"Somethin' to be said for striking while the iron's hot," Jennifer told me. "If we hit the streets and hunt this place down, maybe we can make sure Elmer doesn't have any safe haven to come back to."

She was right, but I could only fight so many fires at once, and that meant picking my priorities.

"Problem is," I said, "we might end up chasing our tails all over town. Meanwhile, I've got a psycho cambion who's here right now, he's hot to kill me, and he doesn't care if civilians get hurt in the process. I've got to focus on that."

"Can't argue with that," Jennifer said. "Where's your next stop?"

I didn't know until an hour later, when Pixie got back to me with the registration info on Grimm's license plate. We were half-wrong earlier. As it turned out, my would-be killer was professional enough to steal a car instead of using his own wheels.

Not just any car off the street, though. And he hadn't made a mistake by letting us see his plates. He did it on purpose. He'd chosen his ride to send a very special message, just for me, a message that rocketed me straight back to the past.

31.

Jennifer stayed behind to supervise the cleanup. Officer Santiago would disappear, a new and eternal resident of the missing persons registry. I stopped at home to change my clothes; then Caitlin and I headed northwest on the 95. Her snow-white Audi roared up the open road, desert flats stretching to the rust-red mountains on the horizon, as we chased down a ghost.

"Sometimes cars just drop off the grid," Pixie had told me. "You know, they get mothballed, rust away outside a farmhouse somewhere. Maybe, eventually, somebody comes along and restores 'em."

"Barn finds," I said.

"Exactly. That's when the chain of custody gets spotty. The plates belong to a white GMC panel van, which lines up with the description you texted me. *Technically*, it's not stolen, but its registration has been expired since the late nineties and there's no record of a sale—the paper trail just ends. So my best guess is your guy found it abandoned in a garage somewhere, fixed it up, and helped himself."

"Great, so it's a dead end after all. Out of curiosity, who owned it?"

"Not a who, a what. It was a company van. Belonged to an outfit called the New Transitions Wellness House. Looks like they were a state-funded halfway house for 'youths at risk,' sort of an alternative to juvie. They got shut down after an abuse scandal—"

She said more, but I wasn't hearing her, too lost in the warrens of my memory. I didn't need the details. I knew that house. I used to live there.

"I don't like this." Caitlin lightly drummed her fingers on the steering wheel. She'd said that once when I told her where we were going. And now, after I'd told her about the pre-bomb part of my day.

"I know. I run into Teddy at the same time this psycho is digging into my teenage years and throwing my past in my face? That's too much memory lane in one place."

"I know he's your blood," Caitlin said. She left the *but* unspoken.

She wasn't wrong, and I was having the same suspicions. I hated this. The last thing I wanted, after a surprise reunion with my kid brother, was to think he was mixed up in this mess. All the same, I took out my phone and made some calls while she drove.

I'd already heard of Tall Pines Security; they had a solid rep, solid enough that I wouldn't want to go up against them in the middle of a heist. That said, I poked around and made sure Mayor Seabrook had contracted the *real* Tall Pines. Maybe paranoid, but considering I've been a ComEd repairman, a Polymath Security alarm installer, and a FedEx driver on various jobs—plus another baker's dozen of past disguises—it was worth verifying.

Next I pulled my job-recruiter routine and had a chat with the Tall Pines human-resources department. My brother was a solid employee, with the company for over a year. I was as satisfied as I was going to get, at least until I spent more one-on-one time with him.

"I hate to say it's a coincidence," I told her, "generally because there's no such thing, but...it really does look like a fluke. Seabrook hired a solid security firm, no surprise there, and Teddy's one of their reliable operators. Simple as that."

Caitlin frowned her response. She wasn't convinced. I don't think I was, either, but I was working overtime to tell myself otherwise.

"All right," she said, "leaving your brother's reappearance out of this, we're still heading toward a confrontation. Grimm stole that van as a direct challenge to you; he's telling you that he knows your history. That he knows what he *hopes* are your weak points."

"And he's telling us where to meet him. I'm fine with that. If he wants a showdown this bad, he's going to get one."

I wasn't taking chances. My cards nestled against my chest, my wand up my sleeve in its spring-loaded holster. I hadn't just changed my clothes back at the apartment; I'd rounded out my arsenal. The velvet pouch of alchemist's clay, Bentley's gift, rode snug in my hip pocket. On the opposite side, a nine-millimeter in a shoulder holster under my linen jacket. Whatever Grimm threw at me—magic or hot lead—I was ready with a rebuttal.

"Which leaves the unanswered question," Caitlin said.

One word: *why?*

We rolled into a small town northwest of Vegas just before dusk. It was a sleepy chunk of nowhere, the kind of place you're either born in and die in, or drive through and forget. We refueled at a no-name gas station with an awning painted like a faded circus tent, then followed the back roads until we reached the end of the line.

"Are you all right?" she asked me.

The Wellness House rose up to blot the setting sun behind its Victorian-styled gables. A central tower speared the sky with a sharp, steep peak and a shattered window for a heart. The white paint was peeling from the clapboard now, and the first-floor windows lay sheathed under nailed boards and signs reading *CONDEMNED BY ORDER OF THE STATE.*

Red spray paint defaced the once-grim sign out front, a childish scrawl that proclaimed *FOCK YOU.* The misspelling gave the defiant statement more power somehow. Maybe it was hidden in the faint smile it brought to my lips. There was a reason I usually resorted to a wisecrack in moments like this. I carried two weapons up my sleeve when it came to fighting fear: laughter and anger.

I had a feeling I was going to need both. For now the house sat dormant, rusting in its sleep, like an elderly tiger that might spring awake to claw and bite at any moment. Caitlin stared at me, waiting for an answer to her question.

"It's just a building," I said and got out of the car.

We circled the property on foot. No sign of the panel van, but that didn't mean he wasn't inside, waiting. All the doors were secure, fixed with extra padlocks on the outside, and the windows were boarded up tight.

"This one," Caitlin said. She had been appraising the windows with an architect's eye and singled out one for her personal attention. She hooked her fingers around a board and heaved. Nails popped free from the groaning wood one by one, until a board wriggled loose. She tossed it aside, letting it clatter to the dirt at her back, and reached for the next in line.

Eventually she cleared an opening big enough for us to invade. The window beneath the boards was long broken, nothing left but a ring of jagged glass teeth. I broke out the shards with the butt of my pistol one by one. I wasn't worried about the noise; if the cambion was inside, waiting for us, he already knew we were here.

I pulled myself over the window frame. My feet touched down on rough floorboards, coated in twenty years of dust and neglect. I gazed across an old industrial kitchen and memories flooded in. In my mind's eye the stark overhead lights—shattered and dead now—were buzzing and bright. The chipped particleboard counter, host to cobwebs and mummified flies, was lined with corroded, moldy cans of bulk-bought green beans and generic potted meat.

We both took out our phones and turned them into flashlights, with the outside light fading fast. Once we left the open window behind, there would be no light at all beyond what we brought in with us.

I stood still for a moment, ears perked, listening to anything the

Wellness House wanted to say. It kept its secrets. Nothing stirred in the bottomless gloom, not even the rats.

We weren't its only recent visitors, though. As we walked along a narrow corridor, my phone's beam trailed across smears of dust on the floor. There were footprints, signs of shuffling, dragging.

"He's been here," I said.

I poked my head into a half-open doorway while I tried to get my bearings. It was strange returning after so many years; some halls I knew by heart, down to the detail of the striped wallpaper or a particular crack in the baseboards, and others seemed utterly alien to me. My memory had reshaped and twisted this place, altered it under the weight of over two decades of nightmares, and being confronted with concrete reality again was jarring. We passed a dorm room I knew—absolutely *knew*—was on the second floor, not the first. I expected a pair of bathroom doors on the left wall, and they were actually on the right.

I pushed open another door and froze.

"Pet?" Caitlin asked. She looked between my face and the cramped room, barely big enough for the wire-frame bed inside and its rotting, yellowed mattress. And the old, dangling hospital-grade restraints with their white buckled straps.

"You know those cigarette burns on my back?" I asked her.

I went inside. I had to. I don't know why. Some bone-deep command pulled me over the threshold, to stare at my teenage ghost on the mattress.

"This is the 'segregation and discipline' hall," I told her. "Six rooms, all just like this, but...it was this room. Once a week, twice sometimes. This was where they put me."

Caitlin put her hand on my shoulder. She didn't speak, letting me process whatever I needed to. I think she wanted me to know I wasn't alone.

"The abuse that got this place shut down," I said, "it wasn't...*deliberate*, if that makes sense. It was born out of neglect. They had too few doctors, too many kids—the state funding paid them by the head, so they packed us in like sardines. Their solution was to hire minimum-wage 'orderlies' with no training, most of them barely a year or two older than we were. Kids watching kids. And when kids get frustrated, they lash out."

"That doesn't excuse what happened to you," Caitlin said. Her voice was barely a whisper.

"No. It doesn't."

I didn't have anything else to say. There was nothing else to see. We backed out of the room and kept moving.

We climbed a wide staircase, the runner rotted to scraps of vaguely floral fabric. A musty odor, like old books and mothballs, hung in the air and tickled the back of my throat. I wasn't sure what I was looking for. A hunch pushed my footsteps, or maybe I was just feeling masochistic and wanted to wallow in the bad old days.

No. Something was significant about this place, outside my own checkered past. Grimm had taken the Wellness House van—and I assumed he'd would have had to put some elbow grease into making it run, after it had been sitting under a tarp or something for twenty years—and gotten his plates caught on camera. He wanted me to see it, wanted me to follow him here.

So where was he?

I strobed my light across an open doorway. I didn't find the cambion, but I found his lair.

32.

"He's *living* here," Caitlin said.

He had been, anyway, if the missing van meant he wasn't coming back. This side room had been swept more or less clean, broken furniture shoved to the corners, and he'd carved out a little sanctuary for himself. A down-stuffed sleeping bag and a pillow lay near a hotplate and a can of Sterno. He had a battery-powered camping lantern, the green plastic hood pulled down tight, and junk-food wrappers spilled from the half-open mouth of a garbage bag. From the food debris and empty soda cans, I figured he'd been here for a week, at least.

A black plastic case sat at the foot of his bedroll. I crouched down, ran my fingertips across the grainy surface and unclasped it. Inside, foam had been cut to securely carry a single pistol and a couple of magazines. Empty. Wherever he was right now, he had the piece on him.

"Only one firearm?" Caitlin asked.

I shut the lid. "Only need one bullet, if you know how to aim. This doesn't make any sense. Why would he camp out here?"

Caitlin glanced to a boarded-over window. "He would have had to fix the van up to get it running again, yes? If he was working alone, and not familiar with that kind of engine, it could have taken him a few days."

I pushed myself back to my feet.

"Hell of a lot of effort. Too much effort."

"The man is clearly insane," she said. "You heard him at the party."

"Sure. I heard him say he was, what, the great-grandson of the king of vampires or something?" I poked my head into the hallway, looking both ways before I stepped out of the room. "One of the first things anybody learns, coming into the occult underground, is that vampires aren't real. No, he looked ridiculous because he was *trying* to look ridiculous. It's an act."

"To what end?" Caitlin asked.

"Once we figure out why he wants me dead, I imagine we'll know that too."

Of course, even if he was putting on a show at the party for reasons we couldn't puzzle out yet, it didn't mean he wasn't crazy.

We made our way to the administrative offices. Now I was definitely playing tourist. Patients—inmates—weren't allowed in this part of the house. I hadn't missed much, just a jumble of bulky desks, a few swivel chairs on rattling casters, and pile upon pile of old, yellowed record boxes. A row of file cabinets stood with their drawers open, empty, and gathering dead flies.

"Looks like they were getting ready to move all the records off-site," I said, gazing from the cabinets to the stacks of cardboard boxes. "Maybe the funding got pulled, the paychecks stopped coming, and they just...left it like this."

Curiosity sent me thumbing through the nearest box. Caitlin opened another and did the same. They were patient files. Each label bore a set of initials and a registration number. I grabbed one at random. Inside was a fragment of a life, treatment and discipline reports and a staff assessment on pink carbon paper.

"I just realized I never asked," Caitlin said. "What's your middle name, pet?"

"James, why?" I figured it out as she pulled my file from the box and opened it up. The label read *DJF / 882.09*. "Oh, hey, c'mon."

She flashed an impish smile. "I want to see your mug shot."

"It wasn't a mug shot, technically." I walked over to stand at her side. "The point of this place was to be a kinder, gentler alternative to juvie hall. We were patients at risk, undergoing treatment to become productive members of society."

There I was, paper-clipped to the edge of the folder, all acne-pocked cheeks and thin, hard angles and unfocused anger. I looked like I wanted to grab the world by the throat and squeeze. I remembered feeling that way pretty much all the time, and nobody was in a hurry to give me a reason not to.

"You matured nicely," Caitlin murmured. One scarlet fingernail stroked my photograph's cheek. "Filled out, but not too much, cleaner skin, better hair."

I didn't think I looked any different. Maybe I'd just taken my face off at some point and flipped it inside out, so all the acne and hate were on the inside now. I didn't want to look at my file anymore. My eyes drifted to the box, to the parade of initials and numbers.

HMG / 796.88

"Hold on a sec." I tugged out the folder and opened it up. As soon as I did, I felt a momentary flash of disappointment. The name inside wasn't Hunter MacGregor Grimm, it was Harry Michael Grimes. But then I leafed over a pink carbon page and found his photograph underneath. Younger—too young to be trapped in the justice system, he'd been twelve at the oldest when it was taken—with smoldering eyes and baby fat on his cheeks. The eyes were what drew me in.

"Cait, look at this. Age him up by twenty years—you think this could be our guy?"

She tapped her finger against her lips, brow furrowed as she studied the picture.

"Same facial structure, jawline is identical...if it isn't him, he could be his brother."

The staff had done half their job before they'd packed up and moved on to greener pastures. Whatever crime he'd committed to land himself in the caring hands of the Wellness House had been expunged from the file. What remained didn't tell me a damn thing, just a smattering of incident reports and—

My finger froze on a single line. "*HMG remanded to Seg/Disp for time-out after fight w/ other patients. Patient DJF initiated altercation, claimed to be defending HMG.*"

"Cait," I breathed, "I *knew* him."

* * *

I needed fresh air. There wasn't anything left to find inside the musty, stifling halls, so we took the files—Harry Grimes's, in case there was more to see, and mine, so I could burn it later—and climbed out the first-floor window. It was dark now, and the desert sky was a cold onyx slate streaked with wispy gray clouds.

I sat on the porch steps. Caitlin perched beside me. I paged through the file by the light of my phone one more time. I had just been given a lesson in the fallibility of memory, the halls and doors of the Wellness House rearranging themselves to defy my expectations, and I wanted to be sure I hadn't confused some half-remembered nightmare with reality.

But I remembered. I mostly remembered feeling helpless. All the time. Powerless, trapped, bound by pointless rules and the orderlies' casual brutality. My hands were shackled, even when they weren't.

It's good to know the things we fear most, the Lady in Red whispered in my ear.

There had been a pecking order among the patients, a hierarchy of wolves and sheep, and I wasn't having that. Syd and his boys had just cornered a new patient, this chubby kid, couldn't have been more than twelve. My first swing cracked Syd's chin open and split my knuckles, and the pain was like a blessing. I was angry for myself and I was angry for this kid who didn't deserve the shakedown, and I only knew one way to let all that anger out. So I punched and punched and the entire world became a beautiful chorus of broken skin and blood and I tasted copper in my mouth, and I think I was screaming but by then the orderlies were dog-piling us, dragging me away, shouting at me to stop resisting.

I would never stop resisting.

"So...you helped him," Caitlin said. "Tried to protect him."

"I think so, yeah."

"Then why is he trying to murder you now?"

I didn't have an answer for that.

I needed more intel on Harry Michael Grimes. I suspected Gary wasn't in the mood to do me any favors right now. I'd let him cool off some, and come to grips with the Santiago situation, before I darkened his doorstep again. That left one other contact with inside access.

"Is this good news?" Mayor Seabrook asked.

I shifted on the rough porch step, phone loose against my ear. "I have a suspect who might pose a credible threat. I'm not sure if he has a police record, but if he does, I need to know where he's been and who his known associates are."

I didn't say what kind of credible threat. If she took my words to mean that Grimes was connected to the ink trade or that he was dangerous to her personally, well, I didn't *technically* lie.

"I can put in a request through Earl's office," she said. "How does this help me?"

"Well, he's in Vegas with a stolen van, a gun, and some real bad intentions."

I gave her a name, date of birth, all the hard facts from Harry's partial file. Once again, vagueness saved the day. The mayor filled in the details with her imagination, and whatever she decided, she found me worthy. I gave her one of my throwaway email addresses; they were free and didn't require any ID to create, so I always kept a couple on standby in case I needed one.

"I'll see if I can have it expedited." She hung up. No goodbyes required.

"Home?" Caitlin asked.

"Home."

Nothing more we could do here, not tonight. We walked back to her car together. I turned in the driveway, hand on the passenger door, and took one long last look.

"Are you all right?" she asked.

"It's just a building."

We drove back through the desert, two more hours on the open highway. As the hot lights of Vegas loomed up ahead, welcoming us back to the neon playground, the mayor returned my call.

"My admin just sent the details to your email," she told me. "This Grimes character is dangerous. Earl wanted to know why I wanted his records."

"What did you tell him?"

"That he's the commissioner, and he serves at the pleasure of the mayor's office, which means he's to do as I say and not ask questions. But I put that in much nicer words. I'm going to be out of touch after tonight, getting ready to head to the conference."

"I really wish you wouldn't go," I said. "Not until I'm absolutely certain it's safe."

"It's fine. Earl is coming with me, we have Tall Pines on security detail, and Metro is giving us a full escort to and from the hotel. I'll be safer than I am at home."

I wasn't so sure. A bunch of civic-minded mayors coming together in one place to discuss how they were going to tackle the ink epidemic—and with it, the Network's cash cow—felt like a disaster waiting to happen. But Seabrook had a cast-iron backbone and she wasn't going to bend for me or anybody. I wished her luck.

"Anything useful?" Caitlin asked me. I was flipping through the scattered files Seabrook's assistant had sent over. It was a haphazard collection of scanned documents, some of them nearly two decades old, tracing the edges of a hard-knock life.

"The Wellness House was just the start for this kid," I said. "In juvie, out of juvie. In county jail, out of county. Graduated to an assault with a deadly weapon charge two days after his twenty-first birthday. State pen for that."

In between the lines, a pattern started to form. Allegations, lists of known ties, suspicions. Everything came together to point a red arrow in a too-familiar direction.

"I know what he wants," I said. "And I know who sent him."

33.

The proof of intent came from all the crimes Harry Grimes *didn't* go down for. He'd been seen at the scene of a Smaldone family hit, two members of the "Mountain Mafia" gunned down in the middle of dinner, but the feds couldn't make a concrete connection. He was linked to the death of an heiress who committed "suicide" by diving into her soaking tub with a plugged-in toaster, but his hands were cleaner than the water. Then he'd been questioned in the disappearance of a Teamster boss. His alibi was airtight for that one, just like the construction drum that the boss's tortured corpse turned up in two years later.

"He's an assassin," Caitlin said after I read some choice excerpts to her.

"Pay for play," I said, "and considering these are just the killings they think he had a hand in but can't prove, I can't guess how many he's gotten away with. Forget all the BS he spouted at the party, it was a smoke screen. Harry Grimes is being *paid* to kill me, pure and simple."

She frowned. Her hands flexed on the steering wheel.

"And you believe you know who sent him?"

"He's a cambion, so even if he doesn't have formal ties to the courts of hell, he's aware of them. He moves in both underworlds—infernal and criminal."

"With you so far," she said.

"He's legally a transient with no fixed address, but check the pattern for the last five years. Every time he's been hauled in for questioning, it's been in Colorado. Aurora, Fort Collins, Pueblo..."

"Denver," Caitlin said. She'd already put it together.

"And who do we know in Denver? Same person who just happened to show up at the party, and threw me off-balance just in time for 'Hunter Grimm' to make his grand entrance."

"*Naavarasi.*" Now her knuckles were turning white. She swerved onto an off-ramp, too sharp, leaning into the wheel.

"Which might...well, not explain all this other weirdness, but it's Naavarasi. We can figure ninety percent of it was just there to confuse us or throw us off the scent."

"Or there are more layers to this," Caitlin said. "As is likely the case—we know that from hard experience. I suppose your attempt at mercy, in your teens, won't be enough to stay this man's hand."

I shook my head. "Nah. Murder for hire is a sociopath's game. I can't expect him to sit down with me and laugh about old times."

Then the idea hit me.

"Cait...if we can prove Naavarasi hired him, what does that do for us?"

"It makes her fair game." Her lips pursed in a grim, determined smile. "Dispatching an unlicensed assassin to kill a member of another court—*if* we can prove she did it, which is always the challenge—is just as bad as using her own hands. Prince Malphas will have no choice but to cast her to the wolves. What did you have in mind, pet?"

"Forget what I just said. I want to sit down with him and laugh about old times," I said. "And then I want to flip him. I was thinking about something Royce said to me, back at the party: 'defection is always an option.'"

* * *

Grimes was out there, somewhere, hunting me down in the urban wilds. I couldn't sit around waiting, so I decided to make it easier for him. He didn't know where I lived, or he already would have hit my place, and he couldn't track my ride now that it was a smoking piece of wreckage. The one place I knew he could watch for me—would watch for me—was where we'd first met. Winter.

Caitlin called ahead. A pair of bouncers met us near the nightclub's unmarked double doors, pushing the line back so we could get right up to the bare brick wall. One handed me a can of cherry-red spray paint. I shook it up, aimed, and wrote my missive in big, curling letters.

CALL ME – DJF

One of the partygoers in line shook his head. "She ain't gonna call you, bro! Give it up."

"Aw," his date said. "I think it's romantic. For an old guy."

A streamer of paint drooled down the bumpy brick off the bottom of the *F*, darkening as it dried, like a rivulet of blood. We left. I wanted him to see my message, not to actually take a shot at me on-site. Caitlin and I were driving around, thinking about grabbing a bite to eat, when my phone rang twenty minutes later.

"I can read the writing on the wall," Harry Grimes told me. "Can you?"

"Sure. It says, 'you picked the wrong target this time.'"

"I never pick wrong. And I never miss."

"What if I could convince you otherwise?" I asked.

"I'm listening."

"Listen to me over a drink instead. There's a bar on the casino floor at the Monaco. Nice and public and well-lit, and nobody shoots anybody there."

"First time for everything," he said.

"The Monaco is CMC Entertainment property," I said, "and you aren't going to start shit on CMC Entertainment property."

"How do you know?"

"Because your name isn't Hunter MacGregor Grimm. It's Harry Michael Grimes, and you're only *pretending* to be crazy."

He went silent for so long I thought he might have hung up. Then he said: "The Monaco. Twenty minutes."

* * *

I always came back to the Monaco. That innate masochism

again, I guess. Back in the day, I'd exorcised a stubborn ghost from the penthouse floor. Well, not *exorcised* so much as *relocated.* Then, when I was scrapping with the Redemption Choir, I'd brought a supposedly innocent priest here to keep him safe while I tried to line up an escape plan. That night had ended in a betrayal and a vicious beating. Basically, I didn't have a lot of good memories to keep me coming back. Maybe just the ramen dishes at Umami—and as I passed through the smoked-glass doors into the casino, moving from the desert night chill to the perfectly regulated air-conditioning, I realized that entire side of the casino floor was covered in heavy sheets of plywood. Everything was shut down, the resort under heavy renovation from its hairline down to its toes, wiping away the old to bring in the new.

And I had worked up an appetite for ramen on the way over. Some nights, I just couldn't win.

At least Ignition, the lounge on the edge of the casino, was open for business. A bar circled a central pylon, and plush chairs and two-seater tables radiated out all around it like the ripples of an explosion. Slow lights shifted across the cherry-red carpet, painting the tourists in simulated fire, while chimes and shrill melodies burst from the gaming floor.

Caitlin came in two minutes after me and disappeared into the crowd. She'd be there, watching. Close enough to move if Harry pulled his gun? Probably not, so I'd just have to make sure he didn't. Or if he didn't leave me any other choice, take him down before he got the chance. I found an open couple of chairs, staked my territory, and got as comfortable as I could. I looked around, taking it all in. The construction made me think of the American, my own little piece of Vegas. The principal construction was done and now it was all down to the detail work before our grand opening. Details, and the liquor license I still didn't have. I almost got lost in minutiae, making mental lists of the calls I needed to make, the cash I had to shuffle around to make this opening happen, when I spotted my guest pushing through the smoked-glass doors.

Harry Grimes had shed some of his rock-star flamboyance from the party. He'd traded the skintight leather pants for battered jeans and thrown a tank top on. One arm was still sheathed in blue Viking runes from his shoulder to his wrist; apparently the tattoos were real. He swaggered to the two-seater and dropped down across from me. Before I could get a word out, he held up two fingers to a passing waitress.

"Jack," he said, "neat."

"Jack and Coke, please," I added.

He snorted at me as she headed to the bar.

"A real man doesn't have to cut his liquor."

"A real man drinks what tastes good," I told him, "and doesn't worry about what other people think."

"Oh, you care. You care plenty. Client told me that little crazy act at your party would rattle you good. You were all twisted up, not sure how to come at me. And in the end you buckled, just like they said you would."

"Let's talk about your client," I said.

"Let's not," he shot back. "I'm a professional."

"A professional would have taken me out. I showed you my back and you stood down."

"As if I was going to make a move in the middle of that crowd?" He laughed at me. "They would have torn me to shreds. I needed you to swing first. That'd leave my hands clean. Us lowly cambion have to abide by the letter of the Cold Peace, after all. Even when it means the higher-ups can do whatever they want, up to and including hunting us for sport."

"Is that what this is about?"

"Not your problem to worry about. Oh, no, Daniel Faust, a pure human, not one *drop* of demonic blood, and *you* get a knighthood."

"That's what this is about." I sat back in my chair. "You're jealous."

"Wrong. I don't want a damn thing you've got."

The waitress came around. We stared in silent détente while

she drew the battle lines on the laminated table between us, laying down napkins and drinks. Harry didn't move a muscle. Apparently, I was buying. I paid cash, added a ten on top, and told her to keep the change.

"Do you even know who I am?" I asked him.

"Sure. You're the hound's pet human. Oh, and you think you're a tough guy because you've got half the gangs in this city ready to fight for you. And that's your problem. You're *insulated*. You're *fake*."

"Okay." I sipped my drink. Tiny icebergs clinked against the glass, floating on a caramel sea. "First of all, I've never described myself as a tough guy. If people want to put that label on me, that's their problem."

He looked down his nose at me. "Got that right."

"Second of all, is that all you know? Do you even remember me? From the Wellness House."

"You kidding me, man? That's why I *took* this contract, once I saw who the target was. Once I saw how soft you'd gone...biggest disappointment of my life, right there."

I shook my head at him, feeling like I'd lost the plot.

"How do you mean?"

"You stood up for me in that shithole," he said. "More than once."

Memory tricks again. I only remembered the one time, but I'd take his word for it. Felt like something I would have done, at that age.

"Sure," I said.

"You remember what you told me? I was this sniveling, pudgy little nothing, and you took me aside and said that unless I started standing up for myself, unless I started punching back, those guys would keep jumping me."

"It's good advice."

"You told me that I had to stop being afraid—afraid of losing, afraid of getting hurt—that I should take all that fear and get angry. Get so angry that I didn't feel anything *but* angry, and then *hurt* those fuckers. Fists, teeth, fight with anything I had, any way I could. Cripple them if I could. Kill them if I could get away with it."

"Yeah, well," I said, "I wasn't exactly healthy back then. We were kids in a bad place."

He waved an incredulous hand at me. "See? That's what I'm talking about. Why are you apologizing? You were *right*."

"I wasn't right. Yes, you should have defended yourself, and I'm glad you did, but that was some messed-up stuff to say to a twelve-year-old. I didn't know any better back then. I do now. You can't let anger rule you; it's a tool, not your master."

"I got out, and I hit the road." He tossed back a swig of Jack. The five-o'clock shadow glistened above his lip. "Found out that philosophy worked everywhere. Stoke the anger in me, put the fear in everybody else. If somebody got in my way, bang. If somebody stepped to me, bang. Turns out, when you're a genuine, no-nonsense tough guy, the world's your oyster. You can take anything you want. Do anything you want."

He raised his glass to me and pounded back the rest of his liquor.

"And I owe it all to you," Harry told me. "You made me the man I am today."

34.

The waitress came around and Harry ordered a second glass of Jack, neat. I was still nursing my first drink. Not that I didn't want it—and two or three more chasing right behind the first—but I needed to keep my head on straight.

"See," he told me, "when I realized how pathetically *neutered* you are, I said to myself, 'he's gotta go.' It's like putting down your pet dog when he gets too sick to walk. Has to be done, and after what you did for me back in the day, I wouldn't want anyone else to do the job."

"You've got a weird definition of 'neutered.'"

"Do I? You didn't get that knighthood because you're tougher than anyone in Sitri's court. You got it by sleeping your way to the top. And this 'New Commission' garbage? So, what, you sit behind a desk and send other people to commit crimes? What kind of bullshit is that? That's no way for an outlaw to live. And don't get me started about how your little friends come running every time the heat is on, all ready to bail you out."

The casino vents gusted cool air across the backs of my hands. My fingers tightened, ever so slightly, on the leather arms of my chair. I felt like I was wearing a jacket of ice. Buried deep underneath, a serpentine vein of angry heat started to pulse. And grow. I took a slow, deep breath, keeping it under control.

"The party," he said, "that was all the proof I needed. After I talked shit about you, your girl, and your entire court? A real man would have thrown hands right there on the spot. You're weak."

"Have you ever heard the phrase 'when all you have is a hammer, everything looks like a nail?'"

Harry squinted at me. "What about it?"

"You said you hit the road when you got out of the Wellness House. I'm guessing you didn't have a family to go back to."

"Not one I wanted to go back to. I stopped back a few months later, just for one night. Just long enough to thank my dad for all that 'strong parental discipline' he showed me for so many years, and my mom for letting it happen."

The waitress swung around again with a fresh drink for my guest. I paid her. He waited, silent, until she retreated out of earshot.

"I made him watch while I cut her throat. Figured it'd hurt the old man more that way, watching her die before I took my time with him. Anger. Fear. I did it just the way you taught me." He reached for his drink. "We are what the world made us. Fighting that's a waste of time. Look at us. I embraced everything we endured, and I became an apex predator. And you? You're a sad, washed-up pile of nothing."

I wanted to get through to him. I *needed* to get through to him. I didn't know how much of this was my responsibility, how much of this monster I'd created in the nightmare laboratory of the Wellness House—how much was me, how much was the other inmates, the abusive orderlies, his own father long before I even crossed Harry's path—but some of it...some of it was on me. I had to make things right if I could.

"Look," I said, "sure, we are what the world made us. We're gladiators, predators, whatever messed-up metaphor you want to go with, it's all the same. But we can change. My brother Teddy, he went through worse than we did. I went to the Wellness House, but he had to go back to *our* house, with our violently insane father, for years, all alone. Know what he does now? Private security. He makes his money by *protecting* people. He's a good guy."

"Yeah? If it's so easy...why don't you do it?"

I didn't have an answer for that.

"Because you don't want to," Harry told me. "Because this life, this world we live in? You love it. You love the blood and the gunsmoke and the smell of somebody else's money. Don't even try to deny it."

I thought about that. Then I sipped my drink, eyeing the ring of condensation it left behind on the napkin. He was right. I couldn't take the high ground here, and I couldn't show him the light when I didn't live in it.

"When all you have is a hammer," I said, "everything looks like a nail."

"Second time you've said it, second time I don't know why."

I fixed him in my gaze, locking eyes over my glass. My jacket of ice became a suit of armor and I spoke very gently, very firmly. It was the voice I used when I explained why someone was going to give me what I wanted, when I wanted it, and the only threat I needed was in the tone of my voice.

"You see me as weak because you only know one way to be strong. You think it's weak when I rely on my friends, because you don't understand that we rely on each other. That I'd shed blood—mine or anybody else's—for any of them without question. I've done it before and I'll do it again, proudly, because they're my family."

He sneered at me over his glass. "A real tough guy doesn't *need* a family."

"And as for Caitlin? She's my rock. My motivation to get my shit together and build a life, to build something real. When people are in love, when they're partners—partners down to the bone—that's not weakness. That's a force multiplier. Together, we're more than twice as strong as we are apart."

Harry rolled his eyes. "You're embarrassing yourself."

"Oh, I'm embarrassed, all right. By you."

That got his attention. He sat up straight.

"The fuck did you say? I'm twice the man you are."

"Right. Because you're 'tough.' You want to know what being

tough really means? It isn't about being good in a fight. It's about having something to fight *for*. You don't stand for anything, Harry. You don't fight for anyone but yourself, and that means you could win a hundred battles and it still wouldn't mean a damn thing. But I can help you."

"You think *you* can help *me*," he said.

"Come work for me," I told him. "Join the New Commission. Join my crew, and I'll show you a different way of doing things. A better way."

"Not happening."

"I pay better than Naavarasi does."

I watched his face, hoping for a sign. A flicker of recognition, the momentary fear that I knew more than I was supposed to. Anything at all.

"Never heard of him," Harry said, his poker face unbreakable.

I'd done my best. I'd appealed to his heart, I'd made a sales pitch, and it had all bounced right off. He wanted this one way and one way only.

"I guess I'm going to have to teach you something else, then," I told him.

"I'm all ears."

"How to be a professional." I contemplated my glass, barely looking at him now. "You *talk*, Harry. You talk, and you talk. That car bomb would have killed me if you could have stopped yapping long enough to set it off on time. It's important to you, isn't it? You want your victims to see you coming. You like the fear too much. You get off on it. I bet you have a little speech you like to give before you pull the trigger."

"Something wrong with that?"

"It's sloppy and it's stupid," I said. "A real professional doesn't talk. Save the quips for the movies. You get in, you do your job, and you get out. And that's what I'm going to teach you."

For the first time since he sat down and started drinking on my dime, I saw a flicker of uncertainty in his eyes.

"How are you going to do that?" he asked.

"When I kill you," I said, "I won't say a word. No speeches, no drama, no one-liners. You'll be alive, then suddenly you won't be. You won't even see it coming."

His heavy-lidded gaze slid up and down my body. Patting me down with his eyes and trying to guess what I was carrying.

"How about we get this over with?" he said.

"My thoughts exactly. I know a place."

"Yeah?"

"The parking garage on Lamb Boulevard," I said. "Only one security guard, the upper deck is clear, and we can dance there. We can dance all night long. Meet me there. Two hours."

"Better be there, Faust. If you run, I'll find you."

He stood, stretched, and downed his second drink. He tossed the empty glass onto the table between us and let it rattle.

"That little speech I like to give, before I pull the trigger?" He pointed a finger-gun at me. "Can't wait for you to hear it."

I watched him go; then I took out my phone.

"Nicky," I said, "you know that favor you're going to owe me, for helping out in Reno? I need to cash it in early."

* * *

I didn't go to the Lamb Boulevard parking garage. Caitlin drove me two blocks south, to a condo tower under heavy construction. Taped windows looked in on dark and empty homes. Seven stories up, the tower became a fleshless skeleton of bare girders and flapping, ghost-white tarp.

"You're sure about this?" she asked me. The Audi's engine purred as we idled at the curb.

"On the off chance he survives, I need someone at the garage and in position to follow him. We can't let this guy slip away. If he does, we'll be fighting on *his* terms again and waiting around for him to take his next shot. We've got the advantage tonight. Let's make the most of it."

She grabbed my shirt collar and yanked me close, pulling me into the kind of kiss I wished would never end. Foolish hope.

Eventually, all kisses did; that's how you knew it was time to go to work.

The lobby door had been left unlocked for me. So had the stairs. I climbed up to the fifth floor, one long slog up granite steps painted in yellow lines, by the light of my phone. An industrial light sconce and a stenciled number marked every turn, but there were no bulbs in the sconces and no juice to power them.

The fifth floor was finished and model-home ready. All they needed was light, furniture, and to clear out the painters' tarps still taped over half the walls. The stairwell opened up onto a long corridor tiled in ivory and lined with open doors. Brand-new apartments waited over every threshold, with shag carpet and floor-to-ceiling windows looking out over the Vegas lights. The air smelled like fresh paint.

"Down here!" Juliette called, waving to me from the door of apartment 503. She grabbed my wrist and pulled me inside, bouncing with a sugar-high buzz. A cold breeze rippled through the empty apartment and ruffled the tarps. It came in from one of the windows, where her sister had cut out a ring of glass the size of a manhole cover.

"Hey, Danny." Justine sauntered over with a military-grade range finder, twirling the olive plastic box on her finger by a lanyard strap. "Nicky says you want to play with our toys."

Juliette's hands closed over my shoulders from behind, nails digging in like ten black-painted needles. She leaned close and whispered, "Sure you wouldn't rather *be* one?"

"Ladies," I said.

"We're just saying," Justine added as she trailed a finger down my chest, "we could teach you some new games."

"We've got games for *days*," Juliette whispered. She blew a puff of hot breath across my earlobe.

"As...enticing as that invitation is," I said, "I have work to do. Did you bring what I needed?"

"*Ugh*." Juliette's hands suddenly gave me a shove, pushing me deeper into the apartment. "Party pooper. You never want to have any fun."

Her sister sighed and pointed with a melodramatic flourish. "If you insist on being boring, fine. There you go."

They'd gone above and beyond the call of duty. There was the ring of glass, sliced away with laser precision and opening up the night. Beside it, a three-legged stool and a long, low table set up with a folding tripod. And perched in delicate balance, with its elongated barrel aimed out across the city, a sniper rifle.

35.

I settled onto the stool and squeezed one eye shut, leaning into the rifle's scope. The lens showed me distant visions, like a witch's crystal ball; it honed in on the sodium lights of the parking garage's upper deck, a span of concrete, and a few forlorn cars, scattered between the yellow lines.

"That's called a scope," Juliette said, hovering over my left shoulder. "It lets you murder people who are far away."

"Yes," I said. "I'm aware. Thank you."

On my right, Justine showed me her range finder. "We've already dialed you in. Do you know what that means, Danny?"

"I have fired a gun before."

Both of the twins clasped their hands to their mouths in horror.

"He did *not*," Juliette said.

"He *did*." Justine gaped at me. "This is not a *gun*, Danny. This is a Barrett MRAD bolt-action sniper rifle. It is chambered for .300 Winchester Magnum rounds, it features a single-button length-of-pull adjustment and a polymer bolt guide that keeps dust from getting into the action. The magazine release is ambidextrous, the safety is reversible, and it has a twenty-four-inch barrel! It is a model of modern warfare, it's been adapted by the armed forces of Israel, Norway, and New Zealand, and it is available in multiple colors, *all of which are shades of black!*"

"You apologize," Juliette hissed in my ear. "You apologize to our rifle *right now*."

I gave the stock a gentle, if awkward pat.

"I...apologize for besmirching your good name."

"That's better," Justine said with a relieved sigh. "See? Now the four of us are friends again."

"We don't know why you want to take the shot yourself, though," her sister said. "We're so much better at shooting than you are. I mean, we're better at *everything* than you are."

"But mostly shooting," Justine said.

I wasn't sure how I could explain it to them. I wasn't sure if I understood it myself, beyond some fumbling gut instinct. I had tried to reason with Harry Grimes. I had failed. And now, at his insistence, I was out of options: one of us was going to die tonight.

Letting the twins handle this was the smart play. I'd seen them in action; up close or at range, the only person I knew deadlier than Juliette and Justine was Caitlin herself. I'd even picked the site of Harry's execution with them in mind. Back in the bad old days, Nicky had put a hit on one of his own men. I was standing next to the poor sap, on that very garage rooftop, when Juliette blew his head off from twelve hundred meters away. This perch was a lot closer. She wouldn't miss.

All the same, I needed to do this.

I understood Harry Grimes. He'd been a scared, hurting kid in a bad place, and inside the walls of the Wellness House he made the same discovery I did: that monsters didn't feel pain. Our lives had branched in different directions, but how much of that was simple luck? If Bentley and Corman hadn't pulled me off the streets and taught me a better way—if they hadn't taught me that the world had value, that *I* had value—I would have ended up just like him.

I didn't create Harry Grimes, but I had a hand in what he'd become. And that made killing him my responsibility.

"I need you downstairs with the getaway car," I told them. "Just in case the shot gets called in by some solid citizen and I have to leave in a hurry."

It was a flimsy excuse, but they let it slide. Justine pointed to the rifle.

"This part is the trigger. You pull that when you want the rifle to go bang."

"I'll make a note," I said.

"You can make it go bang five times," her sister added. "After that point, until you load more bang-making devices, it will no longer go bang."

"I should only need it to go bang once."

Damn it, now I was doing it. They left arm in arm, finally, thankfully.

"So explain this again," I heard Juliette ask in the hall. "Are we *not* having a threesome now? I'm so confused."

"No, he just wants to use our rifle."

"But...okay, no, still confused. He wants to use the rifle *then* the threesome? Hasn't he heard of multitasking? Why does he have to make everything so difficult?"

Their voices faded as they reached the stairwell. Then there was nothing but me, the cold night wind streaming in through the circle of cut glass, and the sounds of the streets below. Distant horns, engine hums, the background noise of ordinary people living their ordinary lives.

Right now, while I prepared to commit a murder in cold blood, my brother was home with his wife and kid. I imagined them sitting around the dining table and sharing a meal, talking about their ordinary day. Washing dishes together, settling in on the couch with a bowl of popcorn to watch television.

Me, my brother, Harry. Some people like to think they're the masters of their fate, but the bends of our lives are so much luck and chaos. One missed call, one change of heart, go left instead of right, and your future is transformed. A twist of fate, and Teddy could have been up here instead of me, watching the rooftops through a high-powered scope and waiting for a victim. I could have been in Harry's shoes, a killer with no friends, no family, no future, confusing brutality and cruelty with strength.

I couldn't control the tides of fate. I could only make the occasional tiny adjustment. That's what the rifle was for.

Nothing to do now but watch, and wait, and shiver as I leaned into the scope and the cold. Harry still hadn't shown, and we were twenty minutes past the two-hour mark. I wondered if he was on some other rooftop, with some other rifle, looking for me the same way. No. He was an up-close-and-personal kind of killer. He was addicted to the last words before the trigger pull, savoring the fear in his victims' eyes. He'd need me to face him, to get some kind of acknowledgment that he'd bested me.

I heard the stairwell door clang and stifled a groan. Asking the twins to sit patiently for more than ten minutes at a stretch was like begging for a miracle. They'd probably driven around the block five times already, then gotten bored.

"Seriously," I said, keeping my eye on the scope. "This won't take long. Just watch the car, okay?"

"Damn right it won't take long," Harry said.

I spun as he charged at me, coming on like a mad bull and lunging through the open apartment doorway. For a big guy he was faster than he looked. No time for the scope, and he'd just be a blur at this range. I hip-fired, the Barrett bucking wildly in my grip. The round went wide and blasted open a chunk of freshly painted wall. His fist buried itself in my gut, doubling me over as the breath burst from my lungs. I staggered back. My shoulders bumped against the glass and I swung the rifle like a bat. The steel cracked against his shoulder but it didn't slow him down.

He swatted the rifle out of my grip and sent it tumbling across the new shag carpet, then grabbed me by the lapels and swung me around. A second later I was tumbling too, flying free and hitting the floor hard on my back. He flexed his tattooed arm. The ink flared to life, blazing sapphire blue as the Nordic patterns flowed like serpents under his skin. Then his cupped palm erupted with blue fire.

I rolled left as a gout of wildfire splashed across the carpeting. It like a meteor, leaving a charred trail and spreading flames in its wake. I scrambled to my feet, going for my pistol. One beefy hand locked around my wrist and the other, glowing azure and hot as an oven, clamped down on my throat.

Harry swung me around again and slammed me against one of the floor-to-ceiling windows, hard enough for the glass to rattle in its frame. Then again. The room crackled as the fires spread, going hazy with swirling smoke.

"What do you think will break first?" he asked me with a brutish smirk. "You or the window? Let's find out."

The back of my skull slapped against the glass. I gasped, sucking down smoke, then coughed it up while Harry shook me by the throat like a rag doll. My vision blurred, eyes tearing up. I knew I'd be out like a light in less than twenty seconds. And then I'd be dead, either left for the flames or thrown to the street below.

Not today. I had one free hand and one shot left. I fumbled in my pocket, tugging open Bentley's velvet pouch, and felt crusty clay under my fingertips. I scooped up two of the alchemist's clay marbles, curling them against my palm, and used the last of my strength to charge them with a jolt of raw magic.

"C'mon, say something," Harry demanded. "*Say something!*"

I'd read him right. He could have finished me by now, but he needed the fear response. He needed the power high. He killed for money, but this was the part he lived for.

I answered with my fist. Not to throw a punch, but to hurl the marbles of clay to the floor at our feet. They exploded, violent and raw, spewing columns of choking green gas with a cobra's hiss. I knew to hold my breath when they went off. Harry didn't. As the green mist blotted out the world in a heartbeat, I heard him cough and his grip went slack.

I twisted my other wrist, pulling free, and slipped loose from the clinch. Then I sprinted, blind, heading for what I hoped was the apartment door. I broke from the mist and the spreading fire smoke, green and black weaving together above the flames like a nightmare hellscape, and stood in the doorway just long enough to pull my nine-millimeter.

I spent all seven rounds into the smoke, firing fast and free.

I couldn't see Harry, didn't know if I'd hit him or anything at all, but I had to try. I holstered the empty gun as I ran for the stairwell door. Then it was one long sprint to the bottom, leaving me breathless and my shirt caked in sweat. My lungs strained for air, throat raw from the smoke and the panic.

A cherry-red Jaguar screeched up to the curb. Justine and Juliette stared at me from the front seats.

"I don't know if you know this, but you set the building on fire," Juliette said, pointing upward. Flames roiled behind broken glass, spreading to the neighboring apartments. "Did you mean to do that?"

"Where's our rifle?" Justine asked.

I jumped in back and slapped the seat. "Go. *Drive!*"

"Okay," Juliette said, stepping on the gas. The Jag lurched into the street and picked up speed. "So...I'm guessing you didn't mean to do that."

I looked out the back window as we veered away from the burning building, watching the street for any sign of Harry Grimes. I wanted to think I'd hit him from the doorway, but I knew better than to hope; I'd heard breaking glass but not a single grunt of pain. I had to assume he'd gotten away in one piece.

That wasn't the part that bothered me. Neither did his occult tattoos and burning hand, even as I poked at my raw, aching neck. He was a cambion, after all, and a hit man who worked in the occult underground would have to pick up a magic trick or two along the way. I'd seen weirder forms of attack.

But nothing explained how, with an entire city to battle across, he'd not only picked up on the double cross but found my sniper perch. I could only figure it one way: that he'd told one more lie, back at the party. He wasn't a one-man army and he sure as hell wasn't a lone wolf. Someone—if not Naavarasi, whoever was pulling Harry's strings—was backing him up from the shadows, keeping track of my movements, and pointing him at me like a loaded gun.

36.

Lately, when I needed to think, I went to the American.

It was starting to look like a club. The drywall was up and wooden floors were down, waiting to receive their coats of paint and tile. Areas had been roughed out: the kidney-shaped curve of the stage, big enough for a live band, and the span of the dance floor. Strips of tape marked where the bar would be installed, where shelves would hold top-grade liquor, where plush leather booths would run along a short stretch of wall. We had built the rough outline of a dream.

Usually, a slow walk around the place picked my spirits up. This was going to be my legacy, my piece of Vegas history. Tonight, it was nothing but an empty nightclub. Of course, I'd just gotten my ass kicked, I had first-degree burns on my throat in the rough shape of a hand, and my ribs were aching, but that wasn't it. I had a head full of questions and I couldn't navigate my way to any good answers.

"Got your message," Caitlin said, standing in the doorway. She held a bottle in one hand and two glasses in the other. "Thought you might want a pick-me-up."

She knew me. Better than anyone. We set the bottle—Veuve Clicquot Yellow Label—on a board stretched between a pair of sawhorses, and I popped the cork while she held out the glasses. I poured for us both. A standing work light shed its low, dusky beam across the floorboards and framed us in the gloom.

"Feels sacrilegious, drinking champagne in here before the grand opening," I said.

"Oh goodness." She lifted her eyebrows at me. "Not sacrilege. I can't be a party to that."

"Cute."

She took out her phone and eyed the screen. "By the way, the twins are demanding reimbursement for their missing rifle. Also they want a formal apology from my court and one pound of imported Swiss chocolate as well as, and I quote, 'four hours of violent angry sex followed by six hours of make-up sex.'"

"With you, or with me?"

"They didn't specify." She glanced to the phone again. "Should I ask?"

"Nah, don't encourage them."

I clinked my glass against hers, and we drank.

"Also," she said, "word from Jennifer. She has some people—the ones she can trust to be discreet—combing through the rest of Donaghy Waste Management's paper trail. She's hoping to find some kind of lead to another Network front. Now that we know there *is* one nearby, thanks to the late Officer Santiago."

"I'd help if I could, just..." I waved my free hand, biting down a wave of frustration. "Little distracted right now, you know? I've got to take care of Harry Grimes before Elmer realizes I'm not chasing him and doubles back. I don't need *two* assholes trying to kill me at the same time."

"And, we can presume, Naavarasi."

My brow furrowed. I stared into the flute of champagne like the bubbles might tell me the future.

"I'm not so sure," I said. "When I dropped her name to Harry, it bounced right off him. Of course, he could just be good at playing his cards close."

"Or he doesn't know who he works for. She can be anyone she wants to be, after all."

"What I do know is I'm only standing here because Harry's got one weakness: he's addicted to the kill. Likes to draw it out." I leaned against the drywall while my neck and my feet competed to see which could ache harder. "He's got a résumé, sure, but he's still an amateur. He could have taken me out with that car bomb if he didn't love the sound of his own voice so much. Could have killed me tonight, too, but he wanted to play with his food."

Caitlin folded her arms and cradled her glass. "A weakness like that can be exploited. Let's find a way."

"I was thinking, before you came in...I think I mentioned once or twice, I had an apprentice, before we met."

"Right," she said. "Desi, wasn't it?"

I nodded, smiling, distant as the memories flowed back to me. The good ones I could smile at.

"Desi Srivastava. Everybody called her Dizzy. Anyway, one night I was telling her how to handle it if she ever had to fight another magician. Forget duels. Duels are for suckers. The best way to take out a magician, I said, was to come up behind him, jam an ice pick between his ribs, and keep walking. If you've got anything to say, say it to his tombstone. You never give your enemy a fair warning or a fair fight."

"You've been thinking about her a lot lately," Caitlin said.

I guess I had. Not that I ever forgot about her. Normally, though, I only saw her face when the whiskey flowed and my walls cracked around the edges.

"It's the Melanie thing," I said. "I'm thinking Bentley might be right. She's going to find a teacher, one way or another. And there are a lot of shitty teachers out there. At least I'd know, with me, she wouldn't get pushed in the deep end too fast, or taken advantage of."

"But," Caitlin said.

"But...it's a lot of responsibility. I gave Bentley and Corman a lot of sleepless nights." I shrugged. "I think I still do. Probably more now than I used to, really."

"Is that all that's staying your hand? Just the responsibility?"

I stared at the floor. The work light's beam cast a line down the dance floor, drawing a fuzzy border between a soft white glow and darkness.

"Desi died on my watch," I said. "I've replayed that moment in my head a thousand times, seeing a thousand ways it could have gone different. One decision here, one second of hesitation there, and she'd still be alive today."

"*Might* still be alive," she said. "You can't know that."

"No. All I know is I'm going to carry her with me until the end of time. And I'm not sure I can go through that again."

Caitlin stepped closer. Our shadows brushed, then our bodies, as she curled her hand around my waist and pulled me in.

"You never told me what happened that night," she said. "Not the details."

"I...thought she was ready. This was back when I was working for Nicky. He'd gotten a line on an easy score. A stack of bearer bonds—untraceable, good as cash—sitting in an investment manager's office safe. So I put a crew together, and we hit the place. When we broke in, the safe was already open and empty. Then somebody—not us—tripped the alarm."

Caitlin's eyes narrowed. Glints of copper swirled in their depths.

"You were set up," she said.

"And ambushed, on our way out. It was this...construct, a crocodile made of sand. Desi, she..."

The words didn't come. My throat wouldn't let them through. Caitlin held me until the blockade opened.

"She was trying to impress me," I said. "But she didn't know what she was up against. She thought it was a demon, tried using a banishing spell, and it just...cut her down. Her and everybody else on my crew. I was the only one who made it out alive. If I'd been a better teacher, if I'd trained her better—"

She pulled me closer. Tighter.

"Did you avenge her?" she asked.

Echoes of grief faded, swallowed by colder, harder memories of vengeance. I felt my heartbeat slow, along with my breath.

"Yeah. I did. Nicky's tipster was in on it, as it turned out. He'd arranged to empty out the safe and frame us for it. His magician was supposed to kill us all, then make the bodies disappear off the face of the earth. When I survived, it wrecked the plan."

Caitlin tilted her head. Her fingertips played at the nape of my neck.

"They wanted you to disappear, so Nicky would assume you'd betrayed him and absconded with the bearer bonds," she said.

"Exactly. He'd be hunting ghosts, never realizing his own informant was laughing behind his back. The guy even laid a paper trail to make it look like we'd fled the country with the score. He bought airline tickets in our names, for the day after—"

I froze. My body went rigid, cold stone, as my mind raced.

"Pet?" Caitlin asked.

I pulled away from her, just to arm's length, and gazed into her eyes.

"The truth has been right in front of us this whole time. Right in my damn face, and I didn't see it. Elmer Donaghy didn't expect me to chase him to Paris and fall into another trap. The trap was right here in Vegas all along. *He. Never. Left.*"

* * *

We were chasing dawn. Good thing I had a bunch of night owls on my crew. Jennifer was first to arrive at the American, stifling a yawn behind her hand, followed by Bentley and Corman. Pixie didn't even look tired, though the can of Red Bull she plowed through on her way in—and the second one she plucked from her laptop bag half a minute later—might have accounted for that.

"When Elmer ran from the fight at his waste management plant," I said, "he left the receipt for his flight to Paris behind. Making it look like an accident, an oversight."

Jennifer nodded and rubbed at one bleary eye. "Right. And then you'd fly to Paris to chase him down, he'd lure you to the company HQ, and kill you on his home turf."

"The creepy little fucker is still playing chess with us. He wanted us to think we saw through his plan. He also wanted us to think we had some time to kill before he came back to Vegas."

Bentley shook his head. The wrinkles on his brow got deeper.

"To what end?" he asked. "To arrange another trap?"

"His so-called 'phase two,'" Caitlin replied. "The project he's been undertaking for his masters in the Network. He needed time to bring it to fruition."

"And he got it, courtesy of Harry Grimes," I said.

Pixie opened up her laptop and cracked a third can of Red Bull. She was starting a row of empties along the sawhorse.

"The guy who's trying to kill you," she said. "Wait, so he's been working for Elmer all along? I thought *Elmer* had to kill you, to get what he wanted from the King of Worms."

I pointed her way. "Exactly. And that's why it didn't even occur to me that they might be on the same team. The king said that Elmer has to kill me with his own hands. If Harry gets the job done, Elmer's shit out of luck. Natural enemies, right?"

"Maybe I'm just overthinking it," Jennifer said, "but lemme take a stab. They're the same person, wearing a magical disguise. Or they got a surgeon and did a hand transplant."

"You are...definitely overthinking it," I said.

"It's after three in the morning, sugar. You're lucky I'm even coherent."

"It's okay, I was overthinking it too, which is how I missed the obvious. Bottom line? Harry *isn't* trying to kill me."

"He put a bomb under your car," Corman said.

"Sure. And he gave me plenty of time to pull over, get out, and run out of the blast range before he set it off. He has a gun—I saw the empty case where he'd been holing up—but he's never even pulled it on me. He beat the hell out of me tonight, but he could have ended me if he had really been trying."

"So Elmer hired an assassin," Jennifer said, "and told him *not* to kill you?"

"Right, because killing me—eventually, on his own terms—is Elmer's job. Harry's job was to do exactly what he did: to keep me chasing him all over town, and give his boss some breathing room. Every step of the way, we've *known* we need to go after the Network, but with Elmer supposedly in Paris and Harry Grimes out for blood, I made Harry my top priority. It was a distraction. A big, elaborate distraction, making me spend all my time and energy hunting a phony threat."

Bentley steepled his fingers, deep in thought. "And in the meantime, Elmer Donaghy has been free to finish his project in peace. For all we know, 'phase two' is already underway. So what do we do about it?"

"We set a trap of our own," I said. "And I'm the bait."

37.

It was a little after four in the morning, inside that momentary pause of breath where the city almost slept. I walked alone down a desolate street, one block from Fremont and a stone's throw from Container Park, where my long-distance death match with Elmer Donaghy had begun.

A short hiss of static burst from the walkie-talkie in my hand, followed by Caitlin's voice. "I still think this plan is too dangerous."

I squeezed the call button. "It's the best way to find Grimes. We know he's going to be looking for me, and we know he's got a means of tracking me across the city. Best thing I can do is give him a nice, juicy target away from any collateral damage."

"And thank you for that," he said, rounding the corner in front of me.

I came to a dead stop. We squared off, ten feet apart.

"I'll call you back," I said to Caitlin and hooked the walkie-talkie onto my belt.

Harry didn't look any worse for wear after our fight in the apartment. He spread his legs in a gunslinger's stance.

"Nice shooting back there," he said. "You *almost* parted my hair."

"In my defense, I couldn't see what I was shooting at. I'll do better this time."

"Let's make a bet."

"That I'm faster on the draw than you are?" I asked.

"Too easy. How about I close the distance between us and take that little gun away from you before you even get a shot off?"

I had to steel myself for what was coming next. We had a plan. It was a good plan.

It was an okay plan.

Most of all, it was a plan that required me to be exactly one-hundred-percent *right*. If I'd misjudged Harry's motives, or my hunch about his secret employer turned out to be wrong, well...my backup wouldn't get here before I was reduced to red paste on the sidewalk.

"Let's do this," I told him.

I threw back my jacket. He charged, coming at me head-on, a high-speed juggernaut of muscle and bone. I had just cleared my holster when he plowed into me, tackling me to the sidewalk. We rolled end over end in a clinch and his fist cracked across my chin hard enough to leave me seeing double. Then he ripped the pistol from my grip, raised it high, and smashed the butt across my forehead. Blood spattered his face and ran down my scalp, a hot, salty river on my cheeks.

He tossed my gun aside, grabbed my shoulders, and wrestled me onto my hands and knees. I had crimson in my eyes and a branding-iron burn across my hairline, drowning out anything but animal panic. I think I flailed at him. He caught my wrist and wrenched it behind my back. My cheek smacked the concrete.

"C'mon, pretty boy," he snarled. "Bite the curb. Let's give you a brand-new face."

If I was right, Harry wouldn't kill me. That left everything else, up to and including disfigurement, on the table. It was now or never.

My walkie-talkie squawked. "Dan, it's Jen. You there?"

Harry grabbed it off my belt, leering at the plastic shell as he raised it to his mouth. Probably thinking of something badass and witty to say to her before he pulverized me.

"Did you lead him away?" Jen's voice crackled. Harry blinked at it, slow realization dawning.

"*Jen*," I croaked, straining one hand up like I was reaching for heaven. "*Help*."

"Just stay ahead of Grimes, keep him distracted and chasing you so he can't get in our way," Jen said. "We've got Elmer Donaghy and the second Network safe house surrounded. The strike team is in place and we're rolling in five minutes. Soon as we snatch Elmer and we've got the place on lock, we'll come and pick you up."

Harry's beefy hand curled around the walkie-talkie as his face went red. "The *fuck?* You...you *tricked* me!"

I managed to flop onto my back. Somehow, I even managed to smile.

The walkie-talkie shattered on the pavement and spilled its electronic guts. He turned and ran, bolting up the alley, heading back the way he came. I tugged my phone from my hip pocket.

"He bought it," I breathed.

"We got eyes on him, kiddo," Corman said. "He's running eastbound, hell-bent for leather. Looks like he's headed for his van. You in one piece over there?"

I sat up, groaning, and stripped off my jacket. I pressed the rumpled fabric to the split in my forehead. One hell of an expensive bandage.

"Just don't lose him. Stay tight, swap pursuit cars every few blocks, and I'll be right behind you."

I hung up. Then I reached over and scooped my pistol off the sidewalk. The safety was still on. It didn't even have a magazine loaded, not that he noticed.

"Putz," I muttered.

Harry Grimes thought you had to be a tough guy to win a fight. He wasn't wrong, but you had to be even tougher to get in a fight and lose on purpose.

* * *

Convinced he was racing to Elmer's rescue, Harry led us on a chase across town. Well, not far across. His final destination was a foreclosed storefront in East Vegas, a hop, skip, and a punch away from where he'd jumped me. My crew kept on him, running an alternating pursuit and putting plenty of slack in his leash.

"Left side of the street," Corman said over the conference line. "He's pulling up...looks like a deli. Shut down, though, old newspaper taped over all the windows. Two floors of apartments above it. I'm driving past so he doesn't make us."

"I'm on it," Jennifer shot back. "Coming up the alley opposite. Yep, he's unlocking the front door."

We couldn't track down Elmer Donaghy on our own, but Harry knew exactly where to find him. And he'd just led us straight to his hiding place.

"He left the front door wide open," Jen said. "Man's definitely in a panic. Can't see too much unless I get closer, but it looks stripped to the bone inside."

I wiped some crusted blood from my left eyelid. It clung to my hand like flakes of rust. The place was just up ahead; a long, low storefront with paper-shrouded windows, *Marino's* in faded gold leaf over the open front door. Hard light spilled from the open doorway and etched a razor-sharp angle on the sidewalk.

"He's coming out alone," Jennifer said. "Looks like he's leaving, and he is *pissed*."

Elmer wasn't here. And now Harry knew he'd been tricked, twice. His stolen van was curbside, up ahead near the deli's doorway. I stood in an alcove to the left of the door and pressed my back to the wall. The cut on my forehead still hadn't clotted over all the way. It oozed down in a slow, warm trickle, tickling the side of my nose and pooling on my upper lip. I tasted copper on my tongue and waited.

Harry boiled out of the deli, slammed the door shut behind him, and headed for the van. I pushed away from the wall and prowled in his wake. My footsteps matched his beat for beat, my stride longer, closing the gap between us.

Then I lunged in, clamped one hand over his mouth, and punched him with the ice pick in my other fist. Five quick jabs, tearing into his kidneys, his lungs, turning his back into a mangled slab of raw meat.

Harry Grimes collapsed to the sidewalk, glassy-eyed, dead. He never knew what hit him. Just like I promised. He'd figure it out when he woke up in hell.

My crew swarmed in, guardian angels with lockpicks and guns. Bentley went to work on the deli's front door and Jennifer popped the side of the panel van. We grabbed Harry's corpse under each arm and hauled him along the sidewalk, leaving a slug smear of scarlet behind.

"How much of that blood is yours?" she asked, nodding at my face.

"All of it. Why? Bad?"

We heaved, once, and tossed the body into the van. The door rattled shut. He'd keep for a couple of days, until somebody noticed the smell and called it in.

"Nothing's that bad if you're still breathin'. All the same, oughta get some stitches on that cut."

"If we have time," I said. "If Elmer's not here, there's a good chance Harry got a warning out to him. I want this whole operation mopped up *tonight*."

Tonight was turning into today, with the glow of dawn on the horizon. Bentley got the door open—faster than my best time, the man still had a magic touch—and we got off the street. The deli was stripped bare, just a long counter, a dusty glass case, and stark light from a couple of humming fluorescent tubes over our heads.

On the far side of the abandoned shop, a backroom door hung open with a keypad lock set into the wall beside it. Harry was in too much of a hurry to close up properly. Either that, or Elmer was just beyond the doorway, waiting for us.

"Jen, Cait, you're with me. Bentley, Corman, and Pix, hold until we give the all-clear."

I slid a fresh magazine into my gun. No more play-acting tonight.

We crossed the threshold in single file, Jennifer and Caitlin splitting left and right, all eyes hunting for danger. What we found was half private apartment, half mini laboratory, where a wall-mounted cot and a chemical toilet shared space with computer tables and racks of analytic equipment. My gaze drifted to a rounded platform of metal with a drain in the floor, ringed in Plexiglas. I thought it was Elmer's shower, until I saw the dangling, open manacles.

"The hell were you doing in here?" I muttered to the empty room. Hand-written notes lay scattered across a folding table, with incomprehensible graphs etched onto green-lined graph paper. A camcorder stood on a tripod, pointed toward the empty plastic-walled cell, and a scattering of cassettes joined the clutter beside it. Each tape was marked with symbols, not words or numbers, spiky, boxy glyphs that spoke to some kind of common hierarchy.

Language, I realized, as I saw more of the symbols adorning his charts and notes. Elmer Donaghy was an alien, not from outer space, but a parallel Earth. He'd learned to speak English at some point, but he naturally kept his personal records in his native tongue.

"Clear over here," Jennifer called out.

"We're clear," Caitlin said. She waved the others inside.

Pixie made a beeline for Elmer's personal computer. She ducked under the desk, yanking cables, tugging his boxy tower out onto the floor and going after the back-panel screws with a multi-tool.

"Touch *nothing* electronic," she said. "Leave it for me. If it's anything like the gear at the waste plant, it's all booby-trapped ten different ways."

I pointed to the tripod. "How about the camcorder? This thing looks vintage."

"Huh?" She glanced over, uncertain for a second, then nodded. "Sure, knock yourself out."

I picked up a random tape from the pile, fed it into the bulky camcorder's slot, and leaned into the eyepiece. I rewound and set it for playback. I wanted to see what Elmer had been up to while we were chasing our tails all over the city.

I saw it, all right.

"You sick bastard," I breathed.

38.

Elmer had a twelve-inch monitor on a rolling cart near the back of his lab. Pixie scrounged some cables, and we hooked up the camcorder for playback so we could get picture and sound. Everyone gathered around the screen and I played projectionist.

"I fast-forwarded through five of the tapes," I said. "As far as I can tell, this one is the first."

The camera's eye was fixed on the cell with the Plexiglas walls. A man, bleary-eyed, wavering on his feet, stood with his wrists in the dangling manacles. They were almost too big for him. He had spindly arms and a shirtless, emaciated chest, ribs poking through his jaundiced skin. The feed was too grainy to show the tracks on his arms, but I knew they were there; I knew a junkie when I saw one, and this guy was a long-term member of the heroin weight-loss program. He had blurry tattoo squiggles on his hip, another over his right nipple that looked like Minnie Mouse. Amateur ink, maybe prison-grade.

"I told you," he drawled, sounding half-asleep, "this kinky shit costs double."

Off camera, Elmer's voice drifted over the speaker like he was trying to put a baby to sleep. "Of course, of course," he soothed. "Just like I promised."

His hand appeared in the corner of the frame, opening a leather case. He tugged out a syringe and a band of rubber tubing. The guy in the cell opened his eyes a little wider.

"We gonna party? All right, man. You're pretty cool."

"Sure," Elmer told him. "Let's party."

I pressed eject and fed in a second tape.

"This one's later," I said, "but I can't read his writing and these aren't time-stamped, so I can only guess how long he had this guy locked up in here."

The prisoner's hair was one clue. It had been scruffy in the first video; now the tangled locks brushed his shoulders. And now the manacles were just right. He'd put on weight, growing out, and his skin had a healthy sheen to it. He still seemed half-asleep, though, disoriented, his eyes refusing to focus as his head lolled from side to side.

"Subject is...healthy," Elmer murmured from off-screen. "Taking to the supplements, no rejection of initial treatment. Having to hose him down and shovel out his feces every morning is laborious and irritating, but I can't risk losing him to a bacterial infection. The humans of this world are fragile. Then again, if *they'd* had to survive three generations of nuclear fallout, plague spores, and weaponized necromancy, I suppose they'd grow into a more resilient species. One can only hope for the future."

He chuckled. His hand came into focus, holding up another syringe. Something oily and yellow burbled inside, flecked with gnat-sized black specks.

"No more o' that stuff," the prisoner mumbled. "Makes me sick."

"Oh, it's just a little something to help with the rigor mortis," Elmer told him.

"Huh?"

"You're dead." He tittered. "You've been dead for two hours and fourteen minutes."

"Man, tha's...s'not funny."

"Six times I've attempted this experiment. First five subjects were all nonviable long before this point. You, sir...you're a prize."

I ejected the tape and reached for the last one. "Brace yourself," I warned them.

All the same, once it started rolling Pixie grabbed my arm and squeezed, hard.

The man in the cell had gained at least two hundred pounds. His gut, solid flab, hung over his sweatpants and he'd sprouted a double chin. His beady eyes poked from folds of fat, his face swollen. His hands were blue, curled and dead, circulation murdered by the manacles that had buried themselves in the flesh of his engorged wrists.

"Success," Elmer's voice whispered, trembling, proud. "Candidate six is a quantified success. We have full bio-factory conversion."

The man raised his head, as far as his wobbly neck would allow, and let out a faint, wheezing moan. His bulk jiggled, and as the camera zoomed in, we saw movement under his skin. Fist-sized forms scurrying, crawling, infesting his body.

"What Santiago was trying to tell us when he died," Jennifer said, her voice low. "The breeder is a—"

"Human," Caitlin replied. "The breeder is a human being."

I looked over to the empty cell. The dangling, open manacles.

"Clearly," Elmer said, the camera's eye running like fingers over his prisoner's body as he savored the moment, "we have a long way to go before we create genuine urban-infiltration breeders that can act autonomously, but this...this is a milestone. The breakthrough I've been working toward."

The prisoner moaned again. Something squirmed deep inside his throat.

"Time for phase two," Elmer said. The video died in a burst of static, and then the screen went dark.

"He's on the move and he's got that thing with him," I said. "Pixie—"

She was already hustling. "His computer. On it."

"Everybody else, fan out and tear this place apart. Books, notes, photographs, anything you can find. We need to know where he's taking it and what he's going to do next."

Bentley pored over his scattered loose-leaf notes, turning a piece of graph paper like he wasn't sure which way was up. "I doubt we'll get much out of this. Deciphering a foreign language—even one from *our* world—is a skill outside any of our wheelhouses."

I stood beside him and chipped in. I tried to sort the material into piles: one for charts, one for journal entries. It was busywork, organizing data we couldn't even read, but I didn't know what else to do. All this time, while Harry Grimes was changing personas on a whim, leading me out of the city and back again on a pointless chase, Elmer had been right here and hard at work. No telling when he had left or how much of a lead he had on us.

"I have something," Caitlin said. She held up a color printout. "It looks like a Google Maps search. What's in Boulder City?"

Jennifer and I locked eyes from across the room.

Phase two is about targeting more valuable hosts, Elmer had told me. *Setting our sights a bit higher than the rabble we have pushing our narcotics.*

"The United Conference of Mayors," I said. "Damn it, Seabrook—"

"I'm callin' her," Jen said, tugging out her phone.

"They're holding emergency talks about the ink epidemic," I said. "They want to coordinate a nationwide police and PR response, make a united front against the Network. There's going to be reps from at least twenty cities there."

"If that thing were to...*erupt* in the hotel," Caitlin said, pointing to the empty cell.

"All at once, the Network would turn some of the most influential mayors in the country into their mind-controlled puppets. And this is just the beginning. We have to get out there. *Now.*"

Jennifer held up her phone. "I'm gettin' voicemail."

"Try Commissioner Harding, he's with her." Then I realized with a jolt: *so is Teddy*.

My brother didn't know the Network was real—hell, he didn't even know *magic* was real—and he was standing at ground zero.

* * *

We tore down the 515, southeast to Boulder City. Caitlin was behind the wheel. I sat beside her and drummed my fingertips on the armrest. Jennifer sat in the back, sliding fresh rounds into her chromed .357 one by one.

Earlier Caitlin had tugged me by the arm, halfway out the door, and held me tight until I'd gotten some sense back. Then she washed my face in Elmer's sink, sluicing away the blood, while Bentley found some gauze for the jagged cut along my scalp. Now I was fresh as the rising, boiling sun. I had the window down, and the arid morning wind ruffled my dress shirt. With no jacket, hair rumpled, bristle on my cheeks and a bandage on my forehead, I looked like I'd just pulled an all-nighter and maybe gotten into a bar fight along the way.

I didn't need sleep. I needed to save my brother and put a bullet between Elmer Donaghy's eyes. Adrenaline would see me through. I knew I'd crash at the end of the line, but that was fine. I could crash when the job was done.

We rolled up to the Boulder City Hyatt at 9:14. The parking lot was standing room only, and Cait had to swerve to the back end to find a spot. Lots of limos were taking up four spaces at a time, along with more unmarked police cars than I could count. The three of us jogged to the revolving doors out front and ducked into the air-conditioned embrace of the lobby.

The whiteboard in the lobby read *Welcome United Conference of Mayors*, but I felt like we'd walked into a cop convention instead. Half the attendees had brought an escort, and they were all right here, drinking coffee and giving a visual pat down to anyone not wearing a badge. Their suspicion washed over me like a heat wave as I made my way to the front desk.

"The mayors' conference," I said. "Is it in session?"

The woman behind the counter checked a clipboard. "Um, yes, looks like they got started at nine. They're in conference room A, looks like."

I held up my phone. I'd pulled up the official website for

Donaghy Waste Management on the way in; Elmer's photo was on the board of directors page.

"Have you seen this man?"

She leaned closer, squinting. "You know, I think I did. Maybe half an hour ago? He was headed that way."

She pointed down a side hallway on the opposite side of the lobby. I tried to move one step ahead of the chess master. Elmer was here to attack the conference and snare as many people with his walking roach farm as he could. How would he do it? He couldn't just walk into the conference room with that thing; he'd start a panic. No, he'd have to be more subtle, slower. The conference was supposed to run for two days, meaning he'd have all day and all night to get the job done.

I thought about Santiago. And Jennifer's response, after she'd blown his passenger to pieces. *I didn't want that sucker getting loose and escaping into the vents*, she'd said. *I'd have to start sleepin' with a helmet on.*

"Is there any access to the HVAC system down there?"

"Well, yes, a utility stairwell," the woman replied, looking half-confused and half-worried now. "But that's for employees only."

Jennifer and Caitlin followed behind me as I cut a path through the milling cops. We ducked down the side corridor.

"He's going to release the roaches into the vents," I said. "Then tonight, when everybody's snug in bed...mass infestation. By tomorrow morning, half of the people in this hotel are going to be Network slaves, and they won't even know it."

"We need a plan," Caitlin said. "If he's cornered, he won't wait."

Right. If we couldn't guarantee neutralizing the roaches, we'd have to deny him his targets. A couple of cops in state trooper garb were jawing around the corner, drinking coffee. I stepped between them.

"Excuse me, gentlemen," I said and pulled the fire alarm.

A klaxon broke, shrill and strong, echoing through the hotel floors. One of the troopers grabbed for me. I pivoted on my heel, threw a right cross, and dropped him to the carpet. His buddy's hand shot for his belt, but Jennifer was faster on the draw. She pressed the barrel of her revolver to his forehead and plucked the gun from his holster.

"Don't you hear that alarm goin' off, sugar?" she asked. "You'd better evacuate."

He half stumbled, half ran up the hall. The entire hotel was stirring like a kicked-over anthill. Doors opening, heads poking out, feet rumbling down the stairwells. We waded upstream through the crowd and found the utility access door. A steep flight of concrete steps shot down into a dim, cool tunnel. The door glided shut behind us, muffling the sounds from above.

Elmer was down in this maze, somewhere, with his living weapon in tow. It was time for the endgame.

39.

We made our way into the belly of the beast. Great metal boilers thrummed and hissed beneath the hotel floor, as hot steam and water coursed through metal pipes. The tunnels twisted like a maze for rats, junctions marked by stenciled numbers in lemon-yellow paint.

Caitlin's eyes were orbs of molten copper, glimmering in the twilight. She wrinkled her nose, sensing something Jennifer and I couldn't, and pointed up ahead.

We used the sounds of the machinery for cover, staying low, watching our shadows stretch along the tunnel walls. I glanced left and poked my head into a storage closet. The walls were stocked high with cleaning products, a mop and bucket lying abandoned in the corner, but no sign of life.

A flicker of motion caught my eye up ahead. A short, crooked shadow loped along the corridor. Elmer.

Jennifer passed me the pistol she'd taken off the state cop upstairs. I braced it with both hands as I took point, easing along the wall. The tunnel opened onto a second boiler room. The long, iron-bellied machines took up most of the floor space, with gaps and narrow aisles between them.

Muzzle flash erupted from a blind corner and I threw my back against the wall as a slug tore into one of the boilers. A white-hot plume of steam screamed loose, close enough that it felt like the desert sun on my cheek.

"Dan," Elmer called out, like he was greeting a friend. "I have to say, I'm almost pleased to see you."

Caitlin slunk low and broke off. Jennifer did the same, turning and flapping her fingers at me in a mouth-wagging gesture. I got it. *Keep him talking.*

"Yeah?" I called back. "Why's that?"

Another muzzle flash blinded me for a split second. His second shot tore out a chunk of wall and showered me with concrete dust. I answered with gunfire, snapping off three quick rounds and darting between the iron-cast aisles. I huddled low and waited until the reverberations died away.

"Still alive, Dan?"

"I was going to ask you the same thing."

"Still alive. Oh, tell your friends to stop flanking me, please. I can see perfectly well in the dark."

"Well," I said, "we *are* here to kill you."

"Quite."

Movement on my left. He'd gotten around me. I hurled myself to the concrete as his sidearm blazed, punching more holes in the boiler and sprouting deadly lances of steam. I lay on my belly and spent the rest of my magazine, shooting at a phantom while burning air sizzled inches above my head. Jennifer got into the act, her hand cannon booming somewhere off to the left.

I scrambled on my forearms like a soldier in a trench, crawling out from under the ruptured metal, and tossed the empty gun. "Caitlin? Jen?"

"Fine, sugar." Quick footsteps followed her voice, heavier than Elmer's; she was moving to fresh cover. Caitlin didn't reply, but I didn't expect her to. She could take a bullet and keep fighting, and seeing as we still didn't know what other tricks Elmer had up his sleeve, I figured she was angling to get the perfect drop on him.

On *him*. That was his game. He would have known trouble was coming the second he heard the fire alarm going off. How much time would he need to release the roaches from their living prison? Minutes? An hour? The longer he kept us pinned down and focused on him, the more time he had to get the job done.

Instead of moving closer, I scrambled back—back to the supply closet we'd passed on our way in. Rummaging through the shelves, I shot a quick text to Caitlin: *Need to get past him. Can you hold him off?*

Just say when, she replied.

I found what I was looking for, buried between jugs of bleach and tall cans of floor polish, and jogged back into the fray.

"Dan," Elmer was calling. His voice bounced, echoed, coming from everywhere at once. "Out of curiosity, does this mean Harry Grimes is dead?"

"Afraid so. Friend of yours?"

I couldn't see him, but I could feel him. Moving like a spider in the dark, locking in on the sound of my voice. I put my back to the wall and slid toward the corner of the room. From here, bracketed by the hull of a boiler, there were only two directions he could come at me from.

"Not really," Elmer said. "He was their crowd, not mine."

"The Enemy?"

"Mm-hmm." Something rustled to my left. My shoulder muscles went tight. "He was on loan. You know, that gentleman, the Enemy...he *really* hates you."

"I have that effect on people."

My phone buzzed. I chanced a two-second glance at the screen. A message from Jennifer: *Keep him focused on you. Moving in from behind.*

"Tell me," I said, "that whole thing about killing me in a replica prison cell...was that even supposed to work?"

"Who cares?" Elmer replied. He could play all the echo tricks he wanted, there was no mistaking his voice was clearer, closer now. "You weren't wrong, before. We don't actually *want* him to get his power back. If we can derail his plans and make it look like an unfortunate accident, so much the better."

"So what do you want?"

"Right now?" Elmer *hmm*ed. "Well, mostly I just want to kill you, to be perfectly honest."

"Jen," I shouted. "Flush him out, *now!*"

Jennifer leaped out from cover and opened fire, unloading her revolver and splitting the air with flash after flash of white light. Elmer yelped, off-balance, and I saw his shadow lurch from his hiding space. Then a second shadow swooped down like a hawk: Caitlin, who had been creeping her way along the tops of the boilers, biding her time. Her heel lashed out in a snap kick that caught Elmer in the belly, doubling him over and knocking him to the floor.

I didn't have time to join in. I sprinted past them, up the corridor he'd been keeping us away from. The tunnel twisted hard left, and thick, boxy AC vents sprouted along the ceiling. I skidded to a stop.

Elmer's experiment squatted in the middle of the floor, in the heart of a nest of wiring and vents. His body had swollen, his bent legs disappearing under the spill of his fat, and he only wore an open raincoat over his naked bulk.

The man turned to me, his eyes so sunken in his face that they looked like tiny black marbles. His stomach rippled and swelled with the outlines of fat roaches crawling in a frenzy under his skin. He opened his mouth, his puffy lips wriggling. No sound came out. It didn't need to; I knew what he was asking me to do.

I raised the can of roach spray I'd taken from the janitor's closet, with a second swinging from my belt, and aimed. Then I flicked my lighter six inches in front of the nozzle and pulled the trigger.

The stream burst into flame and washed over him. His cheap coat ignited first, then his skin. I moved in, firing short bursts with my improvised flamethrower, and hit him again and again. He toppled over, twitching. I heard the roaches scream. Rents in his skin began to tear open, the passengers struggling to escape the burning ship. A few roaches skittered free and I caught them with gouts of fire. They raced down the concrete tunnel, burning like fireflies.

More followed, a river of them now, the blazing roaches fleeing in a glistening tide. The dead man's body deflated like a limp balloon, even his skull flattening out, as if his bones had been replaced by gelatin. The empty can clattered at my feet. I grabbed the backup from my belt and kept firing.

The last hissing scream faded, and nothing remained but the low crackle of flames. Dead roaches littered the tunnel floor like tea lights, filling the air with the stench of charred flesh and sewage.

I figured Elmer would be torn to shreds by the time I ran back to the boiler room, but he was holding his own. I saw Caitlin lash out with a bone-breaking punch and he flipped back on his heels, a court-jester cartwheel that pulled him just out of reach. He spun, dropping low and swinging around on the palm of one hand, and Caitlin leaped over his kick.

The crooked little man was faster, more agile than I imagined. Caitlin couldn't land a hit on him. He couldn't land one on her, either. He was still prolonging the game, trying to keep all eyes on him while his "bio-factory" prepared to burst in the next room.

"Hey, Elmer!" I shouted.

He looked my way. I used the last burst from the can of roach spray to send a burst of fire into the air, painting him a picture. Then I threw the can and my spent lighter to the ground.

"Phase two is canceled," I said.

His face contorted in sudden, feral rage. I braced myself, expecting him to come at me. Instead, he took a deep breath.

A cloud of bilious yellow gas burst from between his lips, streaking through the air on a howl of anger. I leaped to the left, diving clear, as it blew past me. Iron turned to pitted, rusted ruin as the cloud washed over it, and the concrete sprouted a carpet of fuzzy black mold in its wake.

"He's movin'!" Jennifer shouted. I saw him scramble up a boiler, flipping like an acrobat, and leap clear to the other side.

By the time we rounded the corner, he was gone.

Caitlin had a flush in her cheeks and a faint smile on her lips.

Not many people could give her a workout. She leaned against me and I slid my arm around her waist.

"You both okay?" I said.

Jennifer dangled her empty pistol from her fingertip. "Little embarrassed I didn't even wing him, but there's always next time."

"The breeder?" Caitlin asked.

"Dead. A couple of roaches might have gotten loose, but there's nothing we can do about that now. We have definitely overstayed our welcome."

* * *

Evacuating an entire hotel takes a while, and while it felt like we'd been battling in the basement for an hour—that's what my aching muscles told me, anyway—we'd barely been down there for fifteen minutes. There were still lines of stragglers making their way to the parking lot, hotel employees scurrying in all directions, enough confusion to cover our escape. A couple of fire trucks had parked right out front, responding to the alarm. At least a hundred civilians were standing outside the hotel, milling around aimlessly or breaking into knots of conversation, and we used the edge of the crowd as a shield.

"Low profile," Jennifer muttered in my ear, slinking alongside me. "That cop you punched is out here somewhere."

"Probably right next to the cop whose gun you stole."

"I'd like to not have to bail *either* of you out," Caitlin said, "so step lively and keep your heads down."

I caught sight of Teddy, moving fast between a couple of parked limos with his phone to his ear.

"Grab the car," I said, "I'll be right back."

I circled around, waving to catch my brother's attention. He blinked. "Gotta go," he said and hung up his phone.

"Get Seabrook and Harding out of here, right now," I told him. "You too. Do *not* go back inside that hotel."

"Dan? What—what are you even doing here? And what happened to your forehead? Did you get hurt?"

"Listen to me very carefully. You know what I told you, when you asked why I was having a meeting with the mayor?"

He nodded, wary. "Using a bad guy to catch another bad guy. That fire alarm—"

"This particular bad guy might still be around. Grab the mayor and the commissioner and *leave*. Go back to Vegas. Tell Seabrook I said so. She'll take my word for it."

"Okay." He took that in, and I watched his uncertainty slowly turn to steel. "I'm on it. I'll call ahead and make sure the Metro escort meets us on the highway, and I'll ride with the VIPs myself. Don't worry, they'll get home safe."

"Good thinking. Hey." I squeezed his shoulder. "You got this."

"You know, someday you're going to have to tell me the whole story here."

"Someday," I said.

* * *

We were crossing the Vegas city limits, home again, and I couldn't unclench. Jennifer leaned forward in the back seat and her hands worked at my shoulders.

"They're *fine*, sugar. We won. I mean, stalemate, Elmer's still out there, but we gave him one hell of a black eye. It's over."

I wanted to believe that, but I couldn't make it stick in my head. Maybe it was because my brother was involved. Maybe it was because Elmer Donaghy had been a step ahead of us since this sick little game began. We'd taken out two of his fronts, killed his science project, stopped him from infesting the mayors' conference...so why didn't I feel like it was time for a victory lap?

"You'll feel better with a stiff drink in you," Jennifer said. "Cait? Come with us? Drinks on the town?"

"With relish," she said. "I think we've earned a bit of pleasure."

Elmer's plans had all fit the same format so far. The feint, the real plot, and then one last layer. A fail-safe. He always had a fail-safe.

My phone buzzed. It was Seabrook.

"Mayor?"

"We've got trouble," she said. "We're halfway between Boulder City and Vegas. The Metro escort just left."

"Wait." I hunched forward in my seat. "*Left?*"

"Earl is calling HQ and shouting up a storm, but nobody claims to know anything about it. The entire escort just peeled off onto an exit ramp. We're all alone out here."

"Turn around," I told Caitlin. She gritted her teeth and swung hard into the left lane, angling for an open divider on the highway.

"Okay," I said. "Tell your driver to keep moving. We're coming to meet you, but do not, for *any* reason, pull off that road. *Keep moving.*"

The only answer was a crumpled *bang*, then dead silence.

40.

I knew what we would find before we reached the scene. One limousine pulled off to the side of the highway, with a front tire shredded down to the battered rims. We hooked another U-turn and came up behind it. The back doors hung open, nothing inside but a few tiny spatters of dried blood on the leather bucket seats.

I opened the driver's-side door. The chauffeur sat slumped sideways with a forty-five-caliber hole in his face and the back of his head splattered across the privacy divider.

Teddy. Mayor Seabrook. Commissioner Harding. Gone. I punched the side of the limo. My knuckles stung as I stomped back to the car.

"Drive," I said.

We headed back to the fortress. Jennifer kept an operations room ready to roll, if we ever needed one. It wasn't much, just a long and rickety table salvaged from one of the tenement's abandoned basements and a whiteboard stained with marker-trail ghosts, but it was a convenient place to rally the troops in a hurry. Jennifer stepped out to make a few calls. I paced, mostly. Pacing kept the walls from closing in.

"This isn't your fault," Caitlin told me.

I stopped in mid-stride. She was leaning against one wall, arms crossed, watching me.

"This is absolutely my fault," I said. "We should have stayed with them. We should have rode convoy all the way back to Vegas."

"And give the Network a bigger target? And what about when we returned? Would you babysit them for the rest of their lives? Donaghy clearly had a contingency plan in place. If he didn't strike at the mayor today, he would have done it tomorrow."

She was right. I knew she was right, but I was desperate to be furious at someone for losing Teddy and I was the only candidate in sight. I didn't have anything to say, so I started pacing again. I reached the far wall, turned—and Caitlin was standing in my path. She put her hands on my shoulders, stopped my stride, held me fast.

"This," she said, "is not productive."

My nervous energy didn't have anywhere to go. I stood there while it knotted up my stomach.

"Help me," I said.

She pulled me into her arms. It was the best place to be right now.

Jennifer came back, brandishing her phone. "Y'all need to see this."

She'd cued up a news report, a breaking bulletin on KTNV. Helicopter footage swirled across the city streets and hovered over a sprawling lot of vintage casino signs. The dead neon sat out under the afternoon sun, unlit and rusting away, while police lights flashed in the distance.

"—and gave pursuit," the anchor said. "One of the suspect vehicles crashed into a lamppost near the Neon Museum, at which point the gunmen in both vans, with three confirmed hostages including Mayor Seabrook, made entry into the museum itself. At least one employee was shot in the attack. Police have cordoned off the surrounding area, and residents are advised to avoid North Las Vegas Boulevard, North Encanto Drive, and East Wilson—"

"What the hell are they doing?" I said.

Jennifer shrugged. "Near as I can tell, troopers spotted their getaway cars actin' fishy, tried to pull 'em over, and the bad guys went all Rambo on 'em."

"This is...no. Running from the cops, crashing the getaway ride? This is sloppy and loud. The Network doesn't *do* sloppy and loud. It doesn't make any sense."

"Are you sure?" asked our new arrival.

He strode through the doorway like he lived here. We'd met once before; he had a bland face and a bland gray suit, his alligator-skin attaché case the only notable thing about his ensemble, but I wasn't about to forget him.

"It makes sense if they did it on purpose," I said. "Cait, Jen, this is Mr. Smith. He's with the Network."

Smith inclined his head. Jennifer eased back her utility jacket and flashed her holster. Caitlin took one step to the left, keeping a hand light on my shoulder.

"How the hell did you get in here?" Jennifer said.

"Oh, doors and guards don't inconvenience me much when I'm on the company clock." He cupped his hand to one side of his mouth, a bit of conspiratorial folksiness. "And I'm always on the company clock."

Jennifer didn't pull her piece, not yet. I was itching to draw mine, but I needed answers more than I wanted Smith dead, and he knew it.

"Let's cut to the chase," he told me. "We have someone important to you, and we'd like to discuss a trade."

"Mayor Seabrook. She's safe?"

"She is, but that's not the person in question. We have one Theodore...Faust." Smith flashed a bloodless smile. "It's funny, we'd barely checked into your family tree. But then you went and told one of our contractors about him. Your brother is safe, for now. Sound, for now."

Grimes. Damn it. I'd brought up Teddy when we met at the Monaco, while I was trying to flip him over to our side, and even told him how my brother worked in security. He must have passed on the info to his bosses before I killed him.

The biggest threat to my brother's safety wasn't the Network or Elmer Donaghy. It was me.

No sense wasting time. "What do you want?"

"A trade. Your brother, in exchange for you, Howard Canton's wand, and his top hat."

I'd already returned the hat to its more-or-less rightful owner, but I didn't say a word. As far as I was concerned, they weren't getting a damn thing.

"You've got the commissioner and the mayor in there, too," I said, feeling him out. "You want three things, I want three things."

He shook his head. "Mayor Seabrook dies tonight, that's nonnegotiable, but you can save your brother's life. Surrender yourself at the museum with the relics we want, and he'll be free to go. Frankly, he's useless to us except as leverage over you. We have no reason to harm him once you've been taken off the grid."

"Is that it?" I asked.

"That's all, but you'd better decide quickly. Right now, our operatives are holding the police at bay. Eventually Metro will decide to engage a tactical solution, and at that point, well...it's all over but the shooting. It's been a pleasure, sir, ladies—good day."

He turned and headed for the door.

"Hey," I said, "just one more thing."

Smith looked back. I drew my pistol and fired. The slug punched through his forehead, blew out the back of his skull, and spattered gray jelly across the eggshell paint. He hit the wall and slumped, slow, all the way to the floor with his eyes wide open and a look of surprise frozen on his face.

"You don't fuck with my family," I told him.

The gunshot settled into distant echoes. I nudged Mr. Smith's corpse with the toe of my shoe.

"Huh," I said.

"You were expecting something different?" Caitlin asked.

"Actually, yeah. From what we've seen of these Network guys so far, I figured he'd explode out of his skin or sprout tentacles or something." I nudged him again. "Talk about anticlimactic."

Jennifer stood beside me, frowning down at the body.

"I don't get it," she said. "Why all the hullabaloo? They don't need to gin up a hostage crisis—if anything, that's going to make it a lot harder to do a swap."

I had been thinking about that, and I circled back to one conclusion.

"They're being efficient. This isn't about me. You heard the man: Seabrook dies tonight. They want her out of the picture, presumably so they can put their own candidate in office—"

"One with a roach in his gullet," Jennifer said.

"Exactly. This is Elmer Donaghy's contingency plan in action. At some point, Metro's going to roll in hard, and the hostages are going to be 'accidentally' shot in the chaos. One public tragedy, made to order. But they've got Teddy in there too, which makes this a golden opportunity to put pressure on me."

Caitlin tapped her chin with a scarlet fingernail, pondering. "One problem. This clearly isn't a suicide mission, if they're expecting you to hand over Canton's wand and hat. How do they plan to leave once they get what they want? The lot is surrounded."

"That's not a problem at all if you've got an ally who can literally carve holes in the world and walk on through."

Her eyes narrowed. "Fleiss."

"She's got to be there," I said.

I turned my arm. The crisp linen bulged, just a little, showing the outline of my wand's spring holster. Fleiss wasn't the only one who could jump from place to place in a heartbeat. I could work that trick too, when the wand felt like letting me.

"If this doesn't qualify as saving people from danger, I don't know what does. If I could get in there, grab a hostage, and teleport out—"

"There's three hostages," Jennifer said. "Whose life are you gonna save? You'll only get one shot."

"He won't even get one," Caitlin replied. "These people aren't stupid; they won't let him anywhere near the hostages. And I suspect the first thing Fleiss will do is take his wand away."

I thought so, too. And that's when I got an idea.

* * *

"Don't make me regret this," Gary said.

"Look on the bright side," I murmured as we walked up to the police cordon, "there's a really good chance I'm going to die tonight. You'd like that, right?"

Squad cars blocked off the street, just behind a line of sawhorses and orange construction cones. Farther back, at the corner, uniformed officers were waving traffic toward a detour. Night had fallen, red and blue strobes flashing in the dark. Off to my left, a ridged wall ringed the open-air lot of the Neon Museum. The police had cut the power; there were no lights beyond the wall, no glimmering signs, just a graveyard maze of cold steel and glass.

"Detective Kemper," Gary said, flashing his shield at the closest uniform. "Got the hostage negotiator here, straight from the FBI."

The cop squinted at me. "We didn't hear anything about a negotiator. Who called the feds in?"

"Were you planning on *not* negotiating?" Gary shook his head like he'd just heard the dumbest thing in the world. "Look, you can let this guy do his thing, or you can be the one who explains why you, yes, you, personally, kept us waiting while the commish and the mayor were being held at gunpoint. I don't want to tell you how to live your life, pal, but it's not a good career move."

He let us through. In passing, he nodded at my shoulder. "What's the sack for?"

I patted the canvas mailbag. It trailed behind me, swaying across my back like a beggar's cloak.

"Pizza," I said. "Trust me, I'm a negotiator. The bad guys always want pizza."

The entrance to the park was through the visitor's center, a glass-fronted building with three sharp white peaks, flaring out like a nun's wimple. A woman's body lay facedown on the sidewalk out front, sprawled between a pair of pebble beds with a bullet in her back—the employee they'd gunned down on their way in.

I glanced up the street, past the front doors. The museum shared a block with the Siegel Suites, a three-story motel ringed by palm trees. One look, that's all I allowed myself, catching the distant glimmer of movement on the motel rooftop. Caitlin and Jennifer were getting in position, laying the foundation for my plan, but the rest was all on me.

On me, and on Canton's wand. My experiments, my attempts to control its dormant power, had all ended in failure so far. And here I was, about to try again. This time, though, there was more at stake than a little pride: I was betting my life, Seabrook's, Harding's, and my brother's on it.

One of the doors opened, and I stared down the barrel of a gun. A man in a black balaclava grunted at me.

"That's close enough," he said. "Your gun. Toss it."

I took the pistol out with two fingers, nice and easy, and set it on the pebbles.

"*And* your cards. We know you, Faust."

I had a vague, fuzzy hope that they might slip up and let me in with my deck of cards, but I knew better than to count on it. Unlike most of the goons I went up against, the Network actually knew who they were dealing with. The cards joined my gun on the ground.

A stiff night wind kicked up. The breeze took my cards and sent them flying, fluttering across the cordoned-off street, forming ribbons at my back as they scattered and danced away.

"What's with the sack?" he asked me.

"You wanted me to bring Canton's top hat and his wand, didn't you? C'mon, I'm not going to wear a top hat in public. Who does that?"

He thought it over, shrugged, and waved me closer with the barrel of his gun.

"Come inside," he said. "She's been waiting for you."

41.

Beyond the visitor center, double doors opened onto the museum lot. The grounds were a loving tribute to Vegas history, a sprawling maze of salvaged signs from the city's birth through its golden years to today. There was the jagged flair of the Stardust's marquee, the Arabian Nights spire of the Sahara Hotel, the sleek red lines of the Riviera. Memories of casinos long gone, nothing left of them but siren calls forged from neon and steel.

The signs and the footlights sat dark tonight, shadows under a muddy sky, and the only light came from the strobing police barricade beyond the perimeter wall. My host in the balaclava gave me a nudge with the barrel of his gun, marching me deeper inside.

They had five hostages, not three. Along with my brother, Seabrook, and Harding, a pair of employees sat kneeling and cuffed with zip ties in the heart of a small clearing. They were sweating, but they weren't bleeding. Teddy was the most disheveled of the bunch, his shirt torn and his face scuffed. He'd tried to fight. I figured he would. My escort in black had a pack of friends. I counted eight heads and eight guns, mostly rifles with a few sidearms in the mix. A couple circled the kneeling hostages like sharks. Another walked the top of a low steel sign, patrolling like a prison guard on a catwalk. They didn't look nervous.

Teddy's eyes went wide when he saw me, but he kept his lips tight. I didn't have time for a family reunion anyway. Ms. Fleiss, back in her human form, was striding my way.

"If he takes one step toward his brother," she said, "shoot him. In fact, shoot them both."

Now I had eight muzzles pointing right at me. Fleiss stood before me, imperious.

"That was the plan, wasn't it?" she asked. "We are aware of *some* of the wand's properties. You were going to feign a surrender, lay hands on your brother, and teleport him to safety."

I let my shoulders sag, just a little. "You got me."

"And leave the others to die." Fleiss tilted her head. I watched my reflection in her onyx sunglasses.

"What can I say?" I replied. "I'm ruthless like that."

"Hand it over. Now."

I gave her the mailbag. She shook it out between us, opened it with both hands, and peered inside. Then she looked up at me, somewhere between puzzled and irritated.

"What is this?"

"Oh, that's an empty sack," I said.

"You're playing games with me? Now? With your brother's life hanging in the balance? What do you think you're doing, Faust?"

"We were already playing a game. Your game, Elmer Donaghy's, the monsters you both answer to. I didn't have a choice. You forced me to join in. But here's the thing: I've always believed that if you don't like the rules of the game you're playing, *change* the rules. If you can't do that, cheat like your life depends on it."

Fleiss glanced to the closest gunman and snapped her fingers.

"You. If Mr. Faust doesn't produce the wand and the hat in the next ten seconds, shoot his brother in the left kneecap."

Teddy had kept his silence, not sure how to play this, but now he shot a nervous look in my direction. "Uh, Dan?"

"We will *start* with the left kneecap," Fleiss told me.

"I came here with a gamble in mind," I said. "Did you know the wand only works when you're trying to save a life?"

She curled her lips in a sneer. "Yes. And to transport someone away from danger, it only works with direct physical contact. There's ten feet between the two of you, and unless you've developed some remarkable new abilities since we last met, you can't outrun a bullet."

"That's not the gamble I'm making. And it's not *his* life I'm trying to save."

I flexed my wrist, triggered the spring sheath, and Canton's wand dropped into my outstretched fingers. A spark of raw magic surged along my arm and the wand kicked in my hand like a conductor's baton.

I touched the bone tip to Fleiss's heart, grabbed the rim of the sack with my other hand, and pulled it over both of our heads. The canvas billowed down and the darkness swallowed us whole.

* * *

The first and only time I'd teleported with the wand, it had been almost instantaneous. One moment I'd thrown myself into a locker and shut the door, the next I was bursting out onto a catwalk twenty feet above a firefight.

This time, the darkness in-between lingered. I felt the bag trying to open, straining against my willpower as it struggled to disgorge its passengers. I breathed slow and steady, steeling myself.

Beside me, Fleiss wheeled around, flailing in all directions and clawing at the void.

"Where are we?" she snapped. "Let me go. Let me *go!*"

"The wand wouldn't work if you weren't in danger, isn't that right?"

"Meaningless."

"It wouldn't work if I wasn't trying to save you," I said. "If I didn't want to help you."

She turned on me, seething. "I don't need your help."

A thin gray rectangle opened in the darkness, off to our left. The exit. I wouldn't be able to hold the bag back much longer before it spewed both of us out into the world again.

"Listen to me," I said. "Who taught you?"

"What?"

"Simple question. You're a witch. Who taught you how to use magic?"

"My...my lord did." Fleiss took a halting half step back. "He created me. He taught me everything I know."

"Really? Is he a witch?"

Her jaw clenched, her bottom lip starting to tremble. "No, but he *knows* things."

"Tell me about one time," I said. "One memory where he taught you something. I mean, you must remember, right? I could tell you stories for days about when I was learning magic. Tell me one of yours."

"I don't...I don't want to."

"There's one thing no magician ever forgets: the first time a spell actually worked. Everybody has a story about that. Tell me yours. What was it? What did you do?"

The fuzzy gray oblong kept growing. Fleiss spotted it. She ran over, hooked her fingers around the edges, and tried to wrench it open.

"He didn't create you," I said. "He just stole you. But this is your chance. You can run. You don't have to go back to him. Let me help you. Let me take you home."

"He *is* my home," she shouted, her voice edged with jagged-glass desperation.

I only had a few seconds before the spell would shatter, before she'd escape and I'd lose any hope of saving her. There was one card left to play, the words of the Lady in Red.

"What is a witch's creed?"

She froze. The oblong grew to the size of a door, crackling with static and cold gray fog. Wide open, but she didn't step through.

"You're a witch," I said, "so tell me: what is a witch's creed?"

"*Freedom*," she whispered, in a voice too soft for the power of the word. A voice that didn't believe.

Then she plunged her arms into the gray and the spell ruptured, spitting us both into reality with a dizzying, ear-popping lurch of motion. I spilled onto hard gravel, rolling, and Caitlin's hands caught me. She helped me up and Jennifer rushed to stand at my side.

Wind whipped by, icy and swift, and I snatched the second half of the plan—the other canvas sack, my intended destination—before it could blow off the edge of the roof.

We were on the other end of the block, up on the roof of the Siegel Suites. Fleiss looked to the distant cordon and then to the neon boneyard on the far side of a wall of cops. Her nails stretched, turning jagged and black, as she turned to face us.

"I will kill you all," she whispered.

"*Thank* you," I said. The wand flared, sensing the threat, and Caitlin and Jennifer both touched my shoulders. One riffle of canvas, a glimmer of shadow, and we were gone.

* * *

Caitlin was the first to burst loose on the other side, breaking free from the billowing sack in a full-on sprint. She ran, low like a panther, drawing a crackle of gunfire as she scrambled up a cold neon sign. The shooter on the makeshift catwalk had just enough time to scream before she was on him, her shark's teeth tearing into his throat.

The distraction turned heads and bought us the two seconds we needed, popping out right on her heels. One for Jennifer to toss me the backup deck of cards she'd been holding onto, and one for me to let it fly. The cards flew in a hornet swarm toward the hostages and I twirled my wand, evoking Canton's Multiplication. Fifty-two cards sprouted and became five hundred and twenty, forming a whirlwind. A desperate peal of bullets plowed into the cards, dropping a handful to the dust, but the hostages inside the fluttering shell were still in one piece.

Jennifer broke right, chrome gleaming in her fist. She let off two shots and a gunman's head snapped back, blood spray trailing him down like an arc of wet rubies in the dark. I grabbed his fallen rifle, swung the barrel around, and let it rip, lighting up the park with short staccato bursts.

A thunderclap sounded from the visitor center. The cops had

heard the gunfire and assumed the hostages were being executed. They were coming in.

I'm a lousy shot with a rifle, but all I had to do was keep the shooters by the exit pinned down. A ragged, wet howl off behind my left shoulder told me Caitlin was on the move, picking off anyone who tried to get close. Jennifer crouched low outside the whirlwind of cards, adding to the hail of bullets.

My rifle ran dry as white smoke erupted from the visitor-center doors. More shots echoed from that direction, the hoarse shouts of the incoming SWAT troopers ringing out over the dying groans of one of Fleiss's men. I tossed my empty weapon to the ground and let the whirlwind fall; playing cards clattered to the pavement in a cardboard hailstorm.

Then I got on my knees next to the other hostages and laced my fingers behind my neck. Commissioner Harding was right beside me, looking like his eyes were about to jump out of his head.

"Great job," I told him. "Getting yourself free and grabbing a gun like you did, shooting all those bad guys. You saved us all."

The wind shifted and the white fog washed in. Sudden tears stung my eyes, and the back of my nose burned like I'd snorted a fistful of chopped red pepper. I looked to my left, seeing dark figures storm in through the smoke. And Caitlin and Jennifer, kneeling on my other side, following my lead and playing hostage. I figured I should say something pithy, but then I got a lungful of the smoke and the racking, heaving coughs began, and I couldn't think about anything except how much I hated tear gas.

42.

Never underestimate people's willingness to accept an obvious lie if it means they don't have to think or work too hard. How had Earl Harding managed to slip his cuffs, overpower a gunman, steal his rifle, and kill at least six assailants without being shot? Because he was a goddamn hero, that's why. Why did two of the bodies have .357 rounds in them, when the rifles were loaded with steel-cased 7.62? Silly question. You might as well ask why one of the corpses had his throat torn out and another was found with his chest ripped open, his shattered ribs bent outward like the bars of a broken cage.

Or better yet, don't ask at all. Especially when the police commissioner, the mayor, and six hostages all recited the same story. Anyone who poked around beyond that would get a very firm, very brusque phone call from city hall. At the end of the day, one thing was clear: people who wanted a long and happy career didn't ask questions, and people who toed the line got a nice, discreet bonus with their next paycheck.

My phone didn't ring that night. Or the next day, or the next night. Teddy had just seen some impossible things, and he wasn't ready to talk about it. I didn't call him because...I want to say I don't know why, but that's not true. It was the realization that I'd managed to endanger his life just by brushing up against it.

We'd been out of each other's worlds for over twenty years, and the day after our reunion, I put him on the Network's radar. Now they knew I had blood in town, they knew he was leverage, and they'd shown they weren't afraid to use him. They'd do it again if I gave them the chance.

So I couldn't give them the chance.

The first thing I did was call up some of my Commission buddies and swap a few favors. From that moment forward, Teddy and his family were under a discreet twenty-four-hour watch by hard-eyed guardian angels with guns. I couldn't kid myself into thinking that would be enough. If I wanted to keep Teddy clear of the Network, I had to go after them head-on. Tear the whole thing down, or at least convince them that crossing me was the most expensive mistake they could ever make.

Two days later, I got a chance to send a message. It came courtesy of Pixie, who had been tearing into Elmer Donaghy's computer with a pair of tweezers and a microscope.

"Still haven't cracked their messaging protocol," she told me, "but I'm getting closer. Need more samples. I did get something, though. Right before he left his hideout, Elmer was doing some online banking. He had a discretionary account, tied to the waste-management company."

I leaned in over her shoulder and nodded my admiration. "If it leads us to another Network front, we might just get that data you need."

"Oh, it led *somewhere*, all right."

She rattled a few keys, showed me what she'd found, and a light clicked on.

* * *

"Sir? Sir, you can't go in there. Sir?"

I ignored Harding's receptionist and pushed my way into his office with a smile. He had a wall of awards, a folded flag under glass and another standing proud in the corner, and a credenza littered with photographs of him glad-handing every celebrity he'd ever coordinated a security detail for. He pushed himself up from behind his cluttered desk, scowling at me.

"I just want to shake the hand of a hero," I said. "You know this man saved my life? He's a national treasure."

"It's fine, Dottie." Harding waved her back. "He can come in. *Briefly.*"

The door swung shut behind me. He took his seat. We didn't shake hands.

"I don't know what kind of deal you've got going on with the mayor," he told me, "and I don't want to know, but get this straight: do *not* show your face around here. The last thing I need is anyone seeing us together."

"Sure," I said. "Under present circumstances, especially."

His brow furrowed. "Present circumstances?"

"You really are a hero. I hear you've been getting phone calls. *Today* wants to have you on the show. Might even get a five-minute spot on Jimmy Kimmel if you play your cards right."

His smile was more of a smirk. Tiny and mean.

"Well, I *did* fight off a gang of terrorists and save the day. Hell, I've got people asking about the movie rights. Might have to hire an agent."

"You know, it's funny," I said. "In the aftermath, once the smoke settled, I started thinking. And there was one thing, one...little detail that just didn't ring right. You ever speak to a man named Mr. Smith? He's a fixer for the Network."

"Never heard of him," Harding said. The sudden shift in his eyes told me something different.

"He's dead now, so I can't introduce you. But, see, when he told me I could trade my life for my brother's, I asked him about trading for you and Mayor Seabrook too. And he told me that Seabrook was going to die, nonnegotiable."

"Not surprised," he grunted. "These people are crazy."

"The odd thing is," I said, "he didn't mention you at all. Then this morning, one of my people found a paper trail originating in a Network-linked bank account. Ten payments over the last three months, four thousand dollars each time, to a newly formed political action committee."

I leaned in and laid my hands on the edge of his desk.

"The Committee to Elect Mayor Harding," I said.

His head tried to bury itself in his neck, and his eyes landed anywhere but on me.

"Can name a PAC anything you goddamn want," he said. "Sounds like they're trying to set me up."

"Come on, Earl. Give it up. *You* gave the order to call away the police convoy. You were in on the entire plan. And who could blame you? You've got your sights on the throne, or maybe it's just a step stool to even bigger ambitions, but we both know Seabrook's welded to her seat. With her polling numbers, it'd take one of two things to get her out of office and out of your way: a massive scandal or a convenient death."

He held his stubborn silence until it crumbled in his hands. I waited, patient as a spider.

"You want to know what's funny?" he asked me. "This worked out even better than it was supposed to. Plan was, Seabrook would eat a bullet and I'd get some public sympathy points for losing my dear, sweet friend and colleague. Now? You said it: I'm a hero. Hell, I can probably run against her and win clean, if I keep my momentum."

"You can," I said, "but you won't."

Harding locked eyes with me, squinting hard. He might have had the law on his side, but he carried himself like a back-alley thug.

"Think real careful before you make any threats."

I showed him my open hands. "Hey, quite to the contrary. I'm here to extend an offer. You want to be the next mayor? We can make it happen for you."

His anger gave way to suspicion. And the tiniest sparkle of greed.

"You'd stab Seabrook in the back?"

"What's she done for us lately?" I said. "I can't even get her to put a little weight on the Board of Liquor and Gaming. Not even a phone call. If you'd be more willing to play ball, well...we can make things happen for you. Fast."

I had him now, a fish on a line. "How fast?"

"One well-timed tragedy, some backroom pressure in the right places...you could be *Mayor* Harding by this time next year."

He made a show of taking his time. He drummed his fingers on the desk and licked his lips.

"Ground rules," he said. "I've built my entire career on being a hardliner. Integrity, you understand? You never come here again, and we never meet in person. When we have to talk, we use third-party cutouts."

This wasn't his first tango. I wondered just how many dirty little secrets the commissioner had buried in his backyard.

"Of course," I said. "And hey, just to prove my friendship and good intentions, I'd like you to accept a small token of my regard."

I slid a gray velvet box across the desk. He took it, suspicious again, and popped it open.

"A tie clip?" He turned the box from side to side. The diamonds along the platinum glittered in his eyes. "These real?"

"Absolutely. Go on, try it on. Live a little, Earl. You earned it."

He fumbled with the gem-studded clip, prying it from the case, and clipped it onto his tie. It looked garish on him, but he nodded with smug approval.

"Not bad," he said. "I could get used to this kind of thing."

Then he winced. He pressed one hand to his belly.

"You okay, buddy? Doing all right?"

"I just—" He shook his head and pushed his chair back. "I think I ate something I shouldn't have."

He stumbled to his private bathroom as beads of sweat broke out on his ruddy cheeks.

"Breakfast burritos, Earl," I called after him. "They always seem like a good idea at the time, but one hour later—"

The bathroom door slammed shut. I shrugged and circled his desk, jotting a note on his legal pad. Then I ambled out of his office, pausing just long enough to have a word with his receptionist.

"Hey, Commissioner Harding says not to disturb him for a little bit. He, uh—" I pitched my voice low. "He's got some intestinal issues."

She slapped her pen down on her desk. "He ate dairy again, didn't he? I tell that man, every single time—"

"He did," I said on my way out. "Terrible. Do *not* go in there, and when you do, bring air freshener."

Technically, I was misusing my cursed gifts from the knighting party, and I was probably committing some gross breach of court etiquette. Tough. Sitri knew I was a rebel when he hired me. Besides, I could always steal the tie clip back later. It'd be with the rest of Harding's personal effects, down at the morgue.

I needed to send a message, and a simple bullet wouldn't have done the job. Harding had been working for Elmer Donaghy, directly or through a middleman, and eventually his gruesome fate would filter up the ranks. So would the discreet note I left on his desk, the one that simply read, "*Your move*."

I had one more job to take care of today, and it didn't involve killing anybody. I was actually going to do something nice for a change and make somebody happy. So of course, I was sweating bullets.

* * *

"Don't make me regret this."

Emma punctuated her words with a hard poke at my shoulder. Then she stood, a stony sentry at the edge of the conference room. The lower floor of Winter wasn't all fun and dark games; the nightclub sported a pair of meeting rooms—sleek, modern, with warm lighting and ergonomic chairs—for handling court business.

When someone like Melanie ended up in here, it was usually to have a chat with Caitlin. Not the good kind of chat. The two of them were sitting at the end of the beechnut table, Caitlin silently staring, Melanie looking like she was about to slide out of her chair and try to tunnel to freedom.

"I really don't know what I did," she said.

"Are you absolutely sure about that?" Caitlin asked her.

Caitlin's lips curled in the faintest of smiles. Then she giggled, the sound coming out in a tiny sputter.

"I can't," she said. "Melanie, you have this delicious frightened-rabbit affect that makes me *want* to terrorize you, but I just can't keep a straight face."

Melanie looked from her to her mother to me and back again.

"What is going on here?" she whispered.

"What's going on," I said, "is that the three of us had a long talk, about you and...things, and...so, uh, did you still want to learn magic?"

I was not prepared for the scream of joy. Or for Melanie to bound from her chair, race at me, and jump. I suddenly had a hundred and twenty-five pounds of teenager hanging around my neck and squeezing for dear life.

"There are *rules*," her mother announced, but she was glaring at me when she said it. I gently extricated myself as best I could.

"There are," I said. "First and foremost, you've got to keep your grades up. School comes first."

"Totally." Melanie's head bobbed like it was on a spring. I could have told her she'd have to walk a tightrope across the Grand Canyon, and I would have gotten the same answer.

"And," Caitlin added, "I expect I won't be receiving any more disciplinary reports. You'll be on your best behavior at all times and comport yourself as a dignified representative of our court and our prince."

I looked her way. "Which one of us are you talking to?"

"Both of you."

That was fair.

"Okay," I told Melanie, "that's it, then. Report to the Scrivener's Nook tomorrow after school, and we'll get started. You'll need two pairs of black shirts, two pairs of black pants, one pair of combat boots, two pairs of black socks—"

"Wait, wait!" Melanie grabbed her phone, tapping with both thumbs as fast as she could. "I need to write this down, start over."

"No, I was quoting a—" I blinked at her. "I mean, have you never seen *Fight Club*?"

She looked up from her phone. "You do know that movie came out the year I was born, right?"

"Subconsciously, I think I must have realized that on some level, but pointing it out really drives home how old I am. Thanks for that."

"Anytime."

Emma folded her arms and met my gaze.

"Welcome to my world," she told me.

Maybe Jennifer had been right, back when this whole mess started. Maybe I was having a midlife crisis and my search for a legacy was just a symptom. But I couldn't shake the hunger to make some kind of a difference, some kind of an impact before I was gone, and I hadn't been too good at it lately.

I had tried to help Harry Grimes and show him a better way. In the end, all I could do was put him down like a rabid dog. I held out my hand to Fleiss and she slapped it away.

But here was someone who needed a hand, who needed the skills I knew I could teach. The only thing holding me back was Desi's ghost.

And the only one keeping her alive was me. Besides, I think she would have liked Melanie if they'd ever met. And if anyone would approve of me getting back on the horse and taking on another student, it was Desi. She would have kicked my ass for waiting this long. It was time to let go of the past. *Learn* from it, yes, but let it go. And try again.

This time, I'd get it right.

Epilogue

There used to be a village nestled deep in the province of Nuevo León. It isn't there anymore. Survivors streaming into Monterrey, lugging the remnants of their lives in bags and backpacks, told an all too common story. A cartel had been hiding product in a farmer's storehouse. The mayor talked to the *federales*. And by night, men with guns came to deliver their punishment.

That was the story, anyway.

A dusty, bone-dry day brought new arrivals, rumbling in a convoy along a broken road. Four semi trucks—trailers unmarked, plates mismatched and stolen—ran convoy behind a single white limousine. They followed the ping of a satellite transmitter and left the road, tearing across scrub grass and dirt.

At the end of the line, they circled ranks and stopped at the edge of the dead village. From a distance, their passengers might have been astronauts, buried under bulky helmets and lime-green Tychem pressure suits. They rolled out hoses and drove stakes into the barren earth, erecting sealed plastic tents.

By sunset, the village had become a CDC-grade biohazard unit.

The most prominent—and most secure—encampment was dead center, erected over a lonely pit in the earth. Rough-hewn steps led down to a tunnel where a couple of the new arrivals swept bright white LEDs across the ancient masonry.

"They didn't know it was here?" one asked, voice muffled under his hood.

"The old-timers knew. Didn't know what it *was*, but they knew it was bad news and to keep people away from it."

"And here we are. Not too bright."

"Shh," his partner said. "*He's* here. You don't want to get downsized, keep your mouth shut."

The tunnel dipped and turned and dipped again, a black corkscrew gouging a wound deep into the earth. Then the passage leveled out, and a putrid yellow glow rippled, like light on water, off the walls ahead.

"Is that..." one of the men breathed.

They stood before the portal and froze in abject horror.

"Eden," said Mr. Smith.

He stepped up behind them, beaming. The glow washed over his face, his forehead pink and soft like the skin of a newborn baby.

"Isn't it beautiful?"

* * *

Northlight Tower held vaults within vaults. This one was secured close to the Enemy's penthouse, so he could keep a close eye on the treasures within. Fleiss often found him wandering the room, muttering to himself, his flickering form reflecting off the polished stainless-steel walls.

"*Not so smart now, are you?*" he would say. "*No. Not smarter than me.*"

This time, she stood alone, surrounded by pedestals of white Italian marble. Each plinth bore a tiny brass placard and a red velvet pillow, and each pillow bore the tools of a stage magician's trade. Brass linking rings, a length of sturdy cotton rope with a knot on one end, steel cups and red foam balls.

Two of the pedestals, reserved for Howard Canton's wand and top hat, stood empty.

The terror gripped her, like it always did when she had to report her failure. It sank bone-deep and nailed her feet to the floor.

"Amazing," her creator said from the doorway. "Everything going swimmingly, our allies from the Network were doing their part, then you were placed in charge of the final phase. And promptly *didn't* obtain the hat, *didn't* obtain the wand, and *lost* Faust."

"That isn't fair."

She froze in shock as the words fell from her lips. So did he. She felt his power wash over her, probe at her, as his shadow loomed.

"Excuse me?" he whispered.

Fleiss bowed her head. "I...I just mean...my lord, you can't trust these people. The Network will betray you in a heartbeat."

"Of course they will. I'm certain they're planning on it. But if I can buy their momentary cooperation with the gift of a trifle I don't even care about, it's worth the risk. Do you think me a fool, Fleiss?"

"No, my lord! I just want to watch out for you. Care for you." She looked up at him. "I love you."

He nodded. "I know you do. It pleases me."

Daniel Faust's words on the rooftop, when Fleiss cornered him at Elmer Donaghy's lair, drifted back to her now.

"*He does love me*," she had insisted, infuriated by his disbelief.

"*Has he ever told you that?*"

And now she realized—as if a patch of fog had been lifted from some far corner of her mind, unveiling something that had been right in front of her all along—that the answer was no.

"Do...you love me, too?" she asked.

His flickering fingertips traced the curve of her jaw.

"You are a very valuable servant," he replied.

Then he turned and gusted away without another word, leaving her standing alone.

She deliberated in silence, then took out her phone. She had arrangements to see to, matters to contemplate further.

Decisions to make.

Afterword

Change isn't easy.

I'm writing this afterword from my new office in North Carolina, sipping a Diet Coke on an eighty-degree afternoon. One week ago, I was looking out the window at Chicago snow. There's nothing like a cross-country move to shake your world apart, but now that it's finally over and I'm settling in, I'm glad I did it. That's the other thing about change; it's stressful and it's crazy-inducing and it can feel like hell, but more often than not, there's something good waiting for you on the other side.

It took a while for Daniel to break out of his inertia, and now he's found the world never stops moving. Birthdays keep coming (with midlife hovering on his doorstep), challenges keep looming, and the city keeps changing. He has to change along with it. I think that's a feeling we can all relate to, in a wild and uncertain world, though hopefully most of us aren't getting shot at quite as often as Daniel is. If there's a takeaway, I'd say it's this: if he can survive the combined fury of the Enemy and the Network *and* teach magic to a teenager, we can survive anything. And change is a lot easier when you face it with friends.

Speaking of friends (see what I did there? *Segue.*), let me give a big shout-out to Team Schaefer: Kira Rubenthaler, my editor (sorry about the roach-pit scene, Kira); James T. Egan, my cover designer; my awesome assistant Maggie Faid; and also-awesome audiobook narrator Adam Verner. I couldn't do what I do without 'em. And now it's time for me to bravely venture into the living room, and unpack some more boxes.

Want to know what's coming next? Head over to http://www.craigschaeferbooks.com/mailing-list/ and hop onto my mailing list. Once-a-month newsletters, zero spam. Want to reach out? You can find me on Facebook at http://www.facebook.com/CraigSchaeferBooks, on Twitter as @craig_schaefer, or just drop me an email at craig@craigschaeferbooks.com.

The Daniel Faust Series

1. The Long Way Down
    1.5. The White Gold Score
    2. Redemption Song
    3. The Living End
    4. A Plain-Dealing Villain
    5. The Killing Floor Blues
    6. The Castle Doctrine
    7. Double or Nothing

Also by Craig Schaefer

Sworn to the Night
Harmony Black
The Complete Revanche Cycle

Made in the USA
Middletown, DE
10 September 2018